The Diary

by

Sarah D. Gordon

The Wild Rose Press, Inc.
PO Box 708
Adams Basin, NY 14410-0708
Visit us at www.thewildrosepress.com

Publishing History
First Edition, 2024
Trade Paperback ISBN 978-1-5092-5368-5
Digital ISBN 978-1-5092-5369-2

Published in the United States of America

Dedication

To Gordon and those that said, "Of course you can."

Acknowledgements

I acknowledge the traditional custodians of the lands on which this book was written. I acknowledge the cultural diversity of all First Nation peoples and pay respect to Elders past, present and future.

Chapter 1

2022

"Look what I've got!" Becca announced.

Sophie Harris swiveled around on her stool, her excitement at hearing the words equaling that in her assistant's voice. Becca carried a large cardboard box, her smile just seen over the top of it. She dropped the box onto the worktable, a flurry of dust particles erupting into the air. An older woman trailed behind her. "Sophie, this is Mrs. Sadler," Becca said. "Mrs. Sadler called last week about donating some items from their property, Lang Hill."

Sophie smiled and held out her hand. "Of course. We can't thank you enough, Mrs. Sadler," she said. "We are grateful for donations such as yours. It helps give a voice to the past, every little piece telling another part of the story." This was the usual speech given when a donation to the history center was made, but she meant what she said. Donations didn't come often, time taking many of the treasures people left behind, so Sophie was always grateful when she was entrusted with those time had spared.

"You're most welcome. When I saw your poster in the museum, I remembered we had this box—some clothes, I think, and some documents and the like. We found them wrapped in an oilskin coat in an old trunk just after we bought the property. My husband moved them to a box and put it in the shed. We'd forgotten about them. The trunk itself is over a hundred years old, so I'm guessing what's in the box is too. I don't imagine it's anything of financial value, but historically it might be of interest to you."

Sophie smiled, finding it hard to disguise her anticipation at revealing what had lain wrapped in a coat for over a century. "Oh, it definitely will be," Sophie assured her. "Do you know anything about the people who may have owned the items?"

Mrs. Sadler shook her head. "No, nothing really. We were told that my husband's great-great-something worked for the original owner in the mid-1860s, but I'm not sure who they were. Then it went to the Lang family, who owned it until we bought it, although it was long abandoned by then. That's all I can tell you. I imagine whatever's in there belonged to one of the families. It's not really of interest to us, and the owner before us is dead, so we thought if there's anything useful, it would be far safer in your hands than in the shed."

Sophie smiled. "Well, thank you again." She nodded toward the box. "I will let you know as soon as we have documented it all. Hopefully, you can come and see what we found when we put it on display."

"I look forward to it."

"I hope we have something to show her," Sophie said when the woman had left. "We either have a treasure trove from the past or an old moldy coat and some dust."

Becca laughed. "All part of the fun. You want a coffee before we start?"

Sophie could already feel the flutter of anticipation at the prospect of seeing the echoes of another past life.

She knew that, to some people, all this looking back in time might seem dull, a hobby taken up by retirees, but to Sophie, it was a job she loved, her fascination for the past never waning. So as much as she wanted to rip open the box and pull out its contents, she knew they needed to be calm and systematic when taking out whatever was inside. As this box had sat for decades, it needed to be treated with care, so yes, a coffee and a moment or two to temper their eagerness was a good idea.

"I'll make it," Sophie said, and turned to the kettle, switching it on. She took two mugs from the half dozen mismatched ones huddled together on the countertop and spooned coffee into both. "Sugar?"

Becca held up two fingers. "Please."

Coffee made, she handed a mug to Becca, the porcelain inscribed with the phrase "Don't mistake me for a morning person" arching over a picture of a disgruntled-looking cat. "You know me well," Becca said with a smile.

Sophie picked up her mug—"World's Best Grandma." She smiled to herself at the irony of it. Sophie wasn't even a mother, let alone a grandmother, and she couldn't see a future where she would become either. At 32 and single, she could hear the tick-tock of Mother Nature's clock loud and clear, and the only baby Sophie had was this project.

After finishing her master's degree, she had been thrilled when she was offered this job. The family history center was attached to the city's museum, and Sophie, with Becca's help, was given the task to gather, document, and display any items they could beg or borrow that celebrated the first families to settle in this area and give birth to the thriving place it now was.

Genealogy and colonial history were Sophie's passions, and to now be able to hold some of those histories in her hands was a dream come true.

"Sophie?"

Sophie looked up. Becca had clearly been saying something, and Sophie hadn't heard a word.

"Are you listening?"

"Sorry. Wandered off there for a moment. What were you saying?"

"I was saying that Mrs. Sadler's little boy, Will, died when they first moved to Lang Hill. My mum's known the family for years and told me about it when I mentioned the donation."

"That's awful. What happened"

"Apparently, the house had been empty for decades and they had no clue about some wires that were bare outside. Power went on and the kid was electrocuted. He was only three."

Sophie shuddered. "God, that's awful. That poor family. How would you ever get over that?"

Becca shook her head. "I dunno. Apparently, they stayed on the property because they felt the kid was still there in some way. Lang Hill's a winery, and they make a peach wine called Sweet Will. After the kid, I guess."

The women were quiet for a moment, both lost in thought, Becca finally breaking the silence. "Are you ready?" she said.

Sophie nodded and placed her now-empty mug in the sink, then crossed to the worktable in the center of the room. She opened a shallow drawer and took out a pair of white cotton gloves and a paper mask, the gloves to protect the pieces they were going to handle, the masks to protect themselves from the layers of dust that oftentimes came with the items. She slid them across the table to Becca, then took another pair of gloves and a mask for herself, slipping them on. Laying a white sheet over half the table, she then took a pad and pen from the drawer. She opened the pad to a clean page, writing the date across the top and next to that the name: Sadler donation—Lang Hill Farm / Lang family.

"Ready," she said.

Becca pulled the box toward them and took a scalpel, slicing through the brown packing tape that held the box closed. She opened the flaps, then glanced at Sophie, anticipation written all over her face. With care, she reached into the box and lifted out what Sophie guessed was the oilskin coat, still wrapped around the items they were so impatient to see. Becca laid the coat on the white cloth and inspected it.

"There doesn't seem to be any water damage," she said through her mask. "Nor any perishing of the fabric."

Sophie nodded and wrote on the pad. 1: OILSKIN COAT. BROWN. She would finish the entry after they had time to inspect it further. Right now, they had to see how willing the coat was to give up its contents. Becca slowly teased each fold back until the coat lay open, revealing what had been hidden for over a hundred years.

A yellowed piece of paper caught Sophie's attention, and she reached for it. One corner was missing, and it was creased where it had been folded in half. The ink that would have been bold against the once-white document had faded, but the words at the top were easy enough to read: Certificate of Title. Written in the ornate script of the time, it stated underneath that the land belonged to Thomas Lang.

"Well, we know who owned the land, at least,"

Sophie said. She took a clear plastic sleeve and opened it, ready to receive the document. "Although I'm sure Mrs. Sadler said that Lang wasn't the original owner. I wonder why this isn't a transfer of title?"

Becca shrugged. "I'm not sure. I'll look into it. Hey, check this out."

"What is it?"

"What is it? It's you."

Sophie laughed. "What are you talking about?"

"Look." Becca turned the photograph she was holding so Sophie could see what was clearly a wedding photo. The couple stared back at her. The man was tall and somewhat handsome and stood beside a young woman who without a doubt was a spitting image of Sophie, right down to the small mole at the base of her neck. "See? It's you. The likeness is uncanny, bordering on super weird, don't you think? She could be your twin."

Sophie took the black-and-white photograph from her friend. The young woman's hair was bound up in a bun on the top of her head, but a strand had missed being captured and fell in a ringlet over her shoulder. Sophie's hair too fell in curls, and she spent ages trying to straighten them out. She wondered if this woman disliked her curls as much as Sophie did her own. The photo gave no clue to the color of the woman's hair, but Sophie imagined it could easily have been the same dark auburn as her own. As Becca said, it was weird.

"A great-great-great?" Becca asked.

Sophie pouted in thought. "No, not mine. I've traced my tree a long way back, and there are no Langs that I know of. She looks so sad."

She handed the photograph back to Becca. "Yeah,

she does a bit," Becca agreed.

Sophie opened a clear sleeve, Becca slipped the photograph into it, and it was added to the list: Wedding Photograph. No name. Sadler/Lang donation. "What's next?"

"A jacket." Becca pulled it out, a flurry of dust rising into the air with it. She laid it out on the table. "Looks like a man's working jacket."

"Anything in the pockets?"

Becca felt around in the two exterior pockets. She shook her head no.

Sophie came around the table. She was confident in her colleague's ability but couldn't contain her own need to explore the jacket herself. She splayed the garment open, but the one internal pocket was also empty. The lining material was the same gray as the jacket, but it wasn't the quality of the fabric Sophie was interested in. One of the seams of the garment didn't look the same as the others, the stitching uneven, the fabric puckered. There was something under the lining. Sophie felt along the seam until she found what she'd hoped—a hidden pocket. She reached inside and pulled out a folded piece of paper.

"What's that?" Becca asked.

Sophie unfolded it carefully. "It looks like a cheque. Made out to an Edward A. McLeod."

"McLeod? I wonder who he is?"

Sophie shrugged. "Another mystery."

The cheque slipped into its own protective sleeve, and Sophie added it to the list: Cheque. To Edward A. McLeod. Issuer (Unreadable) Sum (Unreadable).

"Hey, we may have struck gold," Becca said, as Sophie bent to add the details of the now bagged jacket to her list. "I think it's a diary."

Sophie looked up, anticipation fluttering in her stomach. Nothing gave a better snapshot of the time than a diary.

"You want the honors?" Becca stepped away from the table, Sophie taking her place. She reached out for the book that sat in the center of the oilskin coat, eager to hold it in her hands, her fingertips tingling as she brushed across the green marbled cover of the book. She had time only to assume static electricity to be the cause of the strange feeling before her world disappeared.

****

1865

Emma knew the infant was dead, yet still she rocked back and forth, a lullaby hummed quietly behind closed lips as the gray light of dawn gave way to a new day. She'd known the baby wouldn't live long, but that knowledge didn't make the sadness of his death any easier, and a tear rolled from her cheek, dropping onto the blanket she'd wrapped the infant in the night before.

"Emma?"

Emma looked up. Her eight-year-old brother stood in the doorway, his outline blurred by her tears. "I'm here, Daniel."

Daniel made no move toward her. "The baby is quiet now. Is he better? Has his sickness gone?"

Emma looked down at the bundle in her arms and, for a long moment, she couldn't speak.

"Emma?"

Emma took a breath and beckoned Daniel to her. He came slowly across the room, his dark eyes staring into hers. "Daniel, your brother was very sick, and his little body couldn't fight anymore. He has gone to Heaven,

Daniel. Do you understand?"

Daniel's eyes didn't move from Emma's, and he nodded. "To be with Mama?"

Emma put a hand on the boy's cheek, comforted by the warmth of his skin. "Yes, Daniel, to be with Mama."

Daniel looked down at the baby and reached out his own small hand. He traced a finger down his infant brother's cheek. "He won't feel sick in Heaven, will he, Em?" he whispered.

Emma shook her head. "No," she said, fresh tears welling in her eyes, "he won't be sick anymore."

For a time neither of them moved, Daniel's hand frozen on his brother's cheek, Emma's rocking halted, and for that moment Emma let herself believe the infant was just asleep. Then the moment passed. "There are things to be done now, Daniel," she said briskly, knowing only action could keep grief at bay. "We have to make a place for the baby to rest." Holding the still infant, she pushed herself from the rocking chair and gently laid him in his cradle in front of the fire. She turned to Daniel and took his hand. "I want you to find me a piece of wood for us to scratch his name onto, like the one you did for Mama. Can you do that for me?"

Daniel looked up at her and nodded, his glistening eyes reflecting the firelight. "He never got a name, Emma. Mama didn't…" Daniel's words trailed off.

Emma placed her hand on the little boy's shoulder. "I know, Daniel," she said softly. "But we will name him. I know Mama talked of calling him Adam. What do you think? We will name him Adam?"

Daniel nodded.

Emma swiped a tear from her cheek. She took Daniel's hand and they went outside, the rain stopping for the moment as if respecting their sorrow, and for the second time in three days, Emma began to dig a grave, this one tiny, alongside her mother's. When it was done, she went back into the house and stood over the cradle, looking down at her infant brother. She reached out and cupped his cheek, praying she'd made a mistake and Adam was only asleep. But his cheek was cold, his skin rigid under her hand. Pushing away the grief she knew would paralyze her, Emma scooped up the infant and pulled the blanket across his ashen face. Holding him tightly to her breast, she went back out into the growing daylight and knelt beside the place where he would sleep for eternity, Daniel trailing behind her, a rough wooden cross clutched in his hand.

Emma kissed the baby's tiny head for a final time and lowered him into the grave. "Sleep in peace, little one," she said. Daniel, echoing her words, dropped a stem of lavender onto the blanket. Emma began to push the freshly dug earth into the grave, the sight of the dirt covering the small body almost impossible to bear. But she continued until the ground was again level, and together she and Daniel hammered the little cross, Adam's name scratched onto it, into the ground with a stone.

When the sun rose higher, she would cover the infant's grave with white stones as she had her mother's, but for now, they had done enough, and she took Daniel's hand and returned to the cottage.

The fire had done little to warm the damp room, and Emma added another log to the flames. Then she dropped into the rocking chair, Daniel climbing onto her lap, his arms encircling her neck. She held him tightly, rocking back and forth, sobs jolting his little body, and

Emma let her own tears fall, tears for baby Adam, for herself, but mostly for Daniel who was too young to have so much death in his life. First, their father was surely dead, although no report said it was so. What else would stop his return to his family? He'd ridden for the doctor when their mother had gone into labor too early with baby Adam. He didn't return, and Emma had to presume his death to be the only reason for that. Mother died soon after, Emma unable to stop the rush of blood that spilt from her body as Adam slid into the world. Her mother's screams of agony had just stopped, her eyes staring unseeing at the newborn son Emma held in her arms.

Emma had wrapped the baby tightly, rubbing his body briskly until tiny gasps of air filled his lungs. But he would swallow little of the milk she coaxed into his mouth, his feeble mewls filling the tiny cottage for three days. Now he too was gone. Daniel was all Emma had left.

Emma rocked gently, Daniel's sobs lessening, his grip around her neck relaxing. Comforted by the steady beat of his heart against her own, Emma closed her eyes.

Chapter 2

2022

"Sophie. Oh my God, Sophie! Are you okay?"

It took a moment for Sophie to realize she was lying on the floor, a cushion from the sofa propped under her head. Becca was leaning over her. "Becca? What happened?"

"You fainted, I think. I managed to catch you before you hit the ground, but are you okay?"

Sophie did a mental check of all systems and they seemed to be functioning well enough. She knew where she was, what the date was, and even the prime minister's name, which was something, as politics was the least of her interests. She wriggled her toes, her fingers, all seeming to obey the commands she sent them. "Yeah, yeah, I'm fine."

"Can you sit up? Should I get an ambulance?"

Sophie sat up. All seemed okay. She shook her head. "No, no, I'm good. Can you help me up?"

Becca took Sophie's hands and pulled her to her feet, guiding her to the sofa.

"I guess having only coffee for lunch wasn't a good idea," Sophie said.

"No, and I think I have told you that before," Becca replied. "I did offer to share my sushi with you."

Sophie stuck out her tongue in disgust. "Becca,

seaweed is not food for humans. I've told *you* that before."

Becca laughed. "Whatever, but I think we should call it quits for today. I'll take you home and you can get some human food."

Although Sophie felt fine, she agreed it was probably wise not to drive. "Can you bag the diary for me? I'll take it home."

Becca nodded in agreement and turned back to the worktable. She picked up the book and slipped it into a sleeve, then quickly wrote on the notepad, the diary now added to the list. "I'll wrap the rest of this stuff in the coat for the night. They've survived over a hundred years this way, so one more night is not going to hurt," she said and pulled the protective folds of the oilskin coat over the items yet to be documented.

Sophie followed Becca from the office, locking the door behind her. She crossed to Becca's car, glancing over at her own. Her car was nearly twenty years old, but it still took her where she needed to go and back again, so she saw no need to replace it just yet. She prayed it would still be there in the morning. She climbed into Becca's car.

Traffic was lighter at this time of the afternoon, but it wouldn't be long before it became the bumper-to-bumper crawl of rush hour. For now, however, they were moving at a steady speed and Sophie was grateful for that. Although she felt physically okay, she felt a little disoriented, like she had been away for a long time but couldn't remember where. Maybe that's what happened when you fainted. This was her first time, after all.

"You okay?" Becca asked, glancing across at her.

"Yeah, I'm fine. A little tired. Becca, how long was

I out for?"

Becca frowned. "Oh, not long. A minute or two. Any longer and you would have woken up in the back of an ambulance. You scared the crap out of me. Why do you ask?"

Sophie shook her head. "No reason. It's just that I think I dreamt something. I can't remember what, just fragments. Do you dream when you faint?"

Becca shrugged. "I guess you could. I've never fainted, so I don't know. What did you dream about?"

Sophie pouted in thought. "I can't remember. Something about a baby? And there was a little boy..." She shook her head. "No, that's all I've got. It was sad, though."

Becca reached across and patted Sophie's knee. "Oh, it's probably because I told you about the little boy who was electrocuted. Will Sadler."

Sophie shrugged. "Yeah, I guess that makes sense," she said, turning to look out the window. "It just seemed such a long dream, but you say I was out for only a few minutes."

"Yeah, but dreams are weird like that. I once dreamt I was on the space station. I just sort of lived there and went shopping and to the movies like normal. Like I was there for years. As I said, dreams are weird."

Becca flicked on the indicator and turned the car off the main road into a side street, then turned into Sophie's driveway. "Here you go."

Sophie picked up her backpack and opened her door. "Thanks for the lift. Pick me up in the morning?"

Becca nodded. "No problem," she said, "but listen, you're to call me if you don't feel good, okay? I'm only fifteen minutes away. Promise?"

Sophie said she would and climbed from the car, swinging her bag onto her shoulder. She waved as Becca reversed out into the street, then turned to look up at her small weatherboard home, the façade a powder blue with white trim. The main bedroom sat proud from the rest of the building and three steps led up to the covered veranda that wrapped around the front and side of the house. Sophie had grown up here and played on the veranda as a kid. She still loved to sit here on warm days and watch the honeyeaters and parrots that often visited the garden. The house had been bought by her parents in the 1950s and had been lovingly renovated over the years. When her parents decided to downsize and travel, Sophie sold her apartment in the city and bought her childhood home from them. Her parents were of course delighted, reminding Sophie to keep a room free for them when they came to visit.

Climbing the steps, keys in hand, Sophie unlocked the leadlight front door, pushing it open onto the hallway that ran from the front door to the kitchen at the back. For a moment, as she did more often lately, she imagined calling out hello, and for the greeting to be returned. In her mind, she would wander into the kitchen and a glass of wine would be waiting for her. "How was your day?" would be asked, and together, she and her imaginary companion would prepare dinner. But imagination was one thing and whether she called out or not, the result would be the same—silence, except for the hum of the robot vacuum cleaner as it dutifully carried out its task of keeping the wooden floors free of dirt and dust.

Sophie sighed and went into her bedroom. She dropped her bag onto her bed, then changed out of her work clothes, pulling on a pair of well-worn jeans and an oversized cream jumper. In the kitchen she opened the fridge, taking out the chicken breast she'd bought the day before. She would roast it with carrot, sweet potato, and parsnips. Human food.

Sophie turned the oven on, all shiny glass and stainless steel. The original Aga that sat in the alcove near the hall door was just decorative now. She put the kettle to boil and wandered into the sitting room opposite the bedroom. This was her favorite room, with its high ceilings and fireplace. Her parents had added the cream-and-blue tiled Victorian surround under the white wooden mantel. A large pastel-blue-and-white rug covered the refinished hardwood floorboards from couch to the white lowline unit that held the television, the shade of blue matching that of the wingback chair and ottoman that resided in the corner. Although her furniture had sat at ease in her modern apartment, it worked just as well here.

Against the wall, near the door, her desk rested, it too a modern piece that seemed to blend well with its surroundings. She crossed to it and opened her laptop, dropping into the cream leather high-back chair as she waited for the computer to start up. She entered her password as requested, then tapped the keypad, typing in the search bar "Sadler child electrocuted." A list of options populated the screen, and Sophie clicked on a scanned image of a newspaper report dated almost thirty years ago. "Toddler Dies at Family Property" the headline read.

William "Will" Sadler died today in a tragic accident at his parents' property. The boy, 3, was electrocuted when he came into contact with a faulty power cable and couldn't be revived. The property had been recently purchased and was in need of renovation. However, a spokesman for the parents said they were not aware...

The story went on, but Sophie was drawn to the grainy photo of the little boy on what looked like his third birthday. He was smiling at the camera, a cowboy hat on his head. A feeling of sadness washed over her, not unlike what she'd felt in her dream. She guessed Becca was right. Hearing about Will Sadler had been the cause of that dream, and who wouldn't be sad?

After dinner, Sophie washed the dishes, then poured herself a glass of wine. She was tired but felt an unease she couldn't seem to shake. She turned on the lamp and curled up in the armchair with the novel she had so far been enjoying. But tonight, after the fourth time re-reading the same paragraph, she closed it and stood up. Wandering over to her desk, she sat at her computer again. She should work on the information cards for the items that were ready for display, but the document remained blank, her fingers hovering over the keyboard, frozen. She couldn't think. "Time for bed." She sighed and stood up.

She went into her bedroom and switched on the lamp on the bedside table, placing the half-full glass of wine next to it. She undressed, draping her jeans and sweater over the chair next to the door, then pulled a T-shirt from the dresser and slipped it on. She climbed into bed. Her bag was where she'd left it earlier, and she reached inside for the diary. Maybe reading some of the entries would settle her. She reached into the plastic sleeve Becca had put the book into, feeling the smooth surface of the cover under her hand, her fingertips tingling.

****

1865

Sunlight began to creep along the stone windowsill, and Emma stretched her hand out toward it, feeling a little of its warmth through the glass. She didn't notice Daniel waking and slipping from her lap. She listened for sounds of him and heard him playing in the yard. The two chickens that would be better as a meal than as suppliers of eggs were voicing their annoyance at the boy's intrusion into their pen, and Emma stood up and crossed to the open door.

Outside, defeated clouds drifted across a pale sky. Emma rubbed her arms for warmth, her thin cotton dress no match for the chill breeze. Her mother had promised to make new dresses for them both as soon as the baby was born, her own gown as threadbare as Emma's. Her mother had worked as a seamstress, and a talented one at that. Her trade dovetailed perfectly with Emma's father's—that of a tailor held in high regard in London. But business was only good at the best of times in the past few years, and those times had become few and far between.

When her mother's health had begun to deteriorate, the decision was made to leave the damp and pollution of London and try their luck in the new colony on the other side of the world. Her father had put his business up for sale and said when it sold, money would soon be a worry of the past. He would order a new buggy, and then they were to ride to the town of Fremantle and choose not only fabrics but everything else that would make their cottage a proper home.

As it was now, the cottage was nothing more than one large room serving as both sitting room and bedrooms, the bed her parents shared and the one she shared with Daniel divided from the main room and each other with calico sheets nailed to wooden beams. A smaller side room served as the kitchen and bathroom, a sheet hung from a rope strung across the ceiling offering some privacy when bathing.

Her father had talked excitedly about extending the stone building, with bedrooms and a bathroom being the first additions planned. There would be a garden, a proper chicken coop, and two more horses, and the pantry would be stocked with everything they needed. The small hamlet of Rockingham would grow, he'd told her, and they would prosper here.

But Emma knew the future her father had wanted for them wouldn't be theirs now. There was no money to speak of, and prosperity was far from her reach. She would mend as best she could the few dresses her mother had worn, and Daniel would have to take care of the few clothes he had until…

Until what? This question had plagued Emma for the past three days, and still she'd no answer, her mind unwilling to contemplate what future lay ahead of them.

Taking her mother's shawl from the hook by the door, Emma wrapped it around her shoulders and went out into the yard. "Are you bothering those chickens again, Daniel?" she called, smiling at the innocent grin the little boy gave back, his sorrow at the death of his mother and brother hidden away.

"They have two eggs today, Em," he said, holding up the creamy-shelled treasure. "Can you bake a cake with them?"

Emma smiled. Two eggs were a treat, and maybe she should make them something special. "We'll see."

Daniel's grin grew as he skipped across the yard to her, a smudge of dirt highlighting one cheek.

Emma took the eggs from him. "Go and clean up, and then we'll decide what to do with our good fortune."

Emma watched as the child jogged toward the house, envying him the small burden he had to bear compared to hers, his mood buoyed by two small eggs.

Setting the eggs gently in the metal pail that hung from the well, Emma steeled herself for the task at hand. In front of her, a low rough picket fence separated the small front yard from the dirt track that connected this property with others, the closest some two miles away. Eventually, the track led to the road to Fremantle. To her left, a line of scraggly bushes marked the eastern edge of the property. The chickens lived on this side of the cottage, the wire mesh that fenced them in no match for their ability to escape. Each evening she and Daniel would spend a good part of an hour finding, chasing, and catching the disagreeable birds, locking them safely into their wooden box for the night. The few nights they had been unable to catch them, however, had been disturbed by the sounds of hungry dogs finding an easy meal. They had eight birds when they first arrived in the colony, but only two remained.

Emma looked to her right at her mother's grave alongside that of her infant brother's, and an overwhelming sense of loneliness washed over her.

She strained to hear anything that would show there were other people nearby, if not by sight at least by sound. But there were no shouts or whistles, no sound of yapping dogs or squealing children echoing through the endless miles of forest—or bush, as they called it here. Tall trees crowded the landscape in every direction, their leaves never turning brown nor falling in response to the changing seasons. Below them, dotted here and there amongst other scrubby bushes, grew black-trunked plants, some the size of a man, their thin green spikey foliage poking out every which way like a head of green untamed hair.

As well as the flora, Emma knew this strange bush-scape was home to odd creatures, also, many of which were dangerous. Snakes were the greatest fear—a bite from one enough to kill the strongest man, or so she'd been told. Long-legged birds that could run as fast as a horse but couldn't fly an inch lived alongside animals that travelled solely by jumping, carrying their young in natural pockets. The name of these animals she knew well: kangaroo. Daniel had pretended to be one for nearly three days when they first arrived, tying a small teddy bear to his belly with one of Mother's scarves and hopping everywhere with great joy. They were happy days, fresh air and sunlight filling them with the promise of a better life than the one they had left in the murky streets of London. How quickly the happiness had gone, taking promise with it.

Emma felt loneliness weigh down on her as heavy as the rocks at her feet that she would use to cover Adam's grave, and for a moment she wanted nothing more than to lie down between her mother and brother and rest in peace.

"I'm all clean, Emma." Daniel's voice rang through the air, jolting Emma from her thoughts, and she glanced over at the little boy, his hands waggled in the air to prove they were indeed clean. Emma smiled, her despair lifting. She'd need to stay strong for Daniel. She was all he had.

The rocks cut into her cold hands, her fingers raw and red as she laid the last stone over the small mound of earth. She broke more stems of lavender from one of the bushes that grew in unruly clumps amongst the scrub land and stuck them into the ground. But she didn't linger over the grave any longer than she had to. That would only invite more grief, and she'd had her fair share of that over her twenty-five years. There were other siblings as well as Daniel and baby Adam—three sisters and two more brothers. All had died, if not at birth, then soon after. Except for the twins, Alice and Eliza, born just a year after Daniel. They had lived to just before their third birthday, typhoid taking them both within days of each other. She'd grieved for all of them, but it didn't bring them back, and lingering over baby Adam's grave wouldn't either.

Returning to the cottage, Emma busied herself cleaning and cooking, but without the infant to tend to, the day dragged sluggishly into night, and with it came the cold. There was little dry wood left, and she glanced at the empty cradle. It soon would become fuel for the fire. She'd heard people speak of the incredible heat that bathed this country in the summer, but that was something Emma could only imagine. Tonight was as cold as any she'd known in England.

After she'd washed the supper dishes, she sat with Daniel in the rocking chair and told him stories of make-believe places and imaginary adventurers. She hoped the made-up tales would fill his dreams instead of the nightmares that reality could so easily present to him. Then as his head drooped on her shoulder, his eyes heavy with the need to sleep, she ushered him to his bed.

"Good night, my sweet," she said tucking the quilt

firmly around his shoulders to keep out the increasingly chill air. "Sweet dreams."

He murmured a reply, his eyes closing.

Emma bent and kissed her younger brother's forehead before returning to the sitting room. The cottage was illuminated by the small fire in the hearth and a candle stub on the table, a dismal light, but enough to see the blank page of her diary waiting for her hopes and fears. Her diary was her friend and her advisor, and more than ever she needed those things now. She dipped the nib into the ink and began to write.

My dearest friend,

My heart breaks as I write these words. Baby Adam passed this morning, and I buried him beside Mother. I pray Father will return soon, but I fear he too is gone, although this I haven't said to Daniel. He believes Father is away on important business and I cannot break his young heart again so soon after Mother's and baby Adam's passing. With Father's absence, I fear we may be next, as food is becoming scarce. I think we will have enough vegetables to see us through two more weeks, but the flour is running low, weevils eating more than us, I feel. When the rain stops, I will go to the Andersons' farm and tell them of Mother and baby Adam. I'm sure they'll lend any assistance they're able, but I know they're struggling also to make ends meet themselves. I don't know what else to do. I will send a letter to England tomorrow to my uncle, but any aid he could provide wouldn't arrive until six months or more, and then it may be too late.

I will pray for my father's return and for us.

E.

Now Emma flicked to a blank page at the end of the

book and tore the page from the binding, setting it aside. Then, closing the diary, she tied it with the red ribbon her mother had worn in her hair and pushed it to one side. She moved the single piece of paper into the circle of candlelight and stared at it. What was she to write? How was she to break the news to her uncle of her mother's death and of his own brother's also, most likely? Fatigue dulled her mind, and she could find no answer to her question. She wrote anyway.

Dear Uncle Robert,

I'm writing this letter to you under the saddest of circumstances. My mother and my infant brother have both left us, their graves side by side on the edge of this property, and my father hasn't returned five days gone now. He rode for help when my mother's laboring began, her health failing quickly. Now it's just Daniel and myself, and although we have enough food for a fortnight, I have no money to see us any further. Our neighbors, the Andersons, I know will help if they're able, but their position is no better than ours. I fear I will have to leave the cottage and try my luck in Fremantle. I realize there's little you can do so far away, but I'm at a loss. I pray this letter reaches you swiftly and that your reply is swift too.

Your loving niece,

Emma.

Emma held the letter up to the candle, moving it back and forth over the flame for a moment, the ink setting firmly to the paper. Then she folded it and slid it into an envelope in which a letter from her uncle had arrived some months back. She crossed out her father's name and a semblance of an address and wrote her uncle's name in the space left. Then, with a small blob of wax dripped from the candle, she sealed the envelope. That was all she could do, and she rested the small envelope that held their only hope against the copper kettle her mother used to fill with lavender to scent the cottage. The wind that had steadily strengthened throughout the afternoon tormented the tall gum trees outside, their branches creaking and groaning under the onslaught. Little parties of it whispered through the gap in the bottom of the door, sending leaves skidding across the floor. The flame of the squat candle wavered, then retired for the night, and Emma decided to do the same.

She drew the curtain that separated her parents' bed from Daniel's and unbuttoned her dress, letting it drop to the stone floor, her petticoat following. She scooped up the garments and draped them along the foot of the bed.

The wind howled around the cottage, and Emma rubbed at the gooseflesh that rose on her skin. She pulled one of her father's shirts from under the pillow and quickly slipped it on.

Daniel turned over in his bed, mumbling something in his dream, then laughed loudly. Emma waited for more, but Daniel sighed and was quiet, his breathing even and relaxed. The sleep of a child, and Emma hoped she would sleep half as well.

She slid under the quilt and curled up as tightly as she could, her hands wedged between her knees. She wished the wind didn't have to moan in such a pitiful way, and she pulled the eiderdown over her head, closing her eyes, begging sleep to take her. But sleep didn't come, in its place just a suffocating sense of loneliness and fear.

Chapter 3

2022

Sophie jolted awake, her hand searching out her phone, her fingers stabbing at the screen, trying to silence the insistent jingle of her alarm. She sighed and closed her eyes. Maybe she could have five more minutes…but her phone chimed again, this time a call, and she answered it, her voice still hoarse from sleep.

"Hey. It's me. Sorry, did I wake you? I'm a bit early."

Sophie stifled a groan. Becca being here meant no five minutes more. It meant she had to get up and get ready for work. This was usually something Sophie gave little thought to, her work never a chore. But today she was tired, her enthusiasm for facing the day deserting her. Maybe she was coming down with something. But she said none of this to Becca. "That's okay. Let yourself in. I'm just going in the shower. Make a coffee if you want."

Sophie disconnected the call and rolled from bed.

"I'm guessing you were good last night. Did you sleep okay?" Becca called from the bedroom as Sophie stepped into the shower stall.

"Yeah, I was fine," Sophie called back, but it was a lie. She'd been woken by two sparring cats, their yowls winding up to screams as they went into battle. A yell from a neighbor halted the skirmish, but Sophie was unable to fall back asleep. She'd dreamt again about a baby, Adam she thought his name was, and a little boy, and although she couldn't remember much of the dream, she could still feel a deep sense of sorrow. She'd only fallen asleep as the sun began to rise, her alarm awaking her again a couple of hours later. But she didn't want to tell Becca because, to be honest, there wasn't much to tell, most of it fading away as dreams do. For a moment an image flashed in her mind—a stem of lavender. She had been holding it, and for a moment she could smell its perfume. "That would be why," she said aloud as she glanced down at the bottle of bodywash in her hand. "Lavender Dream." She sighed loudly and turned off the water. Dressed in black pants and a white button-down shirt, Sophie wrestled her hair into a clip large enough to hold the unruly curls away from her face. She had no energy for straightening irons this morning.

"Did you get anything good from the diary?" Becca was sitting on Sophie's bed, a cup in one hand, her other hand resting on top of the book enclosed in its protective sleeve.

Sophie frowned. Did she even look at the diary last night? She knew she took it to bed with her, hence it being on the bed now, but whether she took it out of its sleeve and read any, she guessed not. Surely, she would have remembered putting it back after she'd finished. "No. I think I must have fallen asleep before I got a chance." She picked up the diary, looking at the green marbled cover, its cloth binding, all protected by the plastic sleeve. She could feel a faint tingling in her fingers, and she held out the book to Becca. "Does this feel weird when you hold it?"

Becca took the diary from her and weighed the book in her hand. She pouted. "Not really. Why?"

Sophie shrugged. "No reason. Just wondered if the plastic felt different than usual."

Becca shook her head. "Not that I can tell. It's the same stock we've been using for a while. Come on, I made you some eggs." Becca pushed herself from the bed. "At least then I'll know you had something decent to eat this morning."

Sophie made a face at her friend. "Thanks, Mum," she said and followed Becca from the room.

****

"He's a really nice guy," Becca was saying. They had been in the car for only five minutes before Becca launched into her pitch. Sophie had become used to Becca trying at least once a fortnight to fix her up with some guy she knew or a friend of her partners. "He's into history. I think."

Sophie laughed. "Becca, the last guy you said that about was into the history of cars. Interesting subject, but he really didn't have anything else to talk about. I know more about the birth of the automobile than I do my own, and believe me, I was told the story of my mother's three-day labor more than once."

"This guy's different, Soph, honestly. Why don't you just meet him? He's really cute, too," Becca cajoled.

"I'll think about it, Bec."

"Think yes," Becca said. "Come on. When were you last on a date?"

That was a good question and one that needed a little thought to answer. Apart from the car lover some months back, it had been over a year. Oh God, that long? Sophie groaned to herself. It wasn't that she wanted to be alone

28

at this stage in her life, and up until four years ago she didn't think she would be. She'd met Matt on their first day at university. Like Sophie, he was an undergrad, his degree in law, Sophie taking hers in history. A chance meeting in student services was all it took for them to become Matt-and-Sophie to their friends and, for the next seven years, that's what they were.

Although they'd never decided in any formal way, they planned a life together, wanted the same things, marriage and children eventually. Their future together seemed pretty much certain. But when Matt was in his final year, things started to change. He moved in a different world to Sophie's now, mixed with people who shared his passion for the law and the lifestyle some of the lucky few could have if that passion was hired by the right people. Sophie, on the other hand, happily spent her days working at the registry office, recording births, marriages, and deaths of Western Australians. She loved the job, but there wasn't a hint of the affluent lifestyle that could be found in the legal world, and she felt uncomfortable around the people Matt now spent time with. At first, the changes in their relationship were small, just little things stupidly left ignored as if they would go away. But although the evolution was slow, it was an evolution nonetheless, and little things became big things. Within two years of Matt taking a position with a well-known boutique law firm, he was talking of them taking a break from each other, maybe seeing other people for a while. Nothing permanent, he assured her. She assured him it was and moved out the next day.

She couldn't blame him, really—they had been so young when they met—but still, that realization didn't repair her broken heart. Apart from the occasional movie, dinner, and one-night stands, she hadn't allowed herself to fall into anything more serious than that. "Over a year."

"A year!" Becca repeated. "Sophie, I don't like to say it, but…"

"Don't say it then," Sophie interrupted. "I'm aware."

Becca laughed. "Well then, I don't have to remind you that this date may be more a matter of necessity, if you know what I mean. Seriously, Sophie, you don't want to become the old lady with many cats. That's what will happen to you. Trust me."

Sophie laughed. "I don't even own one cat, Bec."

"True, but maybe you should at least give this date a try before you end up buying one. What do you think?"

Sophie sighed loudly. "When is it? And where?"

Becca smiled broadly. "We'll get something to eat in the city on Saturday, then maybe see a movie, depending on how things go. You can see if you like him. If not, you can excuse yourself with a headache or some other excuse, like you have to get to the cat home before closing."

"Very funny."

They pulled into the car park, Sophie happy to see her car was still there. She unlocked the office door and turned on the light. The coat was where it had been left, guarding its valuable cargo like a parent wrapping its arms around a child. Gloved and masked, Becca unwrapped the coat again and removed each item yet to be recorded—a small ledger, "Lang Hills Accounts" penned across the cover, a child's drawing of what looked like a horse with a person atop it, and the bundle of letters tied with a faded red ribbon. The oilskin coat was now free to be examined further.

Sophie took the sleeved diary from her backpack and placed it with the items they had secured yesterday. Although she'd taken the diary home last night, she didn't recall reading any of it, and she was eager to do so. She also wanted to look at the letters, another great way to get a feel for the people who wrote them and what their life was like. But the coat needed to be put away first. And who knew what might be hidden in the pockets? "I'll inspect and bag the coat if you want to get sleeves ready for the rest of the items," Sophie said.

Becca nodded and took out what was needed from the drawer while Sophie examined the coat. But unlike the luck they had had with the jacket yesterday, the pockets were empty except for some lint and a brass button. Although the fabric of the coat was undamaged, there was a rust-colored stain that blossomed across the lining at the bottom of the coat. Sophie wondered if it was blood and noted it down, a question mark next to the notation indicating that further investigation was needed.

"Listen to this," Becca said. She'd taken the diary from its sleeve, and she turned the pages gently with her gloved hand. "This is a bit sad. *My dearest friend. My heart breaks as I write these words. Baby Adam passed this morning, and I buried him beside Mother. I pray Father…*"

Sophie looked up at her colleague, the hairs on the nape of her neck prickling to attention. "What did you say?"

"I said isn't this sad." Becca looked up at her colleague. "Jeez, Sophie, what's wrong? You're as white as a sheet. You're not going to faint again, are you?"

Sophie shook her head. "What did you say?"

Becca frowned. "About being pale or fainting?"

"About the baby?"

"The baby?" Becca glanced down at the diary. "Oh, the baby in the diary? He died, poor little guy. So did his mother. Sophie, what's wrong?"

"His name was Adam?"

Becca nodded. "Yeah. That's what it says here. Sophie, what's going on? You look like you've seen a ghost."

Sophie pulled the stool from under the worktable and sat down, her legs unable to hold her up. "Becca, I dreamt about that baby last night. Adam. And the mother."

Becca laughed. "Well, that's not surprising. I wouldn't recommend this for bedtime reading."

"But that's the thing, Bec, I didn't read it."

Becca frowned. "Sophie, what are you talking about?"

"I didn't read the diary, Bec. It was in my bag on my bed. When I got into bed, I reached for it, and I remember putting my hand on it, but I must have fallen asleep. I didn't read any of it. Not a word."

A smile grew on Becca's face. "Okay, good one, Sophie, but I'm a bit old for spooky stories."

"I'm not telling you a story, Becca. I don't understand it myself, but I know I didn't read the diary, and I *dreamt* of the baby and his mother. In the dream, I covered their graves with white rocks so dogs wouldn't dig them up." She held out her hands. "I can feel the roughness of the rocks. I know it sounds crazy, but I know it like I had written it."

Becca's smile had slipped from her face, replaced now with a frown. "Crazy is a good word for it, Soph,

32

but obviously you read some of it in the diary, put it away, and you've just forgotten you read it."

Sophie could only offer a shrug in response. She knew what she'd done, which was to simply slide her hand inside the sleeve to retrieve the book. When she woke up in the morning, the diary was where she'd left it.

Becca sighed loudly. "So what are you saying? You dreamt of people long dead that you know nothing about? Sophie, you've simply read this part of the diary and forgotten, or you've read something about another baby some time and it's all mixed up in your head. That makes more sense than what you're saying, doesn't it?"

Sophie didn't miss the frustration in Becca's tone, and she couldn't blame her friend for that. What Sophie was asking her friend to believe was simply not plausible. She couldn't have dreamt about people she had no knowledge of, so she had to have known about them from the diary. That's the only explanation there was, despite it feeling so real. Sophie felt her face flush as it dawned on her how crazy she must sound. "Of course, you're right, Bec. I don't know what I'm thinking. I didn't sleep well," she said, offering this as the reason for her ridiculous claim. "The small bits I remember just felt so real, and I was so sure I hadn't read it in the diary."

Becca reached across the table and put her hand on Sophie's arm. "You're just confused after yesterday. You've been working really hard on this project, and we were both so excited about the box coming in. We both knew the rough age of the stuff. That and all the history you've been putting together, and then the story about the Sadler kid and fainting yesterday… Well, it's all just got mixed up in your head. It's understandable."

Sophie looked up at her friend. What Becca said was true. This project was so important to her that she'd worked way beyond the required work hours, reading late into the night, filling journals with all the events that made up the individual lives of those who had come before. Family histories were something she took maybe too much of an interest in, often researching beyond the basic information of births, marriages, and deaths of some of the settlers. She wanted to know who they were, where they came from, what was important to them. They had lived, and she wanted to know them, give them a voice, and she would have to admit she felt unusually sad when she read of the deaths of some, especially when they were children. Somewhere she must have read about the death of a baby called Adam and maybe somewhere else about a woman dying in childbirth. Postpartum deaths and children dying young were certainly not rare events. They were all too common. Becca was right, and Sophie now felt more than a little embarrassed, her face not hiding this fact.

"I feel like an idiot."

Becca squeezed her arm. "You are an idiot, Soph, but that's why I love you."

Sophie couldn't help but smile. "Make some coffee, Becca. Let's get this stuff bagged and logged. And not a word about this ever, ever. Okay?"

They worked in silence for the next hour, the five remaining items slipped into protective sleeves and numbered by Becca, Sophie adding their details to the list on the notepad. The next job would be to scan any documents, do any necessary research, write up a more comprehensive description, and plan what was to be displayed. Although there were still three hours left in the workday, that would be tomorrow's job. Becca was leaving early, and Sophie still had plenty of work to do on other displays.

"If I could have got another time with the celebrant, I would have, but Mike is on night shifts so can't get away when I finish," Becca said as she picked up her bag readying to leave.

Sophie dismissed Becca's comment with a wave of her hand. "It's really fine, Bec. You know that."

Bec smiled. "Yeah, I know, but thanks anyway. So you promise you will leave when the big hand is on the twelve and the little hand is on the four?"

Sophie laughed. "I'll do my best," she said. "Now go before Mike realizes what he's getting himself into."

Becca turned to the door, her hand raised as if to wave, one finger more prominent than the others. "See you tomorrow, Soph."

Sophie smiled as she watched her friend leave, then turned back to the worktable. She couldn't have asked for a better partner in this project. Although they had only known each other for a little more than six months, they had formed a friendship from almost day one. Becca was the logical one of the duo, Sophie not ashamed to admit that she was herself a hopeless romantic and a bit of a dreamer at times. But the differences seemed to work, and any fears Sophie had about taking on more than she could handle straight out of university were allayed to some degree. Becca didn't have the qualifications that Sophie had, but she had practical experience, and that was worth ten degrees as far as Sophie was concerned.

Sophie flicked the kettle on, then fetched the

stepladder from the storage cupboard. She folded down the steps and positioned it in front of the bank of shelving units that lined one wall. They held rows of plastic storage boxes of various sizes. She climbed up and took an empty box from the top and dropped it onto the worktables. Then she climbed down and turned to the box. She unclipped the lid and picked up the coat, folded neatly inside its protective bag. She placed that in the box, laying the other items that the coat had once protected, all in their own protective sleeves, on top of it. Except for the letters and the diary.

Coffee in hand, Sophie took the letters and sat on the sofa. She put her coffee on the side table and then slipped on a pair of cotton gloves. Sliding the letters from their sleeve onto her lap, she pulled at the ribbon that held the letters bound together, a half dozen or so, and then carefully unfolded the first one.

The letter was written to an Emma and was written in a child's hand, one not quite proficient in spelling, if the several instances of crossing out and rewriting of words were any indication. The letter assured Emma that he was well and studying hard and hoped he could return to her as soon as possible. He didn't like it much where he was. He hoped she was well and that she wasn't too unhappy. It was signed Daniel, and Sophie felt a chill for a moment and glanced up at the window. She had a view over the hills and could see that dark clouds had begun to gather. It looked like a storm was brewing, the soft pattering of rain on the glass a prelude. She wished she'd worn a jumper over her shirt.

Sophie sipped at her coffee, and then, putting down the cup, picked up another letter. Carefully she unfolded it and read.

Dear Uncle Robert,

I'm writing this letter to you under the saddest of circumstances. My mother and my infant brother have both left us, their graves side by side on the edge of this property, and my father hasn't returned five days gone now. He rode for help when my mother's laboring began, her health failing quickly. Now it's just Daniel and myself, and although we have enough food for a fortnight, I have no money to see us any further. Our neighbors, the Andersons, I know will help if they're able, but their position is no better than ours. I fear I will have to leave the cottage and try my luck in Fremantle. I realize there's little you can do so far away, but I'm at a loss. I pray this letter reaches you swiftly and that your reply is swift too.

Your loving niece,

Emma.

"What the…" Sophie whispered, staring down at the words. Not only were they in her handwriting, but that she'd written this letter was beyond doubt. She knew this as well as she knew her name was Sophie Louise Harris. "Oh, come on, Sophie," she admonished in her best Becca way. "That's just crazy," but the reprimand didn't help. She bundled the letters together and stood up, crossing to the worktable. She opened a notepad to a clear page and began to write.

Dear Uncle Robert,

I'm writing this letter to you…

She stopped. The script was nearly identical, the letters sloping toward the right, the laziness in the letter N, the dominant loop in the capital letter R. This was written in her hand.

She stepped back from the table, her heart beating a

bit harder in her chest. "Sophie, stop. Come on. What are you saying?" she said aloud, trying once again to see this logically. "A lot of people have similar handwriting. Don't be crazy." She nodded to herself in agreement, but herself countered with, "Yeah, but do a lot of people just *know* they wrote something they haven't seen before?" She took a deep breath, trying to calm herself. "You don't really believe that, do you?"

Sophie didn't answer that question, her gaze drifting to the diary she'd left next to the storage box. She reached across the table, her hands resting on the plastic sleeve. When Becca had read out the entry earlier today, Sophie felt like she knew it, as if she'd written it herself. Was the handwriting in there hers also?

She slid the book toward her. The word "Diary" was stamped into the green marbled cover, and Sophie traced over the indented word through the plastic, her fingertips tingling as she did. It felt familiar, yet she'd never owned a diary, nor any book like this, for that matter. She let the book slide from its sleeve and out onto the worktable. She reached out to open it, and the sense of being pulled backward overwhelmed her until she felt nothing at all.

Chapter 4

1865

Emma awoke with a start. Her dreams had been terrifying, her mother calling to her from a distance, moving away every time Emma tried to run to her. "Take care of him," her mother had called over and over as Emma ran. In her arms, she held the lifeless infant, but it had Daniel's face. "Don't leave me, Emma," the baby had whispered as she ran, its body cold and stiff in the blanket. "Don't leave me."

For a long while, Emma lay staring at the ceiling, waiting for the dream to fade, hoping it would take the feeling of dread that lay heavy in the pit of her stomach. She could hear Daniel outside, no doubt seeing if the hens had any more gifts for them. She doubted they would be that lucky again. The two eggs they did get yesterday were something quite rare. She knew soon she would have to kill the birds if they were to provide any sustenance at all, despite the abundance of rabbits that gathered at dusk. They were too fast to catch. Her father had tried to teach her to shoot, and if she'd been a better student, rabbit could have been on the menu. But she couldn't hit the side of a barn, and it hadn't been important at the time to perfect that skill. Maybe she could try again, but for now, she had other things on her mind, and she climbed from her bed.

She called Daniel inside, eggless as she suspected, and told him of her plan to ride to the Andersons' place. They ate a breakfast of oatmeal, the final dribble of honey sweetening the stodgy mash. Then Emma, eager to get to the Andersons' before the clearing sky had a change of mind, ushered Daniel out to the paddock behind the cottage. She watched as he led the young mare from the lean-to and saddled her. He climbed up onto the docile animal, an upturned pail giving him the extra height he needed to reach the stirrups. "Okay, Emma," he said, looking down at his sister. "Get on."

Emma hitched her dress up to her knees and took her turn standing on the pail, steadying herself against the warm body of the horse. She grabbed onto the worn leather of the saddle and swung one leg over the mare's rump, her dress tearing at a seam as she did.

"Are you on, Em?" Daniel asked, and Emma nodded, wrapping her arms around Daniel's waist.

Daniel set the horse in motion, and Emma squeezed her eyes shut as they began to move forward. The pony wasn't a big animal, but it still seemed a long way to the ground, the rocking motion of the animal beneath her threatening to push her that distance any minute. Daniel guided the mare through the gate and out onto the dirt road. The wind had blown most of the threatening clouds to the east, the few remaining ones holding little if any rain. Branches torn from the towering gum trees in the night's storm littered the track ahead of them, but the horse picked its way through.

As they rounded the last bend, Emma was glad the journey was almost over. Her feeling changed as they approached the property, however. Emma now wished they hadn't come at all. She'd been here a few times with her parents, the Andersons' five children running to greet them, their red setter Marie barking a welcome. But today there were no children, no welcome, no one, the yard quiet.

Daniel reined the horse in, and Emma slid to the ground. She looked across at the empty clothesline, the vacant chicken coop, the curtainless windows, and frowned. The property looked deserted.

"I don't think they're here," Daniel said, following Emma's gaze.

Emma agreed it looked that way. The covered buggy was missing, as well as two of the three horses that usually grazed in the field adjacent. One horse remained, however, tethered to the verandah post, and Emma hoped this was a sign that at least someone was there.

"Hello," she called out, turning toward the cottage.

There was no reply, and Emma called out her greeting a second time.

The cottage door groaned open, and Mr. Anderson stepped onto the porch. "Emma?"

Emma smiled with relief. "Oh, thank goodness, Mr. Anderson. I was starting to think there was no one here."

James Anderson pulled the cottage door shut. "You're not far from the truth there, Emma. I was just leaving myself. Five minutes more and you would have missed me."

Emma frowned. "Are you out for the day with the family?" she asked, although she knew their outing was more permanent than that.

The man shook his head, confirming her thoughts. "No. My wife and the children are in Fremantle waiting for me. We decided to return to England. Charlotte finds living here intolerable and misses her family. We sail tomorrow. I was going to ride across to see your father before I left."

Emma's stomach lurched with this news, and she took a deep breath, pulling the letter from what remained of her pocket. "I'm certainly sorry to hear that," she said, although sorry was nowhere near what she felt. She was devastated. She wanted to run into this man's arms and beg him to stay. But she didn't, nor could she cry. She had to be strong for Daniel. Emma squeezed her fingers into her fists, digging her nails into her palms, hoping the pain would stop the tears that waited for her to say the words. "My mother passed five days ago, and my infant brother joined her yesterday." She noted the look of shock on the older man's face but continued. "My father went for help when my mother took ill, and he hasn't returned. I have no news of him, but..." Emma left the rest of the sentence unspoken, not wanting to voice her fear in front of her brother.

"Oh, dear God, I'm so sorry. You've been alone all this time? Why didn't you come to us before?"

Emma shook her head. "The baby was very ill. I couldn't bring him from the house with the weather as it was, and I also couldn't send Daniel on his own. I hoped every day my father would return." She glanced over her shoulder at Daniel and lowered her voice as she said, "Every day that passes it would seem that's more unlikely."

"Oh God, Emma, I don't know what to say. I feel so bad, abandoning you. I...I could postpone my journey. I will ride to Fremantle and tell my wife. She'll understand."

A voice screamed in Emma's head. *Yes, please, please stay*, it cried, but it was only for her to hear, and she shook her head. "No. I appreciate your generous offer, but I cannot ask you to do that." She held out the letter. "What I will ask you to do for me, however, is to put this letter into the mail. It's for my uncle."

Mr. Anderson took the letter from her and looked down at the envelope. "I will, Emma. I will do that first thing. I just wish I could do more."

Emma smiled weakly. "Thank you, Mr. Anderson. Your concern is appreciated, but we will be fine."

Mr. Anderson glanced across at his horse. "Wait. I have something for you." He crossed to the large black animal, unbuckled the saddlebag, and pulled out a calico bag. "It's not much," he said teasing open the string that held the bag closed. "Some bread, cheese, a few eggs, and some sugar. I was going to give them to my cousin in Fremantle, but their need is not as great as yours." He took a breath. "The vegetable garden still has some life in it, some potatoes, carrots. Take everything before the rabbits do."

Emma nodded and took the bag from him. It was heavy, and she set it on the ground by her feet.

"And there's another property about five miles east of here. The Cutlers. They're good people. They'll give you any help they can. Do you promise you will go to them?"

Again, Emma nodded, her mouth clamped tightly closed against the reality of his leaving, which came closer every minute.

The man sighed. "I'm so sorry, Emma. If only…" He didn't finish the sentence. There were too many "if onlys." He turned to his horse, loosening its tether. He swung into the saddle. "My prayers will be with you and your brother, and I will ensure this letter is put in the right hands." He urged the horse forward. "Be a good boy for your sister, Daniel," he said, and guided the horse onto the track.

Emma fought the urge to run after him, watching numbly as horse and rider disappeared into the trees, the thud of hooves fading into silence. Now they were truly alone, and the strength Emma had used to keep her tears at bay faltered. She choked back a sob.

"Emma?"

Would it be Daniel's grave she would be digging next?

"Emma?"

Or would she succumb first, leaving her brother to die alone?

"Emma, please, you're scaring me."

Daniel's cries broke into her thoughts, and Emma turned to face her brother. She didn't want this burden, didn't ask for it, nor did she know what to do about it. She'd not reckoned on being alone in this land with little other than the clothes on their backs and a few weeks of food. But to Daniel she simply said, "Everything is fine, Daniel." She busied herself with the calico bag at her feet, repeating those same words silently to herself until she'd gained some control of her emotions. Finally she straightened up, hauling the bag from the ground. She gathered it underneath and held it up to Daniel. "Can you tie this onto the saddle," she said.

Daniel hoisted the bag up and tied it off, balancing it on the saddle in front of him.

"We will take it home and come back with the bag for whatever vegetables are left."

Daniel nodded, a frown still distorting his features.

"We are going to be fine, Daniel," Emma said with

more confidence than she felt. "I promise."

****

My dearest friend,

I visited the Andersons today, needing the reassurance of adults. I took comfort in the knowledge that they were but a few miles away, a short journey if our situation here becomes too much to bear, but, on our arrival, we were dealt another harsh blow. The Andersons have left their property and are returning to England. Our closest neighbors are now more than five miles east. Daniel knows that things aren't as trouble-free as I tell him. He's young, but I'm sure he can sense the anxiety I'm feeling. He'll soon realize that Father is not returning, and I fear that will be too much for him to bear. The fears that wait in my mind for my attention are too much to contemplate, and I leave them to simmer at the back of my mind. Soon, however, I know I must address them. I miss Mother unbearably, Father too, but for Daniel's sake, I keep these words in my heart and on this page. At least food is not a problem for the time being. Mr. Anderson's vegetable garden has yielded more than our own, and I have potatoes, corn, carrots, and two reasonable cabbages. Moreso, my letter is on its way to England, and eventually Uncle will receive news of us. That's a good thought, and for tonight that's the thought I will go to sleep on.

E.

****

Emma woke, the rumble of thunder disturbing her dreams. She pulled the quilt higher over her shoulders, the smoldering embers of the fire no match for the wind that slipped through any crack or crevice it could find. Another clap of thunder and Daniel cried out in his sleep.

Emma waited to see if he would settle. He whimpered once more, then was quiet, and Emma rolled onto her side. The cottage trembled as thunder again cracked the sky overhead, lightning searing through the dark, lighting the room for a moment, and Emma buried her face in the pillow. She wondered if this would get any easier, if her life or Daniel's would ever resemble what they'd had only a few weeks ago. As she did every night since her mother died, Emma cried herself to sleep.

Chapter 5

2022

Sophie was on a horse with the same little boy she'd seen in her earlier dream. They were going to see someone. She wasn't sure who or why. And there was a letter which seemed important. As in all the other dreams, there was the same feeling of despair. She needed help but there was no one to help her. And there was a melody repeating over and over again.

Sophie opened her eyes. She was once again lying on the floor, her phone ringing from the table above her. Had she fainted again? Her head hurt, and when she felt along her hairline just above her left ear, her hand came away damp with blood. She must have hit her head on the corner of the table as she fell. She wondered how long she'd been out, and she moved her eyes to look up at the clock. Half past four. She'd been out for only a matter of minutes.

Taking a deep breath, Sophie slowly pushed herself to sit up. Encouraged that there was no pain or dizziness thus far, she grabbed onto the stool and pulled herself to stand, steadying herself against the table. Despite the cut to her head, she seemed okay. Her phone fell silent, then rang again, and Sophie picked it up.

"I hope you're answering this at home?"

Sophie cleared her throat and forced a laugh, not

sure if her voice would betray her. "Hi, Becca. Yeah, I'm just leaving."

"You better be."

"I am. Immediately. I promise."

Sophie disconnected the call, dropping her phone onto the table. Despite her promise to go home, she couldn't deny she was a bit shaken by this second collapse. She needed to get herself together before she got behind the wheel. She sat down on the stool, focusing her attention on any worrying physical feelings she may have that would give her a clue for this second blackout. But there was nothing. No dizziness, shaking, numbness, or fever. She'd eaten at lunchtime, although it was only a salad, and she'd had three cups of coffee. Could that be the reason why she ended up on the floor again? Yeah, that sounded reasonable, but she knew at the back of her mind that she probably needed to make an appointment with her doctor.

Her gaze drifted to the diary where it rested on the table alongside her phone. She needed to put that back in its sleeve before she left. A diary provided the best source material of all, and it was the item she was most excited about when Becca had found it. She didn't want anything to happen to it. She reached out for it, but she made no move to touch it, now feeling apprehension more than excitement.

She frowned. Hadn't she fainted both times she touched this book? *God, Sophie, go home. You're tired and not thinking straight. Becca has handled the book multiple times, and nothing happened to her.* But despite her insistence, she didn't move. If she really believed the diary wasn't causing her to faint—because how could any book do that—then why was she so reluctant to touch it? She wanted nothing more than to take it home and read it. So why didn't she just pick it up?

She could feel her heart thump a bit harder in her chest as she reached her hand out, the familiar tingling beginning in the tips of her fingers the closer she got. She snatched her hand away, instead picking up the protective sleeve. Sliding her hand into it, using it as an ill-fitting glove, she slowly lowered her hand over the top of the diary until it rested on it.

Nothing happened.

She let out the breath she'd been holding and laughed. "See? Nothing. You're an idiot, Sophie," she said. But despite her victory, she was completely aware that she'd touched the book both times with only cotton gloves when she'd fainted. "Okay. We'll test that theory, then," she said, feeling a little bolder. She took her hand out of the bag and crossed to the sofa. She laid a cushion against one arm, then returned to the worktable. Feeling rather foolish and glad there was no one to witness this ridiculous spectacle, Sophie slipped her hand back into the sleeve, wrapped her fingers around the diary, gripping the table just in case. Still nothing. With the book in hand, she crossed back to the couch and lay down, her head resting on the cushion, and then she let the diary slip from the sleeve and onto her stomach, feeling the weight of it through her clothes. Again nothing, and Sophie laughed. You're such an idiot," she said. "Now go home." With both hands she reached down and grasped the diary, intending to lift it from her as she sat up, the fainting theory debunked, but she couldn't move. For a moment she was paralyzed, until, with a rush of air, she was being pulled backward at such speed the air was sucked from her lungs. Then there was darkness.

****

1865

The morning sky was hidden under leaden clouds, and Sophie fed the fire with dry twigs, the hot embers hungry for the fuel. But she wasn't Sophie. She was Emma. This was a fact. No surprise or disbelief. No confusion or fear. She was Emma McLeod, and she knew everything that had come before this moment, knew of all the tragic circumstances that had brought her to this point, knew no other life than this.

Daniel rolled from his bed, rubbing his eyes with little fists. He sneezed once, then again, then once more, and Emma prayed it was the smoke issuing from the fireplace, not illness, that caused him to do so. The closest doctor was in Rockingham Town, but he was only there every other Thursday. The next closest one was in Fremantle, the one her father had left to bring back to tend to her mother.

Daniel padded across the room, his small bare feet poking from under his nightshirt. Emma was sure his face looked paler than it had the day before.

"Are you feeling unwell, Daniel?" she asked as he came to her side.

He leaned his head against her stomach, wrapping his arms around her. She felt him shake his head from side to side. He looked so little today, not the same boy who had saddled the horse and taken them without incident to the Andersons' farm.

"Are you sure?" Emma persisted, her hand resting against his forehead. Did it feel hot, warmer than it should?

Emma took Daniel's hands in hers and crouched

down in front of him. "What's wrong, my sweet?"

Daniel's eyes glistened with tears, his bottom lip trembling. "I miss Mama and Father," he whispered, a tear racing down his smooth cheek. "I want them to come back. And baby Adam. You came back, Emma, so maybe they can too."

Emma frowned, Daniel's words a little unsettling for reasons she couldn't place. "Back, Daniel? What do you mean?"

Daniel shrugged. "You came back. I miss you when you go. Please don't go again."

Emma laughed. "Daniel, what are you talking about? I haven't been anywhere. You must have had a dream," she said, but something at the back of her mind, a mere whisper, hinted otherwise. She ignored it. "I won't go anywhere without you, Daniel. I love you so very much. This much, in fact," she said, squeezing Daniel's body close to hers. She held him for a moment, then stood up, taking his hands again in hers. "I love you as much as all the stars in the sky and one hundred more."

A faint smile formed on the boy's face. "I love you two hundred more," he said, the familiar game chasing a little of the sadness from his innocent eyes.

"Three hundred more," Emma replied, Daniel, countering with, "one million more."

He laughed as Emma reached down and grabbed him under the arms. "One million more, eh?" She swung him up and nuzzled his neck. "Well, that is a lot, and I will kiss you that many."

Daniel giggled as Emma deposited loud kisses on his neck and cheek. "I don't want horrible girl kisses," he said, his giggles turning to squeals of laughter.

"You want horrible girl kisses," Emma repeated and

counted to twenty out loud, each number delivering another kiss, the little boy squealing with each one. "There, twenty girl kisses," she said setting the boy back on his feet. "Now let's go out and see if the chickens have any eggs for us."

Daniel smiled and wiped his face.

The storm the night before had battered the chickens' pen, but the chickens, to Emma's amazement, were still in the yard, the pair happily pecking and scratching in the dirt. But there were no eggs to be found, and with Daniel's help, Emma spent the morning strengthening the wire pen so the birds could not wander too far. They really needed the occasional egg these birds chose to lay, or at least the meat from them if Emma was forced to kill one or both.

That afternoon, they ventured out to the property Mr. Anderson had told them about. The Cutlers were kind, but they too had little to offer, their fledgling farm providing only enough for themselves. They introduced Emma to two other families nearby, and they too were just managing to survive. They advised Emma on what she needed to do to fortify her soil and what crops she should plant, but they made no secret of how hard it would be for her on her own, and with no money, buying what she needed was impossible.

It was dusk by the time they returned home, and the chickens were nowhere to be found, the repairs Emma had made to their enclosure no match for the two escapees. They would have to fend for themselves overnight, and Emma could only hope they would return by morning.

After dinner, Emma read to Daniel for a while, then tucked him into bed before she opened her diary and began to write.

My dearest friend,

I have had contact with other families in the area and they have offered words of comfort and aid, but they too are only just managing to grow enough food for their own families and establish themselves. I have no skills nor knowledge in farming, nor the means to purchase what is required to start even a vegetable garden. Having only enough food to last little more than a few days, I think I will have to make plans to leave this place and make our way to Fremantle. I hope I can find work, cleaning or sewing, teaching or nursing. I don't have much choice other than to try. In my darkest thoughts, I think of the women that have been led to the streets to earn enough money to keep themselves alive and wonder if that's my fate also, but that's a thought I give little time to—it's too unbearable and I'm certain there must be another way. I will continue to pray there is a possibility.

Daniel called out in his sleep, something that had become a nightly occurrence, and Emma hurriedly scrawled her customary E at the end of the page.

She moved over to his bed and sat beside him. He rolled over and opened his eyes, the blueness of them dulled by sleep.

"Everything is fine, my sweet," Emma soothed, stroking his soft hair. She'd washed it last night, and his hair now was soft as baby's hair and smelled just as sweet.

"Mama was here," Daniel mumbled. "She told me Uncle is coming."

Emma continued to stroke his head. "It's just a dream, Daniel," she said softly, his eyes fluttering under her caress. "Just a dream."

Daniel nodded slowly and closed his eyes. "He's coming, Emma," he said slowly, his breathing returning to the effortless rhythm of sleep.

Emma sat for a while on the edge of his bed, listening to the wind whining around the corners of the cottage. On the mantel, the clock Daniel faithfully wound each morning showed a quarter to eleven, and Emma pushed herself to her feet. The fire had died an hour ago and she couldn't afford to feed it with what little wood they had left. She carried the stubby candle to her bedside and undressed, slipping under the quilt. She blew out the candle, the cottage now in darkness, and she curled into a ball, her hands tucked under her cheek.

"I'm scared, Mama," Emma whispered, a tear finding its way down her cheek, dropping onto her curled hand. She wanted to hear her mother's voice as clearly as Daniel had in his sleep, but there was no answer except for the lonely wail of the wind.

Chapter 6

"Emma, the chickens have been eaten."

Emma sighed. These were words she didn't want to hear, but she wasn't surprised at all to hear them.

She went outside and went over to where Daniel stood. A scattering of bloodied feathers was all that remained of their last two hens. Clearly, they had been the main course for a dog or two.

"Damn it," Emma said louder than intended, receiving a look of admiration from her brother. She apologized for her language. "Well, there's not much we can do about it now. They're gone."

Daniel looked up at her. "When Father comes back, we will get some more. Don't worry, Emma."

Emma ruffled the boy's hair and turned back to the house. Tonight, she would have to speak to Daniel. Tell him as gently as possible how bad things were. About Father. About their leaving here. But for now, she smiled at her brother. "You're a good boy, Daniel," she said. "Could you see if there's any dry wood around, while I do some laundry? Don't go too far, mind."

Daniel agreed to both requests and ran off toward the scrubland. Emma worried when he disappeared into the trees, her breath held high in her chest until she could see his face again. It wasn't because of the natives that lived on this land and had done so long before any settlers had arrived. Any that Emma had encountered had only shown a passing interest, continuing to wherever they were going with at most a nod of a head in communication. She'd never felt any threat from them. No, she was more concerned about what else lurked in the bush, particularly snakes, and tried to comfort herself with the knowledge that the noise the lad made as he scampered through the undergrowth was enough to scare most living things away.

Emma drew some water from the well and carried the bucket into the kitchen. The well was deep, the water clear, filtered through the limestone far below in the ground. But it was also icy cold and would sadly have to remain that way, there not being enough wood to heat the cottage, let alone a tub of water. Emma filled a basin with the frigid water and submerged her remaining cotton petticoat and apron.

"Emma! Emma! Someone's here."

Emma looked up from her task as Daniel skidded in through the door. "Someone's here, Emma. A man."

Emma frowned. "A man? Do you know who he is, Daniel?" she asked, pulling her reddened hands from the basin, rubbing them briskly with a towel. Once upon a time, the news that someone, a visitor, was arriving was an excuse to celebrate. Providing tea, fresh scones with homemade jam, and a chat was something her parents loved to do when neighbors dropped by. But neighbors were now far and few, and she was alone. Daniel's words only invited apprehension. She chided herself for her growing anxiety. Maybe it was someone from the Cutlers or the Bells. They had assured her they would drop by when they could. She turned to look past the boy, trying to glimpse the new arrival, but could see nothing from where she stood.

Daniel shrugged. "I've not seen him before. He said he was looking for me. And you."

Emma frowned. "What do you mean looking for you and me?"

Daniel shook his head. "I don't know, Emma. He asked if I was Daniel McLeod and I said yes, and he asked if Emma was here. I said yes and I would fetch you." He took her hand and turned to the front door. "Come on, Emma."

Emma followed Daniel to the front door, placing a hand on the boy's shoulder, stopping him at the threshold. She could see the man from here. He sat astride a horse reined in at the gate, his hat in hand, his gaze focused on the bushland on the other side of the track. She studied him for a moment. Dark hair curled a little at the nape of his neck, a short beard marked his jawline, and although she could see him only in profile, Emma was quite certain she'd not met this man before. Her untamed anxiety grew a little more. Emma's eyes darted away from the stranger to the shotgun above the door, and she reached up, lifting it from the twin hooks that cradled it. It felt cold and heavy in her hands, unfamiliar, and she leant it up against the wall next to her.

"Can I help you?" Emma said, attracting the man's attention. He turned to look at her, then swung from the saddle, looping the reins over one of the fence posts.

Daniel stood at Emma's side, and she took his hand, pulling him to stand behind her as the rider pushed open the gate, its hinges squealing with the effort. He entered the yard, stopping halfway between the gate and where Emma stood. He was tall, around six-foot, Emma guessed, and not much older than her twenty-five years.

"I've come to collect Daniel and Emma McLeod." He nodded his head toward Daniel, who was peeking out from behind Emma's skirt. A smile flickered on the man's face for a moment, then was gone just as quickly as his gaze met Emma's. "I have met young Daniel there. He went to fetch Emma, his sister. Are you caring for the children?"

Emma frowned. The children? But she didn't query that, nor answer his question. Instead, she asked, "Who are you and why have you come for the—children?"

The stranger glanced around him as if surveying his surroundings, then turned to Emma. "My name is William Rideout. I'm here on behalf of the children's uncle, Robert McLeod. I'm to escort them to Fremantle."

Emma's breath caught in her throat. For the smallest moment, relief overwhelmed her, the unyielding knot of worry that resided in her belly springing loose, and she smiled. But just for a moment. Fear returned with one thought—Her letter had been sent not a week gone. On God's green earth, there was no way her uncle had heard any word from her. Had Mr. Anderson lost her letter? Had it somehow fallen into this man's hands? But, even so, what would he want with two children? She tried to think of what she'd said in her letter. She'd said she was alone. Settler or freed convict, was this man wanting this property for his own, two small children no barrier to him taking it? A chill raced down Emma's spine.

"I don't think the children's parents would agree to that," she said. "Their father will be home shortly. Do you wish to stay and ask him?"

The man frowned. "Their father? As I understand it, the children's father hasn't returned to this property since he rode for the doctor well over a week ago." The stranger glanced over to the white stone-covered mounds. He nodded toward them. "The graves at the edge of the property, are they not that of the children's mother and an infant?"

Confusion fogged Emma's thoughts. Maybe this man was telling the truth, hope whispered to her. How else would he know about her father and the graves? But doubt was quick to remind her that all that information could have been garnered from the letter which must have come into this man's possession. She held the man's gaze with a confidence she didn't have. "Sir, I don't know where you've gotten your information, but I assure you, my mother is alive and my father is not far from here. Within earshot, I imagine."

The man's frown deepened. "*Your* mother? You're Emma McLeod?"

Emma wasn't sure why the realization that she was indeed Emma McLeod was causing this man so much confusion, but the look on his face indicated he was somewhat bewildered by this. She supposed that being a woman and not a child might pose a problem for whatever his plans were, which could, in turn, become a problem for her. Emma took a step back, urging Daniel into the cottage.

She glanced at the shotgun propped against the wall just inside the doorway. "I am, but I don't think you're who you say you are. My uncle is in England, Mr. Rideout. I sent the letter to him less than a week ago. Unless sea travel has taken a revolutionary turn and ships can sail across oceans at speed never before seen, or man has found a way to fly while I have been in the colony, I don't see how my letter to him arrived so quickly, or his to you." She wished she'd said less and her words not so scornful as the look of confusion on the man's face was now replaced by one of irritation.

He took a step toward her, his left hand reaching into his coat. For a moment Emma was unsure what to do, her brain now flooded with suggestions from *Run!* to *Shut the door!* Instead, Emma twisted around and grabbed for the shotgun, fumbling with it with trembling hands. She swung it around, pointing it at the man now standing not three feet away, but any courage she believed the gun would give her melted away. "I don't know who you are or what you want," she said, her voice faltering. "Just leave now or…or I will shoot."

The man froze for a moment, and for that moment Emma chose to let her imagination turn him around and make him ride away. But he didn't do either of those things, and suddenly he was lurching forward, taking hold of the gun, pushing it upward, away from his chest. He wrenched the weapon from Emma's grip and cracked it open, pocketing the shells. He said nothing, but his fury at her attempt to shoot him was written on his face.

Emma decided the option of closing the door was now her only one, but her trembling legs barely supported her, and she couldn't move. She grasped the door frame and stared up at the man. She was now at his mercy and no amount of feigned fearlessness or concocted saviors would change that. She could no longer feel Daniel behind her and prayed he'd hidden. If she could occupy this man long enough, maybe he could find help. "Please. I beg you. Don't hurt Daniel. He's just a little boy."

The man stared at her for a moment as if she'd taken leave of her senses. "What are you talking about?" Then realization dawned on his face. "You think I'm here to harm you?" He laughed. "If I were, I can assure you I wouldn't need to make up some story to explain my being here. You're not much of an obstacle."

Emma felt her face warm. She knew he was right; she'd thought the same thing herself, but he didn't need to be so condescending about it. He wouldn't be so smug if she'd shot him, now, would he? But she remained silent and watched as he reached into his long coat, taking an envelope from a pocket. He pulled out a letter and shook it open. "Here. Is this the letter you wrote to your uncle?"

Emma glanced at the letter and nodded, recognizing the scrawl of her own handwriting.

He reached inside his coat again and produced another. "And this is the instructions your uncle gave to me." He held the paper out to her.

Emma reached forward and took the letter from him, struggling to read the tightly formed letters of her uncle's handwriting, the paper shaking in her hand.

Dear Will,

I would deem it a personal favor if you would ride to Rockingham Town and escort my young nephew Daniel and my niece Emma to Fremantle. It's under the saddest of circumstances that they have been left orphaned, and I'm beside myself with worry over their welfare. If you could return them safely to my side, I would be more than grateful.

Your friend,

Robert.

The signature had the elaborate flourish that she recognized to be her uncle's. That couldn't be mistaken. "But how can this be? My uncle is in England," she said, re-reading the letter in search of any hint of deception.

"Your uncle isn't in England. He's travelling down to Fremantle as we speak. His name was recognized on the letter and redirected to him at his property. He, in turn, sent a rider to me in Fremantle, and I came directly out."

Uncle Robert had spoken of property he owned, but Emma had never known where. She had never considered it possible that he was already in the colony. Not an hour ago, she'd been preparing, planning, and praying for a way to survive until her uncle could come for them. Six months at the least was the best she'd hoped for. Had her prayers been answered so quickly? She looked up at the man, studying his face for any signs of deceit but could find nothing. Under the circumstances, she'd little choice other than to believe he was telling her the truth. "I-I'm unsure what to say. Under the circumstances, you must understand that… that as a… I had no way of… Well, please accept my gratitude and my apology for any misunderstanding."

William sighed heavily. "No apology necessary," he said, although his tone conveyed more irritation than understanding. "If you don't mind, may I trouble you for some water?"

Emma offered an apologetic smile. "Of course," she said, gesturing for the man to enter the cottage. "Please."

Emma followed him inside and went into the kitchen, returning with a pitcher of water and Daniel.

"As you already know, this is my brother Daniel," she said as she placed the water and a mug on the table in front of him.

Daniel held out his small hand. "How do you do, Mr. Rideout?"

A smile grew on the man's face for a moment, and

he took the boy's hand in his. "You can call me Will, and it's nice to meet you, Daniel."

Emma's attention was now drawn to the fact that their unexpected savior had no doubt been caught in a shower or two on his ride and he was now dripping on the floor, his trousers wet through, his hair sodden. She turned her attention to the fire, feeding it bits of kindling that Daniel had collected earlier, the extra fuel giving life to the smoldering logs. The fire took hold, and Emma placed another log into the center of the flames, the room beginning to warm.

"If you wish to take off your coat, Mr. Rideout, I will dry it by the fire," Emma said in way of a peace offering.

William glanced at her, a look of gratitude crossing his face, and stripped off his coat. Emma took it from him and draped the damp garment over the iron fireguard, watching as the man warmed his hands, turning them back and forth in the warm air that rose from the fire.

"How do you know my uncle?" Emma asked.

"I manage his property. I was in Fremantle to recruit workers. How is it you didn't know he was in the colony?"

Emma shrugged. "My uncle was still in England when we left. His plan then was to arrive here a week or two ago, but he wrote to my father some months back and said he would be delayed until the new year."

"Your uncle completed his business in London ahead of time and was able to sail earlier than expected. He arrived a week ago and had planned to come to see you, but he was taken ill on the voyage over. Nothing serious, but he was confined to bed."

"A week?" Emma said, dismayed to know that help had been so close. "If I had known, I would have contacted him when my…" She stopped, the sentence left unfinished, images she didn't want to see jumping into her mind. But whether her uncle had been in the colony or not would have made no difference to what had taken place. She took a moment to gather herself, aware this stranger was watching her.

"Are you all right, Miss McLeod?"

Emma nodded. "Yes, I'm fine. Thank you," she said, feeling far from it. The past few days she'd had little time to think of the death of her mother and infant brother, her mind taken with the worries of what to do to keep her and her brother alive. Now those worries had simply evaporated, and thoughts she didn't want to have vied to fill the space they left.

"It's…it's just all a bit overwhelming," she said, turning away. She busied herself for a moment with the clock on the mantel, picking it up, winding it unnecessarily. "I will be so glad to see my uncle."

"He's anxious to see you too. He has business in Fremantle tomorrow. We'll meet him there."

"Fremantle?" Emma said, turning back to William. "I was making plans for us to leave here and try our luck there." She shrugged. "I wasn't sure what else to do." She smiled, but it wasn't returned, only contempt showing on William's face, derision in his tone.

"And what do you think you'd find in Fremantle, Miss McLeod?" He raised one eyebrow in question. "Oh, let me guess, you thought you'd find some work, seamstress maybe, or nursing possibly. Or was it perhaps a position of a governess that you believed you'd find? A paid position in a fine home with a respectable family.

Is that what you thought?" He laughed coldly. "You have no idea what the realities of this colony are, nor what you would be faced with out there on your own. That's even if you made it to Fremantle." The man shook his head. "I have to say, it's a blessing your uncle is here to look after you. You wouldn't last five minutes."

Emma opened her mouth but said nothing, shocked into silence by this man's outburst. For a moment, she held his gaze, shaken. Then, turning away, she picked up a log and added it to the fire.

"I saw a mare in the back field. Do you ride?" William said.

Emma shook her head silently.

"I can, and put my saddle on, too," Daniel said. "My father taught me."

William nodded and smiled at the boy. "Good lad." To Emma, he said, "I have some business to attend to this afternoon, but if I can trouble you for a meal and bed tonight, I'd be grateful." He picked up his coat and shrugged it on. "We will leave for Fremantle in the morning."

****

Emma chopped the rest of the vegetables she'd harvested from the Andersons' garden into small pieces, added them to a pot of water, and rested the pan on the stove to simmer. Flour added and the broth beginning to thicken nicely, she sliced the last of the damper she'd made earlier into thick slices. The little butter that was left she spread thickly over the bread.

Mr. Rideout had returned from his business affairs as the sun was setting, wet, cold, and looking a little tired. He sat now in front of the fire in the sitting room, answering Daniel's question about tomorrow's journey.

Emma heard the little boy laugh at something William said, and she scolded herself for feeling annoyed at the liking Daniel seemed to have taken to this man. He was just a child and had no idea how objectionable Mr. Rideout was.

"You won't be able to bring a lot with you," she heard William say. "Your clothes, a few books, that sort of thing."

Emma laughed bitterly to herself. They didn't have anything. What little they had owned had been left behind in England. All their cottage here contained was a rough-hewn table and four chairs, the rocking chair, two lumpy mattresses set on slatted bases, two moth-eaten eiderdowns. a few cooking utensils, a clock, lanterns, and a wooden train belonging to Daniel.

Even the cradle was gone, burnt up in the fire. As for clothes, she wore nearly everything she owned, one of three dresses, an apron, undergarments, and two petticoats. The other dresses hung from a hook in the wall, but they were well worn and stained, not worth more than rags. Daniel hadn't much more—the clothes he wore now, a clean pair of trousers, one shirt, and his Sunday best, an outfit mostly unworn and probably outgrown. They wouldn't fill one bag with the belongings she would take.

"I don't think that will be a problem, Mr. Rideout," she said from the doorway, wiping her hands on her apron. "I have my diary and a few items of clothes, but we have nothing else."

William nodded. "Well, I'm sure your uncle will provide everything you need."

Emma held her tongue, refraining from informing the man that her uncle's hospitality would be enough. As much as he thought she couldn't, she would find a way to provide for Daniel and herself as soon as possible.

"What will Father do when he comes back, and we aren't here?" Daniel asked.

Emma sighed quietly and turned to her brother. Every day it became more and more clear that their father wasn't returning. "We will leave him a note," she said. "He'll come for us as soon as he's able, I'm sure. Now it's time for supper, and then straight to bed, young man. We have a long day ahead of us."

Chapter 7

The sun shone the next morning, although clouds watched from the horizon for their cue. A cold wind tore through her dress and Emma tightened her father's too-big jacket around her. She'd written a note for him, propping it on the table against the tarnished kettle, although she knew in her heart he would never read it. The few items they were taking were pushed into the hessian bag that rested against her leg as she pulled closed the cottage door. Although she'd lived here such a short time, she did have some happy memories and had looked forward to the new life they were to have had in the colony. But as she glanced over at the two graves, at the wooden crosses that bore the names of her mother and baby brother, she felt only a hollow sadness. She said a silent goodbye before she turned away, picking up the bag.

Daniel smiled at her from atop the gray mare. He too wore an overlarge jacket, their father's work coat, thick and mostly waterproof, tied tightly around him with a length of twine. Emma was confident he was well protected from the cold, the jacket covering the boy from neck to near ankle. Their father's hat sat upon his head, a finishing touch to his odd outfit.

William Rideout looked down at her from his horse, a smile nowhere to be seen on his face. "Are you ready?" he said, and Emma nodded, passing the bag up to him.

He took it from her, tying it to hang from the saddle, then reached down and gripped her arm.

"I'll ride with Daniel," she said, pulling against his grasp.

"The boy is not experienced enough to ride with two. You will ride with me."

"He's managed before," Emma protested, struggling against this odd tug-of-war. "We rode to the Andersons two miles away."

William sighed. "This journey is much longer, Miss McLeod. Too much for the mare to carry a passenger. You will ride with me."

He pulled again on her arm, and Emma had no choice but to stand up on the overturned bucket and clamber up into the saddle. She squirmed in behind the man, the forced closeness to this stranger unsettling.

"Hold on," he said and moved his feet in the stirrups, the movement jolting the horse forward. Daniel did the same, his mare falling in behind.

Emma loathed putting her arms around Mr. Rideout's waist, but her fear of falling was stronger than her hatred and she held tight as the animals moved onto the sandy track.

The rain waited a good hour before it started to fall, but then it fell with a vengeance. Emma looked across at Daniel, his smile indicating that neither rain nor anything else, for that matter, was bothering him. To him, this was an adventure, and Emma again envied his youthful naivety. Mr. Rideout too appeared to be faring just as well, his long, oversized, oilskin coat and wide-brimmed hat enough protection from the downpour. Emma, however, wasn't so lucky and was soon soaked through, her father's jacket not waterproof in any way. She could feel trickles of water run down her back, seeping through the fabric of her dress, chilling her to the bone. At first, it was just her fingers and toes she could no longer feel, but before long her shivering became uncontrollable.

"Whoa!" William pulled back hard on the reins, his mount coming to a standstill under a sheltering stand of trees, the animal taking this break to feed off thick clumps of long winter grass. Daniel reined his mare in alongside while William slid from the saddle and looked up at Emma. "Are you cold, Miss McLeod?"

It was a ridiculous question. Her hair was plastered to her face in sodden curls, her clothes drenched, her teeth chattering loudly together, but still Emma shook her head no, her trembling making it impossible for her to answer his question.

He reached up and clasped her by the waist, drawing her to the ground. "Have a break, Daniel," he called across to the little boy, "while we sort your sister out."

Emma's indignation at his comment remained behind her chattering teeth.

Daniel grinned and slid to the ground, looping his horse's reins around a low branch. From a saddlebag, William took a pair of cord trousers and a thick woven shirt. He held them out to Emma. "Take off your clothes."

Emma looked at him in horror. "I b-beg your p-pardon," she said, her words stuttering from her mouth as much from the cold as from the shock of his request. "I w-will do no s-such thing."

Mr. Rideout sighed loudly again, his irritation at her obvious. "We have no time for your argument, Miss McLeod. We have a long journey. Now I will turn around. Take off your wet clothes and put these on."

Emma stared up at him, then at the dry clothes he held out. She wanted to protest further, but to be obstinate was pointless. She certainly didn't want to delay their arrival in Fremantle, nor was she eager to continue the journey in her saturated garments. So she did as she was asked, taking the clothing from him, and he, as promised, turned his back. Quickly, she stripped the soaked jacket and dress from her body. Only her petticoat remained, and she struggled to pull the trousers on under it. With a glance to make sure Mr. Rideout's eyes were focused firmly in the opposite direction, she pulled the petticoat from her body and shrugged on the shirt. The course fabric was rough against her bare skin, but at least she felt some warmth return to her body.

"I'm ready," she said, and William turned around, a smile turning up his mouth.

"Very becoming, Miss McLeod."

Emma didn't get the sense that it was a compliment.

He shrugged off his coat and held it out to her. "Put this on," he said, his shirt now his only protection from the biting wind.

Emma shook her head. "No," she protested. "You will need that. I'm warm now."

William Rideout raised an eyebrow. "Either you wear it, or we both do. I can't have you fainting from the cold."

Emma couldn't hide her annoyance. "Mr. Rideout, I assure you I won't be fainting or anything of the sort. I'm not frail, you know. A bit of cold won't kill me."

The man didn't reply and looked across at Daniel. "Are you ready to go, lad?"

Daniel nodded and hauled himself back into the saddle.

William turned to his own mount and gestured for Emma to lift her foot, forcing it into the stirrup. "Hold the mane," he said, "and swing your other leg over when I tell you."

Emma had no choice but to grab onto the animal as William grasped her by the waist and propelled her upward.

"Swing over," William commanded, and Emma, determined she would mount this horse in as ladylike a manner as possible, pulled with all her might and slid into the saddle, the animal fidgeting under her.

"Steady, boy," William coaxed. Then he too swung into the saddle, behind Emma.

Emma was suddenly wedged before him, the trousers she now wore digging into parts of her body that a dress never did. She realized it was no wonder men were so disagreeable all the time if this was how uncomfortable their attire was. William moved closer to her. He'd put his coat on after her refusal to take it from him, and now, as he'd threatened to, buttoned it around her as well, her arms pinned to her side, her body held tight to his. It smelt strongly of woodsmoke and damp, and she was imprisoned like one would be in a straightjacket. She opened her mouth to make her objection known, her protest cut short as the horse was urged forward.

They headed back out into the rain, it not as heavy as before but wet enough, and Emma had to admit, albeit reluctantly, that she was grateful for the dry clothing and the protection of Mr. Rideout's coat, if not the warmth radiating from the man himself.

They rode in silence for more than an hour, the sun disappearing behind clouds for most of the morning, although the rain had stopped. Occasionally William would speak to Daniel, offering words of encouragement, pointing out objects of interest in the landscape. To Emma he said nothing, and she could only conclude that he didn't like women in general or that he'd taken a dislike to her. Why? She didn't know. She'd not chosen to be in the situation she was in, hadn't asked for Mr. Rideout to personally come for them. But he appeared to take great exception to her, and Emma sighed. Her bottom was numb, her legs ached, and her nose itched, and she'd no way of scratching it except for wrinkling it now again like a rabbit.

"Oh, what's that smell?" Daniel called out, his hand rising to cover his mouth and nose. Emma would have liked to do the same, but her arms were trapped inside Mr. Rideout's coat.

"A dead animal probably, lad," William said, urging his horse into a trot, Daniel following his lead. A crow rose from behind a clump of bushes and landed on the skeletal branch of a dead gum tree.

"It's watching us, Will," Daniel said, twisting in his saddle, his eyes firmly on the large black bird. "Don't they peck your eyes out?"

William laughed. "No, Daniel, they eat carrion. Clean up the dead. It won't hurt you."

Emma didn't think Daniel looked convinced. The boy continued to stare at the bird until it disappeared from sight as they rounded a bend, the track they were on meeting up with a wider white stone road.

"It's the road to Fremantle," William explained. There's a well a few miles along. We'll stop there to eat and rest the horses."

The glare from the white rock—limestone, William

explained to Daniel—was blinding, and Emma was grateful when clouds slid across the sun again. The stop at the well was short, just long enough for a meal of the bread and cheese William took from one of the saddlebags. They washed it down with the clear limestone-filtered water from the well.

"Here you go, Daniel." William tossed a red apple to the boy.

Daniel's squeal of delight was enough of a thank-you, and William passed another to Emma.

"This is a treat, Mr. Rideout," she said, taking it from him. "We haven't had an apple in almost four months now." She bit into the crisp piece of fruit. Its sweet juice filled her mouth and she smiled. "Good," she mumbled.

William polished an apple on his shirt. "You'll have all the fruit you can eat when you get to Eden Hill."

Emma wiped apple juice from her chin with the back of her hand. "Is that what my uncle's property is called? Eden Hill? I imagine it must be quite beautiful, to have such a name. Does my uncle grow apples there?"

William nodded. "Apples, oranges, pears, figs, almonds. He has sheep and cattle, and some crops. Eden Hill is quite extensive."

Emma smiled. "Wonderful. I'm eager to get my hands dirty." She waited for William to at least smile at her remark, but instead, he frowned. Emma wasn't all that surprised and waited for the cutting remark that was certainly coming, a familiar pattern in their interaction, and he didn't disappoint.

"Farming is hard work, Miss McLeod. I imagine your uncle would rather you just take time to recover from your ordeal."

Emma studied the man for a moment, wondering if this was Mr. Rideout's attempt at humor. But there was no hint of a smile, and this didn't surprise her. This man showed little expression other than disdain. If it wasn't for the smiles he threw at Daniel and the small moment of compassion he'd shown her earlier, she could be led to believe his face was frozen permanently in this way.

"Mr. Rideout," Emma said, with all the civility she could muster, "I don't think I will recover from the loss of my family, resting or active. However, I would prefer to feel productive and occupied rather than to have time on my hands in which to dwell on the loss. And as for farming being hard work, I'm sure there are many things I could turn my hand to on the property. I imagine that, given time and the correct instruction, I could adequately learn most things." Emma held the man's gaze, waiting for, at least, an agreement from him, if not an apology, but neither was forthcoming, his eyes giving no clue to what he was thinking.

"Well, your uncle has someone who cleans and cooks, but if you need to keep busy, Miss McLeod, I'm sure he won't mind if you want to take over that role."

Emma opened her mouth to reply that she wanted more to do than cook and clean, but these words stayed in her head. She was suddenly tired and had no energy to debate with this man any longer. She simply nodded and took a final bite of her apple, wondering how much more time she would have to spend in this man's company once she'd reached her uncle's property. Not a lot, she hoped.

"I'm going to plant the apple seeds, Emma," Daniel said breaking into her thoughts. He scraped a hollow in the dirt, dropping the core into it. "Will it grow into a tree?"

Emma smiled, pleased to have her musings interrupted. "It just might. You never know."

Daniel covered the core and stood up, wiping his grimy hands on his trousers.

William also stood. "We should get on our way. We still have a long journey." He extended a hand to Emma, and she took it with grace, clambering to her feet with a silent groan. She ached from head to toe, her body feeling as if it had been pummeled by a thousand bony fists. She didn't look forward to sitting again on the hard saddle for however many more hours it would take to get to Fremantle, but she settled once more in front of Mr. Rideout and held tight as the horse moved off.

The sun had fought its way from the clouds and now shone its rays down onto the creamy rock that made up the road, the reflection blinding. Almost in unison, Daniel and William pulled their hats down low enough to shade them from the glare. Emma didn't have the protection of a hat and could only close her eyes against it. Without sight, she felt more keenly the steady sway of the horse, its plodding gait rocking her from side to side, her head bobbing with each measured step. William shifted slightly in the saddle, one arm tightening around her, and with silent appreciation Emma leaned her head back against his shoulder, the sun warm on her face. She knew she was being dragged closer and closer to sleep but didn't have the strength to fight it. The long nights nursing baby Adam and the nightmare-filled dreams afterward had left her exhausted. Vaguely she heard William ask Daniel how he was faring, but then Emma heard nothing more.

Chapter 8

Someone whispered in her ear.

"Miss McLeod."

The swaying had stopped, and the air was cool on her skin.

"Emma."

For a moment, she thought it was her father waking her to come with him on the early morning walk. Just the two of them in the stillness of the dawn, before the start of the day, the laughter of kookaburras echoing through the endless bush. They had talked about things fathers never did with their daughters—politics, religion, business, and love. She wasn't like the daughters of his friends, he'd told her. They were fragile, giggling children. She had spirit, drive, a strength. She was clever, he'd told her, and if allowed, in this land, would make something of herself.

"Emma."

Now other sounds filtered into her dream. Voices, laughter, the clink of reins and harnesses, the thump of a drum, the shrill wail of a penny whistle, the jingle of a tambourine. And the odor of too many horses. Emma opened her eyes.

Two-storied buildings lined the street on either side, the pavements sheltered by first-floor verandas. Vendors had closed business for the day and now people crowded the pavement, clapping their hands in time to the efforts of a one-man band, the street alight with lanterns. Some revelers danced in the road, their arms intertwined, circling back and forth, paying little attention as a carriage pulled by a team of horses rumbled past, the ground vibrating, a dust cloud left in its wake. The horse under her shifted, snorted nervously, then soothed to stillness by a familiar voice.

Emma turned to look up at William. "We're here?"

William nodded.

Emma looked across at Daniel. He was smiling, his gaze flicking from side to side as he tried to take in all the sights and sounds in front of him.

William slid from the saddle, then helped Emma from the horse. She felt the hard surface under her feet as they hit the ground, but her legs refused to hold her weight, unused to the hours on horseback, and she stumbled. William slipped an arm around her waist. "Are you feeling faint?"

Emma shook her head. "No, no, I'm fine, thank you," she said. "I was just a bit unsteady. I'm fine now."

William nodded and stepped back, studying the crowded sidewalk.

A boy Emma guessed to be about fifteen broke away from the audience and strolled toward them, a frown furrowing his forehead. He raised a hand to tap the peak of his cloth cap in greeting, his frown giving way to a smile. "Afternoon, miss," he said, then turned his attention to William. "Afternoon, Mr. Rideout. I was waiting for you to arrive. You want both 'orses stabled overnight?" He nodded toward William's mount, then to Daniel's.

William passed the reins to him. "Please, Billy, and can you give them both a rubdown."

"Will do Mr. Rideout, sir."

William dropped some coins into the boy's hand. "Good lad. I will collect them tomorrow."

The boy nodded, then turned, taking the reins from Daniel. He led his two charges along the street, disappearing into a side lane.

"Will I get Jess back?" Daniel said, slipping his hand into Emma's.

"Of course," Emma said and gave his hand a reassuring squeeze. "She's just going to have a rest and something to eat. Probably the two things you need. I know I do. Mr. Rideout too, no doubt."

William didn't respond and picked up the hessian bag containing Emma's and Daniel's only possessions. He gestured toward the street. "The hotel is this way, and if you don't mind, I would prefer you take my arm. The crowd can get quite rowdy at night, and an unaccompanied girl is an easy target."

Emma agreed that was acceptable and slipped her arm through his. With her other hand, she held tight to Daniel's.

As William pushed his way through the crowd and led them along the street, Emma was acutely aware of the stares she received from the few women they passed, their gowns clean, their hair in order. She looked down at her own attire. Mr. Rideout's trousers were a good six inches too long on her and almost as much too wide. They were rolled up at the leg and held to her waist with a length of twine. The shirt hung loosely from her shoulders, the sleeves folded up past her elbow. She must look more scarecrow than human, no doubt the reason for the frown the stable boy had given her. She dropped her arm from William's for a moment and tried to brush some stray curls away from her face, her hair a tangled nest, no longer held in the mother-of-pearl clip her grandmother had given her.

William glanced at her. "Don't worry yourself."

Emma looked up at him, his words doing nothing to change the way she felt or, for that matter, looked. The sodden dress she'd changed from was balled up in one of the saddlebags now at the stable, along with her father's jacket. She'd nothing else in the hessian bag and wondered how long she would be forced to wear Mr. Rideout's clothing.

They crossed the dusty street and stepped up onto the pavement. The hotel loomed up ahead, an imposing three-story building, high verandas jutting from the first and second floors. Lights burned in every window, lively music floating out on the night air. A group of giggling young women filed onto the sidewalk in front of her. They nodded politely, their approving stare reserved for Mr. Rideout, their ill-masked laughter directed at her.

William guided Emma and Daniel into the foyer, and for a moment Emma's concerns about her attire were forgotten, her attention drawn to the ornate chandeliers hanging from the high ceiling—three of them, Emma counted—with smaller ones following the broad staircase that swept in a gracious curve upward to the floor above. The light from them bounced off the gleaming white-tiled floor showing between richly colored rugs. Through an open double doorway, Emma had a clear view into another room, a dining room with ten or possibly twelve small round tables populating it. A large fireplace dominated the wall between floor-length arched windows where curtains of gold and orange were held open with magenta ties. The walls were covered in gold and amber floral paper and featured a painting of a gumtree-lined river, one of a sailing ship in a dark treacherous sea, and a portrait of an elegantly dressed woman, all of these hanging from polished picture rails. Two more chandeliers hung from the ceiling, the light from them caught in the silverware set out on the white linen tablecloths. Emma had worked in fine houses back home, many as sumptuous as this, some more so, but it wasn't what she had imagined seeing in this young colony.

A woman watched them from the reception desk, no smile nor sign of welcome showing on her face. Emma wasn't surprised. She knew she must look like a waif. Daniel appeared only a little better. From what Emma had seen of those passing through the foyer, waifs and strays were not welcome in an establishment like this. Emma turned to look as a man descended the stairs, a young woman, her magnificent gown of the deepest pink trimmed with bright yellow, at his elbow. Their eyes met for a moment and a faint smile passed between them. But Emma knew it as one of pity. She turned her attention back to the conversation William was having with the woman at the reception desk, a Mrs. Wheaton, her disdain for the trio not masked in any way. That was until William pushed an envelope across the desk. The woman took it, the look of contempt melting from her face as she read its contents.

She folded the letter, put it in the envelope, and handed it back to William. "This way, if you please," she said.

As they were shown into the dining room, Emma didn't miss the disapproving looks she received as she passed by those more suitably dressed than herself. She smiled self-consciously and was glad to finally sit down, so the table hid at least the lower half of her ridiculous outfit. A chubby, rosy-faced waitress appeared at their table, and William asked for a pot of tea and a plate of scones. "And a lemonade and a bowl of ice cream as well," William added, winking at Daniel.

The girl bobbed in a token curtsy and hurried away.

"What did you say to that lady when we first arrived?" Emma asked, leaning forward a little toward William, her voice lowered. "I thought with little doubt she was going to ask us to leave. She must have thought a tramp had wandered in."

"I said nothing. A letter from your uncle can open doors. He's well thought of." Emma noted a hint of pride in William's voice for a moment before his indifference returned.

"When is the lady coming back with our tea, Em?" Daniel asked, his feet drumming a restless beat against the table leg.

"Hush, Daniel. The lady will be back soon. Now sit still, please."

"When is Uncle coming?" Daniel continued.

Emma shot the boy a look of impatience.

"He should be here around six." William glanced up at the clock. "It's a quarter to that now, so he should be here shortly, Daniel."

The chubby lady returned with their tea, her arrival proclaimed by Daniel's yelp of delight. He waited patiently for his plate to be set in front of him and for Emma to fill a scone with the preserve and cream. Then, with no regard for manners, he bit into it, ignoring the creamy jam that fell onto his lap.

"Daniel," Emma scolded, "use your napkin," she

said, taking small bites of the warm pastry, although she wished she could devour the scone as joyfully as Daniel was. She was starving.

"Can I eat my ice cream now, please, Emma?" Daniel asked.

Emma nodded, watching as William poured tea into a cup for her and then for himself, the delicate china appearing dangerously fragile in his hands.

Emma saw the woman first, her confident strides leaving no question that she was coming to their table. Emma thought she was at least twice her own age, her dark hair graying at the temples only enhancing her beauty. "Why, William, my love, I didn't know you were in town,"

"Good afternoon, Margaret," William said, his eyes firmly on the table in front of him.

"I thought you had gone back to Eden."

Now William looked up, and Emma noted how his eyes didn't stray to the ample cleavage the woman's emerald-green gown failed to hide. "I had further business to attend to."

The woman glanced at Emma, a smile lighting her face. "Oh, I see," she said, extending a milky white hand toward Emma. "Maggie Swanson."

Emma shook the woman's hand and smiled. "Emma McLeod."

"Pleased to meet you, Emma McLeod. I've not seen you in Fremantle before. A pretty young thing like yourself would certainly be the talk of the town. Are you new to the colony?"

Emma opened her mouth to respond.

"Yes, she is," William said dismissively.

But the woman's smile didn't falter, and she held

Emma's hand a moment longer. "And this fine young man?" she said, turning her smile on Daniel.

Daniel wiped his mouth with his napkin and stood up, extending his hand. "My name is Daniel McLeod," he said in his most grown-up voice. "Emma is my sister. We lived in Rockingham Town but our mo—"

"Daniel," Emma interrupted. "I'm sure Miss Swanson has more important things to do than hear our story." She smiled at her brother. "Drink up your lemonade."

Daniel dropped into his seat and picked up his glass.

Maggie smiled. "Well, it's wonderful to meet you both, but I'm afraid I must go." She looked across the room, acknowledging a man with a nod of recognition. "And William, it was lovely to see you again. You know where I am if you wish to visit me. You're always welcome. You know that."

William looked vaguely annoyed at the invitation, a look that Emma was familiar with. "Thank you, Margaret," he said, "but I will be leaving town tomorrow and won't have time."

"Not to worry," the woman said cheerfully, not appearing to have been hurt by his rejection. "As always, if you need anything…" She didn't finish the sentence. "Goodnight, all." The woman turned and crossed the room. Emma watched as the woman greeted her patient admirer and presented her cheek for a kiss laughing at something the man whispered in her ear.

"Who is that?" Emma asked, unable to look away from the woman. "Is she an actress?"

William shook his head, his face illustrating his distaste as he spoke. No, Miss McLeod, she's not. She earns her way through other means."

Emma frowned as the meaning of his words dawned on her. When they did, she could say nothing more than, "Oh." She wondered how Mr. Rideout knew Margaret— or Maggie, as it seemed she preferred to be known—and whether he had used her services. Not that it was any of her business, but she wondered all the same. Maggie's laughter drifted across the room, and Emma watched her with a new fascination. Her father had taught her well: it takes all sorts to make the world go around. Emma could feel William's gaze on her, not a pleasant one, and she looked away from Maggie Swanson and sipped her tea, cold now. Daniel slurped the remains of his lemonade, and she smiled at him. He didn't look tired, and Emma wondered where all his energy came from.

"I'm still hungry, Em," Daniel said, now he had her attention.

"We will no doubt have dinner later, when Uncle Robert arrives," she assured him, hoping it to be true. The one scone she'd consumed was no match for her appetite.

She reached for the teapot, but William intercepted and poured her another cup. Clearly, he thought her incapable of pouring tea, but she chose to ignore that, happier to just drink it while it was hot, savoring the warmth.

Daniel began to fidget in his seat again, and Emma put a hand on his leg. "Keep still," she said quietly, not noticing the man until he spoke.

"Oh, my darlings, my darlings," Robert McLeod said, holding his arms out, his deep voice halting the conversations of the other diners for a moment. Daniel leapt from his seat and flung himself into his uncle's arms. Emma pushed her chair back and rose with a little more grace and fell into her uncle's embrace, refusing to cry as relief at seeing her uncle overwhelmed her.

Finally, the man released them both and stood back. "Emma, I'm so sorry, my darling, for all you've suffered, so sorry that I didn't come for you. I didn't know about the terrible events until your letter arrived. I was planning to visit with you all as soon as I had recovered, and I cannot tell you how…"

"Please, Uncle Robert, there's no need to apologize. Mr. Rideout explained, and I know you would have come for us if you could. I'm equally sorry to have given you so much worry."

The man sighed, his smile returning. "Well, the worry is over now. I'm just glad to see you safe and sound." He turned to William, who stood quietly behind the reunited group. "Will. My friend. Thank you so much for delivering my family safely to me. I'm forever in your debt."

"My pleasure, Robert."

Robert smiled broadly. "Well, you all must be tired. I think we should organize our accommodation. What do you think, young Daniel?"

Daniel nodded. "Are we going to stay in the hotel, Uncle Robert?"

"We certainly are, and I will take you all to dinner in the finest restaurant Fremantle has to offer. He looked at Emma. "Unless you don't feel up to it, Emma. I can understand if a quieter evening might be more to your needs." The sadness in his eyes reflected that in her heart. He felt the loss of her family, his family, as much as she did. But being alone with that sadness was the last thing she wanted right now.

She shook her head. "No, Uncle. Dinner would be

lovely."

He smiled. "Very well. Follow me."

Emma took Daniel's hand and followed her uncle into the hotel foyer, William bringing up the rear. She waited as her uncle organized their room. "Your room, my darling, is number twelve," he said, handing Emma a key. "Will, if you don't mind, I have put Daniel in with you, and my room is next door. Is that satisfactory to everyone?"

There was mutual agreement that it was.

****

Emma unlocked the door to room twelve and pushed it open onto a small but beautifully decorated room with its own small chandelier. A washstand shared a wall with a dresser and wardrobe. The bedstead was a large brass affair, adorned with white oversized pillows and a floral comforter made from the same fabric as the curtains that hung at the window.

Clean and bright as the room was, her surroundings only highlighted how grimy Emma felt. She made no move to sit on the tapestry-cushioned dresser chair nor to go near the bed. She was filthy from her journey here and wanted nothing more than to bathe and wash her hair before dinner, but she knew that was the least of her problems. Even scrubbed to within an inch of her life, how could she go, even to the worst restaurant Fremantle had to offer, dressed the way she was?

A knock came at her door, and she opened it. A young girl in the attire of a hotel employee bobbed her head in greeting. "Mr. McLeod has asked for a bath to be drawn for you, miss." The girl stepped back and gestured along the hall. A sign on the wall halfway along pointed the way to the bathroom. "It's waiting for you, miss."

"Oh, wonderful," Emma said, imagining the pleasure of immersing herself in the steaming water. She made a note to thank her uncle for the kind thought.

Emma followed the girl to the bathroom. Black and white tiles covered the floor, green and cream tiles on the walls. The room was warmed by the fire that crackled in a small hearth, and clean white towels hung over the fireguard. "There's soap, miss," the girl said, pointing to a little stool sitting next to the bath, steam rising from the water, "and a pitcher to rinse your hair. Is there anything else I can get for you?"

"No, no, thank you," Emma said. "This is perfect."

"I will leave you then, miss." The girl bobbed her head once more and left the room, Emma closing the door behind her and sliding the lock into place. She shed her clothes and slipped into the bath with a long sigh of pleasure. It took a growling stomach and cooling water to force her from the water nearly an hour later.

She wiped the mist from the mirror and stared into it. Her skin glowed and her hair hung in soft damp ringlets around her face. Her blue eyes had a sparkle in them, and she felt better than she had in a week, but her heart sank as she remembered that now she must dress in the only clothes she had. She sighed deeply and, having little choice, picked up the trousers. She pulled them on and tied the twine at the waist, then slipped her arms into the shirt and began to button it. A knock on the bathroom door startled her, and she hesitated before answering.

The knock came again, followed by a husky voice. "Hello. Is the bathroom free?"

Emma checked the shirt was buttoned securely and opened the door. Maggie Swanson's wide smile greeted her.

"Oh dear, I'm sorry. I didn't know if anyone was in here."

Emma smiled in return. "Oh, no apology necessary. I have finished anyway."

Maggie tilted her head to one side, and Emma felt as if she was being studied. "You're even prettier than before," Maggie said, "and such beautiful hair. The color of copper. Beautiful." She flashed a smile. "However, I have to say your taste in clothing leaves a lot to be desired. No offense, mind."

Emma smiled in return. "None taken. Unfortunately, at the moment, I haven't anything else. You see, I…well, we…" Emma fell silent. "It's a long story."

"Oh, I'm in no doubt about that. No young lady could end up in…whatever it is you're wearing…by choice. Only the most serious circumstances could be responsible for that. Now, I have plenty of time, if you wish to tell me. I'm a good listener, or so I have been told. But tell or not," Maggie said, plucking at Emma's shirt sleeve, "I think I can help you with at least this. Come with me."

Emma didn't protest as she was led from the bathroom, along the hall, and into a room not unlike her own. What was different was the gowns filling the open wardrobe, draping the settee, and hanging from hooks on the back of the door.

Maggie guided Emma to sit on the edge of the bed. "Now, tell me what has brought you to the point of wearing clothes that clearly belong to a tall man."

And Emma did, surprised how the words tumbled from her mouth, her reluctance to tell this stranger her tragic story disappearing as soon as she spoke. She was equally surprised to have finished her recount without shedding a single tear. "And now my uncle is taking us to a fine restaurant, and this is all I have to wear."

"Oh, you poor lamb. Losing your parents and the infant. What a terrible ordeal. Just terrible. Sadly, there's nothing I can do to change what's happened, but as said, I can help you with one thing." The woman smiled, a twinkle of what Emma could only think of as mischief in her eyes. "What color do you prefer?"

Emma had no time to answer before Maggie turned to the wardrobe. Emma believed she could almost hear it groaning under the strain of its contents, its load lightened slightly as Maggie pulled out three dresses, one of soft green, one midnight blue, and one of the palest pink. She held one up, squinting first at Emma, then at the dress, her gaze darting from dress to Emma to dress. She repeated the process with the next gown, and the next.

"I think the blue," she said finally, but shook her head. "No, no, the pink. But then again, with your hair, I think maybe green. What do you think?"

Emma didn't know what to say. She'd never seen so many beautiful dresses, let alone had the opportunity to choose which one to wear. "I…I don't know," Emma finally said.

Maggie tilted her head again. "I think green. Yes, definitely the green."

She draped the gown across the bed and took Emma's hands, pulling her to stand.

"How long have you known Mr. Rideout?" Maggie asked as she began to unbutton Emma's shirt. Emma couldn't tell if it was a casual question born of small talk or if the woman genuinely wanted to know. Emma wanted to ask the same question of Maggie, wondering what relationship William Rideout had with her, especially considering her dubious occupation. Instead, she said, "I have known him less than a day."

"Oh, I see. Well, a finer man you couldn't meet," Maggie said with genuine affection. "Not many of his sort in the colony."

Emma hoped her smile appeared genuine. "Yes, I must say, he does make an impression."

"Now what are you wearing underneath those garments? Come on, don't be shy, off with them."

Emma hesitated for a moment then shrugged the shirt from her shoulders. She untied the twine that held the trousers to her waist and let them slip to the ground. She stood in her knickers, exposed but surprisingly not as uncomfortable as she'd thought she would be under this woman's scrutiny. There was no judgment in her appraisal, just contemplation.

"Yes, I have just the thing." Maggie spun on her heels and opened a dresser drawer, pulling from it a pair of knickers and a matching camisole. Emma could tell without even touching the fabric that it was far softer than the calico ones she wore now.

"Now these are brand new, never worn, a gift from an admirer who clearly cannot tell what size a lady does or doesn't take." Maggie laughed loudly. "However, they should fit you nicely. Put them on."

Emma took them from Maggie and clutched them to her breast. "Where shall I change?" she asked glancing around the room.

"Right here will be fine. It's just us girls. No need to be shy now. I will turn my back." And as promised, Maggie turned and rummaged in another drawer.

Emma changed quickly, the fabric of the new undergarments, as she'd imagined, soft and silky against her skin.

Maggie turned. "Ah, that's much better. Now, I don't think a corset is necessary with a waist as tiny as yours. And a small, padded bustle is all that's needed. We don't hold much with the fashions of the continent here in the colony." Maggie laughed loudly. "It's far too hot in the summer, far too muddy in the winter, and you can't sit down all year round." She laughed loudly again, and Emma couldn't help but join in, the woman's enthusiasm contagious.

Maggie helped Emma into the padded petticoat, followed by the gown. "Now let's get this beautiful hair away from your pretty face." Emma retrieved the mother-of-pearl clip from Mr. Rideout's trouser pocket and held it out. She sat at the dressing table and watched as the woman piled her damp ringlets high on her head, fastening it with the clip. She pulled a few strands to frame her face, then clapped her hands.

"There. Now stand up," Maggie said and turned Emma to face the full-length mirror.

The dress hugged her body to her waist, then fell in green satin folds over her hips, a waterfall of black-and-green ruffles spilling from the back. The neckline of the gown was edged in black lace and was far lower than she was used to.

Emma frowned. "Is it not too revealing?"

"Oh, of course not. You're beauty personified. Now, the finishing touch." Maggie took a string of beads from a velvet-lined box. "They're fake, of course," Maggie said, her voice lowered as if someone might overhear, "but they look enough like real pearls to suffice." She fastened them around Emma's neck. "Beautiful, just beautiful."

Emma studied herself for a long moment in the mirror. She did have to agree with Maggie's appraisal. She did look beautiful, equal to all and any of the women she'd passed this afternoon and sure to draw attention to herself. But was that wise, proper? Could she—or more so, should she—present herself in public dressed like this? For a moment, uncertainty swayed her toward thanking Miss Swanson but politely refusing her offer. But what was the alternative? To trade this beautiful gown for the dusty trousers and shirt again was unthinkable. In truth, she had no choice. Did she? And never had there been a time when she looked so elegant, so grown up. It really couldn't hurt, just this once. She turned and hugged Maggie tightly. "I don't know how to thank you," she said. "I will take great care of everything and return them to you in the morning."

Maggie waved her hand in the air. "Oh no, you keep them. They seem to have become too small for me of late, and as you can see, I have more than one person can possibly wear and will have more by the year's end. They're a gift to you. You're certain to catch Mr. Rideout's eye tonight."

Emma smiled. She had no doubt she would but didn't know if the result of that would bring admiration or condemnation from the man. She smiled and stepped into the hallway. "Thank you again," she said, "I'm so grateful for your kindness."

Back in her room, Emma dropped Mr. Rideout's clothes onto a chair, depositing her own well-worn boots on the small area of tiled floor under the washstand. From the hessian bag, she pulled out a pair of black court shoes. She'd never worn them, but her mother had bought them for her saying, "Every lady should have a pair of best shoes." Emma had asked when she was likely to wear such impractical footwear, and her mother had replied, "You never know what the wind will blow in."

"Well, the wind has blown, Mama," Emma whispered, and she surveyed herself again in front of her mirror, savoring the scent of the French perfume Maggie had dabbed on her neck. A knock on her door turned her from the mirror, and she crossed the floor, stepping cautiously in her unfamiliar shoes. Her uncle stood in the hallway, his white hair tamed by oil, his ample stomach hidden under white shirt, waistcoat, and jacket. His mouth opened but no words came out. He blinked a few times and made no secret of his admiration as Emma turned full circle.

"Am I presentable, Uncle?" Emma smiled.

"My goodness, my darling, you're an absolute vision. You will drive every man to distraction." Her uncle held out his arm, and Emma hooked her arm through his. "I will be the envy of every man in the colony," he said as they descended the stairs.

Below them, Daniel and William waited. Daniel had changed into the only other set of clothes he owned, his Sunday suit. Although a little short in the leg and not as neat as could be, it looked well enough.

Mr. Rideout had also changed into more formal attire, and Emma believed he could almost pass as a gentleman, an extremely handsome one, at that.

Daniel grinned at her as they stepped into the foyer. "You look like a lady, Em."

Emma laughed. "I will take that as a compliment, thank you, Daniel."

She looked up at Mr. Rideout, aware he was staring at her.

"Good evening, Mr. Rideout," she said, feeling a renewed sense of confidence.

"Miss McLeod," he replied, nodding his head once toward her.

Emma wasn't surprised that he didn't appear to admire her transformation as the other men in her party had.

Chapter 9

Emma dropped into her seat, fanning her face with her hand. She'd danced with three young men, each one particularly attentive, and she was flattered by their interest. It had been a long time since she'd felt this happy. She'd buried her sadness somewhere deep inside her mind and she was free from the burden of worrying over what would become of her and Daniel. On top of that, she felt pretty, something she hadn't felt in a long time.

"Do you wish to dance, Mr. Rideout?" she asked, waving vaguely toward the dance floor.

"Thank you, no, Miss McLeod."

Emma looked at him. His refusal was polite enough but was delivered with the usual tone of disapproval.

"Can I ask why not?" she said, her temper rising a little. She knew she should just let this comment slide by, rudeness seeming to be his way, but she couldn't. Why did he always have to be so unpleasant?

William leant forward in his seat, his hands perched on the table edge. "Can I ask where you came by such a flattering gown?" he whispered. "I know you didn't bring it with you."

Emma frowned, shocked by the intensity in his eyes. "Are you accusing me of something, Mr. Rideout?"

William sat back in his seat, irritation clouding his face "I think that's a rather overdramatic assumption on your behalf."

Emma took a breath, trying to keep her temper even. "I don't believe I'm being overdramatic. I simply asked you a question."

"As I'm asking you."

"Well, if you must know, Maggie Swanson gave it to me. She was most kind."

William stiffened, realization dawning on his face. "Ah. I see. It makes sense now."

Emma held his gaze. "What exactly do you mean by that?"

"It means what it is. You look like you've been dressed by a prostitute."

Emma knew her anger was rising but didn't know how much until her hand swung through the air, her palm striking hard against the man's cheek. "How dare you," she hissed, not shying away from his furious glare. "I believed you could pass as a gentleman when I first saw you this evening. But whatever you cover yourself with, you're still a pig."

Emma pushed back her chair, gathered the folds of her skirt and stood up. She glanced around the room for her uncle. He was standing at the bar, a cigar in one hand and a glass of whisky in the other, engrossed in what seemed to be a serious conversation with another man. Daniel sat on the floor at his feet, the need for sleep now showing on his young face. Emma crossed the room to her uncle's side.

"I have secured buyers for the livestock and the fleece. With the sale of grain and the fruit crop at market, I think we are going to reach our target," her uncle was saying to his companion as she approached.

"Well, I hope so, Robert. It's a fine piece of land you

have, and you've worked hard on it. It would be snapped up pretty quick if it was to be forfeited."

"Indeed."

"Excuse me." The men turned at Emma's words, a frown creasing her uncle's brow.

"Emma, my darling. Are you unwell? You're very pale."

Emma shook her head, choosing to keep the real reason for her pallor to herself, for now at least. "No, Uncle, I'm just tired," she said, "and I think it's well past Daniel's bedtime. It's been a long day."

Robert nodded. "Of course, my darling. I had no idea it was so late. You must be done in. I will get Mr. Rideout to accompany you back to the hotel. I just have a few loose ends to tie up here and I will return myself."

Her uncle's companion pushed himself away from the bar and extended his hand. "In case your uncle forgets to introduce us, I'm Thomas Lang. He's mentioned you but neglected to add how beautiful you are."

Emma returned the handshake. "Thank you," she said, looking up at the man. He was almost as tall as William Rideout but some years older, a hint of gray scattered throughout his dark hair. It didn't detract from his handsome face, however. In fact, Emma felt it gave him an air of sophistication, something Mr. Rideout lacked greatly, along with good manners and consideration for other people. The less time she had to spend with him the better, but she knew that was going to be easier said than done. Her uncle had beckoned for William to join them, and he now stood behind her. Emma didn't acknowledge his arrival.

"William, I was wondering if you would mind

escorting Emma and young Daniel back to the hotel. They're both in need of their beds, and I will follow shortly. Is that all right with you?"

William nodded and gestured for Daniel to stand. "Come on, lad."

Daniel nodded sleepily and climbed to his feet.

Emma kissed her uncle's cheek. "Thank you for everything, Uncle Robert."

"You're more than welcome, my darling. William will escort you to the hotel, and I will see you in the morning."

"Are you ready to leave, Miss McLeod?"

Emma glanced at her escort but said nothing to him, instead turning to her uncle's companion. "Goodnight, Mr. Lang. It was a pleasure to meet you."

"Goodnight to you, Miss McLeod, and the pleasure was all mine. Hopefully, we will meet again soon."

Emma nodded and turned, heading for the street. Ignoring William's offered hand, she climbed up into the buggy that waited at the pavement for them, not an easy feat considering the weight of the gown. Maneuvering in such a garment did take some planning, but she did well enough and sat down, Daniel on the seat beside her. He leaned his head against her shoulder and fell asleep almost instantly.

William clambered into the seat facing her, but Emma ignored him, choosing to focus her attention on the street, not interested in anything William might wish to say or in saying anything to him. If she never saw Mr. William Rideout ever again it would be too soon. She was grateful the distance to the hotel was covered quickly. She shook Daniel awake as the buggy came to a halt, but he looked at her only for a moment before closing his eyes again.

"I'll carry him," William said and scooped up the little boy.

Emma followed them inside and took the keys to the two rooms from Mrs. Wheaton, who greeted them with nothing but smiles now that money was coming her way. Silent, Emma climbed the stairs and followed William along the landing to his room. She unlocked the door and went inside, pulling back the feather-filled comforter and the crisp white sheet from one of the beds. William balanced Daniel on the edge while Emma took off the child's jacket. He flopped onto the pillow, and Emma pulled off his boots and trousers. He could stay in his shirt for the night. She covered him over, tucking the quilt firmly around him. "Goodnight, my sweet," she whispered and kissed his forehead. Then, without a word, she turned and left the room.

She struggled with the key in the lock of her door, a gentle shove required to get the door to move. Once inside, she crossed immediately to the mirror and studied her reflection, trying to see what Mr. Rideout had. Did she look like a woman of questionable morals? Her uncle had never indicated by word or look that she did. Daniel had said she looked like a lady. But Mr. Rideout insinuated she looked like a whore.

"What does a whore look like?" she said aloud, releasing her hair from the confining clip, her auburn curls cascading around her shoulders. Her reflection didn't answer.

A tap on her door drew her away from the mirror and she crossed to the door. "Who is it?" she said, sure her uncle wouldn't have returned to the hotel so soon.

"It's William."

Emma opened her mouth to tell him to go away. She didn't want to hear anything he had to say. But maybe Daniel was ill. She opened the door.

"Is Daniel unwell?" she said frowning, trying to read in his eyes the reason for his presence.

"Daniel is fast asleep."

Emma stepped back, wondering now if he'd come to make his feeling about her earlier attack clear. "Then what do you want?"

William stepped into the room and Emma took another step backward. This was how they'd first met, and she felt the same apprehension now as she had then.

"I wish to apologize, Miss McLeod," he said, closing the door behind him.

Emma, aware her hands had begun to tremble, clasped them tightly together as if in prayer. "Well, I appreciate that," she said, "but I don't think it's proper for you to be here."

William looked around the room. "I assure you, you're perfectly safe," he said, an edge in his voice.

Emma attempted a laugh, but it caught in her throat. "I didn't think otherwise, but it's inappropriate to be in a lady's room unchaperoned. Isn't that correct?"

William shook his head. "Under most circumstances, yes, it would be improper, but you're the niece of my employer. I've only wanted to apologize if I offended you and to say goodnight."

Emma laughed sharply "*If* you offended me? Mr. Rideout, you insinuated I looked like a whore."

William sighed loudly and folded his arms across his chest. "It was my opinion that Miss Swanson dressed you in an unsuitable manner."

"I was dressed no different to any other woman in

the room. I didn't attract undue attention."

"I disagree."

Emma saw something in his eyes she hadn't seen before, a look of uncertainty, and she pushed him to elaborate. "How so?"

"I believe no less than six men asked you to dance. Mr. Lang isn't blind to you, either."

"And?"

William frowned. "And I didn't think that appropriate for a girl your age."

Emma laughed again. "Inappropriate for my *age*? Clearly, it has escaped your attention, Mr. Rideout, but I assure you I'm old enough to make decisions for myself. I don't need someone like you telling me what I should or shouldn't do."

Emma held the man's gaze, the look of uncertainty he wore now joined by embarrassment, masked by irritation. His hands dropped to his side. "No, Miss McLeod. You're correct, and again, I apologize. Goodnight." With that he turned and wrenched open the door, closing it behind him with more force than necessary.

Chapter 10

Emma opened her eyes, the familiar flutter of anxiety turning her stomach. But she was not in the cottage as her nightmare had told her, and she surveyed the room she found herself in. Floral curtains hung at the window and an overstuffed armchair sat alongside an ornately carved dresser. Above a fireplace hung a painting of a white horse, and from the wardrobe resting in the corner hung an emerald-green gown. Although the room was unfamiliar, Emma felt a peace she hadn't felt in a long time. Despite what her dream told her, they *were* no longer alone. "I think we are going to be fine, Mama," she whispered, "and I promise I will take the greatest care of Daniel. You can rest now."

A noise outside her door drew her attention, and she pulled the quilt from the bed, wrapping it around her. She put her ear to the door, but all was quiet now. Still, she called out, "Who's there?"

No answer came, and Emma opened the door a crack. She looked both ways along the hall, but there was no one to be seen in either direction. However, someone had been there and left a large wooden chest at her door, and she read the card tied to the handle with a purple ribbon.

Dear Emma,

If I don't see you before you leave today, I wanted to tell you how much I enjoyed meeting you. Please accept the contents of the trunk as a token of my affection, and I hope we will be able to see each other soon.

Your friend,

Maggie S.

The quilt slipping from her bare shoulders, Emma quickly grabbed the metal handle and dragged the chest through the doorway into her room. She pushed the door closed behind her and knelt in front of the chest. She unlatched the lid and pushed it open, gasping at the sight of three more exquisite gowns to add to the one she'd already been given, several cotton day dresses, petticoats, undergarments, nightdresses, and an assortment of perfumes and toiletries. In a small velvet drawstring bag, Maggie had also left a black bead necklace and a gold chain with a heart-shaped pendant. Emma bundled the clothes into her arms and dropped them onto her bed. No longer did she have to concern herself with what she would wear today, her choice being limited to Mr. Rideout's trousers and shirt or the gown Mr. Rideout so disapproved of.

William Rideout. She was annoyed that the man had entered her thoughts again, and she pushed them aside, focusing her thoughts on which one of the beautiful dresses she should put on. She chose one of heavy cotton, tiny pink, blue, and yellow flowers on a cream background. The sleeves were long, buttoned at the wrists. But more importantly, the neckline was high, a row of pink buttons decorating the bodice. Dressed, she carefully arranged the clothes back in the trunk, adding the gown she'd worn the night before, and closed the lid. A knock on her door drew her to it.

"Good morning, my darling. Did you sleep well?"

Emma smiled. "Very well, thank you, Uncle. Better than I have in a long time."

The man clasped his hands together. "Good, good, I'm pleased. Now, I have ordered breakfast, and after that, I will arrange transport for you and Daniel to Eden Hill."

Emma frowned. "Are you not coming?" She was hoping that today they would be able to talk about her father and what best to do about the property in Rockingham. The thought of her mother's and baby brother's graves being left unattended for too long was unbearable.

"I will come in a day or two. I still have some business to attend to, and then I will join you. Mr. Rideout will accompany you. You will be in safe hands."

There it was again. Mr. Rideout. She wanted to spend as little time with the man as possible, and now she would have to endure another journey with him. Her thoughts must have been less private than she realized, and her uncle took her hand.

"I know we haven't spoken of your parents, and I'm also aware that Mr. Rideout is not the most, what shall I say, forthcoming of people, but he's a good man and I trust him with my life as well as yours. No harm will come to you when he's around."

Emma forced a smile onto her face. She didn't say that great harm would come to Mr. Rideout if he continued to treat her as he had thus far. But she was an adult, after all, and her uncle's life had been disrupted enough by her and Daniel's arrival. A tantrum from her wasn't acceptable. "Certainly, Uncle Robert. Daniel and I will be fine."

The man smiled, concern erased from his face.

"Very good. Now let me escort you down to the dining room. You look lovely again today, might I say."

Emma closed the door behind her and took her uncle's offered arm. As they descended the stairs, she told him of her benefactor, Maggie Swanson, and all the beautiful gifts she'd delivered to Emma's room this morning.

Her uncle nodded. "Maggie has a big heart," he said. "She's a generous lady."

Emma agreed, wondering as they crossed the foyer to the dining room if her uncle was one of Maggie's many admirers. However, she didn't think it a question she should ask.

Daniel was sitting at the table, his sleep clearly as refreshing as Emma's, his eyes bright, and he waved as Emma approached. "You look pretty again, Em," he said, grinning up at her. He jumped from his chair and pulled another away from the table, the high back almost taller than he was.

Emma sat. "Thank you, Daniel. You're becoming quite the gentleman. I think you require some new clothes, though."

Daniel clambered back onto his chair. "Uncle Robert said he'll bring me some when he comes home."

Emma smiled at her uncle as he sat opposite. "Thank you," she said. "I must find a way to repay you. Maybe you can set me to work at Eden Hill. I hear it's a large property. I'm a quick learner."

Her uncle shook his head. "There's no need, my dear. You are family and Mcleods take care of their own." He hesitated for a moment. "I'm sure my wife will be more than happy with some female company."

Emma frowned. "Your wife? Uncle, you never said

you had married. Father never mentioned anything about it."

"Well. No. It was a recent event and a quiet affair. You know me, Emma. I don't like to fuss."

Emma clapped her hands together and smiled. "Well, I can't wait to meet her. I just hope we aren't too much of an intrusion on you both."

Robert placed his hand on Emma's. "You and Daniel couldn't be more welcome, and I don't want to hear any more about it. Agreed?"

Emma smiled. "Agreed."

Conversation was deliberately light as they ate, the subjects of Emma's parents, baby Adam, and even Mr. Rideout avoided by both Emma and her uncle. They were conversations for another time. After breakfast, Emma excused herself and went upstairs to freshen up. As she left the bathroom, a man stepped from the doorway opposite. "Good morning, Miss McLeod."

Emma started at the sound of his voice. "Oh, Mister…

"Lang. Thomas Lang."

"Of course. Mr. Lang."

The man smiled. "I'm meeting up with your uncle later to finish up some business over lunch. I was wondering if you were going to join him. Your company would certainly alleviate the tedium of tallying balance sheets and calculating profit and loss."

Emma laughed. "You're making it a hard invitation to turn down. However, I'm leaving for my uncle's property this morning, so I will have to decline."

The man looked dutifully disappointed. "That's a shame," he said. "I suppose I will just have to comfort myself with the memory of your smile, Miss McLeod.

That will have to suffice until we meet again."

Emma answered with a smile, unsure what to say, then excusing herself, she made her way to the stairs.

Mr. Rideout hadn't joined them for breakfast, but he was here now, looking up at her. Her anger last night at his behavior had been justified as far as she was concerned, but she did feel a twinge of remorse over her actions. She argued whether she should or shouldn't apologize as she made her way down to the foyer.

"Good morning, Miss McLeod," William said, any thoughts he had on the events of yesterday evening not apparent on his face. Emma returned the greeting, then looked past him to her uncle. Apologies, if forthcoming, could wait.

"Are you ready to go, Emma darling? Do you have anything to be brought down from your room?"

"Yes, thank you, Uncle. There's a trunk."

Robert McLeod turned to a waiting porter and directed him to bring the trunk down. Then he took Emma's arm and led her out of the hotel and into the sunshine. There were no clouds to be seen today, the sky a faded blue, the breeze light. A covered buggy waited, Daniel's mare and Mr. Rideout's horse harnessed to it.

"See you soon, my darling," her uncle said and kissed Emma's cheek. He ruffled Daniel's hair. "You behave for your sister."

Daniel grinned and agreed he would try.

Two porters maneuvered the trunk containing Emma's newly acquired wardrobe onto one of the two seats in the buggy.

"What's that?" William asked.

"Some gifts from a friend," Emma said, knowing if she told him they were from Maggie he would no doubt refuse to take them. Why he had such a dislike for the woman she couldn't understand. What Maggie did for a living didn't subtract from her charm and caring nature. Her uncle could see past her occupation. Why couldn't William?

"You will have to sit beside me, then. There's only room for Daniel next to whatever you've brought along with you."

Emma ignored the disapproving tone in his voice and took his offered hand, climbing up into the buggy. If Mr. Rideout's taciturn behavior was the order of the day, then the journey was going to be long and quiet. At least he couldn't object to her attire today.

With Daniel safely wedged in beside the trunk, William urged the horses forward and Emma waved to her uncle as they began to move along the street. They reached the outskirts of the town and headed out on another dusty, well-worn track. But her fear of a quiet ride was unfounded, Daniel thankfully chattering nonstop for the next few hours, asking this and that about all he saw. Twice Emma told him to sit quietly for a while, but William didn't seem to tire of the questions, and Emma noticed that only when he was with Daniel did she see a smile on Mr. Rideout's face. They stopped for lunch in the shade of a willow tree, its graceful bowing branches trailing in a stream of clear water.

The hotel kitchen had prepared a feast for them: ham sandwiches, cheese, hard-boiled eggs and, much to Daniel's delight, chocolate cake. They ate in silence, except for the sound of birds chattering noisily in the nearby shrubs, no doubt waiting to see what crumbs might be left for them by these people.

Back in the buggy, Daniel chatted for a while longer

as they resumed their journey, his voice however not so insistent, his questions fewer. Finally, he fell quiet and leaned his head against the trunk. A few minutes later, he was sound asleep. For a while, the only sounds were the strident cries of honeyeaters and magpies calling from tree to tree and the steady, rhythmic beat of the horse's hooves.

Emma struggled to find something to say. She was still angry about last night but thought it childish of her to act so petulantly. She'd have to talk to Mr. Rideout just to be polite, and the journey would go faster if she had something to think about other than the ache in her legs and the lack of feeling in her behind.

"How long have you been in the colony, Mr. Rideout?"

William glanced across at her, little warmth in his voice as he spoke. "I was born here. In Fremantle."

Emma noted the lack of enthusiasm her companion had for the subject matter but pushed on. "Are your parents still in Fremantle?"

William didn't answer straight away, then shook his head. "No, they're both dead."

Emma felt a jolt of regret asking such a question. "Oh, I'm sorry."

"No need, Miss McLeod. It was a long time ago. I was just a boy."

Emma frowned. "That's awful. Did you have other family here to care for you?"

William shook his head again. "No, no family. It was your uncle who took me in.

"My uncle?"

William nodded. "He offered me a job cleaning out stables in return for a roof over my head and food on the table. When I turned twenty-one, he made me the manager of his property. He's been good to me, and I owe him everything."

Emma could understand that. She too was now being rescued by the same man and felt nothing but gratitude toward him. She smiled. "My father said my uncle was the adventurer of the family, travelling all over the world to places I had never heard of, always trying to secure his fortune. It would seem he was successful."

William nodded but said nothing, urging the horses forward as they neared a fork in the track. The land had begun to rise steadily, and Emma was delighted to see a bank of green hills spread out across the horizon. It reminded her of home. William urged the horses up a particularly steep incline, then turned the animals sharply to the left. This track widened into a fenced laneway. A young boy of about ten stood on the lowest rail of the fence halfway up the lane, watching them as they approached.

"Who was that?" Emma asked, turning in her seat as they rolled past, the boy staring after them.

William turned also but shook his head. "Who?'

"That boy. Didn't you see him?"

William shook his head again. "No, I didn't. It's probably Simon, Lang's son, or the son of his last wife, I should say. That's Lang's property we're passing now."

Emma swung back to face William. "Thomas Lang? Now she understood why the man was so assured he would see her soon. He was probably a regular visitor to her uncle's property.

William glanced at her. "You seem pleased by that."

"I'm neither pleased nor displeased, Mr. Rideout," she said, "I'm happy, however, that Daniel will have someone around his own age to play with."

William glanced at her. "Simon doesn't speak."

Emma frowned. "Some children are just shy. I'm sure he'll open up when he gets to know us."

William shook his head. "No, not shy. He just doesn't speak—to anyone."

Emma again turned to look back the way they had come, but the boy could no longer be seen. "He's mute?"

William shrugged as if the child's lack of a voice was of no importance to him, but there had been something in his tone that led Emma to believe he was sad for the child.

"He wasn't always that way. Not when he first arrived, although he was quiet for a lad. It was when his mother died that he just stopped talking. People who don't know him think he has something wrong with him. That he's dim-witted."

"But he's not?"

William shook his head. "No, he's just as smart as any other child his age, maybe more, and a nice lad. He just doesn't talk. Whoa, there." The laneway opened into a forecourt of crushed limestone, and William reined the horses in. "Eden Hill," he said.

Emma looked up at the long brick building. Four floor-length white-framed windows and a set of French doors interrupted the red brick wall at the front of the house. Three wide steps led up to the equally wide covered verandah that hemmed the front and both sides of the building as far as Emma could see. Thick smokeless square chimneys, one on either end, rose from the iron roof. To the side of the house, a large barn overshadowed a collection of smaller sheds and pens, pigs and chickens residing in the closest ones. In the near distance, the land sloped away from the front of the house down into the valley, the pasture dissected by a wide stream before the land began to slope upward again. Sheep grazed on the low ground, cattle preferring the hillside. To her left, a portion of the land was given to the orchard, hundreds of small trees lined up in neat rows, and to her right was a square dam, the body of water contained by orange earthen walls. "Oh, it truly is wonderful," Emma said, turning in her seat to take it all in. "I can see why it's called Eden Hill."

William nodded but said nothing and climbed from the buggy. He held Emma's hand as she too climbed down. Then he shook Daniel awake. "Come on, lad," he said quietly. "We are here."

Daniel opened his eyes and looked around. "Is this Uncle Robert's house?" He followed Emma's gaze upward.

"It is," she said. "But remember, please, uncle or not, your best behavior."

Daniel nodded and clambered from the buggy.

They followed William onto the verandah and inside into a wide hall. It was cool inside and quiet.

"Martha, are you here?"

Chapter 11

William's call received no reply.

"Martha? Is that my uncle's wife?" Emma asked. "He didn't say her name, and I neglected to ask."

William nodded. "She's probably in her room. She spends most of her time there. Rarely will she be anywhere else." William's tone, as he spoke of the woman, didn't lead Emma to think he was fond of her in any way, but then, other than Daniel and her uncle she didn't know if Mr. Rideout was particularly fond of anyone, especially women, it would seem. "I'll show you to your rooms and then bring your belongings inside."

"I'm starving," Daniel declared. "It has been forever since lunch."

As usual, the words from Daniel's mouth brought a smile to William's face, and he ruffled the boy's hair. "Then food we shall have."

They stood in the foyer, a square area with a high ceiling and polished wooden floors. William pointed to the two closed doors on either side of the space. "This is your uncle's room," he said, nodding to the door on his left. Then he repeated the gesture toward the opposite door. "And this is the sitting room." He then strode off down the short hallway, his boots striking loudly on the timber floor and turned into another corridor, the walls here interrupted by four doors.

"You can have this room, Miss McLeod," he said

and pushed a door open.

Emma moved past him into the room and turned full circle. The room was clean and bright.

"Is it suitable?"

"It's lovely, Mr. Rideout. Thank you." Emma offered him a smile of truce and for a moment, he returned the gesture, but it was gone as quickly as it came.

"Good. The bathroom is across from you, and I will put Daniel in the room next door." He nodded toward a door at the end of the hallway. "That leads to the kitchen, and beyond that, the laundry room." He looked at Daniel. "Shall we go and see if there's something for us to eat?"

Daniel nodded eagerly.

"I would like to cook for us all, if you think Mrs. McLeod wouldn't mind?" Emma said.

William shrugged. "If you're not too tired. I have to admit that cooking is a mystery to me. Mrs. McLeod doesn't seem keen on it, so your uncle usually has someone come in. I don't think, however, he has arranged for her to come tonight, not knowing what time we would arrive."

Emma shook her head. She'd sat all day in the buggy and now needed to move, to encourage the circulation back into her legs. "Not at all. It will be my pleasure. I will see what I can find in the pantry. Daniel, you can help."

"Do I have to, Emma?" Daniel groaned, following his sister down the hall.

The pantry had little to offer, so supper was just a simple meal of vegetable stew with bread and butter, but it was enough to satisfy them all.

When they had finished, Emma washed the dishes,

handing each one to Daniel. He dried them and stacked them on the dresser, all the time arguing his case for not going to bed as Emma demanded he should as soon as they had finished. He maintained that he wasn't tired, but Emma had her way.

Daniel tucked in, Emma wandered into the sitting room. Not tired, a little lonely, and more than a little unsettled in this unfamiliar house, she needed the company of someone, and although Mr. Rideout was certainly not someone who would make her feel particularly welcome, his company was preferable to sitting alone in her room.

The French doors were open onto the verandah, and Emma could see William leaning against the railing. A trail of smoke drifted upward from the cigar held loosely in his fingers. Standing next to him was a woman in her early thirties, Emma estimated. No one had mentioned how old Martha was, and Emma had assumed her to be closer to her uncle's age. But it was just an assumption and one that could be wrong, just as was assuming this woman was Martha. She could well be Mr. Rideout's wife or fiancée. Emma didn't know anything about his private life.

The woman placed her hand on William's arm, and Emma took a breath. She couldn't say it was jealousy she felt—that would be ridiculous—but something was unsettling in the intimate touch. A reminder of her loneliness, she reasoned, and for a moment, she wondered if she should just go back to her room. She didn't want to intrude. She hesitated for a moment, but her need for company was stronger than etiquette, and she stepped out onto the verandah.

William glanced at her for a moment, the woman

remaining silent. Emma immediately regretted her decision, feeling she'd intruded on something unpleasant between the pair. Maybe she should say goodnight and leave.

"Is Daniel sleeping, Miss McLeod?" William said, interrupting her thoughts of retreat.

Emma smiled a little. "He is, finally. He wasn't eager to go to bed, but I think his exhaustion won out over his protests."

William nodded but said nothing further.

The silence resumed, and Emma realized that an introduction to the mystery woman wasn't going to happen. If she wanted to know who she was, she was going to have to find out for herself. She smiled as she held out her hand. "I'm Emma."

The woman had shied away when Emma first appeared, and her nervousness was no less as she took Emma's offered hand. "Martha."

If there had been any other noise, a rustle of the wind through the trees, a murmured conversation, Emma was sure she wouldn't have heard the woman. "Pleased to meet you, Martha. My uncle spoke of you."

The other woman nodded, dropping her hand from Emma's, her eyes not quite meeting hers. "Well, if you'll excuse me, I will retire now. Goodnight, Mr. Rideout. Goodnight, Emma." The woman turned and disappeared into the sitting room, giving no time for Emma to reply, the rustling of her gown louder than her farewell. Emma watched her go. William remained where he was, leaning against the rail, staring off into the distance.

She waited for him to acknowledge her.

He didn't.

"Did you have enough to eat, Mr. Rideout?" Emma

asked, trying to fill the lengthening silence.

"Yes, thank you. I had more than maybe I should. I will need to work harder for the next few days if you're going to continue to cook such satisfying meals."

Emma was surprised by his compliment and congratulated herself on impressing this man with at least one thing. But she said nothing and looked across at the darkened hills. The moonlight painted the landscape in shades of gray, but she could make out the fenced-off pastures and the lines of trees that ran into the valley. Even in monochrome, the McLeod property was impressive.

"Do you manage all the property?" Emma asked.

William nodded. "I do," he said, turning to point into the valley, "and beyond that, there are a dozen or so cattle. It's a small herd, but it's just the beginning. There are also about twenty sheep. What you can't see are the crop fields beyond the hill. Your uncle likes to try a little of everything. We are looking forward to a good harvest this year and expanding farther next year." Emma was surprised at being given so much information. This was a subject he felt she was worthy of knowing about.

"I can see why my uncle was keen for my father to bring us here. He must have thought we had a chance of making a good life here, seeing that he has done so well." For a moment, Emma felt the weight of her sadness pushing down on her. All the hopes and dreams, promises and plans her father may have had for his family were for nothing now. She pushed that thought aside. "I hope I can at least make a good life for Daniel."

"Do you plan on staying on in the colony, then?" William asked. There was a definite tone of curiosity in his question.

Emma shrugged. "I have nothing to go back to. My uncle is the only other relative I have. Not that I expect him to take responsibility for us in the long term."

William shook his head. "Oh, I doubt that's something you need worry about, Miss McLeod. I imagine he's more than happy to have you here, although I imagine he would wish it to be under happier circumstances."

"Well, I hope I can find a way to pay at least some of my way. If not on the property, then a job perhaps, cooking, cleaning, or sewing. I can't imagine it would be that hard to find work of some kind?"

"I think your uncle would prefer you to stay close to home. You're new to the colony. Some might see you as easy prey."

Emma felt a little irritated at his comment, but she laughed, nonetheless. "Prey? You make it sound more like the African plains than a colony of civilized people, Mr. Rideout."

William glanced at her. "If you knew the colony as well as I do, you would see there are some similarities. This is a harsh place, and many are forced to do things they don't choose to, just to survive. You have someone to provide for you, protect you. You don't need to put yourself at risk. There's plenty for you to do right here with cooking, cleaning, and sewing, as you say."

The idea that this man felt she needed protecting and providing for pushed Emma's irritation into anger. Maybe what he was saying was true, but she certainly wasn't naïve or stupid enough to take risks. She opened her mouth to respond to his ridiculous assumption but was suddenly too tired for another disagreement and changed the subject. "My uncle's wife, Martha…she seems shy."

William shrugged. "Shy, maybe, but in my opinion she's much too delicate for this life."

Emma sighed quietly. She couldn't decide whether this was another misguided assumption that women were completely unable to cope in this land, or if they were words of compassion. Did Martha have some condition that made his observation plausible? "Delicate? How so? Is she ill?"

William shook his head. "All I know is that she wilts as a plant does without water and can manage little in the running of the home or helping on the land. Your uncle cares for her as he would an invalid, out of a sense of duty. It's a task he can ill afford, especially now. Why she thought she was suited to this country is beyond me."

Emma glanced over her shoulder, praying that poor Martha wasn't in earshot of Mr. Rideout's unkind description of her. "Maybe she is just out of her depth, Mr. Rideout," Emma said, wondering if there was anything this man could say that didn't infuriate her. "She must feel alone out here without another woman to talk to. I will speak with her tomorrow morning. And what you see as duty, I'm sure my uncle does out of love."

William glanced at her before returning to stare off into the distance. "Love? Anyone that believes you can have that here, Miss McLeod, is either naïve or foolish. Love is the stuff of books and daydreams. When there's no food on the table or clothes on your back or roof over your head, love is the first thing to die. Let us hope, Miss McLeod, that your pleasure at your uncle's finding of it is not short-lived."

Despite her growing anger, Emma was speechless,

truly shocked by this harsh critique. What would cause a man to hold such a terrible view of something that could bring such happiness? Emma only knew love. Her parents had loved each other and their children. To Emma, love held everything together, and without it life was surely poorer. But she kept this to herself, and with nothing more to say to the man, she tightened her shawl around her shoulders and excused herself. "I think I will retire. It has been a long day. Goodnight."

William nodded. "Goodnight, Miss McLeod."

****

My dearest friend,

I can hardly hold the pen to write my thoughts I'm so shocked. I have never met anyone who has infuriated me so much. Of course, I'm speaking of Mr. Rideout. In the two days I have known him, he has belittled, insulted, and ridiculed me. I believe he must have taken a dislike to me, understandably, as I did try to shoot him, and this could be the reason for his animosity toward me. However, now I see this same behavior directed at other women—Maggie Swanson, and my uncle's wife, Martha—so it seems that it's his very nature to be this way.

I feel I have tried my hardest to be pleasant to Mr. Rideout, although—and I'm loath to record it here but will do so as it's the truth—I did strike him just last night. That, however, I feel, was justified after his insinuations.

I will continue to be as agreeable as possible but am hoping I won't be spending any considerable time with this man in the future. If I, however, find myself in his company, I will absolutely avoid confrontation with him, for my sake as well as my uncle's. I don't wish to force my uncle into an uncomfortable position, William being his close friend.

I will put Mr. Rideout from my mind and let this be the last I need to write of him.

E

Chapter 12

The sound of barking dogs and the clink of reins pulled Emma from her sleep, and she rolled from her bed. Crossing to the window, she peeked out through the curtains into the yard at the rear of the house. Two dogs, a black-and-white long-haired and a shorter coated golden-brown animal, raced around a horse, their tails wagging as the rider slid from the saddle. To Emma's relief, it was her uncle. She was happy to see him.

She watched as Daniel raced across the yard and was swept up into his uncle's arms. By the look of the boy's clothes, dusty and stained, he'd been helping Mr. Rideout with whatever work his day had started with. Laughing, the boy was then deposited back on the ground before her uncle took two brown paper parcels from the saddlebags, depositing one parcel on top of the other in the boy's outstretched arms. This was Emma's cue to dress. She planned to make herself useful, so she pulled on the dress she'd worn the day before, suitable for housework or whatever chores her uncle needed her help with. A tap on her door heralded Daniel's arrival, and she called for him to come in.

"Good morning, my sweet," Emma said, as Daniel rushed into the room. She held open her arms and Daniel allowed her a brief hug, his excitement at unwrapping the parcels too much for him to waste time on such things.

"Look what Uncle Robert brought for me, Em. Can I open them?"

Emma nodded.

"Uncle Robert said there was something special inside for me and a letter for you."

Emma frowned. A letter? Who would possibly be writing to her?

Daniel pulled the twine free, then ripped the paper aside, dropping it at his feet. Emma bent to pick it up and screwed it into a ball. "Daniel, slow down."

Daniel didn't and soon had the contents of the parcels strewn across Emma's bed, an assortment of clothing from shirts to underclothes and everything in between that a small boy might need on a farm. His eyes lit up as he pulled out a pair of black lace-up boots, holding them up. "Look, Em. Working boots just like Will has."

Emma smiled. "You're very lucky," she said. "I assume you said thank you."

Daniel nodded and held out an envelope. "This is for you, Emma. Can I put my new boots on?"

Emma nodded vaguely as she looked down at the envelope, not noticing as Daniel skipped from the room. It had to be from Maggie Swanson. She knew no one else. But the handwriting wasn't the same as on the card Maggie had attached to the trunk. Emma carefully teased the seal open and pulled the piece of notepaper from inside. It read:

Dear Miss McLeod,

I wish to convey to you again the pleasure I had in meeting you. I have asked your uncle to forward this letter to you in the hope that you would be agreeable to my paying a visit to you on Thursday week at ten a.m. If

*that's not suitable, please tell your uncle and he'll
arrange for me to be advised of this. I'm hoping that
won't be the case and look forward to seeing you.*

Yours respectfully,
Thomas Lang.

Emma continued to stare at the note long after she'd
finished reading. Thomas Lang was the last person she'd
expected to write to her, and despite his cordiality, his
interest in visiting her wasn't one she shared. Not at this
time, at least. She had no interest in forming any sort of
relationship with anyone right now and she hoped he
wouldn't be greatly offended when she refused his
request. Tucking the letter back into its envelope, Emma
dropped it onto her bed and opened her bedroom door.
But she made no move to leave her room. Just out of
sight in the foyer she could hear her uncle and Mr.
Rideout talking. Their tone and words both conveyed
that this was a somber conversation and one she did not
want to interrupt.

"I think we may be all right, Will. The next few days
are going to be challenging to get the fruit picked and
packed in time, but I'm confident we can do it. I just hope
the weather holds."

She heard William murmur an agreement, but he
said nothing else, and Emma took this as her cue to make
her presence known. "Good morning, Uncle."

Her uncle greeted her with his usual smile. William,
as expected, just nodded toward her.

"Emma, my darling. As usual, you look delightful."

Emma smiled. "Thank you, Uncle Robert. I'm so
glad you've returned. I didn't expect you so early."

"My business dealings concluded earlier than
expected. Thankfully. I'm glad to be home. I hope the

items I brought back for young Daniel are suitable."

"More than suitable, Uncle. Thank you so much. I also received a letter today. It was in the parcel you gave to Daniel. Did you know it was there?"

Robert nodded, a shadow crossing his face. "Yes."

"Did you know what its contents were?"

"No. Mr. Lang simply asked that I give it to you. I was in two minds about whether to or not but realized I had no place to decide that for you. Has he said anything to upset you?"

Now Emma noticed the look on William's face. It was anger she could see in his eyes, but the reason for that she couldn't guess. Was it her very presence, as she'd said nothing to him? What could she possibly have done to make him angry? Her only choice was to ignore or confront him, but after the promise she'd made to herself last night, Emma chose to ignore. "No, Uncle. He asked for permission to call on me next week. He said if it wasn't suitable, you could send a message to him."

"I'll go if you like, Robert."

Emma turned to look at William. "I beg your pardon?"

"I said I'll go directly to Mr. Lang. Tell him the arrangement is unsuitable."

Emma looked at the man for a long moment. At the hotel, he'd scolded her for attracting the attention of men. Last night he'd advised her that she would be viewed as prey. Was he now again dictating who she should or shouldn't see? Not likely. Emma made her own decisions, even if they were just to make a point. "Thank you, Mr. Rideout, but that won't be necessary. I will be glad to have Mr. Lang call on me."

William's expression was one of disbelief. "What?"

"I said that it won't be necessary for you to take a message to Mr. Lang. If he wants to call on me, then I'm agreeable to that."

"Robert?"

Robert McLeod held up his hands. "This is Emma's decision, Will, not mine."

"And to be frank, Mr. Rideout," Emma added, "none of your business."

William's words were measured and controlled, only his tone hinting at what he was feeling. "I apologize, Miss McLeod. I made a presumption, and I was wrong. Now if you'll excuse me, I have work to do." With that, he turned and strode through the open door and out onto the veranda.

Emma watched him go and breathed a sigh of frustration. "That man is impossible, Uncle Robert. I'm sorry, I know you're fond of him, but really, he's insufferable."

Robert had also watched the other man's departure and now turned to Emma. "Some do find him a bit brash, but there's another side to him."

Emma sighed. "Well, I hope it's a little more agreeable than that one," she said, nodding toward the open door through which William had left.

Robert McLeod put his arm around his niece's shoulders and turned her toward the kitchen. "He's a good man. Give him time. Now let us see if there's anything for our breakfast. I'm ravenous."

"I will have to take your word for it," Emma said, following her uncle into the kitchen. She turned her efforts to preparing breakfast. "I met your wife briefly last night," Emma said, taking one of the eggs from the basket. Daniel had collected them this morning, telling her proudly that Will had appointed him the task of looking after the chickens. "I thought I might make her breakfast and chat for a while. It would be nice for me to have another woman to talk to."

Robert smiled a little. "Martha doesn't eat breakfast." He shrugged. "Martha doesn't eat much of anything. She does worry me at times."

Emma tapped the egg onto the side of the mixing bowl, a neat crack separating the creamy shell. Its contents slipped into the bowl, and she added a second, then a third. "She seems shy." She looked at her uncle and he shrugged again, his smile somewhat sad.

"Shy maybe, but I think it's more that she's not happy living here."

"At Eden Hill?"

"In the colony. I think she would be happier returning to England. The summer was terrible for her. I think the doctor was called almost every other day. Eventually, he gave her something for her nerves. It helps. Part of the reason she's so quiet, I suspect. Maybe with another woman in the house, she may open up a little."

"Hopefully, Uncle. I'll try and talk to her if you think it would be suitable."

Her uncle nodded. "I would appreciate it, Emma. I hate to think she's so unhappy, and I can't seem to find a way to fix it. To be honest, I don't know what it is that needs fixing in the first place."

"Don't worry, Uncle, I will try to speak to her," Emma said and turned to the window at the sound of Daniel's laughter.

She could see him sitting on the wooden fence that separated the pigs from what looked like a long-ago vegetable garden. It was overgrown with weeds now, but Emma believed she could revive it. It would be something productive, at least, for her to do. Daniel was watching William, and her gaze drifted toward him as he raised a large square hammer over his head, swinging it down on the top of a fence post, pounding it farther into the ground. His shirt discarded, draped over the fence rail, Emma could see how hours of labor on the farm had toned his body, his skin tanned golden by this land's abundant sunlight. He gave the post a shake, another hit, then dropped the hammer to the ground.

He said something to Daniel, then straightened his back, stretching, his gaze coming to rest on her. She stared back, her face flushing, not knowing whether to acknowledge him, that being a silent confession to her watching him, or to pretend she didn't see him at all, which would be ridiculous.

"Emma, darling. You're miles away. You will stir the eggs to powder at the rate you're going."

Emma started at her uncle's voice. "Oh, I'm sorry, Uncle, I was miles away," Emma said turning from the window. She picked up the jug of milk, added a little to the bowl, then poured the mixture into the waiting skillet. She stared down at the pan, not allowing herself to glance again out of the window. She served the eggs on two plates, alongside thick slices of ham, warm rolls, and freshly churned butter, then sat opposite her uncle.

They ate in silence until Robert pushed his plate away and wiped his mouth with a napkin. "Just what I needed," he said, patting his stomach. "A good start to the day."

Emma smiled. "You're welcome, Uncle. I'm glad I can make myself useful."

"Emma, you're useful just by being here, and this is your home for as long as you want it to be." He laughed. "But I certainly won't deter you from keeping your hungry uncle fed."

Emma smiled and reached across the table. She took her uncle's hand. They were rough, weathered hands that had worked hard. "Thank you, Uncle Robert. From me, and Daniel. It's such a relief to see him happy."

Robert squeezed her hand. "And how about you? How are you? You've been through a terrible ordeal. Dreadful as it sounds, there will come a time when that must be realized. It's not pleasant but a necessary part of life to grieve."

Emma said nothing for a moment. In the two days since Mr. Rideout had delivered her and Daniel to her uncle, she had allowed little time to think too closely about the previous weeks. She felt the weight of sadness on her, and carried it, but she would keep those feelings locked away. She took a deep breath and forced a smile onto her face. "It has been a trying time, but my only concern is the house in Rockingham. There's not anything of great value left there—a table, a few knickknacks—but what I wanted to know is…my mother, baby Adam…what will happen to…" Emma faltered.

Robert squeezed her hand and answered the question she couldn't finish. "The land and cottage are in your father's name. I purchased it until the funds from the sale of his business became available. It's not worth much as it is, but in a while, when we know more, we will decide what to do. Until then, I will send some men to secure the property."

Emma could only nod her agreement, clamping her

lips tightly together as if this would prevent the words that chilled her from being spoken. But she had to ask. "Do you think my father is dead?"

Her uncle looked suddenly tired, and Emma felt regret at bringing another problem to his plate. "I can't begin to believe your father is dead," Robert said, shaking his head, "but I'm sorry to say that I also can't find an explanation for his disappearance. I would have hoped to have heard word from him by now, even if he'd met with an accident and was injured. However, let us not assume what we don't know. For now, at least, we will continue to hope."

Emma nodded again, having little to add to her uncle's hopes.

"This week," her uncle continued, "will be a busy one, but as soon the harvest is in, we will discuss things further." Robert squeezed her hands tightly, then dropped them from his. He stood up. "We will speak more about this later."

Emma smiled weakly. Thank you, Uncle," she said. "And if I can be of any help with the harvest, I would be more than happy to be put to work."

Her uncle smiled and patted his stomach. "A few more meals like that would be help enough, Emma, a mighty help. I'm sure Mr. Rideout would appreciate it also."

Emma frowned. "I cannot guarantee I won't try to poison him if he doesn't change his ways."

Robert laughed. "Well, maybe I should warn him to have someone taste his food from now on."

Emma agreed that may be prudent. "But I can help in other ways, Uncle," she continued. "I'm used to being busy."

"I will keep that in mind, Emma, but for now I must get on. The fruit won't put itself into the baskets."

I can pick fruit, she wanted to call after him. She didn't want to be left alone in the house, her thoughts her only company. But he was gone, and she stood up, carrying their plates from the table to the sink. Through the window, she could now see her uncle had joined William and Daniel near the pigpen. Daniel was smiling at something his uncle said. As he slid from the fence, he caught sight of Emma through the window and waved, then followed his uncle, both disappearing from view. William too looked at her, but there was no wave nor smile, no acknowledgement of any kind before he too disappeared.

Emma washed and dried the few dishes she'd used to make breakfast, but there was little else to be done in the kitchen. The pantry, although not full, was neat and ordered. She imagined it was the woman that baked and brought the bread who had brought more supplies earlier this morning, as there was more than when Emma had looked last night, and all the plates were racked neatly, pans and pots stacked tidily, floors swept and mopped. There wasn't anything left for Emma to do.

Emma took off the apron and returned it to where she'd found it hanging from a nail hammered into the kitchen door. She wandered into the hall and stopped, listening. The house stood silent.

Was Martha still in her room? Would she appear at all today? Mr. Rideout said she rarely did before tea. But surely, she needed to eat, and Emma moved down the hallway, coming to a stop outside her uncle's room. Emma listened again, hoping to hear some noise to show the woman was awake.

Silence.

Emma raised her hand and tapped lightly on the door, then a little harder. She waited, knocked again, but still the woman didn't appear. "Martha," Emma called, her mouth up close to the door. "Martha, would you like some tea?"

There was no reply and Emma turned away, her gaze drawn to the room opposite, the sitting room, and she crossed the hall to the threshold. She'd passed through this room last night, leading her to the verandah and the unpleasant conversation with Mr. Rideout. This morning the drapes were drawn over windows and doors, and she flung them back, the room instantly brightening.

A floral settee took pride of place in the center of the room, this piece the only thing unfamiliar to her. Her uncle had brought everything else with him from England when he'd sailed to the colony. The oak dresser that held his best dinnerware and glassware, and more than a bottle or two of fine whisky and brandy, rested against the far wall. The long dining table that had hosted many dinner parties, along with the eight chairs, their legs curling as if they were slowly giving way under the weight of the occupant, stood off to the side. The familiar rolltop desk claimed its space against one window, the drawers, compartments and shelves no doubt stuffed full of papers and letters, documents, and other sundry items. This was filing, as far as Uncle Robert was concerned, and Emma didn't imagine that his organization skills had improved any. There were lamps and paintings and mirrors and a huge clock she remembered clearly from his home in England.

And finally, the leather armchair she used to climb up onto when she was a girl, curling up as small as she could be, sure she was invisible, giggling when her uncle proclaimed loudly that he'd no idea where she was. She ran her hand over the smooth red leather, bent to smell the rich scent that brought back so many memories. A lump grew in her throat and her vision blurred for a moment. One memory stood out more than the others, and she let it grow.

Her mother, father, the twins, and a newborn Daniel, all gathered in her uncle's sitting room in his house in Oxford, a wood fire warming the room, snow falling silently outside. She'd sat perched on the worn footstool at her uncle's feet, listening to every word as he told them all about his plan to return to Australia. He had a small plot of land there but had applied for a larger parcel, having big plans for his new life on the other side of the world. He told them of the endless land and the bright sunshine, the bluest of skies, and of animals that you would never see anywhere else in the world.

Emma remembered the feeling of excitement in her stomach as he spoke, could see the dream he'd had for this new country in his eyes. And when he asked her father to join him, she could hardly contain herself, held her breath as she waited for her father to answer. Please say yes, she'd silently begged, dreaming of never being cold again, of wide-open spaces, freedom from the dark, dirty streets, fresh air for baby Daniel and her sisters. And she thought she would burst when he said, "Yes, it's worth giving it some thought." But thought was all it was for the next seven years.

A sound from the hallway pulled Emma back into the present. Her cheeks were wet with tears she didn't realize she'd shed, and she wiped her face with the back of her hand. She turned to the sound, at first not noticing

Martha's door ajar. The door opened a little more and Emma could see Martha peering out at her.

"Martha?" Emma moved slowly forward, fearful she would scare the woman away should she move too fast.

Finally, face to face, it didn't take long for Emma to coax Martha into having a cup of tea.

"Would you like to take it on the verandah? It's a beautiful day," Emma coaxed.

Martha shook her head, and Emma didn't push her any further. This was progress enough for one day.

After delivering tea to Martha, Emma took her own out onto the verandah, the view down the valley beautiful. The sun was out, not a single cloud interrupting its warmth. She set her cup on the railing and closed her eyes, turning her face to the warming rays.

A shout from the orchard drew her attention and she looked down into the valley, watching as workers scrambled amongst laden trees, picking and dropping whatever the bounty was into baskets. A child scurried back and forth under the trees, gathering that which had rolled out of reach of the less nimble adults. She assumed it was Daniel and felt a pang of jealousy. Was she not as useful as her young brother? Could she not pick fruit as well as anyone else? As quick as that thought spat itself into her mind, she chided herself for being so childish. But still her frustration remained, urging her to go down to the orchard anyway. She was sure her uncle would see that she was as capable as any man.

She stood up, gathering her skirt to take the first step from the verandah, stopping as William Rideout emerged from the foliage of one of the closer trees. He certainly wouldn't welcome her presence in the orchard.

He would tell her to return to the house, her uncle pulled in to defend her right to stay or to back his long-time friend's position that she should go. Emma sighed again. She didn't want to put her uncle in that position nor make herself the center of that sort of attention. Still, she didn't want to return to the house.

She continued down the steps to the forecourt but turned away from the orchard, walking instead to the rear of the house, passing the barn and adjoining pigpens, stopping at the edge of the vegetable garden. A wooden fence surrounded the long narrow stretch of dirt, weeds growing with far more success than the few carrots and turnips Emma could see. It hadn't been attended to for a long time. A monstrous sow, her barrel-like belly swinging back and forth as she moved, shuffled out of the shelter in the adjoining pen, snorting at the fence. Emma reached out a hand to scratch at the bristly head. "Hello there," she said. The sow snorted again, pushing her head harder into Emma's hand.

"Oh, you like that, do you?" Emma said scratching a little harder at the base of the sow's ear. With a snort and a snuffle, the sow flopped to the ground, her swollen belly rippling with unborn piglets.

"Oh, you poor darling," Emma said. "How many babies are you having? I think one is enough, but you may end up with six or even eight."

"She could possibly have ten."

Emma stiffened. The absurdity of questioning the pig hadn't been foremost in her mind, as there had been no one to hear her do it. That now had changed, and she turned to face the owner of the statement. What surprised her more was that there wasn't only one, but two people, both on horseback, and she hadn't heard them at all, so engrossed she'd been in her conversation with the sow.

"Mr. Lang?"

"Miss McLeod." Thomas Lang nodded once toward her in a semblance of a bow. "The sow can have up to ten young," he repeated, smiling, "but that's me presuming she didn't tell you that herself."

Emma smiled back. "No, she didn't. Although I'm sure she would have but chose not to on your arrival. It's a woman thing."

Thomas threw back his head and laughed loudly. "Delightful, Miss McLeod," he said. "A wonderful thought and a sharp sense of humor."

Emma smiled, unsure how to respond to his compliment. "Are you looking for my uncle, Mr. Lang?"

"No. I was looking for you. I was eager to know your reply to my request, hopeful it was a yes, but I'm prepared to plead my case if it was a no." His smile broadened.

Emma sighed quietly. Again, she conceded that Mr. Lang was pleasant enough, but she wasn't interested in the attention of this man or any other. Courtship and marriage were so far away on her horizon she could barely see them. She would apologize and say that with all she'd been through in the past weeks, it wasn't a suitable time for him to call on her. She hoped he understood.

And she opened her mouth to say this—however, she reminded herself, not four hours ago she'd announced to Mr. Rideout, firmly, that she was agreeable to Mr. Lang's visit. Could she bear for Mr. Rideout to have the satisfaction of knowing she'd changed her mind, that she'd decided to see sense? Emma sighed again. No, she couldn't. She and her pride would just have to spend a few hours in this man's company to make sure Mr. Rideout had no ammunition to use against her. He truly was so contemptuous. It was no wonder he wasn't married. No woman would put up with his behavior. His views were truly archaic and patronizing. They didn't belong in this new…

"Miss McLeod?"

Emma dragged herself back to the present company, annoyed that she'd allowed thoughts of Mr. Rideout to consume her again. She looked up at Lang's companion, who sat silently, his horse reined in a few paces behind Lang's. She smiled. "You're Simon, aren't you? I saw you in the lane when I first arrived."

The boy nodded but remained silent.

"You'll have to excuse my son, Miss McLeod. Since his mother died, he has remained silent."

Despite Mr. Rideout providing her with that knowledge already, she still had no response other than, "Oh."

Emma smiled at Simon. He didn't smile back, just stared past her as if he were blind as well as mute. He was young, ten maybe, tall for his age if you could judge that of a person on horseback. His hair was dark, as were his eyes, and although he may not have had a voice, his eyes said so much, the clearest message being that of sadness.

"I'm not sure if you've met my brother Daniel," Emma said, hoping she would see something else in the boy's eyes. "He's eight, nine in a few months. He'll be so excited to meet you."

Simon's gaze drifted back and fixed on Emma's face. He nodded, a twitch of his mouth and for a moment she saw a tiny spark of pleasure in his eyes.

"You would like that, wouldn't you, Simon?" Lang said, twisting in his saddle to face the boy.

The boy turned slowly to look at his father, but the spark had gone, and Emma saw something else. Something cold. Anger? Hatred? Or was she reading this all wrong? Maybe he was just a petulant ten-year-old, sulking from a reprimand or punishment. Whatever it was, the tension between father and son was thick in the air.

"Anyway, Miss McLeod, concerning my request?" Lang said, turning away from the boy.

Emma sighed quietly. She could almost feel the pain as she figuratively cut off her nose in spite. "Yes, Mr. Lang. Tomorrow afternoon will be perfectly fine. Daniel will so enjoy meeting Simon."

The smile slipped from Lang's face. Emma knew he'd not intended the visit to include an eight-year-old boy, nor had he intended to bring his son, but those were the terms, and if he didn't like them, he only had to say. He couldn't expect a lady to entertain a man without some sort of chaperone, could he? But Thomas Lang didn't protest, and he wished Emma well until he saw her again on Thursday. Emma watched as the horses plodded their way back along the side of the house and disappeared around the corner. Then she turned back to the sow. "Well," she said. "I may have cut my nose off to spite my face, but at least I won't have to look at the self-satisfied one of Mr. Rideout."

The supine animal snorted—in agreement, Emma decided—and stretched out as far as her bulging belly would allow.

The sun was past its highest point, the temperature far warmer now than Emma expected for early spring, but if it was work she wanted to do, then she would have to put up with some discomforts. Those working in the orchard were, so she could ask no less of herself as she turned back to the vegetable garden.

The gate to the plot, which was intended to swing inward, was jammed against a mound of dirt that had blown up against it over time. Emma pushed hard against it, but the gate showed no sign of giving way. She was going to have to get a lot dirtier than she'd planned. She blew hard out between pursed lips, then pushed up her sleeves.

Dropping to her knees, she stretched her arm under the bottom railing. With her hand, she scooped the dirt away, bit by bit, eating away at the mound. As she worked, little beads of sweat gathered on her forehead, then banded together to run down the bridge of her nose dropping like raindrops onto the dirt. She swiped at her face with her free hand, continuing to dig with the other until finally the ground was level again, the gate swinging easily inward. She hauled herself to her feet and smiled, pleased by the small achievement she had made.

Now she could make some headway with the garden, and for the next hour, Emma separated weeds from half a dozen passable carrots and one adequate pumpkin. She stood up straight to survey her work, the vegetable garden now weed free and ready to be replanted. But that would have to wait. A dull headache had begun behind her eyes, and she felt a wave of nausea wash over her. She'd not eaten since breakfast, but now the thought of food wasn't enticing at all. At least she'd stopped sweating, even though it felt far hotter than it had when she had started.

"Miss McLeod. Don't move."

Emma's first instinct was to move, to turn. Not to discover who spoke this command, as she already knew his voice, but to ask the reason why. Her muscles tensed and she twisted no more than an inch when the command was said again.

"Don't move."

Now terror replaced curiosity and Emma froze, the reason her immobility was ordered evident not two feet in front of her—a snake, dull mustard in color, bands of black at intervals along its length, and Emma froze, needing no further command to do so.

"Miss McLeod. You're not to move an inch even if the animal comes toward you. It won't harm you if you don't move. Do you understand?"

Emma didn't know whether to nod or not, so she didn't, she just stared at the snake, its tongue flickering in and out of its tiny mouth. For what seemed like forever, Emma and the snake watched each other, the snake finally choosing to turn and slither away under the fence, disappearing into the undergrowth on the edge of the property. Still, Emma didn't move, her fear slowly dissipating, replaced by a lethargy so strong she didn't know if she could move anyway.

"Miss McLeod?"

Mr. Rideout's words reached her, but they had no substance, as if they were not words at all but the sound of the wind in her ears, the same wind that seemed to cause her to sway back and forth like a sapling in a storm. Then her legs gave way underneath her and she was falling, the ground coming up to meet her.

****

"Shall I send for the physician?"

141

"No, Robert. I don't think it's necessary."

"Did she get bitten?"

"No, Daniel. The snake didn't come near her."

"Then what's wrong with her?"

****

2022

"What's wrong with her?"

"It's okay, miss, your friend's going to be fine. Sophie, can you open your eyes for me?"

Emma did as she was asked, her eyes fluttering open to a light that was painfully bright. She squeezed them shut against it.

"Miss Harris. Sophie. Can you hear me?"

It was a man's voice and one Emma didn't recognize, nor did she know who the voice was speaking to. Who was Sophie? Vaguely she thought she knew a Sophie. But that had been a long time ago.

"Sophie? I'm just going to check your blood sugar, okay? You will feel a little nip on your finger."

Emma was surprised that *she* felt it, a sharp sting to her own finger. It would seem that whoever was talking believed her name was Sophie and not Emma.

"Can you open your eyes for me, Sophie?" The voice asked and, despite the confusion about who she was, Emma complied, her lids fluttering open.

"That's it. Great," a man said, smiling down at her as if opening her eyes was a feat that took great skill. "I'm just going to take your blood pressure again, so hold still and don't talk for a minute, okay?"

Emma nodded silently and felt the cuff wrapped around her sleeve tighten.

After a moment the man said, "It's all good. It's back to normal now. It was pretty low when we arrived.

Have you had problems with your BP in the past?"

Sophie shook her head. She didn't recognize the man staring down at her, or the young woman who stood off to one side. But she did recognize the other woman, her black tightly curled hair, her deep brown eyes now full of concern. She knew her face and believed her name was Becca. "Did the snake bite me?" Emma asked, finding that the only reason possible for the look of worry on the faces of the people looking down at her.

"A snake?" The man didn't seem to like these words. "Did a snake bite you, Sophie?"

No, it's Emma, Emma wanted to say, but as she opened her mouth to do so she could find no reason to. Her name was Sophie. Sophie Harris. Why did she think her name was Emma?

"Sophie, did a snake bite you?"

Sophie could see the terrified look on the face of the girl called Becca as she rapidly scanned the room in search of the reptile, her body seemingly poised to run at the sight of it.

Sophie shook her head. She felt as if coming out of a fog, her mind clearing as she did. "No, sorry," she said, her voice rasping, her throat dry. "No, it was just a dream. Why are you here? What happened?" She glanced at the man, but her question was for Becca.

Becca came forward and crouched at the side of the sofa. "Oh, Sophie. I found you here this morning. You were holding the diary. I thought you had fallen asleep reading it. But then I couldn't wake you, so I had no choice but to call an ambulance."

"The diary. Where is it?" Sophie wasn't sure why she needed to know where the book was, but not having a reason didn't stop her anxiety from rising. "Becca, where is it?"

"I think it's just under the sofa," the other woman, who was silent up to now said, her uniform the same as the man that hovered over Sophie. Paramedics, Sophie realized.

Sophie tried to sit up, but the man wasn't so keen on her doing so. "Take it slow. We're going to chauffeur you to the hospital. You have a cut on your head, and you were unresponsive when we arrived, so it's best if we let the docs take a look at you, okay?"

Sophie shook her head. "I don't need to go. Please. I'm fine. Becca, can you find the diary?"

Becca stood up, the book in her hand. "I've got it, Soph. It's fine. I'll put it away. Don't worry. And you're going to the hospital. No argument."

"No. Put it in my bag. Please?" Sophie could see from Becca's look of surprise that her words had come out as harsh as she imagined they had. She hadn't meant to sound so demanding, but she did know she needed the diary to be close. *Why* that was, she didn't know.

****

"What did they say?" Becca asked as she drove from the hospital car park.

Sophie shook her head. "Nothing really, other than they couldn't find anything wrong, which I guess is good. They did think maybe I'd hit my head and then lay down and lost consciousness." She raised a hand to the spot above her ear. It was covered now with a white dressing. "But I don't remember when I did that. If it happens again, I will need to get some further tests done, but after everything they did, I can't imagine what other tests there could possibly be."

Becca laughed. "Oh, they'll find something to do to

you, don't you worry about that."

Sophie smiled in agreement.

"So you take off as many days as you need. I can manage setting up some of the other exhibits," Becca continued.

"I'll be fine, Bec. I don't need any time off."

Becca nodded. "Okay. But if you do, that's okay. Okay? I'm going to get Mike to bring your car back to yours. I'll drive you for the next few days. Okay?"

Sophie laughed. The last "okay" wasn't a question but an order, and Sophie could only agree. "Okay."

"Good. Until we know what's happening with you, I'll be your chauffeur."

The storm clouds that had threatened earlier now made good on their promise, and raindrops plopped one after the other onto the windshield, Sophie watching as they were swept away by the wipers only for more to take their place. Back and forth, back and forth, it was almost hypnotic watching the twin blades faithfully do their work, and Sophie let her mind drift to…to what? Again, she felt she'd been somewhere, but this time it was different. Where before she had had hazy memories, vague feelings when she awoke, this time she'd been someone else, she was living someone else's life. Someone called Emma, and she remembered every detail.

"Soph," Becca said tentatively as if she didn't know whether she should say what she was about to. "Did you dream something about a snake?"

Sophie frowned. A dream? Is that all it was, a dream? But dreams were confused and disjointed. They relied on symbolism and made no sense when you woke. What she had experienced was different. It was like watching a movie that she starred in. She had a family and she loved them, she missed them. Her brother Daniel, Martha, Uncle Robert. And then there was William Rideout. He was a horrible man, pigheaded, rude, arrogant, but still there was something…

"Soph? Are you all right?"

"Yeah, sorry, Bec. I was trying to remember. I think there was something about a snake, but I really can't recall anything other than that." But that wasn't the truth. She remembered it all. From the moment she laid eyes on William Rideout, the journey to Fremantle, the relief at meeting her uncle, the wonder of seeing Eden Hill. She could see it all as if she were there. And she remembered making a vegetable garden and Thomas Lang and his son had come. She remembered William Rideout telling her not to move. Then she'd seen the snake. She'd fainted, but she didn't think it was due to the reptile. The last thing she could remember was being carried somewhere, and then a paramedic was talking to her. That's when she'd come back. That thought startled her. Come back? From where? Daniel had told her he was glad she was back when she was Emma. Now she was back here as Sophie. But back from where? None of this made sense. Maybe she was having a breakdown of some kind, or maybe they missed a brain tumor at the hospital. That could cause delusions, couldn't it? A headache was starting just behind Sophie's eyes, and she was starting to feel a little nauseous. She was glad when Becca pulled into her driveway. She just wanted to crawl into bed and sleep.

But after Becca left, Sophie bypassed her bedroom. Dropping her bag on the couch, she wandered into the kitchen. She hadn't had breakfast, and lunch was a plate of hospital cafeteria "mixed" sandwiches consisting mainly of cheese, some sort of meat, and an unhealthy amount of butter. She'd nibbled on a cheese quarter, but that's all she'd managed. She opened the fridge and scanned the shelves. There wasn't a great deal to choose from that didn't require some level of preparation, and she didn't have the energy for that. "Toast it is," she said.

Her toast generously covered with hazelnut spread, she carried what she could only describe as comfort food to the sitting room. She set her plate and mug of tea down on the coffee table and dropped onto the couch. The television stared blankly back at her. She picked up the remote and pointed it at the screen, watching as the TV came to life, sound and light filling the room. She didn't watch commercial television often, preferring to read and binge the occasional offering on subscription TV. Tonight, however, she needed something mundane to distract her from her thoughts and settled for the game show that both contestants and host seemed to be enjoying immensely.

"Do you want to go for $5000?" the upbeat presenter asked a clearly anxious contestant. But Sophie didn't hear the answer. Despite her efforts not to think about what had happened to her, her thoughts drifted to her dream, regardless, if that's what it had been. "Of course it was a dream. What else could it have been?" she told herself. "Do you really think you were there, that you were Emma McLeod?" She closed her eyes and could see Daniel clearly as day, Martha and her uncle, too. Even William Rideout appeared before her, and for a moment she longed to be with them. She missed them. "This is madness, Sophie," she said. "You might need to get some professional help to get these people out of your head."

That thought led to another. Wasn't she a professional? Maybe if she could prove who was real and who wasn't, it would show her that these were just dreams, populated by a mix of people she knew about and those who were figments of her imagination, just extras, so to speak. Maybe that would be all she needed to stop the dreams from happening at all. Encouraged by action, Sophie crossed to her desk and took a notepad and pen from the drawer. Leaning over the pad, she drew a line down the center of the page, dividing it into two columns. She wrote Documented as the heading of one column and Dreamt as the heading for the second.

In the Documented column she wrote *Thomas Lang*. She knew his name from the deed of land. Next she wrote, *Adam*, knowing this from the small part of the diary Becca had read out to her. From the letters, she knew the names *Emma, Daniel,* and *Robert* and she wrote these down. Finally, from the cheque, she knew the name *Edward A McLeod*. That's what she knew. As fact.

In the second column, she wrote the names she knew only from her dream, *Martha, Simon, William Rideout,* and Emma's siblings, *Alice and Eliza*. Had they all existed too? If so, there would be records of them.

And what if there is? What does that mean?

Sophie ignored these questions whispered to her. She'd no answer to them. At this point, she just needed to know one way or the other, and she would deal with the questions later, if the time came. *Which it won't,* her rational mind assured her. These people were just creations of her imagination. They had to be.

She dropped into the chair, her computer coming to

life with a touch of a button, and she opened the genealogical website. She signed in, then typed the first name on the list of the people she knew were real. Thomas Lang. She pressed search. A list of potentials flooded the screen, and Sophie scanned the various suggestions. Then she saw it. Thomas Lang married Emma McLeod, in Fremantle, Western Australia, 1865.

"Emma is a McLeod," Sophie said aloud. "Therefore, Daniel is too. The Edward McLeod on the cheque must be related. Her father? Robert is her uncle, so is he a McLeod also? Edward's brother?"

Next Sophie searched for Edward A. McLeod in the UK census records. Again, she was presented with a list of potentials. She had no clue where this man had lived or his spouse's name, but she did have his potential children's names, Emma and Daniel. Working with the date 1865 and estimating birth dates, Sophie searched the census records from 1841 to 1871. Finally, she found what she was looking for. In the 1841 census, she found a one-year-old Emma living with an Edward and Susannah McLeod. A possibility.

She repeated the search in the 1851 census, Emma now being eleven. There were other children listed with the family, and although she'd not seen or heard the names before, they were familiar to her. She tried to disregard the knot that had begun to twist in her stomach. She advanced the records to the next decade and again found Edward and Susannah with children Emma aged 21 and Daniel aged 4. But it was the next two names that took her breath away. Alice and Eliza were both aged 2. "What the hell?" Sophie whispered.

Up until now she'd found the names of people she knew had existed and had documented evidence to prove it. That was reason enough for her to dream about them. But how did she know of these little girls, Alice and Eliza? Their names were not written anywhere. How did they enter her dreams? How did she know, if she were to look, that they both died of typhoid, and why could she see their faces so clearly in life and also in death?

Sophie slammed the lid of her laptop closed and stood up. Suddenly she didn't feel good. The knot in her stomach tightened, and there seemed to be no air in the room. She closed her eyes and took a deep breath in, trying to calm herself, breathing out slowly. She took another breath. There must be a rational explanation for this. She breathed out. There had to be. She took another breath, letting it slowly flow from her mouth, some of the tension easing with it. She opened her eyes, her gaze coming to rest on the couch—or more importantly, her bag. The diary was in there.

Sophie took another shaky breath in and held it for a moment. She let it out in one long breath, then crossed to the couch. Picking up her bag, she turned it upside down, emptying its contents onto the couch. The diary slid out next to her wallet. Taking her phone from the coffee table, she set an alarm for five minutes, then took a seat alongside the contents of her bag and reached out for the diary. She could feel the cold of the plastic under her fingers, the tingling in her fingertips as she slid them into the opening of the sleeve, then the smoothness of the cardboard cover. Then nothing.

****

1865

Emma could hear the voices of her brother and her uncle. She could also hear the voice of Mr. Rideout, muffled, vibrating through her. She should open her eyes, assure them all that she was fine, but she just couldn't get her eyelids to do as she asked. She did form, however, the conclusion that she was moving, a rhythmic bouncing to her progress. But she couldn't feel the ground under her feet or a saddle under her behind. What she could feel was arms around her and hear a heartbeat that wasn't hers and the vibration as Mr. Rideout spoke.

"It's far hotter here than your sister realized. That and the shock of seeing the snake caused her to faint. She needs water and rest."

Even in this half-sleep state, Emma still felt a flicker of anger at his words. I didn't faint, and I don't need to rest, her mind said with the expected level of indignation such suggestions would invite, but the words stayed in her mind, Emma finding no energy to say them aloud.

"Daniel, run ahead and wet a towel. And get some water in a pitcher, and a cup."

The rocking motion lulled her further into what must be a dream, and she didn't fight it. But suddenly she was falling, her arms flailing, her fingers grabbing at thin air. Her eyes snapped open, and she found herself staring directly into the face of Mr. Rideout.

"Shhhh. Everything's fine. You fainted. You had too much sun." The palm of his hand touched her forehead for a moment and she closed her eyes. His hand was cool, her face burning as if she'd sat too near the fire. "You're burning up," he said and draped a damp cool cloth in place of his hand.

"Fainted?" Emma looked around the room. She was in the sitting room, supine on the floral settee, a pillow under her head. The clock on the far wall told her it was nearing five. "Daniel will be hungry." Emma hunched her shoulders forward to sit, but small black dots immediately filled her field of vision and she closed her eyes. A hand on her shoulder eased her back onto the pillow. The cloth on her head, now warm, was replaced with another and a glass of water held to her lips. She sipped at it.

"Daniel will be fed along with the rest of us. We managed before you came, Miss McLeod. We will manage again."

Emma cautiously opened one eye. Was there a tone of condescension in his voice now, when only a moment ago there was something different entirely?

"And I suggest you stay inside from now on. You have no understanding of the climate here nor the wildlife, and both can kill. I'm sure there's plenty for you to do in the house."

Emma opened her other eye, for a moment having no idea what to say, finally managing a curt, "Thank you. I will keep that in mind, Mr. Rideout."

The man nodded once. "We will eat shortly. Then I suggest you rest in your room until you feel better. At least until the morning."

He said no more and disappeared into the hallway. She could hear the mumble of voices from, she guessed, the kitchen, but there was no clarity to the words. She wouldn't have heard them anyway, even if they were speaking right next to her, her own words filling her head.

How dare he imply she couldn't understand this country, that she would be happy filling her days with dusting and darning! Was she seen as useless as Martha, bless her, only capable of gentle pastimes lest she swoon or need the physician? She'd delivered her infant brother, watched her mother die, and buried both alongside each other. She'd cared for herself and Daniel and would have continued to do so.

Damn him, how dare he treat her with such little regard? She swiped at a tear, annoyed that he could make her so angry. Why did she care so much about what he said or thought?

****

2022

Sophie opened her eyes. Her phone was vibrating across the top of the coffee table as the familiar jingle of her alarm played, and she reached out her hand to grab it, silencing the incessant reminder to wake up. It took her a minute to realize it wasn't morning and she wasn't in her bed. She was on the couch, the diary next to her, and vague memories began to filter into her mind. She had been carried somewhere, there was talk of a doctor being called, and the little boy was there and the man, William. They had thought she'd been bitten by the snake, but it was the heat that had made her faint. A snake again. That's what she had dreamt about before. Was this the next chapter, so to speak, of this dream? She wished she could remember more.

She turned her head to look at the diary. It didn't glow, it didn't whisper to her, it just sat there like any inanimate object, but as she had before, Sophie stared at it with trepidation as if it were poisonous, something you looked at from afar but dared not touch, even for a moment. A simple brush of the cover seemed to be all it took. That was true of all the times she'd fainted, and each time she'd come to she had only vague memories. Except for when she'd lain down in the office to dispute her theory that the diary was the cause of her blackouts. She woke up remembering everything. Why? Why had that been different? She played the scene out in her mind. The book had been on her stomach, and she'd gone to sit up, grasping the book, but after that, she remembered nothing other than Emma's life until the paramedics had woken her. Becca said she was still holding the diary and she had taken it from her. So if she was going to follow this logic, however illogical it was, maybe the more contact she had with the diary, the more she remembered. "Come on, Sophie. You don't believe that! You're schooled in verifiable evidence, not maybes and could-bes." She felt her heart pick up its pace as a tiny voice at the back of her mind whispered, *Maybe you should verify it, then.*

Allowing no time to debate her question, Sophie rose from the couch and crossed to her desk. She tore a clean sheet of paper from the notepad and wrote in large letters,

Becca,

If I'm asleep on the couch, please take diary from me and wake me.

DON'T call an ambulance.

Trust me.

I'll explain everything when I wake.

Please don't panic.

Sophie xxxx

She knew telling someone not to panic was the quickest way to send them in that direction, but there wasn't anything she could do about that. She took the note and taped it to the sitting room door and closed it.

She shoved everything back into her bag except the diary, which she picked up by its sleeve. She could feel her fingers tingle at the touch, and she put the book on the coffee table. In the light of the lamp, Sophie kicked off her shoes and lay down on the couch. She pulled the thick throw over her and reached for the diary. Her hands shook as she upended the sleeve, the diary sliding out onto the throw. She held her breath, her fingers poised. Then, with one long breath, she brought both hands together, clasping the book between them. Air rushed past her, pulling her with it into a black space. She hung there for a moment, then came out into the light.

****

1865

Emma woke feeling much better than she had the night before. The skin on the back of her neck stung and her head hurt a little. She would stay inside today and would spend the time giving the house a thorough clean and preparing some lessons for Daniel. He'd missed so much schooling, and although she knew he would protest loudly, Emma would insist that part of each day he would devote to his education, like it or not.

She rolled from the bed and dressed in a light cotton gown. She wondered if she could entice Martha to take some tea with her this morning and went into the foyer. She raised her hand to knock on Martha's door, a sound from inside stopping her. Someone, she could only assume it was Martha, was vomiting, the retching enough to cause Emma's stomach to churn in sympathy. The noise stopped, replaced now by breathless sobs, and Emma didn't bother to knock.

Martha looked up, her face as white as the bedsheets that had been tossed aside in the hurry to find the porcelain bowl. She opened her mouth—for words of protest, maybe—but she closed it again, her misery making speech impossible.

Emma crossed to the dressing stand and poured

water from the pitcher onto a hand towel.

Martha took it from her and wiped her mouth. "Thank you," she whispered.

"Shall I send for the doctor?" Emma half turned back to the door. "Does my uncle know you're ill?"

The other woman shook her head. "I don't need a doctor," she whispered. "I have no illness. It is far worse."

Emma frowned. Worse? What could be worse than illness? What else made you sick to your stomach that wasn't an illness? Poison? Was Martha implying she was being poisoned? Her uncle had alluded to the fact that Martha was unhappy here. Had she reached a level of such mental despair that she'd tried to take her own life? Or was there another reason, one that to most would bring joy, but for some reason caused this woman only despair? "Martha? Are you pregnant?"

The question brought a moan from the woman, more a sound of fear than of sadness. She let out a long shuddering sigh and nodded. "About ten weeks, I think."

Emma smiled. "But that's wonderful news. Isn't it?"

The other woman sighed again. "No."

"No? Martha, what do you mean? Does my uncle know?"

Martha swung around to face Emma, grasping both her hands tightly. "Please, Emma, please, I beg you, don't tell your uncle about this."

The plea in her eyes matched the one in her words, and Emma nodded quickly. "I promise I won't say a word, but please, tell me why. Surely, he'll be overjoyed. Has he said to you he doesn't want children?"

Martha shook her head and released Emma from her grasp, clasping her hands tightly together in her lap. She stared down at them.

"No. But he won't have children, as this one will die too."

"Die? Martha, what do you mean? How many others have there been?"

Martha sighed loudly. "Four. All of them leaving my body dead before God had time to fashion them into children. This one will leave me soon, too."

"Four?" Emma repeated still reeling from the revelation. "And my uncle never knew of this?"

Martha shook her head. "I tell him I have problems only a woman can suffer, and I take to my bed. He's always kind and always patient, but he does need what a husband requires, and it's not too long before I'm carrying another child."

"But why can't you tell him?"

Martha sighed again. "Because I have nowhere to go. No man wants a wife that cannot bear him children. But I know he won't send me away if he believes I'm ill."

Emma couldn't help but laugh at the absurdity of the woman's statement. "Oh, Martha. My uncle won't send you away for any reason. He cares for you. He told me himself. He feels bad that you're so unhappy here and worries that your health will only worsen. He doesn't know how to make you happy. He would never send you away unless you wanted it yourself."

This brought more tears, and Emma sat down beside the woman, wrapping her arm around her, rocking her gently. "You must tell my uncle, your husband. He'll want to know, and he'll understand. It's not good for you to carry this burden alone. You need to eat and drink properly and take fresh air, and we will do our best,

Martha, to help this baby grow and come into the world a healthy child."

Emma felt the woman nod against her shoulder. After a while, the tears stopped, and Martha shifted slightly. Emma dropped her arm away from the woman and stood up. "First things first, then. A cup of tea and a proper breakfast."

Martha nodded. "I will try."

Chapter 13

Martha did more than try, devouring scrambled eggs and bread and butter as if she'd been denied food for weeks. Emma didn't think that was far from the truth, believing that Martha had been denying herself. But as a punishment for not carrying her babies to term or to hasten what Martha thought the inevitable, Emma wasn't sure.

After breakfast, Emma shooed Martha outside onto the verandah with a cup of tea, a much healthier place than her stuffy bedroom. Emma was determined to do everything she could to save this baby if it was at all possible. She wondered how Martha would broach the subject of the terrible secret she'd been keeping with her husband and how he would take the news, but Emma did know telling him sooner rather than later would be best for all concerned.

Emma filled the basin with hot water ready to accept the late breakfast dishes. She was just about to lower the first plate into the water when a chill raced down her spine as the cries of her little brother froze her. She recovered her senses and turned from the sink, wiping the suds from her hands on her apron.

"Emma. Emma," Daniel skidded to a stop in front of her, his face tearstained. "Will's going to shoot Meredith!"

Emma had no idea who Meredith was, nor why

William was going to shoot her. "Slow down, Daniel. Who is Meredith?"

Daniel didn't wait to explain, grabbing Emma's hand and dragging her through the house and onto the verandah. Martha stood, her hands fluttering around her throat as if she were the intended victim. Emma motioned for her to sit. "Everything is fine," she assured her as Daniel continued to drag Emma down the steps and into the yard.

William crossed her path, a shotgun slung over his shoulder. "Mr. Rideout, what's happening?" Emma called after him.

William stopped. "The sow can't deliver her young. Can't you hear her? She's in agony." He dipped his head slightly toward the gun, indicating his intention for the stricken animal.

There was no point denying that the animal was in great distress, if the strident squeals coming from the rear of the house, were an indication. Still, Emma said, "Please, can I have a look at her first?"

"There's no point, Miss McLeod. I've seen this happen before, and it's a slow, painful death for the poor animal. Take Daniel inside and let me do what I must. I'll be in shortly to explain it to him. Letting him take care of the pigs was my idea. I didn't realize he would feel so much attachment to the animal. I'm sorry, Daniel."

William resumed his march across the yard, and Emma pulled her hand free from Daniel's. "Stay here, Daniel," she said and ran after the man. "Can I just look at her before you do what you have to, Mr. Rideout?" Emma asked again.

William didn't break his stride. "As you wish."

Emma followed him into the barn, her eyes adjusting quickly to the dim light of the interior. She found the stall instantly, the weakening cries of the sow guiding her.

"I have tried to dislodge the obstruction," William said as he loaded the gun. "But it won't budge. The young are too big for the sow to deliver, and I cannot get a purchase. It's best I put her out of her pain."

"Give me one minute, please." Emma dropped down behind the animal. She rolled her sleeve up past her elbow. The sow was less than happy with Emma's intrusion, her keening growing to a scream, but it was only for a few moments. Then the sow was quiet. At Emma's feet lay a dead piglet. "It was lying sideways across the birth canal, preventing its birth and that of the piglets waiting to come after it." She said this more to the sow than anyone else, the animal giving a hefty sigh as another piglet fell to the ground.

Emma grabbed a handful of hay and rubbed at its little body. For a moment, it lay still, then began to wriggle in her arms. Emma smiled and placed the newborn animal near its mother's teat. She waited for the next deliveries, all the while not noticing the tears that rolled down her face. Emma didn't know how long she sat in the hay, rubbing little pink bodies into life, eight of them in all. Finally, the sow grunted with contentment and closed her eyes, her breathing steady as she slipped into a well-deserved slumber.

Emma looked up at William. "I think that's all of them," she said, looking back at the five little pink bodies contentedly suckling from their much calmer mother. "We lost three, but these little fellows look good."

`William knelt next to her, a frown of concern on his

face. "Miss McLeod. Are you all right?"

Emma wiped her face with a part of her dress that wasn't smeared with blood and muck. A memory she didn't want to have had wormed its way into her mind. She pushed it away and smiled. "I'm fine. Thank you, although I believe I may have the look one can only get from sitting in a pigpen."

William smiled back. "Well, your efforts are greatly appreciated, Miss McLeod, by me, your uncle, and most definitely Daniel, although I believe Meredith here is probably the most grateful." He reached out his hand.

Emma looked at him for a moment, taken aback a little by this unfamiliar behavior. This must be the other William Rideout her uncle had spoken of. Maybe the safe delivery of a piglet or two was a stable enough foundation for building a friendship. She took his hand and stood up.

"Emma?"

Daniel's face appeared over the top of the stall. "Is Meredith all right?"

Emma looked up. "She's fine, Daniel," Emma said, glancing down and pushing hay with her foot over the bodies of the three dead piglets. He didn't need to see them. "She has five babies. They're all well."

Daniel ran to her, wrapping his arms around her waist. "Thank you, Emma. I knew you would save her," he said, then pulled away. "Oowee, you stink. You better have a bath. I'm going to tell Uncle Robert about the babies." The little boy skipped from the barn, a smile on his face now, his earlier distress forgotten.

Emma watched him go. "Well, I think Daniel has a point," she said looking up at William. "But I think also a glass of lemonade is well deserved first. I made some fresh this morning. Would you like some?" She smiled, but the man in front of her didn't. The William she'd seen moments ago had gone.

"No, thank you, Miss McLeod. If you'll excuse me, I have a lot of work to catch up on." Without another word, he turned and left her alone in the barn.

Chapter 14

Emma sank into the hot water and closed her eyes, an image of William Rideout's face forming behind her lids. He was an attractive man when he smiled. But why did his smile disappear so quickly? He was capable of compassion and kindness, she'd seen more than one example of that, but he seemed to prefer to be arrogant and aloof. Emma didn't think she'd ever met someone as changeable as a spring day. He really was...

Emma smiled wryly to herself. Again, she'd allowed Mr. Rideout into her thoughts, and she cleared her mind of him. In doing so, however, other thoughts, waiting for a moment when she'd nothing to occupy her, began to form in her mind.

Her uncle had been right. She hadn't grieved, because grieving made it all too real, and she wasn't ready for that. She'd cried herself to sleep every night before they had been rescued, but since then she'd never allowed herself to think about what she'd lost—her mother, no longer there to advise, encourage and occasionally scold, and little Adam, who although she'd only known him for three days was a new life in a new country. He would have been the symbol of hope and growth. And her father. He was her best friend, and she couldn't bear to think he might be gone also.

A single tear dropped onto her breast, and she watched it travel downward as it slipped onto her stomach. She knew other tears would follow, and she wouldn't allow herself that.

She stood up, letting the water drip from her body for a moment, goosebumps blossoming on her skin. She reached for a towel and wrapped herself in it and stepped from the bath, small puddles forming around each foot. She dried herself and dressed quickly, pulling on only her camisole, petticoat, and a light cotton dress. The afternoon was warm, and she loathed being weighed down by layers. She pulled her hair to the side, coaxing the curls into a braid, and tied it with a fraying piece of ribbon.

Stepping into the hallway, Emma saw that Martha was still on the chaise on the verandah. She was smiling at someone Emma couldn't see. But she could hear, and her uncle's happy voice came to her ears well enough.

"This is grand, just grand. I couldn't be happier."

Emma waited for more. What was grand? Had Martha told him about the child, or was it the piglets that pleased him? Although he said no more to give her any clue, the subject of her uncle's pleasure wasn't a mystery for long.

"Martha might have a baby," Daniel said, as he raced inside. "She said it might not get to be born, but if she's meant to be a mother it will."

Emma hadn't expected such a candid explanation from her little brother and could only say, "Oh?"

But there was no look of sadness or dismay on the boy's face. "Martha said that sometimes babies just go to heaven early before they can be born," he explained, "and that's something we shouldn't be sad for."

Emma smiled at her brother. The little boy had accepted that as how it was, and Emma wasn't about to dispute it. "Well, that's exciting news," she said. "We must do our best to look after Martha, then, so she can hopefully become a mother." Emma followed Daniel out onto the verandah, her uncle beaming at her.

"Is it not wonderful news, Emma?"

Emma agreed it was but had to wonder if Martha had told her uncle about the other babies she'd lost. For Martha's sake, as well as her uncle's, he needed to know there was a chance of losing this one. But Martha looked like a weight had lifted from her and her uncle appeared overjoyed, so that conversation could wait for now.

Mr. Rideout had come to join the group and was shaking her uncle's hand, offering words of congratulations. Would he think Martha still a burden now that she would, God willing, provide an heir? Or was it not important to him? Was this country too harsh for a new life to thrive? If one was to go by Mr. Rideout's opinion, it didn't bode well for this country's prosperity if no one should fall in love, marry, and have children.

But if he was right? Where did that leave her? She did want to marry, one day, and she wanted to have a family. Would that happen for her in this place? Would she ever know what it was like to have a new life grow inside her, or would Daniel be the only child she would ever raise?

"Thank you for saving Meredith," Daniel said later that night as Emma tucked him into bed. "She's my favorite pig."

Emma laughed. "It was my pleasure. But it's time to sleep now." She kissed his forehead. "Goodnight, Daniel."

"Goodnight, Em."

Emma slipped from the room and wandered back

along the hall toward the sitting room to wish her uncle goodnight. Martha had gone to bed, and Emma was eager to go to hers also. But she stopped short of the doorway. Her uncle wasn't alone.

"I don't hold out much hope, Will, I can tell you that, but it would be a great burden lifted from Emma's shoulders if she knew one way or the other. If it's not too much trouble, could you look into my brother's disappearance as soon as the harvest is in?"

Emma listened for Mr. Rideout's reply. "It's no trouble, Robert. I will make enquiries next week when I go to Fremantle. Miss McLeod has had a difficult time. I only hope I can bring her some good news."

Emma smiled a little at his kind words, but the smile left her face just as quickly as he continued.

"She has been dealt a terrible hand but has managed well with little experience of the colony, especially being so young. I don't like to think what would have happened to her if you had been in England, however."

Emma felt her fingers curl tightly into fists.

"Ah, I know my Emma, Will. She's not and never has been a fragile girl. If anything, she's sensible beyond her years."

"Then tell me, Robert, if she's as sensible as you say, explain how she's inviting the attention of Lang, of all people."

"I don't think there's much to be concerned by on that account," her uncle assured the other man. "You know it was only out of pride."

"Pride?"

"She's her father's daughter and, at the best of times, determined and tenacious."

"And at the worst?" William asked.

She heard her uncle laugh. "At worst, stubborn and headstrong, even if the path she takes is not the one she likes. But she's not a fool nor will she suffer one. She may have made a decision she regrets, but she would rather that than have a decision be made for her."

Emma heard William's sigh, one of frustration. "She could do with understanding that some decisions should be made for her by people that know better."

Robert chuckled. "Well, William, all I can say is that it would be a brave man to say that to her face."

The voices fell silent, replaced with the clink of glasses, the pouring of liquid, the strike of a match, the rich aroma of cigar smoke drifting into the hall.

Emma decided to forgo the goodnight and headed for her room.

She took her diary from the top drawer of her dresser. She had a lot to write about, what with her encounter with the snake, Martha's pregnancy, and of course, saving Meredith, but most importantly she would write about the distasteful Mr. Rideout, her feeling best put on paper than said to his face, and she dipped the pen into the ink.

My Dearest friend...

Chapter 15

Emma hadn't slept well, her dreams of dead piglets and crying babies, William Rideout and Mr. Lang. She was glad to see the sun was shining when she opened her eyes, her mood gloomy enough without the weather adding to it. Today, Thomas Lang was to visit.

She didn't know what she was going to say to the man, small talk and chit-chat not being something she enjoyed. But she'd made this bed and must lie in it, and maybe she would be pleasantly surprised. Possibly the man's company would be more enjoyable than she imagined. She would soon find out.

With another sigh, Emma rolled from her bed and stretched her arms over her head. She washed and dressed in a yellow cotton gown, simple but pretty enough for accepting visitors. Despite her somber mood, there was a strong atmosphere of excitement in the house. Her uncle was whistling as he made tea. "Emma, my darling. Would you like some tea? I'm just taking a cup to Martha."

Emma said she would and sat at the table. "How is she today?"

"She's grand," her uncle said. "Still sick, poor lamb, but she says maybe that's a good sign. She was hardly at all with the other bairns."

Emma nodded, glad that the question of whether Martha had told her uncle about the other pregnancies

169

was answered. It appeared the risk of this pregnancy was also understood.

Emma followed her uncle, tea in hand, out onto the verandah. She set the cup down on a small table pulled up next to Martha's chair. "Have you seen Daniel?" she asked, looking around for her brother.

"He said he had some new friends to go and see," her uncle said.

Emma smiled. She knew where he must be. She went down the steps and strolled to the back of the house.

"Daniel?" Daniel's head appeared above the wall of the pigpen, exactly where Emma knew she would find him. "Daniel, come here, please."

The little boy nodded, then turned away. "I'll be right back," he said, but if he was speaking to a human or pig, Emma couldn't tell. The little boy clambered over the fence. "I was checking on Meredith and the babies," he said, with a little nod toward the pen. "They're getting big already."

Emma smiled. "Daniel, I don't want you to go far today. Mr. Lang is coming to visit, and I want you to meet him."

"I have already met him, Emma. At the hotel. I shook his hand and everything, but I don't think he likes children much. He didn't know much about stuff, either, not like Will."

Emma sighed. No, Mr. Lang wasn't like William, but that was probably a good thing. Two arrogant, insensitive men would be unbearable. "Never mind if you've met him. I want you to sit with me while he's visiting. He's bringing his son, Simon. You can show him the schoolwork we have started."

"Why?"

"Because, Daniel."

"Because isn't an answer, Emma. You're always telling me that."

Emma smiled. "Very well. If you must know, I don't know what to talk to Mr. Lang about, and it will be uncomfortable on my own. I need you there so it's not so difficult."

Daniel frowned. "Why did you invite him over, then, if you don't have anything to say?"

"Because, Daniel."

"Emma!"

"Please, Daniel, just do as I ask. I'm making some ham sandwiches. There will be scones and jam. You can have as many as you want."

Daniel eyed his sister for a moment, his hands planted on his hips. Emma knew he was weighing up whether the feast was worth the boredom. Then he grinned. "All right, Em, but I have to collect the eggs first, and can I still go out with Will to fix the fence? It's not far. Please?"

Emma nodded. "Yes, but you must tell Mr. Rideout that you have to be back just before midday. I want you to be clean and tidy."

Daniel promised he would." Can I go now?"

Emma crouched down in front of the little boy. She hugged him to her and kissed his forehead. "Off you go. Midday, do you hear?"

Daniel nodded and climbed back into the pigpen.

Emma busied herself in the kitchen for the next few hours, preparing enough food for the four of them and at least two more, but she didn't imagine her uncle would be free, there being so much work still to do. As for Martha, she seemed to dislike Lang. Although she said nothing of that to Emma, her reaction to Mr. Lang's visit was enough for Emma to guess that was the case. And certainly Mr. Rideout wouldn't drop by for lunch.

The thud of hooves coming along the track heralded Mr. Lang's arrival, and Emma sighed loudly. Her stomach churned and she felt more trepidation than she should for a simple lunch engagement. She untied the apron that had kept most of the flour from her dress and hung it over the back of a chair. Then she smoothed her hair and went out into the foyer. Mr. Lang was waiting on the verandah.

Emma took a breath, calmed herself, and opened the door. "Mr. Lang. Good afternoon."

"Good day to you, Miss McLeod." He took her hand in his and raised it to his lips. His hands were soft, not working hands like her uncle's—or Mr. Rideout's, for that matter. Not that she'd had much to do with Mr. Rideout's hands—the assistance down from a carriage, up out of the hay after the piglet's delivery, the brief accidental brush when he took a plate from her. That was all, but enough for her to know.

"You look beautiful, as usual, if you don't mind me saying," Lang said, drawing Emma's attention back to him.

Emma smiled a thank you and gestured for him to sit down at the small table she'd brought out onto the verandah. She sat opposite.

"How have you been, Mr. Lang?"

"I'm well. Thank you. And yourself?"

Emma smiled politely. "Well, thank you."

"I'm pleased."

Emma smiled self-consciously as the silence began to grow. She cast around for something to add to the faltering conversation. She hoped Daniel would return earlier than she'd asked. "It's wonderful news about Martha's baby, is it not?"

Lang looked surprised, a frown momentarily creasing his brow. "Oh. I wasn't aware. That's wonderful news. A child brings so much joy."

"Yes, they do," Emma said, waving away a fly that buzzed around her face. "Did your son accompany you today, Mr. Lang?" She gazed across the fields in the hope of seeing the boy. Although he was mute, he still would provide another source of attention if he came to join them for lunch.

"He did. I told him to go and introduce himself, so to speak, to your brother if he could find him. He's had no one to play with for a long time, so he was quite eager."

Emma surveyed the valley, looking for any sign of the children, fearing that having a new playmate would divert Daniel from his job as chaperone. "My brother Daniel asked that I call him when you arrived. He would like to meet you, he said."

Lang frowned. "I have already met your brother. At the hotel when you first arrived."

Emma glanced at him. "Yes, I know, but he insisted. It's time for his lunch anyway. I will go and find him and Simon, and we can all eat together." She stood up. "Please don't get up. I won't be long."

Before Lang could voice his objection, Emma hurried down the steps onto the forecourt and went around to the side of the house. Daniel was probably showing Simon the piglets, but an inspection of the pen revealed only Meredith and her new charges. William's horse was tethered to the upper railing of the chicken coop. "Mr. Rideout," she called out.

William appeared at the door. "Miss McLeod?"

"Would Daniel be with you?"

William shook his head. "No. He's not with me."

Emma frowned. "Wasn't he coming with you to fix some of the fence posts?"

"He was. He was collecting the eggs when I went to saddle up. I said I would come for him in ten minutes, but he was gone when I came back." William pointed to the basket of eggs left on a ledge in the coop.

Emma frown grew. Daniel wouldn't miss helping William with the fences, and she didn't think he would defy her request to be home for lunch. "Simon was looking for him. I wonder where they are?"

William's gaze moved from the eggs to meet Emma's. "Simon? Oh, I see. He came with Lang, I suppose. I'll go out and have a look for the boys, Miss McLeod, so you can get back to your-guest."

He couldn't have said the word with more disdain, and Emma sighed. If only William knew that she wasn't enjoying Mr. Lang's company at all. But she wasn't about to tell him so. She went out into the yard, straining to see if the boys were hiding amongst the fruit trees, the shadows and branches providing a multitude of places for small boys to hide.

In vain she called out for her brother and waited, receiving no reply, although she expected that. Her uncle's property was extensive, and although Daniel had been told time and time again not to stray too far, she had no idea how far two boys at play would go. Once more she scanned the orchard and the field. Then her heart stopped dead in her chest.

In the distance, she could see a child, the identity of

which she couldn't determine from where she stood, but she could only assume it was one of the boys. But it wasn't that she could see the child that turned her blood to ice. It was that the child stood on the edge of the dam. Her skirt lifted, Emma was moving down the hill before she realized, the incline propelling her faster and faster.

She stumbled, her legs not able to keep up with the pace, but she righted herself and entered the orchard, racing between rows of apple trees, breathing hard as she crossed the field. Still aided by the slope of the land, she plummeted down the hill, the high side of the dam rising in front of her. Now she could see who stood there, Simon, his face a mask of horror, his body still, frozen. He hadn't seen her yet, his focus on the water at his feet.

"Simon?" Emma breathed.

The boy turned and ran toward her, pointing toward the dam, his mouth opening in a silent plea, and now she could hear screams. Daniel's. Emma sprinted up the embankment, catching sight of her brother's flailing arms rising from the dark water of the dam as he slipped under, two chickens bobbing in the water, riding on the waves created by her brother's struggle to stay afloat.

"I'm coming, Daniel," Emma called, pulling her shoes from her feet. Tossing them aside, she plunged into the water. It was deeper than she realized, the icy water pulling the breath from her lungs, stiffening her limbs. She could swim. Her father had taught her when she was young, but now with her dress billowing out around her, anchoring her, she could not reach the little boy, watching in horror as he disappeared under the murky water.

"Daniel," Emma screamed, clawing at the water.

The boy surfaced in front of her, and she grabbed

hold of him. "I've got you," she said, wrapping one arm around his chest. Daniel thrashed wildly, panicked, his arms flailing, his fingers scratching at Emma's face. "Daniel, stop," she said, spluttering muddy water from her mouth. Vainly she tried to push her free arm through the water, trying to inch herself and Daniel closer to the shallow side of the dam. "Hold on to me."

Daniel flung his arms around her neck, his weight and that of her dress pulling her under. She surfaced, turning her face upward to stop her mouth from filling again with the murky water. Then they began to sink under the surface again. Emma could feel exhaustion beginning to rob her limbs of any strength and knew this was her last chance. With one last effort, she pushed upward, this time finding herself nearer the lower embankment than before. She pushed Daniel away from her and toward the edge, his feet finding purchase on the muddy ground. He scrambled up the side.

Emma, however, found no grip on the muddy bottom, and for the third time, she felt the water close over her head. She struggled to the surface, seeing with complete clarity Daniel's stricken face watching her, his little hand reaching out in vain toward her. Down again she went, exhaustion the victor now, the air in her lungs slowly running out.

Was this it? Was she about to die? Not an hour ago, she was making sandwiches and scones. Now she was drowning, shocked by the idea that soon she would no longer exist. But that thought was overtaken by the realization that Daniel would be devastated and that she couldn't allow it. With a new surge of energy, she struggled to the surface, the bank just out of reach.

Then, without any idea how, she was lifted free from

the water and deposited less than gently on the muddy bank next to two sodden chickens looking curiously at her. Emma spluttered, water dribbling from her mouth as she looked up at her savior, words of utter gratitude ready on her lips. Her rescuer glared down at her.

"You must be the most stupid, idiotic person I have ever come across. It's a miracle both of you were not lost. Your dress alone would have drowned you, even if you could swim." William stared down at her, his fury clear, his trousers dripping with water. Emma glanced to her side to see whether he was talking to Daniel. Daniel was the one who had been in the dam. She'd rescued him. But Daniel was nowhere in sight, and Emma struggled to sit, brushing a muddied clump of hair from her eyes.

"I beg your pardon?"

William's expression didn't change, except to appear even angrier, if that was at all possible. "What the hell were you thinking? I'm at a loss to understand what you…"

Emma held up her hand, stopping William mid-insult, her own anger building. She wanted to spring up to deliver her protest at this man's words, but her sodden gown made that far harder than she'd hoped. With some effort, she untangled herself from the waterlogged fabric and struggled to her feet, water puddling around her. She planted her hands firmly on her hips, ignoring the water that dripped from her hair into her eyes. "How dare you speak to me like that?"

He stepped toward her, "How dare I? Do you know how close you came to drowning?"

Emma nodded, her eyes locked onto his. "Mr. Rideout, I can assure you that there's no confusion on that matter." She was confused, however, by the look on his face. Despite his anger, he looked truly terrified, and if she didn't know any better, she would have said that he'd been as scared as she at the prospect of her death. But she did know better. He looked at her for a moment longer, then closed his eyes and took a breath. When he opened them again, his gaze was directed off into the distance. "Your visitor," he said, the words spoken as if they had a taste, a bitter one at that, "is here. Another one of the many stupid decisions you seem to make."

"Well, if you think me that stupid, Mr. Rideout," Emma hissed, "maybe you should have just left me to drown."

William's eyes darted back to meet hers, his anger clearly equal to her own. "Maybe I should have." With that, he turned and strode away.

"Emma, my darling, are you all right?"

Emma turned to see her uncle shambling toward her. She nodded and smiled vaguely at Mr. Lang, bringing up the rear. "Yes, yes, I'm fine," she said. "A little wet, but completely well."

"And Daniel?"

Emma glanced about for him. He was no longer on the bank, and that worried her. No doubt he feared serious repercussions, as rightly he should.

Chapter 16

Emma tiptoed into the washroom, a trail of puddled footprints marking her journey from the front door to the bathroom. She squirmed from the sodden gown, dropping it along with the petticoat and camisole into the trough. It was little wonder she almost drowned, her clothing weighing almost as much as she. But surely, she didn't deserve the scolding that she'd received from Mr. Rideout. He was the most objectionable person she had ever come across. But she had no time to further critique the man's deplorable personality. Her need to find Daniel was more pressing and certainly more productive.

She poured a bucket of water over her hair—that would have to do for now—then washed the mud from her face. Her teeth chattered as she wrapped herself in a towel. She opened the door a crack and peered out. The house was quiet. Mr. Lang had taken his leave, at Emma's insistence, and her uncle had gone to reassure Martha that all was well. Her path clear to her room, she hurried along the corridor. She dressed quickly, choosing a much simpler, lighter gown more suited to aquatic activities if another need should present itself. She prayed that would never happen again.

Daniel wasn't hard to find once Emma had deduced where a small boy would go when he was scared and in trouble. To his best friend, of course, and Emma crossed to the pigpen. The day had darkened a little, a few graying clouds, an advance party from the bank building on the horizon, drifting across the sky. "Daniel," she called quietly, "Come here, please."

For a moment there was silence save for a small grunt from Meredith. Then Daniel shuffled from the back corner of the pen. His clothes were wet and stuck to his small frame, his hair limp and plastered to his head. He couldn't have looked any more miserable. He stood in front of her, his eyes fixed firmly on the ground.

"Do you know what a fright you gave me today, Daniel? You could have drowned."

The boy nodded silently.

"And although I'm so, so angry with you for being near the dam, I'm so, so grateful that nothing bad happened to you. Do you have anything to say?"

This time the boy shook his head, his gaze not straying upward.

"Do you want to tell me, Daniel, why you were at the dam? You were told to stay away from it by myself, by Mr. Rideout, and by Uncle Robert."

Daniel didn't answer, just glanced at his sister, his eyes pleading with the hope they wouldn't talk about it. "I'm sorry, Emma."

"I understand that, Daniel, but why were you there?"

Daniel shrugged, his lips clamped tightly together, tears filling his eyes. When he did speak, his words were just above a whisper. "I accidentally let some chickens out of the coop. I tried to get them, but they ran and ran."

"They ran to the dam?"

The boy nodded. "Simon was trying to help me get them, but we couldn't catch them. They ran up the side of the dam and then I couldn't see them." Daniel took a shaky breath, and wiped his face. "I didn't know if they could swim, so I went to look. Simon tried to stop me, but I slipped." He looked at Emma, the fear in his eyes heartbreaking. Emma sighed. She was angry at him, but seeing him so miserable touched her heart, and she crouched down in front of him. "Come here," she said and held her arms open. He rushed into them and held tightly to her. She hugged him back, feeling sick to her stomach at the thought of how close she came to losing him. "Puhwee, Daniel. Now you smell like you've been sitting in a pigpen. Let's get you in a bath."

Emma stood and took Daniel's hand and led him to the house.

In the bathroom, she filled the bath with water warmed on the stove and turned to Daniel. "Trousers off." She threw them into the trough. Along with her dress, they would need to soak for a while. However, the shirt was probably beyond saving, stained a reddish-brown, a tear down one side, no doubt where she'd grabbed him. "Arms up," she said and pulled the sodden shirt up over his head. The little boy climbed into the bath, and Emma lathered up some soap in her hands and massaged it into the boy's muddy hair.

"Will Uncle Robert be very angry at me?"

Emma sighed. No doubt he would be, but she was unsure who dealt out the punishment, or what it would be. "Let's get you cleaned up," she said, "and we will go and speak with him."

****

"Miss McLeod."

Emma stopped her pacing and glanced at William. He stood in the sitting room doorway, a hesitancy about him that she hadn't seen before. "I wanted to ask how Daniel is?"

Wanting nothing more than to ignore the man, Emma didn't respond for a moment. She was, despite being grateful to be alive, still so infuriated by this man's less-than-gallant rescue. But there was an uncertainty written on his face, a shadow of the fear that she'd seen earlier today. A little of her anger abated.

"Daniel is unharmed, Mr. Rideout, although he was extremely frightened by the whole experience. I'm sure he won't go near another body of water bigger than a bathtub. Uncle Robert, however, doesn't feel that's punishment enough." She frowned. "He's no doubt receiving a spanking." She turned slightly, a distinct slap and a yelp, more indignation than pain, lending proof to her theory. Emma clamped her lips tightly together, tears welling in her eyes.

"Don't fret over the boy, Miss McLeod. He'll be none the worse for it. If nothing else, he at least will think twice before he acts. I imagine it's a lesson you have learned also."

Emma didn't know if it was a change in his look or his tone, but Emma sensed the conversation, amiable up until now, was about to take a turn. "What do you mean?"

"Your attempt to save your brother was admirable, but you need to put aside pride and consider your capabilities before you act."

Emma closed her eyes and sighed loudly. She was in no mood to fight with this man or defend herself against his ridiculous opinion of her. She could swim, that was true, though not at all well when weighted by so much clothing, and yes, maybe she should have called for someone that could do better, but—and this was the most important part—Daniel was alive due to her

182

actions. "Mr. Rideout, I'm grateful to you for pulling me from the dam," she said, her tone conveying neither anger nor apology, "but Daniel is alive and well because of my pride. That's all that matters now."

"Pride? Miss McLeod, pride had nothing to do with it. Only pure luck. But there's no guarantee that next time you will be so lucky."

It wasn't Emma's intention for her anger to get the better of her. She'd been in this situation so many times with this man, and she wouldn't be drawn into another argument. But intention and action were two different things, and a storm of words rushed from her mouth before thought could intervene. "Next time? Why would there be a next time? I cannot foresee a time that I will need to jump into a dam pond to save Daniel, or anyone else for that matter. Or do you think, Mr. Rideout, that I'm so without common sense that I may just fling myself in for no good reason? Do you think me that stupid?"

If William thought she might require an answer to that question, Emma gave him no time to give one before she continued.

"And it may surprise you that I have and still do possess the ability to think and act rationally and reasonably. I do admit that since a person was drowning in front of my own eyes, and that person being my flesh and blood, I may have acted impulsively, but that's certainly something I don't regret. Love, Mr. Rideout, a concept you clearly don't understand, does and will always compel people to behave in ways that seem unthinkable." Emma took a deep breath and straightened her shoulders, ready, waiting for the attack surely coming her way.

But when William did speak, it wasn't what she expected. He held her gaze for a moment, his expression unreadable, then he reached into his trouser pocket. "I made this for the lad. Could you see he gets it?" He held out his hand and Emma opened hers to receive a tiny wooden horse, intricately carved. Emma studied it for a moment, then looked up at the man. "You made this?"

William nodded. "I hoped it might cheer him up." Without another word, he turned and headed for the door.

"Is there a problem? I heard raised voices."

Emma's gaze darted to her uncle. He stood in the sitting room doorway, first looking at her, then he turned to William. "Will?"

"It's nothing, Robert," William said. "Everything's fine. It's just a misunderstanding. If you'll excuse me, I'll turn in. I'll see you in the morning."

Robert frowned. "Er, yes. See you in the morning, Will," he said, stepping aside to let the other man pass, his frown remaining as he turned to Emma. "A misunderstanding? Anything I need to know about?"

Emma shook her head, confusion hampering her ability to provide a reasonable answer. If Mr. Rideout was capable of anything, it was most certainly his ability to leave her speechless.

"Emma?"

"No, Uncle, it was nothing," Emma answered. "It has just been a trying day and tempers flared a little."

"I must say, you two are like a pair of spitting wildcats."

Emma forced a smile onto her face, but it was embarrassment she felt more than humor. What must her uncle think of her? Ever since she'd arrived, she'd done nothing other than spar with Mr. Rideout and even though he may have deserved it, it had to stop.

"I'm sorry, Uncle. I do seem to attract Mr. Rideout's anger, and I believe he sees me as completely incompetent, but that's no excuse for my behavior. All I can say is I hope that, over time, Mr. Rideout and I can become more amicable, and I again apologize for the disagreements between us. I will make sure it doesn't happen again."

Her uncle smiled. "Not to worry, Emma. As I have said before, there's a different William from the one you see at the moment. Time is all that's needed." The man studied her for a moment. "Do you have an interest in Thomas, Emma?"

Emma frowned. "Thomas? Do you mean Mr. Lang, Uncle?"

Her uncle nodded.

"No, not at all," Emma said, shaking her head, surprised at the question. "He appears to be a pleasant man, but, no, I have no interest in him. Why do you ask? Has he asked you to enquire? Any feelings he may have toward me aren't reciprocated."

Robert smiled. "No, nothing of the sort, my darling. I was just curious. Come, I will take you to your room. We could all do with a good night's rest after the events of today. Daniel is in his bed now, his pride smarting more than his backside."

Emma's heart sank. Daniel! She felt terrible that she'd forgotten about her brother, that she'd not been to comfort him, but she remained silent and allowed herself to be guided into the foyer and along the hall to her room.

Emma closed her eyes as her uncle kissed her forehead "Tomorrow will be a better day," he said.

****

But tomorrow was far from better. With dawn's arrival came the rain. Clouds that had gathered the day before and blanketed the sky by nightfall, waited until daybreak to relieve themselves of their burden, and it rained, fat drops hammering relentlessly on the iron roof, turning the forecourt into a muddy lake, rivulets of water rushing over the slope and down into the orchard. Lightning speared through the sky, illuminating the sodden valley. William and Robert wore the faces of unhappy men.

Emma pulled her shawl tightly around her. The verandah offered shelter from the rain that poured from the roof in a series of waterfalls, but it did little to protect them from the chill that had arrived with the storm. Across the valley, lights burnt in the windows of the farm workers' cottages, more concerned men watching from their shelter to see what damage this storm would do. Emma didn't understand the ins and outs of running Eden Hill, but she did know, from what she'd seen and heard, that this harvest, the sale of it, along with the wool and grains already stored away in the barn, was the difference between having a home or not. Thunder rumbled across the sky, and Robert raised his voice to be heard.

"As soon as the lightning passes, we must get what's left of the fruit from the trees."

William nodded but said nothing, his eyes resolutely on the deluge that fell in what appeared to be a single gray sheet. And for the next five days, the rain fell with hardly a break, the men working nonstop despite the downpour. Emma could do little to help other than prepare meals and keep Martha company. Mother and child seemed to be doing well, the morning sickness helped with hot tea and a piece of dry bread before she climbed from bed. Although still concerned about the stability of the pregnancy, Emma was pleased to see that Martha was putting on weight and had some color in her cheeks. She'd shed her corset and petticoats, bustle and overskirt, and appeared much happier in a simple cotton shift with a shawl for warmth. Now there was plenty of room for a baby to grow. She looked healthier and happier than Emma had ever seen her, a good sign, she hoped.

Daniel, on the other hand, was far from happy, protesting every day at not being allowed out with William and Uncle to help with the harvest. Emma reminded him that a week at her side was a lenient punishment considering his impromptu swim in the dam. So although he grumbled, he got on with his lessons while Emma made bread and biscuits. Martha came to sit with them in the kitchen, the warmest room, the temperature outside having plummeted with the storm's arrival.

Martha spoke little but was happy to sit and peel vegetables for soups and stews that Emma cooked for the evening meals. The vegetables didn't come from Emma's garden, however. That had been forgotten about since the encounter with the snake, but she would get back to it one day, determined to grow as fine a specimen as the ones provided by one of the farm workers' wives.

The trio worked in comfortable silence at the kitchen table, Daniel bent over his work in great concentration, Emma kneading a pillow of dough, and Martha deftly slicing the skin from a potato. Mutton was stewing in an iron pot over the fire, waiting for the addition of vegetables and dumplings. The rain still pummeled the iron roof, but the rhythmic tapping was more soothing than an annoyance. Over this noise, Emma could just make out the heavy thud of boots and a knocking on the front door.

Daniel jumped from his chair and raced from the room. Emma opened her mouth to call after her little brother, closing it again, seeing it as pointless now as she could hear him talking to whoever had knocked. She plopped the dough into a pan and covered it. Then, wiping the flour and dough from her hands onto her apron, she followed Daniel's path into the foyer. She suppressed a sigh at the sight of Mr. Lang on the verandah, his wide-brimmed hat and long leather coat dripping, a testament to his journey in the rain. What could possibly have been so important to bring him out in this weather?

"Yes, please," Daniel was saying as Emma approached.

"Yes, please, to what, Daniel? Good afternoon, Mr. Lang. Would you like to come in?"

"No, that's fine, Miss McLeod. I'm drenched through and wouldn't like to drip on your floors. I came to invite you and Daniel to Simon's birthday tomorrow afternoon. If you can attend? Hopefully, the weather will be more agreeable." The man smiled.

Emma frowned. "Oh, I'm not certain, Mr. Lang. Daniel has a lot of schoolwork to catch up on, and…"

"I understand it's a busy time," Lang said. "It's just that the poor boy's mother passed just after his birthday, and the day is such a sad reminder. He has no other friends close by, and I was hoping the presence of Daniel and yourself would cheer him up a little. I don't want to interfere with Daniel's studies, however."

"Can we, Emma?" Daniel begged, hopping up and down beside her. "Please. I have been cooped up in the house for days. I want to play with Simon. Please, Em, please?"

Emma looked down at her brother. She'd no real reason to say no other than her preference not to go, so she nodded yes. "Of course. We would be delighted."

Thomas smiled, as did Daniel. "I will send a buggy tomorrow for you both." He glanced over his shoulder. "A covered one."

Emma agreed that would probably be best and that they would expect it around noon. She closed the door and ushered Daniel back to the kitchen, glancing at the collection of vegetables Martha had worked her way through. She took a carrot and began to chop it into slices. Then another and another.

"Was that Mr. Lang?" Martha asked quietly.

Emma looked at the other woman. "Yes, it was. He has invited Daniel to Simon's birthday celebration. To cheer him up, seeing his mother died so near the date."

"Just Daniel?"

Emma sliced the next carrot. "No, he asked for me to attend with Daniel." She waited to see if Martha had more to say. She'd the feeling that she might. And she wasn't wrong.

"Are you fond of Mr. Lang?"

Daniel looked up from his schoolbook. He'd taken a slice of carrot, crunching it loudly as he too waited for Emma's answer.

"Daniel, close your mouth when you're eating. And get on with your work, please."

Daniel did as she asked, or at least pretended to.

Emma snatched up a potato. "No, Martha, I have to be truthful and say that although I'm sure Mr. Lang is a perfectly nice person, I'm not fond of him in any way."

Martha slid the knife down the side of a potato, the thin strip of peel curling as it fell to the table. "He's not."

Emma stopped her slicing. "He's not what?"

Martha looked up at her, her gray eyes earnest. "A nice man."

Emma fell silent, aware that Daniel's interest was no longer in the use of capital letters in proper nouns. "Daniel, you may go and play in your room for a while."

The boy didn't move.

"Daniel," Emma repeated.

With a sigh, the boy stood up and left the room.

Emma waited a few moments. She didn't like idle gossip, seeing the dangers of it firsthand when she was young, her best friend a victim of vile untruths that nearly ruined her life, but she couldn't deny she was curious. "What do you mean, Martha?"

Martha pulled another potato from the sack on the floor at her feet. Her cheeks had flushed, and she kept her eyes firmly on the potato, but she made no move to peel it.

"Martha?" Emma didn't want to push the other woman to speak, but she did want to know what she meant. Emma was going to his home chaperoned only by an eight-year-old boy. Why this man may or may not be nice she believed to be an important matter.

Martha took a breath, her voice dropping to almost a whisper. "He has a temper."

Emma nodded and waited. Was that it? The man had a temper. It wasn't the most sinister thing she'd heard said of someone.

"Everyone has a temper, Martha. I know I do. But I hope that's not what determines a nice person from one that's not."

Martha's face reddened more, and she shook her head. "No, of course not. It's just that he…he can be unkind."

Emma sighed quietly. Again, an accusation that wasn't particularly damning. "Unkind in what way?"

Martha looked up. "Please, Emma. Just be careful about inviting Mr. Lang's attention."

Emma opened her mouth to say she had no intention of doing any such thing and Simon's birthday invitation would be the last one she would accept, but the sound of heavy footsteps in the hallway and Emma's name being called left the words unsaid.

Emma turned from the table, Martha's hand on her arm stopping her for a moment. "Please, can we keep this between us?"

Emma was unsure what they were keeping, as nothing had really been said, but nodded her agreement anyway.

****

Emma set a bowl on the table and guided William's arm onto a folded towel, then unwrapped the blood-sodden rag that had been tied to stem the bleeding. The gash in his forearm was long but not too deep.

"It should heal without stitching," she said, not missing the look of relief on the man's face. "But it needs to be cleaned." She reached for the kettle cooling at the end of the table. She maneuvered William's arm over the bowl and poured the warm water over his wound. Small bits of debris dropped into the bowl, swirling for a moment in the bloodied water before sinking under the surface. When Emma was satisfied the wound was free of debris, she rested his arm back on the towel. Then she tore a strip from a piece of clean cloth and held it against the open top of a bottle of vinegar. She upended the bottle and, with the vinegar-dampened cloth, dabbed at the wound.

William let out a stifled grunt and Emma looked up. "I'm sorry if I'm hurting you."

William shook his head. "I will manage, Miss McLeod," he said through clenched teeth. "You're quite skilled at this."

Emma smiled a little. "I've had a lot of practice, having younger siblings."

William nodded. "I can imagine. Daniel does seem to like to get himself into mischief."

For a moment, Emma wondered if she was about to receive another Rideout lecture about her inability to judge a good decision from bad, but even if she were, she was resolved this time to keep her outrage to herself. She stole a glance upward and studied her patient's face. It was, as she had assessed the first time she saw him, a handsome face, framed by dark hair that brushed the top of his collar in unruly waves. The recent weather had also not allowed time for grooming, and a short beard highlighted his jaw. But he looked tired, something Emma wasn't surprised at, considering the hours he'd worked these past days. Her gaze drifted from his eyes to his long straight nose. It gave him the appearance of seriousness, arrogance, detachment, all the characteristics Emma knew already. But she also knew that when he smiled, his appearance changed, his eyes softened, and a dimple appearing in one cheek as his mouth turned up.

"You said 'siblings.' Did you have other brothers or sisters?"

His words catapulted Emma from her thoughts. Her face warmed with the knowledge that he must have seen her staring. She set aside the vinegar-soaked cloth and busied herself for a minute assessing his wound. It was clean, and the bleeding had stopped. She would leave it uncovered for the moment to dry, then bandage it, but really her assessment was more to give her time to gather her thoughts.

William's free hand came to rest on hers. "I'm sorry. I shouldn't have asked."

Emma looked up, noting genuine compassion in the man's eyes. She shook her head. "Please, no apology necessary. It's just how it is." Her father had said those same words to her each time they had lost one of their family, and she felt a wave of sadness wash over her. Would she ever hear his voice again? She pushed that thought aside. "Baby Adam you know of, but there were two other brothers and five sisters. None lived long except for twin girls. They were three when typhoid took them." She fell silent, seeing the faces of those she'd loved and lost pass through her mind.

Strong fingers gently squeezed her own, and Emma bit down hard on her lip, fearful the expression of sympathy would make her cry. But that couldn't happen. Not here, not now, and she turned her attention to the roll of cloth. She picked it up and began to bandage his arm. "It should heal without too much trouble," she said, tying off the ends to secure it in place. "Try to keep it dry if you can, but it will be no trouble to redress it if you can't."

William looked at her handiwork. "Thank you—

Emma."

Emma looked up. She'd only heard him use her first name once before. "Oh, it's nothing," she said. "Just think of it as payment for pulling me from the dam." She held his eyes for a moment, searching, fearful her jest may have been a step too far.

William frowned momentarily. "And the snake?"

Emma took another step. "That was compensation for my saving the life of your pig."

The man looked thoughtful, but the smile in his eyes was unmistakable. "Then I believe we are even."

Emma smiled a little. "I believe we are."

"Did you need stitches?" Daniel skipped into the room, stopping at the table to stare at William's arm.

William's eyes jolted away from Emma's. "Er, no, Daniel, luckily no stitches needed."

"I did once. Look." Daniel pulled up his sleeve to reveal a lumpy scar. "I fell from a tree. It only hurt a little bit. Emma fixed me."

Emma smiled. "And you were very brave, Daniel. Although you really had no business climbing that tree at all."

William's gaze flickered to Emma for a moment. "She fixed me too, Daniel," he said, looking back at the boy. "I hope I would have been as brave as you if I had needed stitches."

"We are going to a party."

Emma took a moment to recognize that the subject had been changed, and she felt the color drain from her cheeks. "Daniel. Could you please go and wash up for dinner?"

"I will, Emma. I just want to tell Mr. Rideout about the party."

"Daniel, now!"

"What party is this, Daniel?" Although William gave the boy a smile, Emma knew it wasn't going to last long, watching as it dropped from the man's face as Daniel answered.

"Mr. Lang has invited me and Emma to his house tomorrow for Simon's birthday."

William looked up at Emma, no good humor in his gaze now, only disappointment, anger, all Emma expected to see as clear as if he'd shouted his contempt for her aloud. But there was something else. A look that didn't shout. Instead, it whispered, but Emma heard it loud and clear. It declared defeat. Silently she tried to tell him it was a misunderstanding, that it wasn't what he thought, but she knew nothing would change the look on the man's face.

"Just you and your sister? No one else?"

Daniel shook his head. "No. But if you want to come, Will, I'm sure he won't mind. I can ask."

William shook his head. "Don't worry yourself, Daniel. I'm afraid I'll be far too busy with the harvest, but I'm sure you and your sister will have a good time." He pushed back his chair, the legs squealing as they were slid forcefully across the floor, and he stood up. "Thank you for your assistance, Miss McLeod." He turned and strode from the kitchen.

****

2022

"Sophie, wake up. Come on. Open your eyes. Sophie. You said not to call an ambulance and I haven't, but if you don't open your eyes by the time I count to 10, I will. I mean it. 1…2…

Emma forced her eyes open. She didn't understand

why the person so much wanted her to open her eyes, nor why this person was counting, but she opened them, nonetheless.

"That's better. Jeez, Soph, you have a lot of explaining to do. A shit load, and it better be good."

Emma was shocked by the words that came out of the woman's mouth, and she seemed angry, but Emma didn't know why or what she wanted an explanation for. The party? Why did this woman want to know about it? Who was she?

"Soph, look at me. Do you know where you are? Do you know me? It's Becca."

Becca. The name was familiar, as was the face, and the fog began to lift. "Becca?"

Becca smiled, and Sophie could see the relief in her eyes, but her anger was still evident. "Yeah, it's me. Are you okay? What's going on, Sophie? What's with the note on the door? And the diary?"

"Coffee?"

Becca sighed, one of frustration. "Coffee. Is that all you can say?" She shook her head. "Okay. I'll make you a coffee, but then I want an explanation. Understand?"

Sophie nodded and pushed herself up to sit. A wave of dizziness hit her, and she closed her eyes. It was gone as quickly as it came, leaving her feeling well enough if not a little disorientated. She knew where she was now, but she was well aware she'd just been somewhere else, been someone else. She'd been Emma again.

Becca returned with the coffee and two slices of buttered toast and put them on the coffee table next to the diary. She sat down beside Sophie. "I imagine you've not eaten, so I've bought you some breakfast. This is more for my benefit than yours, as you won't be able to use hunger as an excuse to avoid giving me an explanation."

Sophie could hear that Becca's anger hadn't lessened, and almost as soon as Sophie swallowed the last bite, Becca said, "Well?"

Sophie took a breath in and blew it out slowly. How to begin? Becca wasn't going to believe her no matter what she said, so Sophie guessed it didn't matter how she began. She blurted out the first thing that her mouth decided to say. "When I touch the diary, I go back in time, or see into the past or something. I don't know how else to explain it."

Sophie watched the array of emotions play across her friend's face. First came confusion, quickly followed by suspicion, and then she smiled, but the anger in it couldn't be missed. "Okay, you got me. I don't know what the joke is meant to be, but, yeah, you had me going for a minute. Not funny, though, Sophie. I was worried sick when I saw you out on the couch after what happened yesterday. It took over a minute to wake you. I didn't know what was wrong with you, and you not wanting an ambulance. You scared me, Sophie. Whatever this joke is, it's not funny."

Sophie saw the tears well in her friend's eyes. "I'm sorry, Becca. I didn't mean to scare you. but I had no choice."

Becca shook her head. "No choice? What do you mean? Let me guess, someone put a gun to your head and said, 'Hey, play a practical joke on your friend that will really scare her'?"

Sophie sighed and reached for her friend's hand. She took it in hers, her gaze holding Becca's. "Becca, I swear, on my life, I'm not joking."

Becca pulled back as if she'd been slapped. "Sophie,

you need to go back to the hospital."

"Bec, I know how it sounds, but it's true. Look." Sophie stood up, the room swaying for a moment as she did. She took a breath then crossed to the desk. She came back with the notepad. "Look, Becca. See these names? These are people mentioned in the diary, or written on the title, or on the cheque, right?"

Becca nodded, but Sophie could see her friend clearly thought she was having a breakdown. Sophie continued regardless.

"See these names, Alice and Eliza? These people aren't in the diary as far as I know or written down anywhere. But I know these people. I researched them. They were real people."

Becca shrugged. "So? I don't understand what you're telling me."

Sophie took a breath, tried to calm her thoughts so she at least sounded like a sane human being even if her words contradicted that. "Bec, when I touch the diary, I faint, right?"

Becca frowned. "I'm more inclined to say that you had your hand on the diary when you fainted. I don't know if I could say the diary was the cause of your fainting."

Sophie sighed. "It's happened three times now."

"What? Sophie, you need to see…"

Sophie held her hand up, stopping Becca's words. "And when I faint, I dream. But when I wake, I can't remember much, just vague snippets and feelings. But there were two times that were different. When I hold the diary, grasp it in my hands, I seem to live the life of a woman called Emma, for days, weeks, and when I wake up, I remember everything, but I can't wake up until the book is taken from me. Hence the note."

Becca shook her head and pushed herself from the couch. She looked at Sophie and shook her head again. "I...I don't know what to say, Sophie. This is...this is...well, I don't know what this is. A joke, a mental health issue, a...a..." She shook her head again. "I don't know."

"Bec, I know it's a lot for you to take in, and it's impossible to believe. I don't even believe it and it's happening to me, but it *is* happening. Look, see these names, Alice and Eliza? They were Emma's little sisters. I don't think you will find any mention of them in the diary or on any documents. But if you look them up, you can see they were real, and if you can find a death certificate for them, it will show that Alice and Eliza McLeod both died at age three from typhoid. How would I know that? That's got to prove something."

Becca frowned as if she was in physical pain. "Sophie."

"Look, I can show you, if you want."

"What do you mean?"

Sophie glanced at the diary on the table in front of her. She shrugged. "I'll just touch it and you can make sure I don't hurt myself."

Becca shook her head. "Sophie, come on. This has gone far enough."

"I'm sorry, Bec," Sophie said, reaching out from her perch on the couch, her fingers brushing the cover of the diary.

Chapter 17

1865

Emma fell asleep as the sun began to rise, a pale smudge on the horizon. She woke as the sun was nearing its highest point. Her eyes felt heavy, gritty, and swollen, and she knew her face would advertise the terrible night she'd had. She took a deep breath and let it out slowly, her next breath catching in her chest as her door slammed open and Daniel skidded into the room. He was dressed in his best clothes. "Come on, Emma! The buggy will be here soon."

Emma groaned. She was tired, and the last thing she wanted to do was attend a child's birthday party. She sighed loudly. "What time is it, Daniel?"

"It's half past eleven. Come on, Emma. We will be late!"

"I'm not feeling well. Maybe we could visit with Simon tomorrow."

"No, Emma," Daniel moaned, pulling on her arm. "You promised."

Emma sighed. "Very well, Daniel. But we won't be staying long. Is that clear? Simon is welcome to come and visit with us if he wants, later."

Daniel nodded.

Emma shooed Daniel from the room and contemplated going back to sleep. She could feign illness.

"Emma, come on," Daniel called from the other side of the door putting paid to the idea of more sleep. "I can't hear you getting up."

Emma groaned again and rolled from the bed. She dressed quickly, forgoing a formal gown for one more practical. It was, after all, a child's birthday party, not a ball, and she didn't want anyone to assume she would take extra trouble with her appearance for Mr. Lang. She took one final look in the mirror, deemed the light gray high-neck gown satisfactory, and she went out into the hall.

"Emma, are you wearing that?"

Emma ran a hand over her hair, pulled back severely from her face, and smiled at her brother. "It's clean, Daniel, and tidy enough for a child's party. I think it will suffice. Come on, I can hear the horses."

They went out onto the verandah. Dark clouds still wandered the sky, pushed by a chill wind, but at least the rain had stopped. For now. A buggy pulled by two horses came into view, but Emma was blind to them. She searched the orchard below for a familiar figure. If Mr. Rideout saw how she was dressed, maybe he would realize this wasn't a social call and she'd no interest in trying to attract Mr. Lang's attention. Sometime last night, as she tossed and turned looking for sleep, it became clear to her that she needed Mr. Rideout to know that. Why she did was something she didn't know.

"Emma?" Martha came out onto the verandah, pulling her shawl tighter around her shoulders. Emma was comforted to see how well the woman looked, her cheeks flushed with color, her eyes clear and bright, but a furrow in her brow gave away that she was worried.

"Emma, please be careful."

Emma wanted again to question the woman as to what she meant, but there was no time, the horses voicing their displeasure at being kept waiting as much as Daniel was. She hugged Martha to her for a moment. "I will, although, to be honest, I'm not sure what I'm being careful of." She loosened her embrace and looked into Martha's eyes. "I will be back as soon as politely possible. Or earlier. I feel a headache coming on."

The Lang property adjoined her uncle's and would take no more than ten minutes to get there on horseback across the field. By buggy, however, it took fifteen jolting minutes to arrive at what was the start of the lane that led to his house, white wooden fences lining both sides, hemming in green pastures and recently harvested fields. The land began to rise and, from the top of the hill, Lang's home could be seen clearly in the distance. Five towering gum trees, their trunks ghostly white, stood like sentries on the edge of the forecourt, the extensive stone-and-iron house sitting squat in the quadrangle of red dirt. Constructed in the same style as her uncle's home, it was a long rectangular building, a verandah shading all sides, French doors and long windows interrupting the thick stone walls. The roof had been painted white, and it stood out like a beacon against the gray sky.

They made the descent down the hill toward the house, the driver bringing the buggy to a halt in the forecourt. Lang was waiting for them, along with another man, who held the reins of two horses. Simon sat atop one of the animals, a third tethered to the verandah railing.

"Good afternoon, Daniel, Emma," Lang said with more enthusiasm than Emma thought necessary. "I'm so glad you could make it." He extended his hand to Emma, and she took it, navigating the two small steps from the buggy down to the ground as quickly as her gown would allow.

"Happy birthday, Simon," Daniel said as he clambered from the buggy.

Emma echoed Daniel's words, a shy smile appearing on the birthday boy's face for a moment.

"What do you think of Simon's birthday gift?" Lang said, reaching to stroke the nose of the animal Simon sat astride. "I thought he was old enough now to care for a pony of his own. Ned is going to take the boys for a short ride so Simon can become acquainted with the animal. I've had Ned bring a suitable one for Daniel to ride. With your permission, of course, Miss McLeod."

"Can I please?" Daniel said, turning to look at Emma.

"Oh, I don't know, Daniel," Emma said, taken aback by the request.

"Please, Emma. Simon is."

Emma sighed. "Very well, Daniel, but just for a little while. Half an hour and no more."

Daniel whooped in excitement and climbed easily into the saddle of his mount, boy and pony following Ned and Simon back up the lane.

Emma watched them go. "We can't stay long," she said turning to Lang, "but Simon is welcome to visit with us any time he likes."

"Thank you, Miss McLeod. That's very kind. I'm sure he'll be more than happy to hear that. I will tell him when they return."

Emma smiled and turned to the house. "You have a wonderful property," Emma said, although it wasn't like

Eden Hill. Lang's home was at the bottom of the hill, the bush closing in on three sides. Emma imagined the crops and livestock needed the sun, hence the reason they had been given the higher ground. They wouldn't have fared well down here in the shadows.

"Thank you. The land looks a bit bare now we have finished the harvest," Lang said, gesturing to the fields that bordered either side of the deceptively steep lane that led to the house. "Now we just must take it to sale and plant again for next year, providing the sales are enough for this year's repayment, that is."

Emma had heard the same kind of conversations at home. It seemed to be all the men talked about. "And what if the loan is not paid?" She'd tried to ask her uncle the same question, but he always told her she wasn't to worry, that everything would be fine. Maybe Mr. Lang could at least answer that for her.

"Then the land is forfeited and sold to whoever has the money to cover the outstanding debt. Most around here are in their final year of debt. To lose your land now would be to lose three years of hard work. Myself, and I say this without wanting to sound boastful, I am in the fortunate position of not having too much concern on that matter."

Emma nodded, not really understanding what Lang meant by that last assertion but beginning to appreciate now why there was so much stress etched on her uncle's face most of the time. What with the loan, the baby, Daniel's near drowning, and, Emma had to add, the tension between her and Mr. Rideout, not to mention the concerns he would have for his missing brother also, Emma was surprised her uncle could even manage a smile, let alone laugh as he so often did. She knew there wasn't anything she could do to help in any way with money, but at least she would try not to burden him with any other concerns, at least for the time being.

Lang gestured for her to go up onto the verandah, his hand hovering near her elbow as she ascended the steps upward. One set of French doors was open, white lace curtains drifting lazily in and out as the breeze directed, the smell of baking wafting from somewhere inside. Lang guided Emma to one of the chairs at a small table.

"Something smells wonderful," Emma said.

Lang nodded. "That will be Mrs. Taylor's baking. She's a wonder in the kitchen."

At that moment the woman in question came out onto the verandah. "Tea, Mr. Lang?"

Lang clapped his hands together and smiled. "I think sherry, Mrs. Taylor," he said, the woman disappearing inside before Emma had a chance to object. He gestured for Emma to sit.

Mrs. Taylor appeared a few moments later with a silver tray and set it down on the table. The tray held two glasses, sizable ones and not the sort Emma had ever seen sherry served in, and a glass decanter full of rich red liquid. "I have refilled it," the woman said, nodding toward the tray. Her disapproval was clear as day, and it was obvious to Emma that it had been filled much too often by this woman. "The cake for the boy is cooling on the rack. I 'ope he likes it. I will be off now."

Lang thanked the woman, and Emma watched as the woman descended the steps and began her journey up the hill.

"Sherry?" Lang asked, the decanter held over the glass he'd placed in front of Emma.

Emma glanced at the man. "No. No, thank you," she said. She looked around, searching for anyone who might be working close by, but the place seemed deserted, especially now that Mrs. Taylor had disappeared from view along the lane.

"Where is everyone?" Emma asked. She was becoming uncomfortable in this man's presence alone. She didn't know why. Thomas Lang had never given her reason when she'd been in his company before to justify this feeling. She chided herself for letting Martha fill her head with concerns about the man's character, but Martha hadn't said anything at all other than that he had a temper.

"I've given everyone the day off. We have all worked hard over the past few weeks and will again soon, so I thought today was good for some relaxation. Although the wind doesn't seem to want to rest, eh?"

Emma agreed, the soft breeze having now become gusty, the gums sighing as it played through their lofty branches. A few drops of rain plopped onto the roof, followed by a few more, and within minutes the rain again began to fall in earnest, the verandah offering no shelter now. "Shall we go inside?" Thomas said.

Again, Emma felt an uneasiness, but still she was unable to pinpoint the reason why. Hopefully, Daniel would be returned to the house sooner rather than later. Then they could go. She stood and followed Mr. Lang and his sherry tray in through the French doors. He waited for her to enter, then set the tray on a table next to a green velvet couch. He closed the doors against the increasing wind. "Ah, much better."

Emma stood in the middle of the large room. All the noise came from the outside, the house itself so quiet, the sort of silence that told you there was no bother to call out—there was no one else here.

"Please sit," Lang said.

Besides the couch, there was no other seating in this room. No wing-backed armchair like her uncle's or chairs that would make up a suite. In the rug, she thought she could make out the indents of where another chair may have been. Or was it just the pattern in the rug that made it appear that way? But the question of when and if there had been other pieces of furniture in the room was academic. Emma had no choice but to sit on the couch, perching as far on the edge as she could without falling off. Thomas Lang dropped down next to her. He reached for her glass and held it out to her. She took it from him but had no intention of drinking from it. Lang, on the other hand, had no qualms about doing so, downing two more glasses in quick succession.

"A nice drop, that," he said, holding up his empty glass. "You should at least taste it."

Emma couldn't be sure, but did she hear a slight edge to his voice that wasn't there a moment ago? "I imagine the boys will be back soon," she said, turning a little on her perch to look at Lang. "With the rain coming down like this."

Lang's eyes were glazed, and for a moment she wondered if he was seeing her. He shook his head, then pushed himself from the couch, with a grunt that seemed needed to assist him in the endeavor. "Ned will have them sheltered up in the stables," he said, pouring himself another drink. He picked the glass up from the tray, made his turn back to the couch too fast and stumbled, a significant portion of the red liquid sloshing out of the glass and splattering onto the couch, the rug, and down the front of Emma's dress.

Emma jumped up, watching as the stain bled across the fabric of her bodice. Thomas stared down at his glass as if wondering why it was only a quarter full. He shrugged a little and raised the glass to his mouth. Tipping his head back, he swallowed the little that had remained. Then he turned back to the tray and refilled his now-empty glass. "You want some," he said, his words lazy, slurred. He could no longer hide the fact that he was drunk.

Emma shook her head.

"Pick that up."

Emma was shocked by the man's words, unsure if he was talking to her or lost in some intoxicated imagining.

He pointed with his foot, Emma following his indication. She'd placed her full glass on the floor, something that Thomas seemed suddenly unhappy about. "Did you not hear me? I said, pick it up. Now!"

His eyes no longer held any warmth or even intoxicated blankness. They blazed with anger, and Emma picked up the glass, shaken by this outburst. This man had changed, dramatically so. She was shaking as she handed him the glass. "I think I would like to go home, please, Mr. Lang, if you would please call for the buggy. I will collect Daniel on the way."

He smiled now. "Home?" Then he laughed. "We haven't eaten the cake yet."

Emma attempted a smile of her own, but it was fragile. "Maybe another day, Mr. Lang. My dress is stained, and I think it best if I leave."

"Take it off."

Emma's mouth dropped open, the words *I beg your*

pardon forming in her mind. But she knew what he'd said, and she didn't voice her thought.

He repeated it anyway. "Take it off."

Emma shook her head, taking a step back. She glanced over her shoulder at the twin doors. Did he lock them? She could outrun him, that she was sure of, especially in his present state, but she would have to get out of the house first.

Thomas too was looking at the doors, the smile still on his face. He reached out, grabbing hold of her arm. "You're not thinking of running out on me, are you, Miss McLeod? Come on, let's dance."

Emma pulled against his grasp. "Let go of me."

"Oh, don't be coy, Miss McLeod, or can I call you Emma? We both know this is what you want. You did come out here willingly." With his free hand, Lang drained his glass and set it, empty, on the tray. He swayed slightly again, and Emma prayed he would pass out. But he stayed upright, his fingers cutting into her flesh as she pulled away as hard as she could. Any minute she was sure her hand would snap from her arm. Suddenly he jerked her forward, his strength far greater than hers, and she slammed into his chest.

"That's better, lovely," he said. He entwined his other hand in her hair and pulled hard, her face forced upward.

She tried to scream out, but his mouth came down hard on hers, crushing her cry into a gurgled squawk.

He let go of her wrist, his hand now employed in finding a way into her dress, his mouth pressed against hers, the alcohol on his breath enough to make her feel faint. He pulled at her gown, the material gathered higher and higher until she could feel cool air on her knees.

Then his hand was on her skin, fingers crawling their way up her thigh. This man was about to assault her, and she wasn't going to let that happen. She pulled her head back a little from his, not enough to scream out—there was no one to hear her anyway—but enough to be able to close her teeth around his bottom lip. And she bit down, hard.

Lang yelped, his hands called from their duty elsewhere and flying to his mouth. Blood dripped down his chin, drops joining the sherry stains on the rug. Emma stepped back.

"Bitch," he spat at her, blood spraying from his mouth with his words. He took a step toward her, she one more back, but his hand still reached her cheek, the blow snapping her head sideways, little pinpoints of light dancing before her. But she wouldn't pass out, she couldn't, or he would have her. She shook her head and moved to the back of the couch, Lang following like a hunter stalking his prey. She reached the side of the couch, and he smiled. "Where are you going to go?"

Emma glanced around the room, the quick survey for escape routes not encouraging. "What do you think my uncle will do when he finds out what you've done?" she asked, her voice wavering, tears blurring her vision.

"You won't tell him."

Emma frowned. "What do you mean? Of course, I will."

He took a step toward her, Emma moving two back. "Let me explain, lovely. Do you remember what I told you about the sale of the harvest and paying back the loan? Well, think about this. Your uncle comes here, with no doubt that Mr. Rideout, and they beat me bloody, which no doubt they'll do. They'll then be arrested and will miss their opportunity to get their produce to market. No sale, no repayment, and you will all be out on the streets. Now that's not a nice way to repay your uncle for taking you in, is it? And then there's the matter of you coming out here unchaperoned. Wouldn't do much for a lady's reputation, would it?"

Emma couldn't believe what she was hearing. Had Lang planned this? Surely not. Her tears were blurring her vision, and she swiped at them. "Just let me leave. Please."

Lang sighed loudly, his anger appearing to dissolve. "I thought you had feelings for me, Miss McLeod."

Emma shook her head. She felt a little bolder now the man seemed to have calmed down. "I'm sorry, Mr. Lang, if I caused you to think that, but I assure you, it was only out of concern for Simon that I agreed to your invitation. But even if I did have feelings for you, do you think this is appropriate behavior? Now, I would like to leave, and I promise not to speak of this to anyone."

Emma turned toward the door. But the words that followed froze her.

"It's such a shame you feel the way you do, Emma. I had hoped you would have been a willing party, but if you're going to put up a fight, I don't mind."

Emma turned back to the man, her eyes wide, her mouth opened in silent protest. This couldn't be happening. She turned back to the door, only one step taken before Lang lunged for her, grabbing her arm. "Come on, lovely. It might be fun."

Emma squealed, her free arm flailing wildly as he dragged her toward the couch. She glanced around frantically, catching sight of the glass decanter just within her reach. She grabbed for it, her fingers curling around the neck of the heavy glass bottle, lifting it from the tray. The stopper hadn't been replaced and sherry dribbled over the rim onto her arm as she swung it sideways, there coming a distinct thud as the decanter met Thomas Lang's temple. He looked surprised for a moment, a soft grunt stealing from his mouth as he crumpled to the floor.

Emma froze briefly. Had she killed the man or simply knocked him out? Either way, she wasn't prepared to wait and see. On legs that were surely made of rubber, she made it to the French doors. They hadn't been locked, and she flung them open, the wind whipping the curtains out in front of her. The rain hadn't eased any, but getting wet was the least of her concerns. Getting as far away from Lang as she could was the only thing on her mind. If she could find Daniel, surely Lang couldn't harm her in front of witnesses—Daniel, Simon, and the man Ned. And if luck was with her, they would take a horse and return to her uncle's farm before Lang came looking for her.

Emma leapt the two steps from the verandah and bolted across the forecourt, the wind hissing through the top of the gums as she ran under them. A noise behind her, a shout maybe, or just the wind groaning through the trees, forced her on, and she headed for the lane. Lang said Ned would shelter the boys in the stables. She was sure she'd passed some stables earlier, at the top of the hill. She prayed they would be there. Hitching her sodden gown to her knees, Emma continued to run along the lane, the land beginning to rise more steeply, the rutted limestone surface now a series of muddy pools, each one sucking at her shoes, threatening to throw her off balance. Her breath came in ragged snatches, her pulse hammering in her ears, but despite the howl of the wind and the drumbeat of her heart, she couldn't mistake the distinct sound of pounding hooves, of a horse at speed, growing louder behind her. It could only be Lang, and he would run her down in minutes.

Tears mingled with rain as she forced herself to run, her sobs robbing her of the breath she needed to move. She turned for a moment, the animal and rider only a blurred moving shape through the gray curtain of rain. Turning forward, she tried to run faster, mud sucking at her feet, her lungs burning, desperate for oxygen. But it was a futile attempt, the animal rapidly closing the gap between them. She could hear it snorting as air rushed in and out of its nostrils, could feel its breath, and then it was upon her, its powerful body radiating heat as it drew level.

Her legs buckled under her, having nothing left to give, and she fell hard, jagged stones slicing into her hands as she tried to stop her fall, her knees skinned and bloodied as she slid along the ground. She didn't feel any pain, though, terror dominating all other feelings, and she tried to crawl, the horse dancing above her, its rider urging quiet. Then a thud as the rider dismounted, and Emma knew just one thing. Lang was going to hurt her, kill her maybe, any number of explanations of how she came to be dead in the laneway available to him.

****

2022

"Sophie, wake up. What's happening?"

Sophie's eyes sprang open. Her heart was pounding in her chest, her breath rushing in and out of her lungs. She looked up at Becca, her terror reflected in Becca's eyes.

"He tried to rape her."

"What? Who? Who tried to rape who, Sophie?"

"Thomas Lang. He tricked Emma to come to his house and then tried to rape her."

"Lang. The man on the Title Deed? Did she get away? Oh God, I can't believe I just asked that!"

Sophie shook her head. "I don't know. I think she was being chased, but it's all fading now. I was—Emma was so scared."

Becca took her friend's hand. "It's okay, Soph," she soothed. "It was just a dream. Or something. But it's over now. Breathe."

Sophie nodded and took in a deep shaky breath. She let it out slowly between pursed lips.

"You okay?" Becca asked.

Sophie nodded again. "I think so." She looked up at her friend. "Do you believe me, Bec?"

Becca shrugged her shoulders. "Clearly, you were seeing or experiencing something. That I believe. I also believe you passed out when you touched the diary. But that's the best I can do for now. If it's medical or psychological or—saints save me—real, I don't know. I'll need some more convincing to say more than that. What I'm willing to do, though, is follow up on your research. Drink your coffee, and we'll go and see if we can find the death records for the twins."

****

"So yeah, you're right," said Becca from her place in front of one of the computers set up for the public to use for family research. But there would be no amateur researchers today, with the doors of the office locked and a hurried sign posted on the door saying the office was closed due to illness. Becca thought it would be more appropriate to put "due to madness" instead. Sophie had to concede there might be some truth in that. "There were twin girls, McLeods, Eliza and Alice, who both died aged three. They had an older sister Emma and a brother called…"

Sophie saw this as the test it was. "Daniel?"

Becca nodded. "I've ordered the death certificates for both. We will see what those say. Did you say that this Emma married Thomas Lang?"

Sophie nodded. She had told Becca about the research she'd done so far. "Yeah, that's what the marriage certificate said. I can't understand why. She was in love with William Rideout, as far as I could…feel. And as we both know now, she has nothing but hatred for Lang, from what I…saw."

Becca shrugged. "That is the problem, I guess. All we have to go on is what you think you saw or dreamt or remembered or whatever this is, Sophie. Did you find out what happened to Emma or any of them?"

Sophie shook her head. "No. I was going to, but when I saw the twins' names, I sort of lost it. I thought I was going mad, believing I was living this person's life, so I just sort of stopped looking."

"Well, we can at least look, I guess. There's no harm. Especially while the jury is out on your sanity."

Sophie smiled at this and sat at another computer, the women working in silence for a while, the clacking of fingers on keyboards the only sound. "Oh, my God," Sophie whispered.

"What is it?"

"Emma died not long after her marriage to Lang. What, three months, it looks like. It's written about in the *Perth Gazette*. She drowned." Sophie couldn't stop the tears that welled in her eyes. She knew Emma as well as she knew Becca, and that Emma had died in such a terrible way was heartbreaking. But she was confused as well. How did Emma drown? She nearly had once before when she'd saved Daniel, but she could swim if her clothes were light enough, and she'd vowed never to go near water again. How could this have happened? Sophie said this much to Becca.

"I guess these things happen. And I'm sorry to say that I'm going to add to that bleak news. Robert McLeod died, too, in 1865. It says he died at his residence in Fremantle. Did he have a place in Fremantle?"

Sophie felt the shock of this as keenly as she had when discovering Emma's death. Dreams, maybe, and completely irrational, but these people were real to her. She took a breath and wiped her cheeks with the back of her hand. "No. His home was Eden Hill. That's what I don't understand about the title being in Lang's name. My— I mean, Emma's uncle owned the property. Not Lang."

"Well, it would seem Emma's uncle lost it somehow to Lang," Becca said. "Something happened to the family in 1865, apparently."

Sophie nodded. It appeared that way, and the thought made her stomach churn. "Did you find anything about Daniel, or Robert's wife Martha?"

Becca shook her head. "Still looking."

By midafternoon Sophie wished they hadn't begun this search at all, each discovery as painful as the one before, finding only tragic endings for Daniel and Simon, both boys no longer with their families but in the records of a boys' home miles away from Eden Hill. Date 1865. Then came the death of Martha in 1870, just five short years after the birth of her child, if the child had been born at all. There was no record of a McLeod birth, nor were there any records of a William Rideout or a Margaret Swanson.

Sophie was exhausted as five o'clock neared, and more than a little confused. As far as she knew, the last payment on Eden Hill was almost certain to be made as soon as the harvest was sold, and the future was looking to be a positive one for Emma's family. She'd seen it, she'd lived it. But despite what she thought she knew, the record made it clear. At some point, something had gone terribly wrong in 1865.

"Come on. It's time to go home, Soph. You look shattered."

Sophie smiled weakly. She felt it.

They spoke little on the way home, both women lost in thought. Becca turned into Sophie's drive, and Sophie reached for her bag. "Thanks, Becca, and I'm sorry."

Becca frowned. "What for?"

"For dragging you into…into whatever this is. If it's anything. Maybe I'm…I'm just…" Sophie shrugged. "I don't know. My logical brain tells me it can't be real, but I know it is. Doesn't that sound like maybe I'm having a breakdown or something?"

Becca turned off the ignition. "Look, Sophie. I've been thinking about this all the way here. I know all this is really weird, and I doubt any scientist or doctor could tell you why it's happening, other than that you're certifiably insane. But I don't think you are, and you know you're not. So with that off the table, let's be super logical. Let's just say you've researched this family before and forgot, I don't know, maybe when you hit your head. Let's just say that, okay, and that's how you know the things that you've told me. That would be a logical conclusion, right? But if that's not the case, what are we left with? Whatever this is, it's happening. Even if it's just dreams, dreams are there for a reason, and I'm thinking you need to find out what that reason is. I have touched the diary. I feel nothing, but this is happening to you, so you need to find out why."

It took a while for Sophie to get her tears under control. She'd been so scared and so confused about what was happening to her, and now at least she had Becca at her side. She blubbered out as best she could that same sentiment, ending with, "Thank you, Becca."

Becca reached across and squeezed Sophie's hand. "It's okay, Soph. I'm here, whatever happens." She paused for a moment, then asked, "Does it hurt, when you do, er, whatever it is you do…when you…you become Emma?"

Sophie fished a tissue from her pocket and wiped her face. "No, there's no pain. It just feels like I'm being sucked backward really fast and like I can't breathe for a moment. Then I'm okay, and for a second or two I know I'm somewhere else. Then I'm Emma and that's all I know. It's the same when I come back." Sophie shrugged. "From wherever."

Becca nodded in thought. "Is it dangerous, do you think? To your health? Clearly, you can't be out for long, needing food and water and all that."

"I don't think so. The hospital didn't find any ill effects. My blood pressure drops a little maybe, but that's it."

Again, Becca nodded and was quiet for a moment. Sophie could feel there was a question brewing, and she waited. Her wait was soon rewarded. "Sophie, my thinking is that unless you see this to whatever end there is, it's not going to end. Are you up to going back?"

****

"Okay, we're all set. I will keep an eye on your bp and your pulse," Becca said, wrapping the bp monitor cuff around Sophie's arm. She'd gone home to retrieve the items she thought necessary for the "trip" as she referred to it, returning with the monitor, a pulse oxygen reader which was now pegged to Sophie's finger, and three-quarters of a leftover pizza. "Do you need to go to the bathroom?" Becca asked after they had finished the pizza.

Sophie laughed. "That's what my parents used to say before we went on a road trip."

Becca shrugged. "It's sort of the same, isn't it?"

Sophie guessed it was, but there had been no accidents so far, so fingers crossed there were none to come.

"Remember last time you were there, you said Lang had tried to rape you, er, Emma, so you don't know what you're heading into. If I think you look like you're in some sort of trouble physically or mentally, I'm going to bring you back, okay?"

Sophie nodded.

"You ready?"

Sophie nodded again and lay back on the couch.

"Okay, here we go."

****

1865

"Miss McLeod."

Strong fingers gripped her arm, and Emma swung her arms wildly, her fingers curled, clawing blindly at whatever came within reach, only a pitiful squeak mustered from her throat.

"Miss McLeod! Emma! Stop!"

The hands released her, and she crawled forward a few paces, her breath wheezing in and out of her chest, her searing lungs insatiable.

"Emma. Please. Let me help you."

Emma could no longer fight, and she froze where she was on hands and knees, splattered with mud, rain-soaked, tear-streaked, then she turned, sitting hard on the muddy ground. What she saw in front of her should, by all sensible thought, give her nothing but relief and thankfulness. But common sense was no longer in control. "What are you doing here?"

William Rideout was soaked through, his hair plastered to his face, droplets falling from his chin. He frowned, and Emma wasn't surprised at that. It wasn't the response one would expect when someone had ridden to the rescue of another, as she suspected he had.

"I'm inclined to ask you the same question," William said.

"I asked first."

She saw a look of confusion pass across the man's face. "Very well. Martha asked me to come. She implied you might be in some sort of trouble."

Emma swiped one long dripping ringlet from her face. "Well, that's thoughtful, Mr. Rideout, of yourself and Martha, but as you can see, I'm fine. Thank you."

William's frown bloomed into a smile, albeit one of confusion. "Miss McLeod, I don't know if you're drunk, or just being—well, I have no idea what, but you're crawling around in the mud. Your hands and legs are bleeding, and there's blood on your gown. To me, it looks like you could do with some assistance."

Emma looked down, only now beginning to feel the sting in her hands. Blood was splattered across her bodice. If it was her own or Lang's she wasn't sure.

"Can you at least tell me why you're in the mud?" William asked.

Emma stared up at her rescuer. "I fell from a horse."

The rain had eased, no longer a constant thrum but still loud enough to drown out her words. "I beg your pardon. I don't think I heard you correctly."

"I fell from a horse," Emma said louder this time.

"You fell from a horse," William repeated, his disbelief in her story as evident as the rain that pattered on her head. Still, he didn't dispute it, just asked, "Why were you on a horse?"

Emma sighed quietly. "I was having a lesson with Simon and Daniel. Ned was giving us instruction."

"Really."

Emma could only nod.

"Is this also the reason for your torn dress?"

Her gown had indeed been ripped in two places in her struggle to escape Thomas Lang. She gathered one of the seams in her hand, holding it together as if this would hide it.

William didn't wait for her answer and continued, "And this horse is where, Miss McLeod?" He made a show of scanning the track in both directions.

Emma tried to dislodge a lock of wet hair from her face with a toss of her head, but it clung stubbornly to her cheek. "I would have to guess, Mr. Rideout, that it ran away."

William nodded thoughtfully. "Ran away. And I also suppose that Daniel, Simon, and this Ned haven't noticed you're no longer with them. Or have they gone in search of the animal and will return at some point?"

Emma didn't even try to offer a rebuttal. She just stared up at him, raindrops blurring her vision.

"I'm sorry, Miss McLeod, but I don't believe you."

"I don't give a damn if you believe me or not, Mr. Rideout," Emma's said, her fragile emotions merging, coming together as rage, her voice raised so her words weren't misheard or misunderstood. She wanted him to hear clearly. "I'm sorry that you've been sent to rescue me again. I imagine it's becoming a bit tedious, but contrary to your view of me, I'm perfectly capable of taking care of myself. I have never needed your help, nor do I need it now." She felt dangerously close to tears and fought to control them. Being found sitting in the mud was one thing, but crying as well wasn't acceptable. She curled her fingers into her palms and took a deep breath. "So I won't take up any more of your time, and I wish you a good afternoon."

William slowly shook his head, then without saying a word, he reached out a hand to her. For a moment, she stared at it. The last thing she wanted after her outburst was to be assisted by him, but she would gain nothing by refusing it. Lang could appear at any time. Reluctantly she took his hand, and he pulled her to her feet. Face to face with him, she felt all the fight leave her. The charade that a moment ago seemed to offer her some false dignity now seemed as ridiculous as it was.

"Did the horse kick you in the face, too?" William said. He reached up, gripping her chin, turning her face upward.

Emma resisted putting her hand up to touch the place where Thomas Lang's hand had left its mark. She could feel it. Mr. Rideout could obviously see it. She nodded.

His grip on her chin was gentler now, but there was anger in his voice. "Did this...fall, result in any more injuries?"

She shook her head no, fully aware of what he was asking. "Nothing of consequence."

William studied her face a moment longer, no doubt judging the honesty of her denial. Then he dropped his arm to his side and took a long visible breath, turning slightly in the direction of Lang's house that lay hidden behind the sentinel gum trees.

Although she couldn't see the house, she could imagine it, the image of Lang as she left him clear in her mind. But whether he was injured or dead she'd no idea. If she'd killed him, she would surely go to prison. If she'd not, he would certainly have her charged with assault, whether he was visibly injured or not. The fact that he'd assaulted her she didn't believe would absolve her from prosecution. She shivered at that thought.

"He's still alive, Miss McLeod, if that's playing on your mind."

The wind dropped, and the rain stopped, the world falling silent, William's words scattering through the bushland. It took a moment for her to realize what that meant. "You've seen him?"

William looked back at her. Anger was an emotion she'd seen in him often, his eyes darkening, his voice low like a rumble of thunder warning of an imminent storm, and most times she seemed to be the catalyst. But this was different, this wasn't directed at her, and Emma was glad of that. "He has a headache and some bruises, but he'll live. Luck was with him that I found him before I saw you and not the other way around. He may not have fared as well if that were the case, but I will deal with him later."

Emma couldn't deny she was surprised and flattered by Mr. Rideout's need to avenge the insult done to her. But this wasn't the days of knights and fair maidens, and although she'd not intended any of this to happen, it had, and she was responsible, the consequences hers alone. But one consequence was worse than all others, and of this she'd no doubt. William's opinion of her as a silly inept girl was now well and truly confirmed, and any chance of friendship between them was lost. Of all the multitude of thoughts, that one brought tears to her eyes, and she pleaded with herself not to cry, not now.

"I appreciate your concern, Mr. Rideout, but this is my fault, and I don't want anyone getting into trouble because of something I have done." She'd hoped the action of talking would stall her tears, but it didn't, and she covered her face with her hands. "I didn't want you to see me like this."

She didn't resist as William wrapped his arms around her and pulled her close, his coat damp, his unshaven chin rough against her cheek, but she cared about neither. "It's not your fault, Emma. The blame lands on Lang alone."

Emma looked up at him. "I only came here because of Simon," she said, it suddenly seeming important for him to know that.

His anger had lessened, but his eyes gave fair warning that it hadn't gone. "I know. Martha told me. She overheard the conversation you had with Lang. I would've stopped you, but I thought maybe it wasn't my place, that you had feelings for…"

Emma shook her head vehemently. "I have no

feelings for Mr. Lang, not now, not before. It was my stupid pride and your arrogance that instigated my entertaining Mr. Lang in the first place. I didn't want to, but I couldn't back down once I had agreed. I decided, however, that I wouldn't see Mr. Lang again, but his plea for Simon's sake touched my heart, and I…

Emma had been kissed before. Once when she was sixteen, at her birthday party, by a skinny, spotty, awkward boy called Arthur, a peck really. Then again by a man who professed his love when she was eighteen, a more grown-up brief brushing of lips she supposed, but she'd never been kissed like this, her face held between William's hands, his mouth lightly on hers at first, judging to see if the gesture was welcomed. It was, that Emma couldn't deny, and it only took her a moment to assure him of that.

****

Daniel led the way back to Eden Hill on Lang's pony. Ned had urged him to take it, assuring the boy he would collect the animal tomorrow. The man offered his apologies to Emma. He didn't say what for, but Emma believed it hadn't taken him long to guess what had happened to her. Simon wouldn't look at her at all, just took her hand for a moment, silent as always, then turned his pony toward the stables. She didn't think either of them knew what Lang had planned to do, but neither of them seemed surprised that he'd done it—sadly, not even a ten-year-old child.

Daniel just looked confused, asking one question after another. William explained that Mr. Lang had become ill and taken to his bed, and Emma, trying to ride home, had fallen from the horse she'd borrowed. William had returned the horse to the stable and took

Emma onto his. This had explained most things with at least an element of truth, and Daniel seemed happy with the explanation.

"You must have riding lessons as soon as possible, Emma," Daniel said, concern furrowing his brow. "You were lucky William found you."

Emma could only nod her agreement, the motion of the horse rocking her from side to side as it picked its way along the track toward home, tiny birds feasting on the insects that had emerged with the rain, darting up from the ground, chattering their annoyance at the disruption of their feast.

Emma relaxed against William's chest and closed her eyes, exhaustion washing over her. The closeness to him was equally comforting and confusing. She felt both protected and vulnerable. Their relationship up until now had been that of spitting wildcats, as her uncle had put it, with occasional episodes of amicability. But never in all the short time she'd known William Rideout did she ever think he would feel anything more for her than tentative friendship.

She could still feel his mouth on hers. But was she reading more into the kiss than she should? Was she in love with him? But more so, was he in love with her? She knew his thoughts on that subject. Had they changed? She was fully aware of how mercurial his mood could be and had seen this tender side of William before. Tomorrow, would their relationship return to its original form? That thought weighed heavily on her.

"Why did you tell me you fell off a horse?"

This question, although derailing Emma's troubling thoughts, led her to others equally uncomfortable. She sighed. There was no point telling him other than the truth, and if anything was going to alter his mood, this was it. If this new intimacy was the beginning of something or just a transient moment, she supposed knowing sooner was better than later. She hoped. "Because to tell you what really happened was unbearable," she said. "I felt your derision at my fall from a horse far more bearable than admitting I had found myself in the situation I did. You had clearly shown your disapproval of me inviting Mr. Lang's attention, and I wanted to avoid a 'told you so.' "

William's reply was simple, a soft "hmmm" of thought, and Emma wondered if she'd hurt his feelings.

They rode in silence for a few minutes, until William broke it. "Is it important to you what I think?" This question Emma had asked herself and annoyingly the answer was that it did matter. Somehow, at some point, having Mr. Rideout's friendship and respect had become important to her.

He continued, saving her the need to voice an answer. "I suppose I have been a bit...off-hand with you."

Emma couldn't help but laugh. "Off-hand? I hadn't used that one when listing your shortcomings."

"You have a list?"

Emma couldn't see his face but could hear the frown in his voice. She continued anyway. It was all or nothing. "I do. When you made me angry, I would list as many unpleasant names for you as I could think of."

"Such as?"

Emma hesitated. Stomping around her room, near paralyzed by her anger, her less-than-flattering adjectives seemed perfectly acceptable, as they were on the occasions when she said them, deservedly so, to his face. But now the words felt churlish, distasteful to voice out loud. She braced herself, not knowing what reaction her words would bring. "Arrogant, pig-headed, patronizing, rude, conceited." She took a breath. "Shall I go on?"

"There's more?"

Emma didn't miss the tone of wounded surprise in his question. "Some."

"Anything not quite so damning?"

Emma shook her head "Not really. Not when I was furious with you."

He was silent for a moment, then asked, "How many times was that?"

Emma felt a stab of sadness. Was she sabotaging this new relationship, if that's what this was, by answering his questions so truthfully? Should she not adopt a more tactful approach? But she decided not. It had to be the truth or nothing at all. This didn't, however, ease the pang of regret as she answered. "On most days that we spoke, in one way or another."

William didn't reply. Emma had no way of knowing if he was angry, sad, or indifferent to what she'd said, the lengthening silence giving her no clue as to what he was thinking.

"In my defense," William said, startling her from her thoughts, "I did find you at times infuriating and, might I add, a danger to yourself."

There was no malice in his words, and Emma smiled. He was probably right. Not that she would tell him that, but she didn't argue the point.

"But I can honestly say I have never found you tedious, nor that you're incapable, as you seem to think I do."

228

The sun, finally showing itself, was warm on her face, and Emma allowed herself to enjoy this moment of truce, happy at least to not be fighting with this man. Tomorrow everything could go back to the way it was, or worse, but right now she would just savor this time. There was one thing that troubled her, though, a question gnawing its way into her mind.

"Will I go to prison?"

She felt him shake his head. "No, Emma. You're not going to prison. I doubt *any* further action will be taken. It's his word against yours, and I'm sure his reputation precedes him. There's nothing for you to worry about."

A kookaburra called in the distance, its laughter echoing through the bush. It was so unlike the soft call of the cuckoo in the springtime back home in England. But never judge a bird by its call, Emma thought to herself. Kookaburras didn't murder the young of other birds.

Emma had expected her uncle to be in the orchard and Martha to be resting in her room. Instead, they were on the verandah, and by the look of their smiles, there was a pleasant reason for them being so. But all smiles faded as they came to a stop in the forecourt. Both herself and William were soaked through, Daniel too. Riding in the rain was an easy explanation for that, but her tear-swollen eyes, the rip in her dress, and the splatter of blood, something she hadn't realized until William pointed them out, were going to be harder to explain. Not to mention why they left in a buggy and arrived home on horseback.

Her uncle was first to react, leaping from his seat. He reached up, catching Emma as she slipped from the saddle. "Good God, Emma. What has happened to you?"

"I'm fine, Uncle. Just a little accident."

The man didn't look convinced. "Will?"

William swung from his horse. "Daniel, can you take the horse to the barn?" He handed the reins to the boy. "While I speak to your uncle."

Daniel nodded and took the reins, the animals following him toward the back of the house.

"If you will excuse me," Emma said, "I will take a bath now."

Martha stood up. "I'll put the kettle on to boil. Some tea after your bath may be nice." Emma nodded. Martha, she believed, had already guessed what the real story was.

****

Emma and Martha sat side by side on Emma's bed.

"Emma, I'm so sorry this has happened to you."

Emma smiled weakly. "It wasn't your fault, Martha. You weren't to know."

The other woman shook her head. "That's true, Emma, I didn't know he was going to do what he did, but I know what he's capable of, and that I should have told you. I should have tried harder to dissuade you from going." She swiped at a tear that rolled down her cheek with the back of her hand. "I'm so sorry, Emma."

Emma could do nothing other than reach out and squeeze the woman's hand, a gesture of understanding, forgiveness. But that was all she could do, words not possible, her mind struggling to grasp what the other woman had said. It took a moment for Emma to speak. "How do you know what Lang is capable of?"

Martha sighed and looked down at her hands clasped tightly together in her lap. She recounted how she'd met Lang not long after she'd arrived in Fremantle.

Widowed, she and her brother Anthony had hoped for a new life in the colony, hearing talk that the fresh air and warm sunshine were the cure for all ills. But the voyage had been hard, the food spoilt and scarce, and disease rife. For poor Anthony, sickly to begin with, he just didn't have the strength needed and passed away.

Martha showed little emotion as she recounted the loss of her brother, her tone one of weary resignation. She'd little to sustain her when she arrived, just a small sum of money and a few personal items. And little protection. She was a lone woman in a somewhat wild colony. When she saw an advertisement for a housekeeper on a small property east of Fremantle, she applied immediately. Accommodation and a small wage for cooking, cleaning, and schooling a young boy, skills not beyond her, was almost too good to be true.

"And it turned out that it was," she said quietly.

Thomas Lang was to be her employer, a gentleman, a widower for the third time and now the sole parent of a young son who had lost the gift of speech.

Things had started well enough, Martha finding the work fulfilling and pleasant. Her new charge was a sweet child and did as he was told but wouldn't utter a word. Even his tears were silent. Lang was well-mannered and respectful. For a time.

Then things changed. Lang became more familiar, uncomfortably so. He liked to take a drink occasionally, or so Martha thought, Martha soon coming to realize that Lang drank often, quantity rather than quality being his preference. When he was drunk, what gentlemanly ways he may have owned disappeared. Then he became quick with his belt at any transgression, real or imagined, and apparently, Mr. Lang had a fertile imagination.

"Did he beat you?" Emma whispered, horrified.

Martha simply said, "Yes," and continued. "But poor Simon took the brunt of the drunken rages. And there were many of those."

"How long did you stay?"

"Longer than I should."

"Because of Simon?"

Martha nodded, the action causing a tear to overflow her lashes and roll down her cheek. She didn't seem to notice. "But I realized it made no difference to the way Lang treated the boy if I was there or not. At times, it seemed to make it worse. When I wouldn't submit to his advances, which were becoming more and more frequent, he would take his anger out on me, but that was restrained compared to what the poor boy endured. Simon learnt fast how to disappear and did so for days, sometimes. I would leave food out for him in the barn, hidden, and sometimes it would be eaten, sometimes not. He never seemed hungry or dirty, though. I think he was going elsewhere for food and, God willing, some comfort."

"But Lang seems to dote on the child," Emma said, trying to make sense of the two different sides of Thomas Lang that she herself had seen.

Martha smiled sadly. "It's all a show. He was the same when I first met him. It's his way of trying to impress. This time it was you he wanted to make a good impression on."

Emma's eyes widened in surprise. "Me?"

Martha nodded.

"But I have no interest in Mr. Lang."

"He thought differently. You agreed to him calling on you."

Emma sighed loudly. She had, that she couldn't deny, but how could she explain to Martha why? It wasn't because of her affection for Mr. Lang. "I-I…"

"I know why you did, Emma, but Lang wants a wife to give him an heir. You're young, beautiful, healthy, and unspoken for, so you're more than he could have hoped for. I imagine he thought that if you weren't to give yourself willingly, then force would work just as well. He probably believed you would marry him rather than let the shame of what had transpired be made public. I should have made more of my warning to you about the man, but I didn't think he would go as far as he did. I thought there would be more time for us to talk. I'm truly sorry, Emma."

"But my uncle? Why, if he knew what the man…" Emma stopped. She already knew the answer. "That's why you wanted to keep it between us. He doesn't know, does he?"

Martha shook her head. "I never told him."

Emma shifted on the bed. "Why?"

Martha sighed. This was a secret she'd kept to herself, and Emma could see that the effort to recall the reason why, let alone disclose it, wasn't an easy task.

Martha closed her eyes, as if not seeing Emma's face would make the task easier. "Lang raped me," she said, her words as shattering as a sledgehammer to glass.

Emma sat frozen. She had nothing to say and waited for Martha to go on.

Martha did. "It was the day I told him I was leaving. I knew it was no longer any good for myself or Simon if I stayed. He'd been drinking, as usual, but I was so in a hurry to go that I misjudged his mood." The woman opened her eyes, but although she stared into Emma's,

Emma didn't think the woman was seeing her at all, her mind seeing another time and place.

Martha took a ragged breath. "Suffice to say, he wasn't pleased with my resignation and demanded I repay his hospitality. I refused, but that didn't stop him…" She fell silent, and Emma reached out, putting her hand on Martha's.

"Did you tell anyone about what he did?" Emma whispered.

Martha shook her head. "It would have made no difference if I had," she said. "He was friends with most, and it was my word against his. He made it clear that rumors spread quickly in the colony. A woman that cooked, cleaned, and gave herself freely was one step up from a prostitute. When I met your uncle, I felt blessed to find such a kind and affectionate man that I didn't want to risk losing him by telling him what Lang had done. There was nothing to be gained from that except heartache and anger." Martha's shoulders dropped. Although the burden of the secret no longer had to be carried, the telling of it to Emma seemed to have drained the woman. "But I wish now that I had. It would have saved you from what could have been a similar fate."

Emma shook her head. "But it didn't get to that, Martha. You're not to blame yourself. I should have known better. I was foolish."

Martha sighed. "In truth, Emma, it's neither your fault nor mine. There's only one person to blame, and he's not worthy of another second of thought." Martha smiled, dabbing at her eyes with the back of her hand. "Tomorrow is a new day, and we won't ponder the past. There are people who love us, and they're the only ones we will give our thoughts to."

Chapter 18

"Baaaa."

Emma's eyes sprang open, and she looked straight into those of a lamb that for some reason was standing on her stomach, another plaintive *baa* issuing from its little mouth. Her eyes drifted upward meeting those of her young brother.

He grinned back at her. "This is Daisy."

"That's lovely, Daniel, but why is Daisy sitting on me?"

Daniel's grin remained. "Will said I could bring her to show you."

"Did he, now?"

Daniel nodded. "Her mother died."

Emma nodded and pushed herself up a little, her woolly bedfellow hopping from foot to foot trying to balance against the sudden movement. The right rear leg came down hard, and Emma let out a gasp as the bony hoof pressed into her belly. "Oof! Daniel, could you please take the da—Daisy off the bed."

Murmuring words of comfort, Daniel gathered the creature in his arms, Daisy baaing her displeasure at being restrained.

Emma took a breath and sat up against the pillows. "So what do you feed your new friend with?" she asked running a hand across the quilt to satisfy herself the lamb hadn't left any gifts behind.

"Will said she must be given milk until she's old enough to eat grass. Will says I can feed her next. Or you can, if you like."

Emma pouted and nodded. "William certainly says a lot, doesn't he?"

Daniel nodded. "He knows a lot of stuff."

Emma agreed he did. "Well, take Daisy out onto the verandah while I dress, and we can feed her together."

Daniel smiled, his new charge clutched in his arms. "Okay, Em. And don't forget we are going to the party tonight."

Emma groaned. The harvest ball. She'd forgotten, even though her uncle had told her only a week ago, and any excitement she may have felt turned quickly to dread. Everyone attended, her uncle had said, and that would probably mean Lang would be there. Martha said to give him no thought, thoughts being a gift given only to those who deserved it, and Emma tried to focus her mind on William. But that only sent an equal ripple of anxiety through her. She'd seen nothing of him after they arrived home yesterday. She'd gone straight to her room after bathing and seen no one other than Martha for the rest of the night. She didn't know what—or should she say "who"—to expect when she came face to face with him today.

Her stomach grumbled loud and long in response to the aroma of bacon and fresh bread, and the choice of staying hidden away was no longer an option. She hadn't eaten since yesterday morning. She threw back the blankets and swung her legs out of bed. Angry grazes crisscrossed the skin on both knees, but she didn't want to think about the events that had caused the damage, pushing them into the recess where she kept all memories she didn't want to think about. She'd become quite adept at that lately. She feared the day when the thoughts would all demand attention, but today wasn't going to be that day.

She dressed quickly, choosing a simple but pretty sky-blue gown, and stepped out into the hall, the smell drawing her toward the kitchen.

Martha was alone, humming to herself as she took another loaf from the oven and set it to cool on the table. She appeared to glow with contentment, her pregnant belly showing ever so slightly under her gown. She smiled as she caught sight of Emma and dusted her flour-coated hands on her apron. "Good morning," she said. "Did you sleep well?"

Emma smiled. "Mostly." She came into the room and leaned against the table. Absently she drew a pattern in the leftover flour on the cutting board. "I appreciate your help last night."

Martha set down the bowl of eggs she'd been stirring and looked at Emma. "I should thank you. I feel like a weight has been lifted from me by confiding in you. I hope you're hungry?"

Emma nodded, "I'm starving," she said, resisting the temptation to pick at the crust of one of the cooling loaves. "Can I help with anything?"

"You could call the men in from the verandah. Breakfast is ready."

Daniel was sitting on the verandah railings, swinging his legs back and forth. "Careful you don't take a tumble from there," Emma heard her uncle say. "Oh, good morning, my darling," he said as she came out onto the verandah. The sun was just rising above the edge of the roof, and she raised her hand to shade her eyes against its glare. She offered her cheek for his kiss. "Good morning, Uncle."

"Did you sleep well?"

Emma smiled and assured her uncle that she had. She wondered what explanation William had given the man about her appearance yesterday, but whatever it was it didn't seem to give the man cause to question her. She delivered Martha's request that they all attend breakfast.

Her uncle beamed. "Come, Daniel," he said, swinging the boy from the railing. "Your clever, beautiful aunt has a feast ready for us."

They disappeared inside, leaving Emma alone with Daisy, who paid her no attention at all, and William, whose attention was solely on her, but he seemed guarded, and Emma wondered if, like a rainbow, his affection for her had disappeared now the storm had passed.

"Breakfast is ready," she said, in case he'd not heard, and she gestured toward the house, suggesting he follow Robert and Daniel inside. But he made no move to do so.

"Your kindness and attention have transformed Martha. I didn't think it was possible," William said, nodding toward the house. "Your uncle too. He's like a lovesick schoolboy."

Emma smiled and looked at the man across from her, trying to read his feelings on the matter of this renewed love. But his expression remained unreadable, his opinion only known to himself.

"I think Martha just needed someone to talk with, to voice her fears," Emma said. "And her happiness has probably lifted a burden from Uncle Robert. He clearly cares for her."

William frowned, and Emma steeled herself for his thoughts on that, but he said nothing. Instead, he reached out his hand, tilting her face upward to the morning sunshine. She'd studied her face this morning before leaving her room. The red mark left by Mr. Lang had faded somewhat, but it was still there to see if you looked, and William was doing just that. His thumb was warm as he softly traced the faint patch of pink on her left cheek. "Does it hurt?"

Emma shook her head. "No. There's far more damage to my pride." She smiled, waiting, hoping he would too, but instead he dropped his hand away and stepped back, and for a moment Emma thought he looked nervous. This wasn't going the way she'd hoped, but it was going the way she knew it would.

"I need to speak to you about yesterday," William said, confirming her fears. "I feel that my behavior was thoughtless, especially after what happened to you, and I want to apologize. I shouldn't have acted that way."

Emma's father had always told her that her emotions were written so clearly on her face anyone could read them. William was the opposite, his thoughts usually a mystery. But not this time. The emotions he usually hid so well played across his face—confusion, fear, uncertainty, and shame were all there to see as she studied the man in front of her.

"Are you saying you regret kissing me?"

William sighed, shook his head. "Regret?" He shrugged. "Yes. It wasn't the right thing to do, and I'm sorry. I overstepped a line, Miss McLeod."

Emma's heart sank. There it was again. She was Miss McLeod. Whatever had transpired yesterday was gone with the rising of the sun, it seemed.

For a moment, Emma was speechless. Then she said, "I have no regrets, William. None at all. But I need to know—am I Miss McLeod to you, the niece of your friend? And yesterday was just an error in judgment on your behalf? Or am I Emma, the woman you kissed yesterday? I know my feelings, William. I need to know yours." Emma continued to study his face, searching for anything that might show what impact her words had on the man, but his face told her nothing now. "William?"

There was no reply, only Daniel skidding to a stop in front of them. "Come on, you two," the boy said. "Martha said breakfast is getting cold."

Emma dragged her eyes from William's and looked down at her brother. She struggled to understand what the boy was saying, her thoughts focused only on hearing William's answer to her question. "What?"

"Breakfast," Daniel said again, smiling up at her. "It's getting cold. Martha said to be quick, as we have a lot to do today. She wants you to help her get ready for the party."

Emma nodded, forcing a smile onto her face. "We will be in shortly, Daniel," she said, turning to usher the boy inside, her efforts halted by the sound of hooves heavy on the ground. Emma turned to look along the track but couldn't see who the rider was, scrubby trees blocking her view. Was it Thomas Lang coming to demand an apology or worse?

William obviously was asking himself the same question, and he stepped in front of her as the rider emerged from the bush. But it was Ned, and Emma let out the breath she'd been holding.

Ned slowed his mount to a walk, then reined the animal in as he drew level with the verandah. "Good mornin', Mr. Rideout, Miss McLeod," he said. "I 'ope you're feeling well this mornin', miss."

Emma flashed the man a smile, mostly from relief that it was Ned asking the question and not Thomas Lang. "I am, thank you, Ned."

"Glad to 'ear it, miss," he said. "I'm sorry to cause you any trouble, but I've come to get the pony before Mr. Lang notices it's not there. Save any discussion, see."

Emma nodded that she did, indeed, see. "It's no trouble at all, Ned. Daniel, could you fetch the pony from the barn?"

Daniel skipped down the steps of the verandah, jogging across the forecourt to the stable.

"Your help was much appreciated yesterday, Ned," William said as the trio watched Daniel emerge from the barn, the pony in tow.

Ned took the lead rope from the boy. "No problem, Mr. Rideout. Wish I could 'ave done more." His meaning was clear and the regret obvious in his words. "Good mornin' to you both." Ned turned his mount back toward the way he'd come. He raised a hand in farewell and urged his horse forward, the pony falling in behind.

Emma watched until the bush swallowed them up, then turned back to the house. She ignored her brother's tug on her hand, her eyes focusing on William, questioning.

He didn't look at her, however, his words for Daniel. "Please tell Martha I won't be coming in for breakfast," he said. "I have some things to attend to."

Without another word, he turned, taking the two steps down to the forecourt in one stride. Emma watched him until he disappeared around the side of the house, confusion again all that he left her with.

Daniel tugged Emma's hand with more force. "Come on, Em," he said. "I'm starving."

Emma sighed and, not knowing what else to do, allowed herself to be towed along behind her brother into the house.

There was no denying the air of excitement in the kitchen. Her uncle was leaning against the table, Martha resting against him. His arms were clasped around his wife's waist, her hand resting lightly on her swelling belly. Emma couldn't help but smile at this picture but couldn't ignore the stab of sadness she felt. She didn't know what had happened between her and William, nor what would have happened if Daniel hadn't come out. Would she be smiling with happiness like Martha or still as miserable as she was now? Martha broke away from her husband, laughing as he whispered something in her ear. She put a plate down and gestured for Emma to sit.

"Where's William?" Martha asked, setting down another plate.

Emma shook her head silently and dropped into a chair.

"He said he'd some things to do, Aunty," Daniel said, delivering the message he had been asked to. "Can I have some more bacon, please? I'm starving."

Emma couldn't admit the same, her appetite lost somewhere between verandah and kitchen, and she pushed her food around her plate, grateful for Martha's excited chatter about the harvest ball, hoping it would draw any attention away from Emma's obvious lack of hunger. Only Daniel made a quiet comment on how her bacon and sausage were still untouched and could he have it if she was not going to eat it.

After breakfast, Daniel announced that although he

would be happy to stay and help with the dishes, he thought it more important to help Uncle Robert with the last-minute preparation for the sale that would take place the day after tomorrow.

Emma laughed and shooed the little boy out of the kitchen. "Off with you, then, before I change my mind," she said. "But you're to have a bath and lay out your best clothes when you're finished," Emma called after him as the boy scampered after his uncle. "Do you understand?"

Emma heard a call of "yes" from the hall, and she stood up, gathered the dishes, and took them over to the sink. She filled a basin with hot water, but her attention wasn't on the stack of plates waiting to be washed. Her eyes were drawn to the barn door visible through the kitchen window. She wondered if William was inside and what chores were so desperately in need of being done. None, was the answer. She knew that. His hurried departure was just a way to avoid answering her question.

"Emma?"

The sound of her name penetrated her thoughts, and Emma turned her attention to Martha, surprised to see a small frown on the woman's face.

"Are you unwell, Emma? You were miles away."

Emma forced a smile onto her face. "I'm fine, Martha," she said. "Maybe still a little tired."

"A rest maybe this afternoon, then. Before tonight's outing. What do you plan to wear?"

Martha's question sent a ripple of dread through her. Tonight's social gathering was the last thing on Emma's mind, and she hadn't planned to attend. The thought of running into Lang wasn't a pleasant one, and her thoughts on that were clear on her face.

"Your uncle and Mr. Rideout will be there, and we both will be perfectly safe. You're not to worry. We will have a wonderful time."

Despite Martha's determined words, Emma didn't miss the look of apprehension in the other woman's eyes. Emma realized that the risk of encountering Lang would be far harder for Martha, her experience with him more traumatic than her own. She needed Emma's support tonight, and Emma couldn't refuse to give it despite her apprehension. She smiled. "We will," she said. "And in answer to your original question, I have no idea what I will wear."

Emma followed Martha to her room. A wardrobe stood against one wall, and Martha opened it, displaying the few plain dresses in shades of gray and brown. "I never really needed anything else," Martha explained as she pushed one dove gray dress aside, revealing another almost identical one.

Emma reached for another dress, in a more dramatic color, rose pink, but it was just as plain as the others. Sizing Martha up, Emma guessed she was not too different in size from herself, despite Martha's slight belly giving her a more curvaceous figure. "Come with me," Emma said, and took Martha's hand. They went down the hallway to Emma's room, where Emma guided Martha to sit on the bed. Then Emma knelt in front of the trunk and opened the lid.

"Oh, my!" Martha covered her mouth with her hands, her eyes wide in delight.

Emma pulled a coral gown from the trunk and held it up. "I think that might be too pale for your complexion," she said. "Maybe blue would be a better color for you." Emma pulled out an azure blue gown, the

244

silk slipping smoothly through her fingers as she spread out the skirt.

"You're so lucky to have such beautiful gowns," Martha said.

Emma pulled out her favorite, a red satin dress, white lace at the wrist and throat. There was no plunging neckline this time. Despite not knowing William's feelings for her, she did not want to give him cause for disapproval nor draw attention to herself. She'd learnt her lesson. "They were a gift," she said, "from a 'lady' in Fremantle." Emma lowered her voice despite there being no one else in earshot. "However, I was given the impression that she's in a profession where she wouldn't be referred to as a lady."

It took a moment for Martha to catch Emma's meaning. "Really?"

Emma nodded. "But she was so kind to me when I needed someone to be."

Martha smiled. "Well, as she was so kind to you, l won't judge her less a lady because of her profession," she said. "Having someone come into your life at a time when you need them is truly wonderful. I have your uncle and you and your brother as proof of that. You've changed my life, and I hope I can repay the debt."

Emma smiled at the other woman. "There's no debt, Martha," she said. "No one can replace my mother, but I count myself lucky to have you to fill the terrible gap her passing left." Emma felt tears prick at her eyes as images of her mother and baby brother skimmed across her mind. These were thoughts she'd managed to give little time to, and she wasn't prepared to give them any now.

Chapter 19

Martha had retired to her room to rest for an hour or so, and Emma thought she too should try to sleep for a while. She'd not slept well the night before, and it was likely to be a late night tonight. But as much as she tried to rest, her mind wouldn't take part, her thoughts caught in a whirlpool, each one swirling around and around in an unstoppable current of confusion brought about by William Rideout. She rolled onto her side, eyes closed, listening to the silence of the house, willing herself to sleep, but she knew it wouldn't come. She had to speak to William now, put the matter to rest, whether the outcome was favorable or not.

Emma pushed from the bed and stood in front of the mirror. She tucked a stray lock of hair back into her hair clip, smoothing an unruly curl back behind her ear. Then with a determination posing as confidence, she went out to the barn.

The huge door was ajar, and Emma slipped into the dim interior. Flecks of dust glittered like gold in the thin shafts of sunlight that pierced the gaps in the walls and roof. Emma waited for her eyes to adjust, but if it was to see what was in the barn, she didn't need sight—the smell was enough to tell her that her uncle's horses, as well as William's mount, sheltered here. But there were other odors, the sweet scent of ripe fruit and fresh-cut hay, the oily aroma of fleece; the bounty of the harvest.

A horse nickered, a soft call taken up by the other four. But it wasn't fear they communicated, just the murmur from one animal to the other that someone new had come into their space.

"Miss McLeod."

Emma jumped at the unexpected sound and spun around.

"Mr. Rideout. William. I-I was concerned that you haven't eaten today."

William stepped from the shadows, a bundle of hay in his arms, and he crossed to a stall, dropping the feed over the door into it. The animal inside snorted its gratitude. He strode back to what Emma could now see was a barrow of hay, and he gathered another bundle, Emma slowly turning to follow his path as he delivered it to a second stall.

"Don't concern yourself, Miss McLeod. I'm not hungry."

Now she was here, Emma's decision to confront William didn't seem to be as easy as it had in her head, but she also hadn't come here to watch him feed horses. She wanted an answer and was now terrified of what it would be.

"William," she said, letting the words slip from her lips before she lost her nerve, "on the verandah, you didn't answer my question." She took a breath and waited, feeling her heart beating uncomfortably hard in her chest.

Twice more, William gathered the animal feed, crossed the barn, and dropped it into a stall before he spoke. Even then he didn't look at her, his answer directed at a rake he'd taken from a hook on the wall. "Because the answer makes no difference."

Emma frowned. "I don't understand. What do you mean, 'It makes no difference'?"

Again, William took his time answering, his focus instead on raking up the strands of hay that had fallen to the floor. He bent and scooped them up, dropping them back into the barrow, the rake following. Finally, he turned to look at her, and Emma was shocked to see the look of anger on his face. "Goddammit, Emma, can't you just leave it?"

There was no time for Emma to answer his question, or to say anything at all, even if she'd had any idea what to say, for it took only seven strides for William to leave the barn, Emma counting each one of them. And with William went any clarity she'd come to find, the man leaving her more confused now than before.

"Give him time, Emma."

Emma turned to look at her uncle. He had come through a door behind the stall. She was embarrassed that he had probably witnessed her sparring with William yet again, but she couldn't hide her feelings this time. Not that she had any idea of what she felt—confusion, sadness, disappointment—but it was anger that spoke for her. "Time?" she said. "I don't think time is going to change that man at all. Patience and respect haven't, so I cannot see why anything else will. He plays games, Uncle, but I don't know what the rules are."

Her uncle turned a little toward the brown mare that nuzzled his shoulder, the animal unsettled by Emma's outburst. He ran a hand down the length of the animal's nose, a soft hush settling the animal. "People behave in different ways under pressure, Emma. William has a lot on his mind right now, what with the sale of the harvest and all the concerns that brings."

"Concerns? How can his fears be any different than yours, Uncle? In truth, I imagine yours to be greater, having the responsibility of a wife, and a child on the way."

The man nodded. "That's true, Emma, I won't deny it, but everyone is feeling it, Will included. He's the manager of this property and feels a lot of responsibility for the outcome to be successful."

"So that's it," Emma said with more than a hint of sarcasm. "Mr. Rideout behaves the way he does, his moods as changeable as the weather, his behavior unfathomable, just because he's worried. Is he like this every year?"

Her uncle smiled. "No, Emma, for Will, this year is different. He has reason to be more apprehensive than usual. Every year we have been able to pay our debts, and we hope this year will be the same, but everyone who relies on this property doesn't take this year's sale as a certainty until it's done. They all have some sort of backup plan if things don't go the way we all pray it does. Will, too, but this year he feels he has more to lose than he has before."

Emma frowned. "I don't understand. What does he have to lose that you don't?"

Robert opened his mouth to say something, then closed it again. He ambled over to Emma and put his arm around her shoulder, guiding her to sit on a stack of empty crates. He tipped over a half barrel and sat down. Leaning forward, his hands clasped in front of him, he spoke, but it was with measured words, as if what he was about to say was something he'd rather not.

"Emma, Will has feelings for you, ones that he wishes he didn't have. Ones he believes he can't afford."

Emma shook her head. "Wishes he didn't have? Can't afford? I'm sorry, Uncle Robert, but what does that mean? Everything I hear from William and from you, it all sounds like riddles."

The man sighed loudly. "Emma, what I'm trying to get you to understand is that Will honestly believes that love is a luxury, something you can only have if you can afford it. Right or wrong, it's what he believes. It's not an easy life here, Emma, and the colony is full of people whose lives have been destroyed by poverty in one way or another. Will saw it happen to his parents, witnessed firsthand how even the strongest bonds can fall by the wayside under the burden of poverty, and he saw what poverty can force people to do to survive. If the harvest fails and Will has nothing to offer you, then he'll never tell you how he feels. That, however, doesn't stop him from being angry at himself for having feelings for you, or being angry at you for being, well, you."

Chapter 20

The home of Mr. and Mrs. Appleton was warm and welcoming. Women in their finest gowns, men in their Sunday best, smiled and laughed, relieved that at least the harvest was over. And even though success wasn't assured when it came to sales and the security of their home, those here tonight set their worries aside. What would be, would be.

Twin chandeliers, twenty candles in each, sparkled, illuminating the large room and the wonderful spread of food set out on an enormous mahogany table pushed up against the wall. The twelve chairs usually arranged around the table were now spaced along two other walls joining two rich green velvet sofas, seating for wearied dancers. Gold brocade curtains hung at the five floor-length windows, each set drawn aside by red velvet ribbons. The curtains at the French doors were also open, giving access to the verandah.

The final strains of a gentle waltz slipped now into a much livelier composition, couples drifting in from the verandah, from the dining room, some to join in the dance, some to watch. Robert took Martha's hand, and despite her protest, she allowed herself to be led onto the dance floor. She looked breathtaking in a deep green gown, the skirt gathered at the back, the train draped over a small bustle. Emma had convinced her she didn't need to hide her golden hair away in the tight bun that must surely give her a headache. Instead, it was left to fall in soft curls to her shoulders. Emma nor anyone else who cared to look couldn't miss the look of adoration on her uncle's face as he held Martha, the couple turning and stepping in time to the music.

Emma had worn the red dress and felt beautiful in it. However, no one, especially Mr. Rideout, could accuse her of dressing inappropriately, her gown more conservative than those worn by most of the other women. She wished she were on the dance floor and it was William who held her close, but on his arrival, William had joined a group of men, their welcome of him warm and jovial. He smiled and fell into the conversation, his face transformed as he relaxed in their company.

Occasionally, Emma would catch his eye, his gaze lingering, but he gave her no clue what his thoughts were, and he made no effort to speak with her, let alone ask her to dance. She watched her uncle and Martha spin past again before she turned, excusing her way through the spectators, and wandered out onto the verandah, welcoming the cool air and the relative quiet.

Oil lanterns hung from the roof, and Emma moved to the far end of the verandah, away from the puddles of illumination and the myriad of flying insects they attracted. She stared off into the dark bushland that bordered the front of the Appletons' property. A light breeze stirred through the lofty gum trees, their leaves softly rattling, and although it was warm, Emma felt a chill race through her.

In the daylight, the rugged wild landscape of this country was to be admired. But at night, its beauty disappeared into the shadows, and it was then Emma felt the loneliest, the farthest from England. She brought an image to mind of the house that had been home to her family—Mother, Father, her brothers and sisters, and herself. There had been a lot of sad times in that house, but just as many happy ones, and she wished right now she could return to one of those. But wishes never changed anything. It wasn't her home anymore and could never be. She had to make a life here for herself and Daniel, and she wondered if it would be a happy one. Of all the feelings she'd experienced since being delivered to her uncle, true happiness had shown its face rarely, and Emma wondered if it would always be this way, or if this country had taken that from her forever.

Inside, the guests applauded the skill of the musicians as the melody came to an end, cheering as another piece began, hands clapping in time with the beat, the footsteps of the dancers heavy on the wood floor. Emma could hear laughter, and she smiled sadly. How could one feel so alone when near so many people?

A hand fell softly on her shoulder, and she jumped. But she didn't turn around straight away. There was only one person who would touch her like this. No other man here would dare be that forward, her attention gained by a name alone or a polite "Excuse me." A smile blossomed on her face, and she turned to face William. But it wasn't he who stood in front of her, and she backed away. "What are you doing here?"

"I'm a guest just as you are," Thomas Lang said. "I saw you out here, and I came to apologize for my behavior yesterday."

Emma looked toward the house. She could see a group of people just inside, smiling, laughing at something one of them said. She made a move toward the door. Lang stepped in front of her. She could see now that his eyes were glazed, and she could smell the alcohol on his breath as he spoke. "Truly. Emma, I mean it." He reached out and took her hand, raising it to his lips. She tried to snatch it back, but his grasp was strong. "I want us to be friends."

"Take your hands off her."

Emma looked beyond Lang. William stood behind him.

"Did you hear me, Lang?"

Lang's fingers loosened their grip on Emma's hand, and he turned to face the other man. "I heard. But I think it's up to Miss McLeod here, not you."

William took a step closer, Emma not missing that his hands were curled into fists at his side. The last thing she wanted was for William to become involved in a fight with a man not worth a second thought. She stepped between the two men, her attention on William. "William," she said, but he didn't look at her.

"Go inside, Emma."

"William, please, come inside with me. Please."

She had no idea what William could see on Lang's face, but his anger was rising. Emma pleaded with him again. "William, this isn't necessary. Please come inside. Please." She put a hand on his arm, could feel the muscle tense under his shirt. For a moment, his gaze dropped to meet hers. "Come inside. He's not worth it."

It took a moment for William to agree, but to Emma's relief he did, and he allowed her to lead him back into the house.

"He's not worth it, William," Emma repeated, looking up at him.

But William didn't look at Emma, his eyes firmly

on the doors they had just come through as if he was having second thoughts over Mr. Lang's worth. It was only his name being called that turned his attention away.

"Will."

Both Emma and William turned to look across the room to where a man Emma hadn't seen before was gesturing for William to join him. Emma assumed he wasn't a guest, judging by his disheveled appearance.

"Stay inside, please," William said, meeting her eyes for a moment, then, excusing himself, he strode across the room, and again Emma could do nothing but watch him go. He frowned as the stranger conveyed whatever message he had for William and, in unison, both men glanced in Emma's direction. She could only assume they were talking about her. Did this have something to do with Lang? She hoped not. She wanted the incident with that man to fade into the past. The discussion was over quickly, and William made his way through the partygoers to her uncle's side. He said something close to his ear, and her uncle's smile dropped. William glanced at her one more time, then turned away and disappeared into the entrance hall. She waited a minute or so to see if he would return, then excused her way through the crowd to her uncle. "Where did Mr. Rideout go?" she asked, not bothering to hide her need to know.

Her uncle smiled at her, but it was forced. "He had some business to attend to."

Emma felt a chill race down her spine. Had William told her uncle what had happened at Lang's home? Were William and this other man planning to visit with Lang, to demonstrate exactly how they felt about yesterday's event? She couldn't live with herself if William went to prison defending her honor. Emma searched the room for any sign of Lang. As much as he was the last person she wanted to see, at least she would know William wasn't carrying out his plan, if Lang was here. But he was nowhere to be seen.

"Are you feeling unwell, my darling?" her uncle asked.

Emma tried to smile. She was, but she wasn't prepared to explain the reason for it. "No, Uncle," she assured him. "I'm fine. A little hungry, perhaps. Where exactly was Mr. Rideout going?"

"Fremantle, I believe." Her uncle reached out and squeezed Emma's shoulder. "Don't fret, Emma. He'll be back tomorrow."

Emma had no choice but to comfort herself with the knowledge that William had gone in the opposite direction to Lang's property, if she was to believe what her uncle had said.

Her uncle turned the conversation to her hunger and the fine spread the Appletons had provided for their guests. Platters of steaming pies and pastries, sandwiches and canapes, bowls of fruit, and far more cake than should have been allowed in one place were laid out in a sumptuous display, and Emma followed her uncle and Martha to the table, grateful for the diversion.

She collared Daniel as he ran past. His shirt was untucked, and his knees were dusty. He smiled at her.

"This is a great party, Em."

"I hope you're behaving yourself."

The little boy nodded in reply. "Me and Angus are playing hide-and-seek with Simon and Matty."

"Angus and I," Emma said.

Daniel grinned. "You're not playing, Emma."

Emma laughed. "I will ignore that, Daniel. Have you eaten?" Clearly he had, since crumbs and a smear of jam decorated his shirt. She wondered what else the boy had devoured while the adults were distracted.

Daniel wriggled loose from his sister's grasp. "Can I go now, Em?" he said. "We've got to hide."

With Emma's permission and the warning to mind his manners, Daniel ran off after his new companions.

The rest of the evening passed slowly, although Emma knew she was the only one who perceived it that way. Everyone else seemed to be having a wonderful time.

She found herself spending most of her time glancing at the hallway, a fruitless exercise. William had left, and she knew he wouldn't be back. She declined the invitations to dance from her uncle and a few of the single men who seemed to vie for her attention.

Finally, guests began to say their goodbyes, a cue to her uncle that it was time for them to leave also. Martha looked exhausted, and Daniel too was clearly ready for bed. Thank-yous said, and farewells wished, Emma took Daniel's hand, and they went out into the night, their buggy waiting for them.

The journey home was quiet, fatigue dulling conversation, although Martha found the energy to tell Emma the highlights of her evening.

Emma smiled and nodded, pleased that Martha was so happy, but Emma's thoughts were elsewhere.

Chapter 21

The smell reached them first, not an unusual one. Fires were commonplace in the summer months, she'd been told, and caused a great deal of concern. But at this time of year when the ground was sodden, muddy pools forming at the base of any land that sloped even slightly down, the risk of fire was slim. "Can you smell that, Uncle?"

Emma couldn't see the movement of her uncle's head to confirm or deny that he could, but she did see him raise his arm, pointing along the road ahead of them.

The night was dark, the moon a waning crescent, so pointing out the orange glow that lit up what appeared to be half the sky was not necessary. Was it a distant bush fire that had found some fodder to give it life, or a bonfire, some sort of harvest festival? But the urgency in her uncle's voice as he urged the horses on sent a shiver through her. Something was wrong.

The few minutes it took for the horses to climb to the crest of the rise and round the bend seemed to take far longer than it should, trees blocking any view of the cause of this light show. But the reason was all too clear as they came out onto the lane that led to Eden Hill.

"Oh, my God!" Emma whispered, her hands pressed tightly over her mouth. Martha sitting alongside her echoed her words.

Robert pulled back on the reins, the horses coming

to an uneasy standstill silhouetted against the backdrop of flame. "Oh, my God," Emma whispered again, turning to her uncle. But he neither said anything nor moved. He just stared, his body stiff as if he'd been turned to stone.

Daniel had fallen asleep almost as soon as they left the Appletons' party, and his eyes held only confusion now as he woke to the sight of the fire. "Emma? What's happening?"

Emma hugged her little brother to her, unsure how to answer. She knew nothing more than what they could all see. Fire was devouring the barn, although it appeared the feast had been going on for some time, with little left now of the large structure. They could feel the heat even at this distance as it reached out to sear their skin, and Emma raised a hand to shield her eyes. Men, their identities masked by smoke and soot, ran back and forth, hurling water at the roaring flames, bucketful after bucketful. But they might as well be throwing thin air, so little difference did it make to the fire's appetite. The roof had gone before they arrived, the walls now skeletal remains of beams and bars barely visible through the flames. The contents of the barn were reduced to nothing.

The buggy bounced a little as her uncle came back to life, but still he said nothing as he climbed down, Martha's plea to be careful receiving no response. Emma took Martha's hand in hers, her other arm wrapped protectively around Daniel, and they watched as the barn disappeared, its blackened frame collapsing. As it fell, so did Robert, dropping first to his knees for a moment, then tipping over onto his side. Emma scrambled from the buggy, her dress hitched high as she ran to her uncle's side, kneeling beside him. She could hear Martha screaming out her husband's name, and Emma echoed the calls. "Uncle! Uncle Robert!" She shook his shoulder, calling his name again and again, but there was no response.

****

2022

"Sophie, wake up! Come on open those eyes. Sophie?"

Emma opened her eyes as asked. The face that looked back at her was comforting.

"You with me, Soph?"

Emma nodded.

"What's your name?"

Emma thought this a strange question but opened her mouth to answer anyway. "Emma…Sophie."

"Good girl, Soph. You want to sit up?"

The fog began to lift a little, and Sophie let Becca help her up. She felt a little dizzy, but that was all, physically. She could feel she'd been crying again, and her heart still pounded from the shock of seeing her uncle prone on the ground. She didn't know if he was dead.

"What happened, Sophie? Your pulse was all over the place, and you were getting a bit distressed there at the end."

"How long was I out?"

"Only about an hour. Here, have some water."

Sophie took the glass from her friend, her hands shaking as she put it to her mouth. She took a sip, then set the glass on the coffee table next to the diary. She blew her breath out loudly as if she'd just finished a race.

"Can you tell me what happened?"

Sophie recounted Emma's escape from Lang, her rescue by William Rideout. "She's in love with him,"

Sophie said, "and I'm pretty sure he's in love with her too, although he keeps backing away from it." She continued, telling Becca of her talk with Martha. "Lang is a real bastard. There's no doubt of that now. How Emma came to marry him is impossible to understand." She told Becca of the ball and her encounter again with Lang, William's warning to him, and then of the fire. "My... Emma's uncle just collapsed in front of me," Sophie said swiping at a tear.

"Oh, it's okay, Soph," Becca said wrapping her arm around Sophie's shoulder, pulling her close. "At least we know he doesn't die at this point. It says he dies in Fremantle."

Sophie nodded against her friend's shoulder.

"I'm so tired, Bec. I want to go to sleep and not dream of anything or anyone."

Bec agreed it was a good idea. "I'll stay here on the couch, in case you need me."

****

Sophie woke early the next morning, and as she'd hoped, she could remember nothing of any dreams she might have had. She felt refreshed and hungry. She could hear Becca moving around in the kitchen, and she climbed from bed.

She went into the kitchen, the smell of fresh coffee beckoning her. "Morning, Soph. You look a hundred times better than yesterday. Did you sleep okay?"

Sophie smiled. "I did. I feel almost normal. I hope the couch wasn't too uncomfortable for you."

Becca shook her head. "It was fine." She set a cup of steaming coffee on the counter in front of Sophie as Sophie pulled out a stool and sat down. It was Saturday, so there was no hurry to be anywhere, and Sophie relished this thought. She wrapped her hands around her mug. The sun was streaming in through the kitchen window, and she could see a willy wagtail bouncing along the fence line. She felt more relaxed than she had in days. She put that down to Becca knowing about the diary. But with that thought came the memory of what had happened last night when she was *away.* That was the only way she could think of it now.

As if reading her mind, Becca said, "Have you read *any* of the diary, Sophie?"

Sophie shook her head. "No, none at all. Why?"

Becca turned and retrieved the diary from the counter behind her, dropping it down in front of Sophie. "I read some this morning. There are some sad things in there. If I'm to believe you really are experiencing this person's life, then you've experienced some horrible things. But you're right about what you say about Emma feeling something for Mr. Rideout. In a positive way or not is still not clear. She says some harsh things about him. But even though she does seem to write about everyday events, like rescuing Daniel from the dam, the birth of the piglets and how you saved…"

"Meredith," Sophie interjected.

"Yeah, Meredith. She writes all about that, but there's no hint as to why she might be marrying Lang."

Sophie nodded and sipped at her coffee. In the bright light of day, sitting in her kitchen with its modern appliances and shiny countertops, Emma's life seemed a long way away. But Sophie was still so aware of it. She still felt it. She could also feel what Emma did for William. She wanted to hate him, and yes, he was all the things she'd written about him, but she was in love with him.

So why would she marry Lang?

"When was the last entry, Bec?" Sophie eyed the diary.

Becca slipped her hand into the sleeve and withdrew the book. She carefully opened it and turned the pages. "It seems she started to write a little about what Lang had done but then left that entry unfinished. She then wrote about going to the Harvest Ball."

"No mention of the fire?"

Becca shook her head. "No, nothing."

Sophie drained her coffee and put the cup down. "That's because I haven't written it yet."

Becca's expression of disbelief was almost comical, her eyes seeming to want to pop out of her head. "What?'

"Well, if I'm Emma, then I'm the author of these entries. As the fire has only just happened, then either I—that is, Emma, have stopped writing in the diary altogether, or I haven't written the entry yet."

"Are you serious? This diary was written over a hundred years ago. That's an insane thought."

Sophie laughed. "Yeah, because everything else that comes out of my mouth just lately is rational. But insane or not, I need to find out one way or the other."

The two women fell silent as they ate breakfast. Then, just as silently, they went into the sitting room.

Sophie took up her position on the couch and took the diary from her friend.

****

1865

Emma woke. She had managed a few hours' sleep in a chair brought up alongside her uncle's bed. Martha was still asleep beside her husband, both women within an arm's reach of the man, should he need them in the night. But he hadn't. Although he looked like he was just asleep, this sleep wasn't one that a person wakes from in the morning. Nor could the doctor say if her uncle would ever wake from it.

Martha stirred as Emma stood. She looked as bad as Emma felt, lines of worry etched into her face.

"Any change?"

Martha shook her head. "No," she said. "Nothing. He hasn't stirred in any way." She looked up at Emma, a plea in her eyes as if begging Emma to tell her all would be well.

But Emma couldn't, able only to go to the other woman, putting her hand lightly on her shoulder. "All we can do is hope, Martha." Emma knew her words offered little comfort, but there was nothing else to say. "I'll go and check on Daniel and put some water to boil. I will bring you some tea, and you really must try and eat something, too."

Martha nodded, but Emma didn't believe Martha would eat anything she brought for her. Still, she had to try.

Emma stepped out into the hall and stood for a moment, listening. A cock crowed far off in the distance, the announcement that it was time to rise carried on the morning breeze. This same breeze wafted the smell of burnt timber, seared wool, and charred apples into the kitchen, and Emma quickly drew the curtains across the window. The smell was enough. She didn't need a visual reminder of last night's events.

It had taken most of the night for the fire to be extinguished and the loss tallied, the latter more heartbreaking than time-consuming. It appeared everything had been lost. Emma had only been able to watch, helpless, unable to stop the inferno or help her uncle. She'd sat in the dirt, his head cradled in her lap until the doctor arrived. She was thankful Dr. Fenning had been an overnight guest at the Appletons' and arrived not an hour after her uncle's collapse. But there was little he could do, other than diagnose an attack of apoplexy, caused by the shock of the fire. How severe was the damage to the brain, he couldn't tell. All they could do was wait.

A chill had seeped into the kitchen, and Emma snapped some twigs, feeding them into the embers that glowed in the stove. One tiny flame licked at the dry sticks, the fire's appetite awakened. Another piece of kindling ignited, the flames dancing down its length, the heat setting the rest of the tinder alight, devouring it, the flames hungrier now.

She fed it more, thicker branches, and they crackled and blackened as the fire feasted upon them. She pulled a chair up in front of the fire and held out her hands, soaking up the heat that began to radiate into the room. She stared into the flames, mesmerized by the living, breathing force that hours ago had caused devastation and heartbreak.

Now the lively orange flames were the source of comfort. The only one, however, as far as Emma could see. Did her uncle have any insurance against this kind of terrible loss? His collapse led her to think there was no such thing.

Again, in the short time she'd been in this country, an overwhelming sense of desolation washed over her. The fire had taken everything. There would be no sale, there would be no way to repay the loan, they would no longer have a home. She stared into the flames, the branches nearly consumed, but she didn't move to add any more, there seeming no reason to keep warm, to eat, to breathe almost.

"Emma?"

Emma reluctantly dragged her eyes away from the flames and looked at her little brother. He stood in the doorway, his young eyes filled with anxiety, the same look she'd seen on his face the day baby Adam had died. She wanted to comfort him as she'd done then, but she could only look at him, having nothing to say to him other than the horrible truth. There was no one to rescue them this time. Their home was gone, their uncle's health was precarious, and Martha would lose the baby. There would be nothing to save them from a life of destitution.

"Emma?" The fear in his voice now was enough to drag her from the pit of black thoughts she'd fallen into. She sighed loudly and held out her arms. When Daniel crossed to her and climbed onto her lap, she hugged him close and told him what you always tell a child when the truth is too much to know. Everything was going to be fine.

She would make certain of it. There was no other choice. Emma pushed all other thoughts aside, locked them away, and made tea for Martha and herself, milk for Daniel. She encouraged Martha to eat a little bread and jam and to rest, reminding her that when her husband awoke, the last thing she needed was a scolding for not looking after herself and their child. Martha even managed a small smile and agreed.

The rest of the morning dragged, Emma busying herself as best she could. She tried to encourage Daniel to continue with his lesson, but neither of them could concentrate. She allowed him to go to his room to play.

For a while, she sat with Martha, but by late afternoon she could no longer stand hiding away in the house. It was pointless anyway, the smell of smoke in every room not allowing her for a moment to forget what was outside.

She went out onto the verandah, wishing immediately that she hadn't. But it wasn't the sight of what remained of the barn or the look of shock in the eyes of everyone she met that triggered this wish, it was the horse and rider that appeared from around the bend in the track.

For a fleeting moment, she thought it was William. She didn't know if he'd gotten word of the fire, not that it would make any difference to the shock if he had. There was no way to soften the blow that would come when he saw that nothing remained of the harvest, their future now just a pile of ash. Add to that the news of Robert, and it wasn't a homecoming she would wish on her worst enemy. But she longed to see him, with a tiny seed of hope that maybe everything hadn't been destroyed by flames.

But it wasn't William. Thomas Lang was the rider. She backed away to the door, Daniel colliding with the back of her legs.

"Is that William?" he asked, peering around her skirt.

"No, it's not. Now go inside, Daniel," Emma instructed. She turned and pushed Daniel back through the doorway. "Go and wash up for dinner."

Daniel went, protesting his reluctance at returning inside, but Emma ignored him and turned back to the unwelcome visitor. Lang had pulled his mount to a halt, tipping his hat in greeting. "Good afternoon, Miss

McLeod."

"What do you want?"

Lang looked toward the charred remains of the barn and shook his head. "I heard about the fire. And your uncle's collapse. It's a tragedy on both accounts. Any knowledge of how the fire started?"

Emma shook her head. She had wondered what it was that had caused the blaze, all care with open flames being uppermost in everyone's minds, especially since the harvest had been completed. But that was not a conversation she wanted to have with this man. If she never spoke to him again it would be a blessing. "If there's nothing else, I have dinner to prepare."

Lang's gaze drifted from the remains of the barn to look at her, and she saw a hint of anger in his eyes that she'd seen before. She was fully aware of her vulnerability, Martha and Daniel no deterrent if his anger became something more, and although Emma knew where her uncle kept his guns, she didn't know if they were loaded or how to load them if they were not. She just had to hope Lang wasn't aware that William was absent.

As if reading her mind, Lang asked, "Is Mr. Rideout around? I would like to speak with him. I owe him an apology for my behavior last night. And to yourself, of course."

There was no confusion in Emma's mind that what he said wasn't what his eyes told her, and Emma stepped back toward the door. "I will see if he's around," she said and went inside. She stood just out of view of Lang, although she could see him. She didn't want him coming in search of Mr. Rideout himself. But he didn't dismount, just stared off into the distance, his eyes squinted against the late afternoon sun.

Emma waited a long minute, then went back out onto the verandah.

"He's bathing," she said, holding Lang's inquisitive gaze.

"Is he?" Lang said, nodding, the skepticism in his voice not missed. But even though it was clear he didn't believe her, he said nothing to indicate that. "Well, if you could pass on my apologies, I will return tomorrow to speak with him and enquire after your uncle." Lang tugged on the reins, clicking his tongue, his horse following the command to turn back the way they had come.

Emma watched him ride away, then went inside, bolting the door behind her. She checked the lock on the French doors and the door from the kitchen to the rear garden. Satisfied the home was secured, she calmed herself with a few deep breaths. Lang was gone, and she should put him from her mind. Still, she would ask one of the farmworkers tomorrow to show her how to load a gun. Pushing that thought aside, she tried to focus on preparing the evening meal, although it seemed Daniel was the only one eager to eat.

Emma sat with him at the table, pleased to see the boy wolf down his bowl of soup, happy to provide seconds when he asked. She nibbled at a slice of bread, a spoonful of her broth almost too much to swallow. She hoped Martha was doing better. She'd been buoyed by the doctor's prognosis after his examination of her husband earlier that afternoon. He said her uncle was showing small signs of awareness. They could try him with a little broth if he woke further but to take care he didn't choke. Doctor Fenning warned, however, not to get her hopes too high. It was early days, but with complete rest and quiet over the next few months, a full recovery wasn't impossible.

With Daniel tucked in his bed, falling to sleep almost instantly, Emma checked to see if Martha needed anything, then wandered into the sitting room, dropping to sit in her uncle's chair. She prayed this piece of furniture wouldn't be the only thing she would have left of the man.

A memory drifted lazily across her mind, a happy one. She was about nine and was in the garden with her uncle. They had built a snowman, and Emma had taken her mother's best hat to top its icy head. She had planned to borrow it for just a moment to complete the snowman's ensemble, but a sudden gust of wind had blown it from the snowman's head and into the stream at the end of the street. They had chased after it, but it raced away in the current and was lost. Her mother had no idea and searched everywhere for the hat, and finally Uncle Robert bought her a new one, fearing the poor woman would go mad wondering where she'd left the missing one.

Emma smiled at the memory. They had laughed so much that day, but laughter happened a lot when Uncle Robert was involved. He always had treats and jokes, and it was from this chair he would tell her stories of his travels. She knew his stories were embroidered in places to be more exciting than they probably were, but she didn't care and would sit enthralled by the tales.

She felt a lump grow in her throat and pushed herself from the chair. She wasn't going to allow herself to cry. It wouldn't serve any purpose. She went into the hall, checking on Martha one last time, then turned to go to her room. But it was the sound that froze her where she stood—the distant thud of hooves hammering the ground at speed. Her first sickening thought was that Lang, full of drink, had decided to pay a late-night visit, but as the animal drew closer, she could hear it wasn't alone. Two sets of hooves echoed in the dark. Lang wouldn't come here accompanied, surely.

Emma left her lantern on the hall stand and went into the darkened sitting room to peer out into the night. Relief raced through her. The rider was William, another horse tethered to his own. Composing herself, fearing she would run headlong from the house and fling herself into his arms, she returned to the foyer and took the lantern from the table. She held it out in front of her as she unbolted the front door and stepped out onto the verandah. The candlelight was flimsy against the night, but the small glow was enough to see William's face as he looked at her from the saddle. He didn't need words to tell her that, despite the dark, he'd seen what little was left of the barn well enough.

"Robert?"

Emma nodded. "He's alive."

She saw relief flash across William's face before he looked again to the barn, slumping a little as if the enormity of what was lost landed on his shoulders. He urged his horse closer to the verandah. The other horse followed behind, both animals standing patiently as William slipped from the saddle and looped the reins over the railing. She held up the lantern as William loosened the buckles on the saddle of his mount and hoisted it to the ground. William then turned his attention to the other animal.

"How is Martha coping?" he asked.

Emma opened her mouth to reply but no words came from her mouth, a sudden realization slamming into her, rendering her mute. William had unbuckled the second saddle and was sliding it from the horse's back. For a moment, the lamplight illuminated the worn leather and, with complete clarity, she could see the three initials stamped on the side: E.A.M. Then she looked up, searching for the irregularly star-shaped flash on the horse's muzzle.

"Is that my father's horse?" She asked the question, but she was in no doubt who the animal belonged to. What she wanted to know was how Mr. Rideout had possession of it. Hope ignited in her mind, a tiny fragile flame that she struggled to keep alight. Was her father alive, maybe ill or injured, and William had offered to care for the animal until her father was well enough to return to them?

Hope or not, she knew that wasn't the truth, for wouldn't such wonderful news at least bring a smile to William's face? Wouldn't he want to tell her what she so wanted to hear despite the tragedy that had befallen them? Of course he would, she reasoned, but the look on the man's face conveyed none of this, and she knew instantly that there was one reason and one reason only that her father's horse was here. Her father was dead, and the little flame of hope wavered and died.

William looked up at her, his eyes now affirming what she knew to be true. "I'm truly sorry, Emma. There was an accident, a fall. He didn't suffer. I only wish I could…"

But Emma didn't wait to hear what he wished for. She placed the lantern on the railing and turned to the house. She heard William call her again, but she didn't stop, making her way along the dark hallway to her bedroom. Inside, she closed the door behind her, her room no better lit than the hall, and she fumbled for a match, her hands shaking. The fireplace was already laid, and she knelt in front of it, holding the lit match to the nest of straw that lay under the web of kindling. The flame tasted the fuel for a moment, then blossomed into an orange arc, creeping its way through the straw, finding its way finally to the tinder. Names flashed through her mind as each sliver of wood blackened, smoldered, succumbed to the flames. Her little brothers Adam, Edward and Samuel, her sisters, Eliza and Alice, Hannah, Annie, Susannah, her mother, and as the last twig turned to ash, Emma whispered, "Papa."

A victim of its own greed, the fire flickered, then died, plunging the room into darkness again. But she didn't care. There seemed to be nothing but darkness in her world.

"Emma." The sound of her name drew her eyes to the shadow that reared up on the wall, spawned from the flickering light of a lantern. William separated from the shadows and crouched down in front of her, his features distorted in the wavering candlelight. She studied his face, hoping to see something that would tell her she'd made a mistake, misheard what William had said, that her father wasn't dead, but the look of regret in his eyes remained. She sighed heavily. "I always knew he was dead, but I held onto that…that tiniest glimmer of hope."

William put his hand to her cheek. "Emma, I know. I wish I could have brought better news."

She covered his hand with her own. "My father would have said, 'If wishes were horses, then there would be a lot of horses.' " Her mouth twitched into a sad smile, a lone tear escaping her lashes and rolling lazily down her cheek. "What am I going to tell Daniel?" she breathed. "This will break his heart."

William sighed, the thought of breaking this news to Daniel seeming as terrible to him as it was for her. "He doesn't need to know until morning. It will make no difference to wait."

She nodded, silently agreeing to the decision, having no better one herself.

"Please, Emma, you're exhausted. You need to rest." William's hand slipped from her cheek, the warmth that it brought fading. He stood up, extending the same hand to her.

Emma looked up at him. If only rest could return her family to her, restore her uncle to health, repay the loan. But rest wouldn't realize any of those things. It just allowed more time to wonder how much more this land would take from her. Still, she allowed William to pull her from the floor. He guided her to one of the armchairs that faced the now-cold fireplace, draping around her shoulders a blanket snatched from the bed.

Then he turned his attention to the ash-filled grate and built a new nest of kindling for the flames to consume. She watched as he struck a match, the little finger of flame scurrying through the tinder, then igniting in a flash of light and warmth. He added some smaller logs, waiting for the flames to lick at the bark before positioning another, larger one that would keep the fire fed for a few hours.

He stood up and stared into the flames for a moment, then turned to her. "That should burn through the night."

She nodded and stared into the flames, wondering how he could read the amount of time left for the fire to live on the logs. Could you tell the same about a person? Was there a way to see if her uncle would see another dawn? Or Daniel? Could she see when she would lose him?

"Emma, you really must try to sleep. I will check on Daniel before I turn in, and if you need me in the night, I will be…" He nodded to her closed door as if that would be enough to finish the sentence.

"You were wrong, Will," she said, her gaze held by the flames that danced across the grate.

"Emma?"

"You were wrong. You told me that love, here in this colony, is only for books and daydreams, but you forgot to add that happiness, too, is only a fantasy. This is a place of death, where nothing good can survive." She glanced up at him for a moment, his features blurred through her tears. "Everything I treasure has been or will be taken from me, no matter how much I try to protect it."

He sighed loudly and crouched down in front of her. "No, Emma, you're wrong. Look at Martha, her baby. They're thriving here. Daniel too. That's because of you. Your strength has been enough, and they need you to go on being strong for them. You have people who love you, Emma, people who need you."

Somewhere at the back of her immobilized thoughts, she wondered if he was one of those people. Not that she believed she cared anymore if he was. She would only lose him too. But still, she asked the question. "Do you need me, William?"

"Emma, I…" He stood up. "I should go."

She wasn't surprised he didn't answer, and she felt neither angry nor sad. In truth, she didn't feel anything at all and wondered what difference it would make anyway. Whether he needed her or not was of no importance. There was to be no "happy ever after" for any of them.

This one realization was all it took for the wall she had so diligently crafted to crumble under the weight of everything she'd lost. She covered her mouth tightly with both hands as tears fell one after the other.

Taking her by her elbow, William pulled her upward. Silently he led her to her bed and drew her down to lie beside him, holding her as she cried, exhaustion finally pushing her into a dreamless sleep.

****

2022

"What happened, Sophie? You were crying. Again." Becca said, anxiety clear in her voice.

Sophie took the tissue Becca offered and wiped at her cheeks. "I know, Bec. I'm sorry. It was my father, Emma's father. He's dead. She always thought he was, but William just confirmed it." She sniffed.

"Oh, Sophie. I hate this. Whatever you're seeing or going to or whatever is happening, there's so much sadness. I don't think this is a good idea. Maybe you should stop."

Sophie sighed. Becca had a point. She'd never felt so much despair in her whole life as she had in the past few days, but she didn't know how to stop. These people were as real to her as Becca was. There was no logic in it, but she missed them and cared about what happened to them.

"Look," Becca continued, "tonight we're going out. That will give you a break from all this, at least, and then you can see how you feel tomorrow."

Sophie groaned silently. It wasn't so much that she'd forgotten agreeing to the date. She just was shocked it was still Saturday. She felt like days had passed since this morning. "Becca, I don't know if I'm up to going out tonight."

Becca stood up and extended her hand to Sophie. Sophie took it and allowed her friend to pull her to her feet. "Maybe not, but you're still going. So go and wash that pretty hair of yours, and I'll pick you out something to wear. You're going to do this for me, Soph. Okay?"

Sophie nodded and headed for the bathroom.

****

The date went as Sophie expected. Luke Farlow was as nice as Becca had said. He was a graphic designer, loved dogs and the beach, was easy to talk to and just as easy to look at. But there was no connection, no fluttering of butterflies in the stomach, no desire to invite him back to hers or want to see him again. He was just a nice guy, and Sophie made her excuses after the movie when a visit to the pub was suggested. She was tired, she said, had had a hectic week and needed to catch up on her sleep. It wasn't lies, to be fair.

She went straight to bed when she got home, a sleeping tablet guaranteeing she wouldn't lie awake thinking about Emma or trying to fight the temptation to visit her. Emma had been so sad when she'd left her, and she didn't want to return to that right now. She was drained.

She awoke the next morning feeling a little groggy, finding two cups of coffee and a cool shower necessary before she felt awake. She ate a quick breakfast, then grabbed her keys and phone.

Her car stood in the driveway. Becca's partner Mike

had rescued it, as promised, from its stay in the Family History Center car park. She unlocked it and slid into the driver's seat, opening Maps on her phone, typing in "Lang Hill Farm." She clicked directions and slotted the phone into the cradle on the dashboard.

Half an hour later, she reached the turnoff to Lang Hill and followed the single-lane road until she saw the sign: Lang Hill Farm. Here she turned into the long driveway that led to the house, a modern two-story home, a wide verandah shading the six long windows that interrupted the red brick walls.

She had rehearsed what she would say if the Sadlers were home. She was interested in their connection with the property and could she ask some questions about their family tree. But there was no reply to her knock on the door, and she turned to look across the fields to the dam below.

One hundred and fifty years had passed since she saw the vista as Emma had seen it, but little had changed. Fruit trees still lined up in neat rows, their ancestors the ones she had raced through in her attempt to save Daniel from the dam. The dam itself was still there, but it seemed bigger. A road dissected the fields that rose beyond the dam, the property split into two now, but sheep still grazed there.

Slowly she turned. Peeking out from the side of the Sadlers' home was a remnant of the home Emma had lived in, the home Sophie was in just yesterday, small in comparison to its modern neighbor. Now it was home only to ghosts, windows and doors boarded, entry restricted by metal fencing, signs hanging at intervals along it warning of the danger of entering the building. This was in stark contrast to the home Sophie knew. She knew every room in that house, knew how it smelt, how it sounded, how it felt, and she also knew the happiness that had happened inside those walls as well as the grief.

She looked beyond the house to where the remains of the barn had stood. A large steel shed now took its place. There was no pigpen, and Meredith was long gone, but a vegetable garden flourished where once Emma and a snake had had a standoff.

Taking a tissue from her pocket and wiping at a tear that rolled down her cheek, she thought maybe she shouldn't have come here, and she asked herself why she had. Had she hoped that seeing Lang Hill—or Eden Hill, as she knew it—would break this connection to the diary? Had she thought a dose of reality might shake her enough to put an end to the delusion, dreams, whatever they were?

But she knew the answer to those questions was...no. She just wanted to come home, to be with those she loved. But that home was long gone, as were those who had lived there. This thought overwhelmed her, and she hurried back to her car. It took a while before she gained control over her tears, replacing sorrow with anger that she'd allowed herself to come here, to lose all sense of reality because of a few dreams. "Enough now, Sophie," she said. "This has to stop."

Her phone buzzed in its holder, Becca's name appearing on the screen. Sophie let it ring out. It rang again and then a third time. She answered.

"Where are you?"

Sophie didn't hide the fact she'd gone for a drive, but she didn't say where. It would be too hard to explain. "I'll be home in half an hour, if you're looking to come over," Sophie assured her.

Becca's car was in the driveway when Sophie arrived, and Becca rose from the chair on the verandah as Sophie climbed from her car.

"Hey. I know it looks like I'm checking up on you, but yeah, it's how it looks. I'm checking up on you. You seemed preoccupied last night, so I was a bit worried. Considering the circumstances."

Sophie smiled and separated the house key on her keyring from the one for her car.

'So where have you been? Cat home?"

Sophie laughed. "No, just for a drive."

"Anywhere nice?"

Sophie climbed the three steps up to the verandah. Knowing her sunglasses were hiding the fact that she'd been crying, Sophie faced her friend. "No, just up past the inn. I haven't been out that way for ages. Wanted to see what was left of the pioneer village. There's an organic café up there."

"Did you stop in?"

Sophie shook her head. "No. Just looked."

Becca nodded. "Do you want to make me a coffee?"

Sophie knew the game being played. Becca didn't believe her and was hoping she could make her say more. Sophie was well aware that as soon as her sunglasses came off that would say enough.

Inside, Sophie went straight to the kitchen and flicked on the kettle. Then she turned to face her friend, her red-rimmed eyes not missed.

"What's going on, Sophie? Where did you go today? Now, if it was to see your secret lover—" Becca held her hands up—"then hey, tell me it's none of my business. Although you know I'll still want details, like why have you been crying?"

Sophie smiled. She wished she could tell her friend she'd spent her morning in the arms of a man. That would be received with enthusiasm. Saying you went to see the house where your other self's dead relatives, and the man you were in love with, once lived wouldn't be received in the same way. "I went to Lang Hill."

Becca nodded as if she'd known all along. "And the Sadlers made you cry?"

Sophie shook her head. "No. They weren't there, and I was glad about that, as it turns out. They would have thought me as mad as I feel. Some woman crying in their garden over a long-dead family that's not even mine? Grieving for a man I never knew? I thought if I went to see it today, it would help me realize that this isn't—wasn't—my life. It was Emma's." She wiped the back of her hand across her cheek, erasing a tear. "But it didn't work."

Becca sighed loudly. "Oh, Sophie. I know this diary thing is a big deal, but I think you need to take some time away from it. We have plenty of other stuff we need to get done at work, and we can see in a month or so if things are still the same. Maybe the fainting is just a psychological response of some sort to missing your family or being alone. I don't know, but Sophie, I'm worried about you. I'm really trying to support you with whatever is happening to you, but I'm starting to think this is way out of my depth. Maybe you need to give your parents a call. Maybe you're just missing them."

Sophie contemplated this theory. To be honest, she would entertain any hypothesis if it meant there might be a rational reason for her behavior. Her analytical mind began to search for evidence. Didn't these fainting episodes start around the time Becca was planning her wedding? Was she just lonely? Was she stuck in some sort of psychological void, unable to escape until she faced an emotional need she was hiding from herself? She turned back to the kettle, busying herself with making coffee for them both, her thoughts chaotic.

"Look, Mike's working tonight," Becca said. "He'll be glad for me to be out of the house for a bit so he can get some sleep. How about we get some takeaway for dinner and watch old movies tonight? Tomorrow is a public holiday, so we can go shopping and spend a lot of money on new clothes. We can always take them back when buyer's remorse sets in. What do you think? I'll buy you lunch," she added with a grin aimed at winning Sophie's vote.

Sophie smiled. She had to admit she didn't want to be alone and was grateful Becca had offered before she'd had to ask. "Okay. And thank you, Bec. I really appreciate what you're doing."

****

"You wanna watch *The Other Boleyn Girl* or *Fifth Element* next?" Becca called from the sitting room as Sophie refilled their wine glasses in the kitchen.

"You pick. I don't mind," Sophie replied, the glass of wine she'd downed with dinner leaving her relaxed and a little sleepy.

"Well, do you wanna see Bruce with his shirt off or Natalie with her head off?" Becca said, laughing loudly at her joke.

Sophie turned off the kitchen light and went back into the sitting room. Becca was curled up on the couch, and Sophie handed her a glass. "That's the last one for you, I think," Sophie said with a smile. She sat down next to her friend. "Let's watch poor Natalie."

Anne Boleyn's head was still firmly attached to her shoulders when Becca fell asleep, the second glass of wine and way too much Chinese takeaway putting her out cold.

Sophie slipped a cushion under Becca's head and covered her with the throw. She turned off the TV and stood up, Becca stretching out into the vacated space with a contented murmur.

Sophie went into her bedroom. Becca's company and the movies had been an effective diversion, but now she was alone, all Sophie had felt before came flooding back. She glanced at her backpack hanging from the back of the chair by the door. The diary was in there, a fact she'd kept from Becca.

Chapter 22

1865

Emma opened her eyes, listening to the house, trying to hear any sounds of movement inside or out in the yard. But there was silence except for the sound of a dog barking in the distance. The fireplace was cold, the logs having burnt out sometime in the night, and she stared into the ashes, trying to clear her head. But what came, as her mind cleared, tore at her heart. Her father was dead.

She rolled to her side. William had gone, and Emma felt the creeping presence of grief begin to engulf her. She would give in to it, let it drag her down into its depth and stay in that black place. She had no energy left to fight with, and what was the point of fighting it anyway?

"Emma! Emma! Emma!"

The sound of her young brother's excited voice derailed her dark thoughts, and with a flick of her arm, she threw back the covers and sat up as Daniel flung open the door and bounded into the room. "Father is here!"

Her brother may as well have struck her, his words having the same impact, and she struggled to find a response. But it was an inadequate one. "What?"

"Father is here," he said again, his eyes lit with excitement.

"Daniel, what do you mean? You...you've seen

him?" She knew it was a ridiculous question, but she held her breath as she waited for his answer, clinging to a fragment of hope that maybe last night had been a terrible nightmare.

He shook his head. "No. But his horse is here. And his saddle. So he must be with Uncle. I didn't want to disturb them." Daniel jumped onto her bed, bouncing up and down on his knees. "Get up, Emma. Come on. You won't get into trouble if you knock on the door. You're a grownup."

She breathed out in a long sigh, her absurd hope fading with it. Tears gathered in her eyes, not missed by her brother, a frown creasing his forehead. "What's wrong, Em?"

She took hold of his hands. "Daniel, my love, I need to tell you something."

This wasn't how she had planned to tell her brother about their father's passing, but then, she'd not had a plan at all. She'd allowed the thought that maybe she would never tell him, just let the months pass and the knowledge grow in his young mind that their father probably wasn't coming back. But it was a coward's way, and she wasn't a coward. Daniel cried as the words she said sank in, the reason why horse and saddle were here without their owner, and she held him in her arms, murmuring sounds of comfort as William had with her.

"Why does everyone die, Emma?" Daniel sobbed.

Emma smoothed his soft hair, stroking it behind his ear. "I know it feels that way, Daniel. And we have been dealt more than a fair share of sadness. But we have each other, and Uncle Robert will get better. I know it won't bring Father or Mama back, but we will still be a family, and we must be strong for Uncle and Martha and the new baby. You will need to be like a big brother to him, or her."

Daniel sniffed and nodded his head, tears shining in his eyes. "I can do that, Emma. I can be strong," he said with the determination only an eight-year-old could have, "and I will look after you as Will asked."

Emma's hand stilled, and she frowned. "What do you mean, Daniel? When did Will ask you to do that?"

Daniel swiped the back of his hand across one cheek. "This morning. I heard a noise outside and went out. William was saddling his horse. I asked where he was going, and he said he had to leave and for me to look after you." He squeezed Emma's hand. "I said I would."

Fear stirred in her belly, and she steadied her voice. "Did he say where he was going, or when he would be back?"

Daniel shook his head now. "He just rode away. That's when I saw Father's horse."

A tear tracked down the little boy's face, and Emma wrapped her arms around him. "I'm so sorry, my sweet," she whispered into his hair.

"William will come back, Emma, won't he?"

She didn't know what to say. She didn't know the answer to that question, nor did she know where William was to come back from.

****

Emma felt a little guilty agreeing that Daniel didn't have to eat all his carrots and cabbage. She felt the same as she allowed him to have a second and then a third helping of dessert. But seeing his smile outweighed the guilt. After dinner, She indulged Daniel again, allowing him to stay up an hour more than usual, and he disappeared into the sitting room, no doubt to search amongst Uncle Robert's small library for tales of adventure. He preferred books that had drawings of exotic animals like orangutans and rhinoceros or other creatures that stirred the imagination.

Emma washed the dishes, then tiptoed into the hallway. Through her uncle's closed door, she could hear the soft murmuring of Martha reading to her husband. This she'd done every day since his collapse.

Emma tapped lightly on the door, opening it as Martha called for her to come in. "How is he?"

Martha laid the book on her lap and smiled at her husband. He was asleep, although it was difficult to tell the difference between sleep and his short periods of wakefulness. He was yet to smile or utter a word, a few blinks the only clue that he could understand. As much as this was encouraging, the little nourishment he'd so far managed to take in wasn't enough to sustain a grown man, and Emma worried it would be starvation that took his life and not the stroke that felled him in the first place.

"He's doing well," Martha said, smiling now at Emma. "He took a little more broth than usual today, and some bread."

Emma smiled, somewhat comforted by this. "And you, Martha? Do you need anything?"

Martha shook her head. She'd eaten everything Emma had taken to her at dinner, and she'd cleaned the plate Emma had prepared for her for tea. Emma was satisfied that mother and baby were well nourished, at least, but she did worry that Martha might not be resting as much as she should.

"I can sit with him if you would like to rest. You're welcome to use my room."

Martha continued to smile, but there was an element

of sadness in it now. "I'm fine, Emma dear. Really. I feel well, and I do sleep here next to Robert when I need to. Please don't fret over us. You must look after yourself and Daniel."

The women stared at each other for a moment, a silent communication that Emma understood perfectly. All they had left was hope, and that was becoming thin on the ground.

"Everything will be fine, Martha," Emma whispered, wondering if things would ever be fine again. She knew Martha was thinking the same thing.

With nothing further to say, Emma wished Martha good night and went into the sitting room.

Daniel had fallen asleep, an atlas open next to him, his hand resting on a colorful map of Africa. Emma watched him for a moment, then crouched down beside him and shook him gently, waking him enough for him to walk. She guided him to his room and tucked him into bed. He smiled, murmuring something to someone only he could see. Emma hoped that whatever he was dreaming was wonderful, because dreams were maybe all that was left to them now.

Weary herself but knowing sleep wasn't going to come easily to her, Emma returned to the sitting room, dropping into her uncle's armchair, curling her legs underneath her. The house was silent. The fire she'd lit earlier still glowed warm, the trio of candles on the mantelpiece forming a small pool of light on the rug at the hearth.

The smell of burnt timber and fruit still lingered in the air. Although it wasn't an unpleasant odor, the reason for it wasn't forgotten, and despite her words of reassurance to Martha, all Emma felt was a creeping sense of hopelessness. William was gone. And for how long? Would he return tomorrow? The next day? Ever? Although she was willing to try to understand the reason for William's abandonment of them all, if that was what he'd done, she didn't believe he had.

Love was one thing he might run from to avoid losing it, but a sense of duty, responsibility, and loyalty was something not to be underestimated in William Rideout. He would never leave them to fend for themselves under the circumstances. He would return, that she was certain of. And until that time, she would do what she could to stay strong for Martha, Uncle Robert, and Daniel.

Chapter 23

Despite Emma's faith in William's loyalty, he didn't return that night or the next or the next, a week passing with no sign or news of his whereabouts. The days blended one into the other, punctuated only by the arrival of neighbors and friends inquiring after Robert's health. Emma made tea and offered cakes and sandwiches, glad for the distraction.

She tried to busy herself with the day-to-day necessities of life and made sure Martha, Uncle Robert, and Daniel were well looked after and the house was clean. But there was a sense of futility in the scrubbing and polishing. No matter how much the windows shone or how neatly the beds were made, without a miracle, this house would soon be someone else's home.

"William will return before then," she chided herself. "He'll find a way to save the property." But as each day passed, her conviction weakened, replaced by a familiar fear. She'd waited for her father to return. That had also been in vain.

The thud of hooves quickened her heart, and Emma dropped the plate she'd been washing into the basin of warm water and dried her hands on her apron. As each day passed, she hoped more and believed less that the sound of hooves would mean William had returned. Still, she allowed herself to believe again that it was William, and, in her mind, she watched as he dismounted his black horse and strode up the steps to the verandah. He would tell her that everything would be fine now.

But she knew her imaginings were a lie. Any arrivals at this house were all to enquire about her uncle's health. Despite this, she let hope lead her outside, disappointment greeting her yet again in the form of Thomas Lang.

"Good afternoon, Miss McLeod," Thomas said, sliding from the saddle of his mount. "I came to enquire after your uncle. Any improvement?"

Lang had come every day since her uncle took ill and asked the same question. And Emma gave the same reply. "No, there's no change."

Lang nodded at this news, then continued with the usual pleasantries. "And yourself, Miss McLeod. How are you coping?"

"Well enough, Mr. Lang. We are all well."

"Good, good. I'm glad to hear it."

Emma enquired now as to his health, as was the usual dance. He would reply that he was well, and that would be the end of it. He would climb up on his horse, wish her a good day, and—thankfully—ride away. Every day was the same, the exchanges between them polite and short, but it wasn't by want that Emma entered a conversation with this man. It was a necessity. To tell Lang what she really thought, to order him to leave the property, would only invite his anger, and it must be clear to him by now that she was alone out here with a pregnant woman and a child. So she remained polite, grateful that each day he left without incident. Today, however, something was a little different. He turned to his horse, but he made no move to climb into the saddle. A ripple of anxiety rolled through her. "There's something concerning me, Miss McLeod," he said, turning back to face her. "Something that has been on my mind for a time now. I was hoping that it was a subject that may not need addressing, but it appears it must."

She frowned. What subject did he refer to? Her assault on him? His assault on her? Did he wish to exact revenge, or complete what he'd not been able to? Anxiety grew to fear. Although he'd apologized to her the night of the ball, Emma believed it was anger he felt the most every time he looked at her, remorse not even given a passing thought. "And that would be, Mr. Lang?"

For a moment, he didn't look at her, his gaze surveying the land that sloped down into the orchard, to the dam and beyond. "What are your plans?"

Her frown deepened. Now she was confused. "Plans? For what?"

Lang's eyes drifted back to hers, but she could read nothing in them. Nothing to comfort her anyway.

"For your family?"

She shook her head, no closer to understanding his meaning than she had been a moment ago. "I don't know what you mean."

Emma felt as if she was being studied as Lang continued to stare at her, his eyes narrowing. "About the loan, Miss McLeod. Your uncle's payment. I assume you're aware of it."

She nodded. "I am."

"How do you plan to pay it?"

She was relieved the conversation wasn't going in the direction she feared. However, she didn't want to have this conversation with Thomas Lang, either.

Only last night Martha had broached the subject, one they had both avoided since the fire, pretending that everything was going to be fine, as Emma had assured her. But they were both aware that time was running out. Payment was to be made in two days, something Emma didn't want to think about, but Martha had been less reluctant. With no other facts to go on, she made it clear that William had either left them to fend for themselves or he'd met with an accident.

Both scenarios brought tears to Emma's eyes, but tears didn't change anything, and the harsh reality had to be faced. Soon they would be homeless. Every visitor since the fire and her uncle's collapse had offered their desire to help in any way, saying if there was anything they could do, Emma was to just ask. She didn't doubt the sincerity of the offers, but there was an unspoken clause. "Anything" didn't include the one thing they needed most of all—the sum of money required to secure their home. But Emma had asked anyway, knowing that most of those she asked were in the same position as her uncle and would only scrape through themselves. Few could afford to loan her the sum needed to save Eden Hill.

Except for Thomas Lang. It was common knowledge he had fared well financially after his second wife had died.

In the darkest hours of the night, when everything else slept, Emma had imagined this day, imagined the reality of asking Thomas Lang to loan her the money to save her uncle's property. She wondered what the cost of that would be, and this was where her imaginings ended. In the light of day, she had refused to believe it would ever become a reality, but it seemed daylight was wrong.

Pride screamed at her to tell him they would manage. But what good would pride do? It wouldn't protect them, keep them all from the street. Emma took a breath, loathing every word about to be spoken. Lang watched her closely as she did. "I don't know what I'm going to do, Mr. Lang. I have asked for help from others, but most, as you know, have nothing they can spare. I know things haven't been pleasant between us, and I wouldn't ask if it were not necessary, but I'm asking you now to put what has happened aside and assist us, perhaps? For my uncle's sake, if nothing else."

Lang had shown no emotion during her speech, but now he smiled. But it wasn't a smile of warmth, and Emma felt a chill stroke her neck. "Did I say something amusing, Mr. Lang?"

"I wouldn't say 'amusing,' Miss McLeod. naïve, possibly, or a little misguided."

Emma felt a tiny flame of anger and struggled to keep it out of her voice. She needed this man's help, and giving in to her temper wouldn't achieve that. "How so?"

Lang looked away from her and again surveyed the orchard and fields. "The loan office will open at eight o'clock on Monday morning, all debts to be finalized by the stroke of five that same day. Those that can't pay will lose their land. But you know this already, Miss McLeod." Lang's gaze drifted back to meet Emma's. "What you don't know, however, is that at eight o'clock Tuesday morning, any person with the necessary funds and a desire for new land will line up at the door of the land office and see what's on offer. I, Miss McLeod, will be the first in line and will pay the outstanding debt on your uncle's property."

Emma couldn't believe what she was hearing. Was this man really going to help them? "You will pay the loan, Mr. Lang? For my uncle? I don't know what to say.

I can only…"

Lang held up a hand, stopping Emma midsentence. "Miss McLeod, before you embarrass yourself with your outpouring of gratitude, I must correct you. Your belief in my generosity is misguided. I will be purchasing the land for myself. It's prime property. Many would love to get their hands on it. I, luckily, can afford to."

Emma shook her head. Surely, she hadn't heard correctly what this man had said. He was buying the land for himself? Taking away her uncle's livelihood, their home? He couldn't be as callous as that, surely.

"You're going to buy it for yourself?" she asked, in hope she had misinterpreted what he had said. She hadn't.

Lang nodded.

"But why? Why would you do such a thing? My uncle thought you a friend. You cannot take all he has worked for. Where do you expect us to go?"

Lang surveyed the property again. "That, Miss McLeod, is up to you. You will have to find somewhere else to live. And as much as I would like to say that this is just business and nothing personal, that would be a lie. Your uncle has taken a lot from me. I want something back."

Emma frowned. "What do you mean, taken from you?"

Lang nodded toward the house.

"What I mean, Miss McLeod, is Martha. She would have made a fine wife, and that baby she's carrying would have been mine. However, your uncle saw fit to take her from me. Taking his land will be small comfort but will have to suffice."

"Martha?" Emma spat, her anger flaring. "As I'm

aware, you took something from her, something that can never be replaced. She told me what you did. Leaving you was the best thing she could have done, and if my uncle has her love, that's your fault, not his."

Fury rolled across the man's face, and Emma steeled herself for his response, but he simply said, "Make payment or pack your bags."

Emma clenched her fingers tightly into her palms. "My uncle may not be able to fight for his home, Mr. Lang, but, I can assure you that Mr. Rideout is. This is his home as well, and he loves my uncle as if he were his own father. He won't allow you to take this land."

"Mr. Rideout? Is he back, then, Miss McLeod?" Lang's smirk indicated that he already knew the answer. "You clearly don't know the man as well as you think. Last I heard, he was seen boarding a ship in Fremantle. Only rumor, of course, but usually there's some truth in rumors. A man has to earn a living, and there's no future here."

Emma knew the shock of his revelation was written across her face, and she could do nothing to hide it.

"If I'm not mistaken," Lang continued, "I would think you feel something for Mr. Rideout. I hope for your sake that it's only affection you gave to the man and not anything else of greater value. The last thing you need is another mouth to feed."

It only took a step for Emma to close the gap between them, her hand arcing through the air, but it didn't connect with the man's face. Lang caught her arm midair.

"Let go of me," Emma spat, holding the man's stare. "And get off my uncle's property."

But Lang didn't release his grip, his other hand

rising, his fingers curling into her flesh at her throat, choking her. She had no choice but to stare up at him, terrified by what she saw. That he might squeeze the breath from her here and now showed clearly in his eyes.

She struggled to focus on his words as his fingers flexed. "If you ever attempt to strike me again, I assure you I won't hesitate in returning the gesture. And it's not something you would appreciate. This time I will leave as you have asked but think about this. If by five o'clock on Monday you haven't paid the loan, I will buy this land and you will have two choices—leave and find some means to support yourself and your family. I'm sure a beautiful young woman like yourself would be able to earn money quite quickly, or…"

At the edge of her vision, pinpricks of light blossomed like fireworks in a dark sky, and Emma wondered if she would even get to hear what her other choice might be. "…you can agree to marry me, and I will provide a home for your uncle and aunt as long as they need it." Lang held her gaze a moment longer, then uncurled his fingers from her throat.

Emma stumbled back, her hand rising to her neck as she gasped air into her lungs.

"I want an answer by Monday, Miss McLeod." Lang turned away and swung up into the saddle, urging his mount forward.

Emma stumbled to the verandah and dropped onto the step. She didn't cry. She was too shocked by what had just happened, and she was grateful for that, at least. She didn't want Daniel or Martha to see her tears or know about what had just taken place. Not yet anyway. But she knew it would be soon enough. As far as she could see, Lang's ultimatum was the only course of action left to her. Martha would have to be told, of course, but it could wait at least until tomorrow.

****

Emma took a breath and straightened her shoulders. It had been a long time since she had shared her thoughts, the pages of her diary filled with sadness and loss, anger and outrage, and she loathed to revisit that, so her diary and its bleak story had stayed closed and hidden away. But now she pulled the book from under a pile of folded handkerchiefs and untied the ribbon that held it closed. She moved the candlestick closer so light pooled on the blank page waiting for her words, then picked up the pen, wiping ink carefully from the nib.

My dearest friend,

The future of my brother and now my uncle, Martha, and the baby rests on me, and for them I would do anything for it to be a happy one. But to marry a man who has no hesitation in harming anyone who angers him, who has no restraint of that anger, then I can be assured that my future won't be of the same quality. And although I use the word 'choice' as if I'm not bound to marry Thomas Lang, I have no choice at all, as to leave Eden Hill would certainly kill my uncle and leave Daniel, Martha, and myself no future at all to speak of.

As for William...

The tears she'd struggled so hard to keep hidden after Lang's departure, as she prepared dinner, read to Daniel, and sat with Martha, finally appeared, dropping onto the page, and Emma closed the book, the sentence left unfinished. She didn't know how to finish it.

****

2022

"Sophie, can you hear me? Sophie, wake up."

298

Sophie's eyes fluttered open. She stared into the eyes she knew well, but she'd never seen anger in them as she could see now.

"I can't believe you, Sophie Harris! You agreed you wouldn't do this, then you go behind my back. All I hear is you making terrible sounds. I came through and I didn't know what was happening to you. You sounded like you couldn't breathe. I thought you were dying. Then I saw this!" She held up the diary.

Sophie pushed herself up and closed her eyes for a moment, waiting for the usual dizziness to pass. Her throat was sore, and she reached for the glass of water on her bedside table. She sipped at it, but her voice was hoarse as she spoke. "It was Lang. He had me by the throat," she said, as if the explanation was enough to win Becca's forgiveness.

"Really?" Becca laughed bitterly. "I can't say I blame him, Sophie. I could happily throttle you myself."

Sophie coughed, her voice clearing a little. "I know, Bec, and I'm so sorry, but Becca, I know why Emma married Lang. She doesn't know about the money. The cheque. She never knew it was there."

Becca's anger didn't lessen. "What are you talking about?"

Sophie took another sip of water. "You know—the cheque we found in the jacket. The one to Edward McLeod, Emma's father. It was from the sale of his business. Emma didn't know it was there. If she had, she would have used it to pay the outstanding debt on Eden Hill."

Becca shook her head. "I can't believe I'm going to ask this, but what debt?" Sophie realized then that Becca only knew snippets of Emma's story, bits Sophie had told her and bits that Becca herself had read in the diary. Sophie explained about the fire, what it had taken, and the cost to Emma. "So she has to marry him, or they'll be kicked off the land. Look in the diary, Becca. I have written it in there."

Becca held Sophie's gaze for a moment, then reached for the diary. She turned to what should have been a blank page.

"My dearest friend," she read aloud, *"The future of my brother and now my uncle, Martha, and the baby rests on me, and for them I would do anything for it to be a happy one. But to marry a man who has no hesitation in harming...*

Becca dropped the diary onto the bed as if it had burnt her. "Oh! This can't be," she protested. "We both know this entry wasn't here yesterday." She looked at Sophie with confusion, but fear was clear in her eyes also. "How did you do this? Please just tell me you have a fountain pen and ink hidden somewhere in this room and you are writing in the diary. Tell me this is all an elaborate hoax, Sophie. That I could accept."

Sophie shrugged. "I told you. Emma hadn't written it yet."

Becca rose from her seat next to Sophie and started to pace in front of Sophie's bed to the window and back. "You know, it's not that I didn't believe you. I could see something was happening to you, but secretly I was pretty sure they were just dreams." She nodded toward the diary, and Sophie didn't miss the anxiety on her face. "But I don't know what to think anymore, other than whatever is happening is not right. We need to lock this book away."

"Becca, I know. I don't understand it either, but I

can't stop now. I have to keep going."

Becca stopped her pacing and turned to look at Sophie. "Keep going? What are you talking about?"

Sophie clasped her hands together as if in prayer. "Becca, please, I have to. I have to at least try."

Becca threw her hands in the air. "Try what, for saints' sake?"

"Try to tell Emma about the money. Please, Bec."

Becca shook her head. "No, no, no! Soph, this is madness."

Sophie could only agree with her friend's assessment, but despite that, she had to go back. "Please, Becca, I have to, and I can't do it alone. One last time. Please."

Becca took a long breath in and let it out slowly. "Okay, Soph," she said after a moment, "let's just say I agree, and I'm not saying I do, how are you going to tell her? You only remember you're Sophie for a few seconds when you go back."

"I know."

"Then how are you going to do it?"

Sophie chewed at her lip. How indeed? "I'm just going to have to hope that something will trigger a memory. If I go back reciting something, like 'look in pocket' or 'father's jacket' or 'check jacket' or something, maybe that will be in Emma's memory too." She smiled weakly at her friend. "Who knows, Bec, maybe we've been doing this same thing over and over and will until we get it right. I can see their lives through the diary. There must be a reason. Maybe we've never been in the right place at the right time. I have to try. And if it's just all dreams and imaginings, then what does it matter? If it isn't, this may be the only way to end this.

Even if I were never to touch the diary again, it will always haunt me. Will you help me, Becca?"

Becca sighed loudly, and Sophie could see she'd won her case. "I'm not happy about this, Soph, I'm telling you now. This is the last time. I don't care what you say. When you come back this time, I will burn this book no matter if you manage to tell Emma or not. Deal?"

Sophie nodded. "Deal, but please don't bring me back unless you honestly think I'm in trouble. Not for tears or screams or…or anything like that. Only if that pulse thingy says something is really bad. Deal?"

Becca nodded. "Deal."

Chapter 24

1865

"Emma, you cannot marry that man!"

Emma sighed. "I have made my decision, Martha. There's no other choice."

"A choice, Emma? This is not your choosing, this is making a pact with the devil and walking through the gates of hell. I won't allow it. I won't."

Emma couldn't agree with the other woman more and wished that Martha forbidding her to go through with the marriage was all that was needed. But not going through with it wasn't an option she had. She'd tried to think of any other way she could save the property and her family but could think of nothing.

She turned to the doors. They were open to the verandah, framing the view of her uncle's property. She'd only been here a short while, but it was home to her and Daniel. More importantly, it was her uncle's home and that of his unborn child.

A shy breeze brushed her face, bringing a hint of rain. The sky, although blue, was bordered by a gray horizon. Another storm was on its way. In more ways than one, Emma thought.

She sighed and turned back to Martha. "Martha, if there was another way, I wouldn't entertain this idea for even a moment. You know that. But there's not. I have hinted, asked, even begged for someone to help us, but to no avail. We... I have no other choice."

Martha dropped onto the couch. "We will find somewhere else to live, then, Emma. We can find work."

This idea Emma had mulled over many times in the darkest hours when her mind painted a vivid picture of what she faced marrying Lang. But it was an idea that had no substance, made from fear and wishes. "Martha, even if we could find a home, we would need employment to afford the rent and for food. You cannot risk your health or that of your child doing the jobs that might be available to us. And even if you found employment suitable in your condition, when the child is born, you would have to leave to care for it. I don't want Daniel to live a life of just scraping by, living hand to mouth, and having no chance of a decent future. But foremost is Uncle Robert's health. The doctor is adamant that moving him could...would...be detrimental to his recovery. Here we have adequate shelter, food, water, security, everything Uncle needs to get better, everything to ensure your baby is born healthy and remains so. We cannot risk losing that." Emma looked down at her clasped hands. "We both know that leaving here is not an option."

"Maybe Mr. Rideout will..."

"Martha, please." Emma had tried hard to push thoughts of Mr. Rideout to the back of her mind. In her heart, she didn't believe William had abandoned them. But common sense also had an opinion. He'd never declared his love for her nor made any promise to be her savior. This debate left her with only two reasons for him not sending word of his whereabouts. Either he didn't care to or he was unable to, and both these notions were too unbearable to contemplate. They both did, however, lead to only one conclusion. "There's no one coming to save us, Martha. It's just us."

Martha nodded, resigned. 'I cannot tell you, Emma, how much this sickens me, and if I could change place with you, I would. If only Lang would meet with an accident."

Emma smiled sadly. That idea had entered her mind also, dismissed just as quickly. "I know, Martha. But then someone else would buy the property, and they may not be willing to let us keep our home. I need you to be strong for me. I can then at least take comfort that Daniel is loved and taken care of. He'll find it hard without me here all the time."

Martha sighed loudly. "I will, Emma, I promise. I will love him as my own."

"Emma, I'm sorry."

Emma looked up as her brother came into the room. Daniel had expressed his anger at Emma earlier for what she was about to do, shouting that he hated her. Then he'd burst into tears and run from the room. Emma had let him go. There was nothing she could say to him to make him understand there was no other choice. To Daniel, problems were just solved, and this time he believed this one would be too. He couldn't understand it would take marrying Thomas Lang for that to happen.

Emma held her arms out to him. "It's all right, my sweet. Where have you been?"

Daniel looked up at his sister. "In the shed. I go there to talk to Father's horse when I am sad." His face reddened a little. "It makes me feel better. I went there today, and I thought I would clean his saddle. You know how Papa always liked to keep…" For a moment, Emma thought Daniel was going to cry, but he wiped his eyes on his sleeve and continued. "Anyway, it made me think that maybe we could sell Father's horse, Emma. Would that get us enough money?"

Emma frowned. "What did you say?"

A look of regret flashed across the little boy's face. "I'm sorry, Emma, if I said something wrong. I just thought Father would want us to be safe, and I was thinking that maybe we could sell Father's horse and maybe Father's saddle. Would that get us enough money, Emma?"

Emma's frown deepened. There was something about what Daniel had said, but she couldn't work out what it was. "Say that again, Daniel."

Daniel looked confused by the request but did as he was asked. "Maybe we could sell Father's horse and his saddle."

"Father's horse, Father's saddle," Emma repeated slowly.

"Emma, are you all right?" Martha asked. She reached across the table and rested her hand on Emma's.

But Emma didn't hear the other woman's question or Daniel's second attempt to apologize. There was something she could hear in her own head. *Father's horse, Father's saddle, Father's horse, Father's saddle, Father's jacket... Father's jacket?* "Father's jacket," she said aloud, the chair scraping across the floor as she shoved it backward, rising to stand. "Father's jacket!"

She noted the look of confusion on both Daniel's and Martha's faces, but she didn't know how to explain why those words came from her mouth. She didn't know herself. "Daniel, where's Father's jacket?"

Daniel looked both puzzled and scared, and Emma

smiled at the boy. "Daniel, you haven't done anything wrong. I just need to know where Father's jacket is. The one you wore when we left the cottage. Do you know?"

Daniel nodded. "It's in the trunk in my room, Emma," he said warily.

Emma hated that Daniel looked so scared, and she took a breath. "Could you just get it for me, please?"

Daniel nodded again and trotted from the room.

"Emma, what is going on? Why do you want your father's jacket?"

Emma looked at Martha. She shrugged. She had no answer and hoped that seeing the piece of clothing would trigger some clue. But Daniel was back before Emma was forced to offer the woman a reason. She took the jacket from him and laid it on the table. She stared at it for a moment. No great revelation came to her.

"Emma? What are we looking for?"

Emma bit at her lip. Looking for? She didn't know, but if she were to look for something, where would she look? In the pockets. There were two outer pockets in the jacket, and Emma slipped her hand into each one. Empty. She opened the jacket, her fingers searching the one inside pocket. Again, she found nothing. For a moment she stood frozen, then her hands were moving, her palms sweeping back and forth across the jacket lining. She stopped. There was a lump in the fabric where one shouldn't be, a pocket, well hidden, just inside the seam where the back of the jacket joined the front.

She slipped her hand in and pulled out an envelope. It held a single piece of paper, and Emma slid it out. Her hand rose to her throat. "Oh, my God."

"What is it, Emma?" Daniel said, Martha echoing the little boy's words.

Emma turned to them. "A miracle."

"A miracle? What do you mean? What is it?" Martha said.

"It's a check, Martha. Made out to my father. I can only think it's the funds from the sale of his business. I didn't know he'd received the money."

"Is it enough to pay the loan?"

"I don't know." The piece of paper that had taken Emma's breath away was hidden back in its envelope. As it dawned on her what she was holding, she told Daniel to close and lock the doors, then draw the curtains over them. Still, she felt she was being watched and lowered her voice as she said, "Did Uncle Robert ever mention how much money was needed to finalize the debt?"

Martha shook her head. "He never really talked about those matters with me. He said it was boring."

Emma looked at Daniel, her eyes questioning. Maybe he'd overheard the men talking? But Daniel shook his head. Emma sighed. William would have known the answer to the question and if the cheque in her father's name was enough.

"Lang would know," Martha said sourly. "But he's the last we can ask."

Emma nodded. She swore Daniel to strict secrecy, cautioning him not to tell a living soul, human or animal, about this find. Not even Simon, although the boy hadn't been seen for days. Thomas Lang wasn't to know. There were only two days to finalize outstanding debts, and there was no way Lang was going to let Emma or anyone else meet that deadline.

Emma leaned back in her chair and sighed. "Well," she said after a moment of silence, "I will go to

Fremantle anyway and speak to the financiers. It may be enough."

"But that can only be on Monday. Lang will come Monday expecting your answer," Martha said. "What do we tell him? What will he do when he finds you're not here?"

Emma bit at her lip. There wasn't a chance Thomas Lang would miss his daily visits, his way of keeping an eye on his impending purchase, ready to thwart any last-minute plans they might have of saving Eden Hill. And he would especially not miss Monday, eager no doubt to hear her decision, as if she had a choice. "Tomorrow is Sunday," Emma said. "Lang will no doubt come and check on me tomorrow, so we will just have to hold out nerve for one day, give nothing away. I will leave early Monday morning. If all goes well, I can be back by midday. Lang doesn't visit until midafternoon."

"I will come with you, Em."

Emma shook her head. "No, Daniel, you must stay here. If Mr. Lang comes early, then it will be harder to explain both of us not being here. You can tell Mr. Lang I have gone to call on a sick friend."

Martha didn't look happy about the idea, and Emma was no less worried. But there was nothing else for it. This was their only chance.

My dearest friend,

I cannot describe the hope I feel. I don't know why I knew to look in my father's jacket. Maybe he's watching over us, but whatever the reason I'm beyond thankful. It's only my fear that's equal to the enormity of my gratitude.

There's a chance we can secure my uncle's property, and this requires me to ride to Fremantle, alone. But my fear is not only the danger of the journey, but if my journey is for nothing. We have no idea if this cheque will cover the loan or if it will even be accepted as payment at all. And if not, then fear becomes terror as my only option then is to marry Lang. I won't think of this now, however, and pray that never becomes a reality.

E.

****

Sunday passed like any other day, if anyone were to observe. Martha tended to her husband, Emma cooked and cleaned, and Lang paid his usual afternoon visit, his exchange with Emma cordial and short. He made no mention of yesterday's assault, offering no apology, showing no remorse. But Emma didn't expect either. He enquired about her uncle's health and that of Emma herself. She did the same in return and then he left, but not without reminding her that her deadline was tomorrow. She'd not forgotten.

Monday dawned bright and clear.

Emma hadn't slept well, nightmares waking her more than once during the night. But at least today the sun was shining, the storm clouds of yesterday gone to drop their deluge elsewhere. Emma decided to take this as a good omen. Daniel had saddled their father's horse, and Emma suddenly felt sick at the thought of riding the beast to Fremantle at speed. She had to get to Fremantle and back before Lang came to Eden. Could she do this? What if she were to fall or became lost? And even if she did make it in one piece, how did she find the office she needed? But her biggest concern of all was the cheque. Was it enough to make payment, and would it be accepted?

"You will be just fine, Emma," Daniel said, reading her mind. "Galaxy will look after you. Just hold tight and keep your feet firm in the stirrups."

Emma nodded. She could do that, she hoped.

"And don't go too fast."

Emma wanted to laugh at this bit of advice, sure in the knowledge that the horse would decide its own speed and direction, or if it was to go at all. She didn't think she'd have much say.

There had been a lot of debate about where the cheque should be carried, hidden on her father's horse—under the saddle, maybe—or carried on Emma's person. In the end, it was decided that if Emma and the horse were somehow separated, then the document was best to be with Emma. The envelope and its contents were tucked into a leather drawstring purse, which now hung from Emma's neck as valuable as any precious jewel. Emma hugged Martha and Daniel, reminding them that if Lang should show up before she returned, they were to say she was visiting a friend and would be back later. Then, with a jolt of her heels into the horse's belly, she set off along the lane.

Her first hurdle was to cross the road to Lang's property, her anxiety growing as she reached the fork. But she passed the turning without incident and tried to relax a little. Tucking the pouch inside her bodice, she urged the horse on a little faster, less fearful now as to whether the sound of its hooves would attract Lang's attention if he was nearby.

She rode for another ten or so minutes, settling into the rhythm of the animal that carried her. Gum trees lined the track on both sides, offering shade from the morning sun, long shadows a perfect camouflage for horse and rider. Emma rounded one bend, the track stretching out in front of her, and she urged the horse on a little faster still, the animal covering the distance quickly.

Then, without warning, as they approached the next bend, the animal slewed to the left, skidding to a stop. It reared up onto its back legs, squealing in fear. Emma had no choice other than to drop the reins and fling her arms around the horse's neck to save her from being thrown from the saddle.

"Whoa, whoa!" she called out, not knowing what else to say to the animal, hoping this would settle it. With a final snort, the horse quietened, and Emma felt for the reins, grasping them tightly. She closed her eyes for a moment, feeding long slow breaths into her lungs. When she opened them again, she could now see what had startled the animal.

"Simon?"

The boy emerged from the shadows.

"Simon, what are you doing out here? Mr. Lang will be looking…" Emma stopped and swung around in the saddle, frantically scanning the surrounding bushland. "Simon, are you here with your father?" she asked anxiously, looking back to the boy.

The scowl on his face and the aggressive shake of his head told Emma that he wasn't. She hoped he wasn't lying. "He said you had been gone for nearly a week. Is it because of the fire, Simon? Did you burn down the barn?"

Simon shook his head violently back and forth again, his mouth set into a firm line.

"What are you doing out here?"

Simon opened his mouth and for a moment Emma thought he was about to speak, but he just gestured she follow him and turned away.

Emma watched him go, unsure of what to do. Was this a trick? Was Lang waiting for her?

The boy went a little way along the track, then half turned to see if she was following. He gestured to her again. Still, she hesitated, and he turned fully to face her. He gestured again, his hands waved frantically, his expression one of pleading. He really wanted her to go with him.

Emma took a breath and let it out slowly. This was the way she had to go anyway, and if Lang already knew she was out here, he certainly wouldn't be shy about it. Emma urged the horse on.

Simon trotted on again, Emma following slowly behind. The bush was silent as they moved through it, Simon stopping where the track split into two, a thinner and less worn path winding off to the left. Emma could see no more than three feet in, the track almost concealed by scrubby bushes. The boy turned to her, pointing excitedly.

"You want us to go that way?"

Simon nodded and smiled, the first time Emma had ever seen him do so. But it was short lived, the smile dropping from his face, fear filling his eyes.

Emma opened her mouth to call out to him, but her words froze in her throat. She could now hear what had scared the boy, and she twisted around in her saddle. A rider rounded the bend, the hooves of the mount hammering the ground.

She glanced back to where Simon had stood, but he had disappeared into the shadows, his presence known only to her. Her horse grumbled and pawed at the ground as her nervousness passed to the animal. She knew she could neither outride the approaching rider nor hide from him. She tried to convince herself that her anxiety was unfounded, that the rider would pass her by, continue the journey to wherever it was he needed to be in such a hurry, and she would carry on with hers.

But as she pulled hard on the reins, her father's horse turning to clear the path, she knew she was wrong, her mind going blank with dread as the face of the rider became clear—Thomas Lang. She knew she'd been seen but she couldn't let him find what she carried. She urged her horse into the entrance of the second track, and then, pulling the cord over her head, she swung the purse into the scrub. She turned her animal and Lang appeared in front of her as she did, his horse snorting with exhaustion.

"Miss McLeod? Would you like to tell me what you're doing out here?"

Emma was surprised to see anger in the man's eyes. When did he come to believe she should inform him of her plans, even fictional ones? The words "none of your business" gathered on Emma's tongue, but she swallowed them, common sense assuring her that to anger this man further wasn't wise. Especially out here. Instead, she chose to avoid the question.

"I might ask you the same thing, Mr. Lang. Is it just an early morning ride you're taking, or are you on an errand?"

His smile didn't comfort her in any way, his eyes cold and dark, his answer causing the hairs on the back of her neck to prickle to attention. Her horse shifted under her, it seeming to be as eager to end this exchange as much as she was. "I'm riding to Fremantle to finalize my loan, Miss McLeod. It's a particularly important day, as you well know." He looked away, surveying the track ahead. "Although not for all, I'm afraid."

Emma had nothing to say to that.

Lang's gaze drifted back to meet her. "Anyway, I thought I would ride over to Eden and speak with you before my journey. I must say, I was surprised to find you were not there and had to wonder where you would be going so early."

Lang had been to Eden already. Had Martha or Daniel given him any cause to be suspicious? Emma felt as if a trap was closing around her. If Lang had any idea she'd outwitted him, found a way to save her uncle's property, Emma was certain he'd do anything to stop that from happening—leaving her dead in the bush was not beyond imagination.

Emma tried to order her thoughts. She had to remain calm. She had to believe that what she was about to tell this man was the truth.

"Well, if you must know," she said, adding a hint of annoyance to her words, "I'm going to visit with a friend."

Lang frowned.

"Martha and Daniel informed me of the same thing. Who would that be, exactly? They didn't seem to know."

They wouldn't, Emma thought. Even she didn't know, never expecting to be questioned over the topic. Her hands began to shake, and she gripped the reins more tightly.

"It's no one you would know, Mr. Lang."

Lang leant forward in his saddle, his eyes meeting hers. "Try me."

Emma could see the challenge in his eyes, and she knew he could see fear in hers. And she was scared, alone out here with this man. He'd been violent toward her twice now. If he were to catch her in a lie, she knew there would be a third time. She pulled her eyes away from him and looked back the way they had come. She prayed for someone to appear, be it bushranger or priest, she didn't care. But there was no one to see or hear, just the sound of a bird calling deep in the bush. Emma took a breath in and let it out slowly. She straightened her shoulders and looked at the man. "Mrs. Everett, if you need to know," Emma said, dragging the one name she could remember from the many women she'd met at the Appletons.

Lang's expression didn't change, and Emma felt a chill run down her spine. He knew something she didn't, something that would make what she said implausible if not impossible.

"Then I believe you're going in the wrong direction, Miss McLeod. The Everett property is beyond mine. This track leads to the Jacksons', as well as the Reynolds and McGregor properties, and if you had ridden long enough you would have been on the road to Fremantle. Are you not aware of where your friend lives?"

Emma groaned silently, forcing a smile onto her face. "I came to the same conclusion, Mr. Lang. I was turning back just as you rode up." Emma knew the man didn't know why, but he did know she was lying.

"Really? Well, it's fortunate I'm here. I will escort you to your friend's property."

Emma waved a hand in dismissal. "There's no need. I can manage, and I wouldn't want to divert you from your business. I'll be fine on my own."

"Oh, I insist, Miss McLeod. I have all day to attend to my business, and maybe, on the way, you might tell me what choice you've made regarding my proposal."

Anger displaced some of Emma's fear, but still she kept her tone even. "Choice? I don't think you gave me any choice, Mr. Lang. Marry you or be thrown out on the streets? Most would refer to those terms as blackmail."

Lang pushed out his bottom lip in feigned indignation. "Miss McLeod. You make me sound like such a monster."

Emma laughed bitterly. "Oh, not at all. I'm sure you only have my best interest at heart."

Lang smiled, but his cold eyes met hers. "I'm glad you understand. Now shall we go?"

Emma could almost hear the trap snap closed around her. She couldn't continue to the Everett property. She was a stranger to Mrs. Everett, and turning up on the doorstep at this time of the morning was certainly not going to prompt a warm welcome. Maybe she could convince Lang to leave her at the head of the track. If not, then she would feign illness and return home. Either way, she could wait for him to continue to Fremantle and then return to where she'd dropped the pouch. If she could find it, she still had time to ride to Fremantle before the deadline.

Putting her first idea to the test, Emma suggested Lang leave her to make her own way as they approached the track that led to Lang's property and Everton beyond. However, as expected, Lang wouldn't entertain the idea of her going on alone. This was a dangerous place for a woman, he reminded her. This left her the only other option, and she sighed loudly and raised a hand to her head. "To be honest, Mr. Lang, I think I will return home. I'm feeling unwell. I didn't imagine horse riding could be so tiring."

Lang showed no surprise at this change of plan. "You do look a bit pale, Miss McLeod. Maybe such an early start wasn't a good idea. Lead the way, if you will."

Having no other choice, Emma continued up the lane and brought her horse to a standstill in the forecourt of Eden Hill. She slid from the saddle. Daniel jumped from the verandah, throwing his arm tightly around her waist. She looked across at Martha. The woman looked pale and more than a little nervous, her eyes questioning, darting from Emma's gaze to Lang.

"I got lost, Martha," Emma said. "I didn't realize the Everetts were the other way. Luckily, Mr. Lang found me, and I decided to come home. I'm not feeling well." Emma forced a smile onto her face. "Thank you, Mr. Lang."

"My pleasure, Miss McLeod. It would be a tragedy if you were to have become lost."

Emma studied the man's face for a moment. His smile was as fake as her own, and there was something in his look that chilled her. He knew. Not the details, of course, but he knew she'd found a way of paying her uncle's debt. And now he was toying with her, as a cat would a mouse. And as she thought it, Lang's smile grew.

Emma tried to keep her voice steady "Well, thank you for rescuing me. I won't keep you any longer. I know you have business to attend to."

Lang nodded and swung from the saddle. "That's true, Miss McLeod. But may I trouble you for a glass of water before I continue? Daniel, be a good lad and bring me some, will you?"

This wasn't an innocent question—there had to be a reason behind his request. Emma just didn't know what it was, and that made her nervous. However, she could not refuse, having no cause to. Daniel still clung to her, and he looked at her, questioning. "Daniel, could you please get Mr. Lang some water."

Daniel nodded and dropped his arms from her. He ran inside, returning moments later with a mug of water. "Here you are, Mr. Lang," Daniel said, stopping in front of the man.

"Thank you, Daniel. You are a good boy," the man said, putting his hand on the boy's shoulder. "I think I would like for you to accompany me to Fremantle. Give us time to get to know each other. What do you think, Miss McLeod?"

Emma knew very well what she thought of the idea. Daniel was not going anywhere with this man. "No, I don't think so, Mr. Lang. He's far too young to go that distance. Come here, Daniel."

Lang took hold of the boy's arm. "Oh, I think he will be just fine, Miss McLeod. I'll return him to you safe and sound. I trust you will be here all day?"

"I said no. Now let him go," Emma demanded, crossing the distance quickly between Lang and herself. "Let him go *now*," she repeated. "You're hurting him."

"I don't want to go with you. Let me go," Daniel cried, pulling against the man's hand, his pointless attempt to free himself earning him a stinging slap across the head. "Be quiet."

Daniel's face drained of color, his eyes blinking rapidly from the shock of the blow.

"You bastard," Emma growled.

She spun on her heels and marched toward the house. Inside, she went into the sitting room, taking her uncle's shotgun from its mount on the wall. She'd followed up on her idea to learn to load the weapon, and she'd kept it so since. She went out onto the verandah, taking the steps down to the forecourt as one.

Martha saw her first. "Emma?"

Emma glanced at the other woman, but her focus was on Lang.

A smile grew on his face as he too caught sight of her and he raised one hand in appeasement, the other still gripping the boy. "Miss McLeod, I think you should put that down."

Emma lifted the gun to her shoulder.

Lang pulled Daniel in front of him. "Miss McLeod, you will hurt the boy."

Emma nodded and shifted her aim, the gun now pointing at Lang's horse. "The boy for the horse, Mr. Lang," Emma said. She could see uncertainty in the man's eyes, and she took great pleasure from that.

"Very well, Miss McLeod. You've made your point," Lang said and released his hold on Daniel.

"Go into the house, Daniel," Emma said, watching as the boy bolted across the yard and scrambled onto the verandah. His footsteps faded as he disappeared through the door. She turned her attention back to Lang, the man raising his hands in mock surrender.

"You can put the gun down now," he said, taking a step toward her. "I mean it. Put the…"

The recoil jolted her backward a step, her ears ringing from the blast, but she had no trouble hearing the howl of pain issuing from Thomas Lang's mouth. He stumbled backward, one hand raised to his shoulder. Blood blossomed on his shirtsleeve.

Emma hadn't planned to shoot Mr. Lang, and she certainly hadn't planned what to do if she had. But she had shot him and now wished she'd done a better job. The man was furious and still on his feet. It took no more than four strides for him to reach her, and he snatched the gun from her hand. "You stupid bitch, you shot me!" he snarled.

Emma saw the butt of the gun coming toward her, but it was too late to move.

Chapter 25

Emma couldn't bring herself to look in the mirror, to see herself in the yellowed gown that was her wedding dress. It had belonged to Lang's first wife, a woman twice the size of Emma and more than a few inches taller. It had been bundled in the back of a cupboard for years, obvious by its smell alone, and it hung from Emma like a sack. But that was the least of her concerns. In less than an hour, she was to marry Thomas Lang, and whether she was beautiful or not made no difference. She was more hostage than blushing bride, the discoloration on her jaw the proof of that. She didn't remember much of what happened after she'd pulled the trigger, the recoil of the gun stunning her. But she was grateful for that, not wanting to have the memory of yet another assault at the hands of the man she was about to marry.

What she did remember was waking on the verandah, a pillow under her head, a blanket over her. Martha and Daniel were staring down at her, and both had been crying.

She'd tried to smile, overjoyed to see Daniel was safe, but the action of moving her mouth was too painful, resulting in something more like a grimace than a smile. Her look of confusion brought an explanation from Martha. Lang had been enraged at her for shooting him. He'd hit her with the gun, then dumped her, unconscious, on the verandah. Neither Martha nor Daniel could take her any farther and could only make her comfortable. Lang had left, nursing his shoulder.

"He was in a lot of pain," Martha had told her with satisfaction, "but not enough, as far as I'm concerned." Tears welled in her eyes. "He said you wouldn't be going anywhere now, and if you didn't die, he would be back in the morning to marry you."

As shocking as it was to hear what Lang's parting words had been, the realization that it was dusk was far worse. Time to pay the debt had long passed, and any hope of not becoming Mrs. Thomas Lang was gone.

The next morning, as promised, Lang arrived, wedding dress in hand. He was pleased, he told her, that she'd not died, but said nothing more about the incident, nor the purple bruise that had blossomed on her jaw. Emma in return made no mention of the wound to his shoulder, something that didn't seem to bother him a great deal now. No doubt the pain was lessened by analgesic properties of the alcohol she could smell clearly on his breath.

The ceremony was to take place in her uncle's house, a final insult, but Emma reminded herself that her uncle, Martha, and Daniel would at least have a roof over their heads. She had it in writing. But as much as she took solace from that, she also knew her life was never going to be the same. She was to live with Lang, Daniel to stay with Martha, although she could visit as much as she liked, Lang had assured her. But Emma knew that even if she were to spend twenty-three hours and fifty-nine minutes a day with Daniel, it wouldn't be enough to erase the one minute she'd have to spend with Lang.

For one short frivolous moment, Emma allowed herself to think it was William waiting to make her his wife. But as it was, with these kinds of thoughts, they only brought misery. This wedding was happening, and that could mean only one thing: William was gone.

And that thought took her breath away.

Emma wiped her eyes with the corner of her sleeve, and without a glance in the mirror, she left her room for the last time.

In the sitting room, Martha sat on the couch, her arm wrapped around Daniel's shoulders. Both had been crying, but Emma had nothing left to console them with. She just glanced at them, then turned to look at her husband-to-be. He was leaning against the mantel, a fat cigar pinched between his fingers. Once she'd thought him handsome, but now the sight of him repulsed her as if the cruelty that lived in his soul had physically disfigured him into the monster that now stood before her. He smiled as he caught sight of her and raised his glass. Emma didn't acknowledge him in any way, looking past him to the priest.

Father Ryan was a small man in all ways, short and thin. Emma didn't know if he'd been paid or coerced to perform this wedding ceremony or if he was a priest at all.

"You look lovely, my dear," Lang said, but it wasn't with the affection of a lover, more that of a lion about to devour its prey. "Let's begin, shall we?"

Emma imagined this was what it was like to take those final steps to the gallows. She too prayed for salvation as she took her first step. But death wasn't going to give her a quick end. What she was facing she couldn't bear to think of.

She stopped in front of the priest and stared straight ahead. Lang came to stand alongside her and took her hand. She wanted to snatch it away but hoped the loathing she felt for him would pass from her hand to his. She wondered if this was how his other brides had felt or if they'd had some affection for this man, something she couldn't even imagine.

Lang made a rolling motion with his free hand instructing the priest to begin.

The little man straightened and opened the volume he held, finding a marked page. "Dearly beloved…"

"Wait." Martha stood up. "You must have two witnesses or you cannot continue."

The priest looked a little surprised by this revelation but nodded his agreement. "That's true," he said eagerly.

Emma began to think the clergyman didn't want to be part of this any more than she did.

Lang sighed in frustration but didn't insist that the other man continue. Instead, he pulled a watch from his pocket and glanced at it. "Very well," he said. "My man will be here shortly with the deeds to this property. I'm sure he and Mrs. McLeod here will suffice."

Emma pulled her hand free from Lang's and smiled weakly at Martha, glad for the reprieve no matter how short it was to be.

In silence they waited, no one having anything to say that hadn't already been said. It wasn't long before the thud of hooves told them a rider was coming along the track.

Lang rubbed his hands together. "That will be him now," he said to no one in particular, his eyes on the door.

A single thud denoted the rider had dismounted, wood creaking as the steps to the verandah were negotiated, footsteps marking a path from the front door to the sitting room. Emma didn't bother to look. She didn't know who Lang's "man" was, nor did she care.

"What are you doing here?"

Emma was slow to react to Lang's words, and it took her a moment to realize that whoever he was talking to wasn't who he'd expected. Emma's gaze travelled to the door.

"Simon?"

"Where have you been, boy? I have been looking for you for days. Come here."

But Simon had no intention of obeying Lang and stood his ground.

"I said, 'Come here, boy.' " It took Lang only a few strides to close the gap between himself and the child. Simon made no noise as Lang grabbed him by the arm and swung him into the room, the boy falling and sliding into the wall. Then Lang was on him and pulled him to his feet by his shirt. "Get up, you little bastard. You're a cretin just as your mother was."

Simon regained his footing and shook Lang free, staring up at the man, his eyes narrowed, a growl rumbling from the boy's throat as he sank his teeth into Lang's forearm. Lang yelped, batting Simon away with his free arm, sending the boy again to the floor. "I should have killed you along with your mother," he roared, as Simon scrambled backward across the floorboards.

A collective gasp from the room froze Lang in place, the realization of what he'd just revealed dawning on him. He turned slowly, looking at each person in the room in turn, and it was clear what he was saying without a word being spoken. Their silence on his utterance was expected or a price would be payable. "Miss McLeod. I believe we shall resume the ceremony now."

"The witness is still not here," she whispered, knowing this card had already been played.

Taking hold of her arm, Lang dragged her to stand in front of the visibly shaken priest. "Damn the witnesses," he said. "We will marry now!"

The clergyman's voice shook as he spoke. "Dearly beloved…"

Emma didn't listen as the priest rattled off the rules and regulations of the marriage contract. She was just glad her uncle couldn't witness this.

"Emma Rose McLeod, do you take Thomas Montgomery Lang to be your wedded husband? Do you promise to…"

A tap on her hand drew Emma's gaze from the painting above the mantel, a peaceful scene of sheep grazing in a meadow. She looked down to see Simon had crawled across the floor and was now crouched beside her, hidden from Lang's view by the voluminous fabric of Emma's wedding sack. He pushed a folded piece of paper into her hand.

"…honor and obey…"

Emma frowned and unfolded the note with her fingers, her action hidden in the folds of material that hung from her.

"…in sickness and health…"

She glanced down to see what if anything was on this paper that Simon so urgently wanted her to have.

"…to death do you part."

She read *Certificate of Title*

"Miss McLeod?"

Property of Misters Robert J. McLeod & Edward A. McLeod.

"Miss McLeod?"

327

Full ownership of Eden Hill. Free and clear of all debt.

"Emma, for God's sake answer the man."

Emma pulled her eyes away from the most important piece of paper she'd ever held in her hand and looked into Thomas Lang's eyes. "Oh, my apologies, Mr. Lang." To the priest, she said. "No, I don't. Not to any of it."

Lang's confusion turned rapidly to anger. "What are you talking about?" His attention was drawn to the piece of paper in Emma's hand. "What's that? Give that to me." He snatched the paper from her hand.

"No, give it back." Emma grabbed at his arm, but it made no difference as Lang caught hold of her with his other hand. "How did you get this?"

"Simon gave it to her."

Emma's eyes darted to the woman standing in the sitting room doorway. She was dressed in a somber gown, but there were still enough jewels and ruffles for the average woman to wear this gown to a Royal Gala without anyone questioning its suitability.

"Maggie Swanson," Lang said slowly, his displeasure at this woman's arrival not hidden.

"Sorry to interrupt your nuptials, Thomas."

"More a freak show, I would say, Miss Swanson. First an imbecile and now a whore are amongst my guests. If Robert were here, we could add a cripple."

"How dare you," Emma hissed, struggling to free herself from Lang's grip, but his fingers only tightened. "Let go of me! You're hurting me."

"Oh, this is nothing, Miss McLeod, compared to what comes later if you don't stop this ridiculous farce," Lang growled.

Emma could see that not only was the threat he made real, but he was looking forward to carrying it out. "You're correct, Mr. Lang. This wedding is a farce, and one in which I no longer need to take part."

"Because of this?" Lang laughed. "This is a forgery. A fake. I own this land. And I own you, Miss McLeod."

"I think you will find you're wrong, Thomas," Maggie said from the doorway.

"And why is that?" Lang said turning to her.

Maggie came into the room. "Well, for one, I distinctly heard Miss McLeod here say a resounding no to being your wife. Isn't that right, Father?"

All eyes turned to the priest. He seemed to have come down with a fever, sweat beading on his brow. "Yes...I...I would have to...to agree," he stammered. "The...the young lady didn't agree to...to the marriage."

"Rubbish," Lang blustered. "Unless she wants me to put her family off my land, I think she may reconsider."

"Well, that's where you're wrong again, Thomas. The document is genuine. This is Robert McLeod's land. Paid for in full by Robert and his brother Edward McLeod. You are trespassing, it would seem."

Lang looked back at the document in his hand. He was silent for a long moment. Finally, he shook his head, then sighed loudly, seeming to accept his defeat. "Well, it seems you win, Miss McLeod. Well done. I can't say I'm not disappointed that we won't have our wedding night." He let go of her arm and bowed theatrically. "I will take my leave of you all."

"Where do you intend to go?" Maggie asked.

"Go? Home. What do you care?"

"But Thomas, you don't have a home."

Confusion washed over the man's face. Although he

spoke with derision, his eyes exposed a measure of uncertainty. "What are you talking about?"

"Tell me, Thomas, did you send your man, Ned Tanner, to Fremantle yesterday to finalize your debt?"

Lang's frown deepened. "Ned? That idiot. Yes."

Maggie shook her head. "Well, I'm afraid your idiot, as you refer to him, was offered an opportunity he couldn't turn down. Maybe if you had been more generous to your employees, he may have thought twice about it, but it seems he only needed the one thought. Your property belongs to me."

Emma's mouth dropped open, and she watched as Lang's face first reddened, then deepened into an alarming shade of purple. He was silent for a moment, seeming to not even breathe, and Emma wondered if the man's heart had stopped. But suddenly, with a roar, he grabbed Emma by the waist, hurling her away from him, clearing his path to Maggie. Emma slammed into the priest, both crashing to the floor. Emma turned to see Lang rush at Maggie, but suddenly he was falling, arms flailing as he too went down. Simon crawled from under the man, and Emma saw the boy smile for a second time.

Emma untangled herself from the priest and the folds of her ridiculous dress and helped the winded clergyman into a chair. It took a while for Lang to clamber to his feet. But he made no further move toward Maggie. Emma wasn't sure if it was an injury that stopped him or the pistol that Maggie held in her hand. The deadly piece of steel should have looked completely out of place with the powder-blue gown the woman wore, but somehow Maggie made it look as natural as carrying a purse.

Lang looked around the room, all eyes on him,

before he stumbled to a chair and fell into it. He sat almost frozen, his eyes closed, and it was a few moments before he spoke. His voice a little above a whisper, he asked, "Is this payback, Maggie, for…for…well, we both know what."

Maggie looked at the man, her eyes darkening as if she too was remembering. "Yes, we do both know, but no, this is for something far worse. I warned you never to hurt me again, Thomas. But you obviously didn't listen."

Lang looked up at her, puzzled. "I don't know what you mean. I've been nowhere near you."

"Yet still you hurt me. You shot my son, and that's far more painful than any beating you've given me."

Lang's frown deepened. "I—I don't know what you're talking about. I didn't even know you had a son."

"Maybe not, Mr. Lang, but when you shoot a man, you can be certain he's someone's son. Don't you agree?"

Lang was silent for a moment, his head bowed, his brow furrowed in thought. Then he looked up, realization growing on his face. "William Rideout?"

Emma gasped at Lang's words and turned to Maggie, her heart stopping as the woman nodded, confirming what Lang said to be true.

William was dead. Thomas Lang had killed him, and a rage unlike anything Emma had known before grew inside her. Emma knew this man in front of her would always be a danger to her family and someone had to put him down as they would any dangerous animal. So for the sake of Martha, Simon, Maggie, William, herself, and any other poor soul that had been a victim of the man's cruelty, it was up to her to make sure he couldn't harm anyone again.

It took only two strides for Emma to reach Maggie's side, a questioning frown creasing the woman's brow as Emma approached. But Emma had no intention of explaining herself. She reached out, snatched the gun from Maggie's hand, and swung around to face Lang. It pleased her to see the fear on his face as she pointed the gun at him.

Lang rose from his seat. "Really, Miss McLeod? Do you plan on shooting me? Again?"

Loathing to voice them not twenty minutes ago, she was more than happy to say the words to him now. She smiled a little, aware of the irony. "I do." She took a step toward the man. "I'm going to do what someone should have done a long time ago. The world will be a better place for it."

Lang snorted. "You actually think you can hit something vital this time?"

Emma took a step closer. "I plan to keep trying until I do."

"In front of all these witnesses?"

Emma shrugged one shoulder. "I don't see anyone here, Mr. Lang." But she could hear them, Daniel calling her name, Martha too, Maggie pleading with her to put down the gun. Other sounds filtered into her consciousness—a dog barking in the distance, the clink of a bridle, the soft grumble of a horse, uneven footsteps across the verandah. But none of this mattered to her.

She took another step.

"Emma? Put the gun down."

The words were whispered close to her ear, the speaker's breath warm on her neck, and it was a voice she knew. Emma knew this could mean only one thing.

When Emma was a little girl, she remembered people whispering about an old woman in their town that had gone mad. They spoke of how the poor soul heard voices and saw things that weren't there. When Emma asked her father what people meant, he'd explained to her that something terrible had happened to the woman and her mind had broken, that what she saw and what she heard were just imaginings, even though to her they seemed real.

Emma didn't understand then, but she understood perfectly now. She'd gone mad just like the old woman, not surprisingly after all she'd lost, all that had happened. The fact that her broken mind had conjured the voice of William Rideout didn't surprise her either. She loved him and now he was gone.

"Emma," the voice whispered again, commanding this time. "Put the gun down."

A hand slid along her outstretched arm, meeting her hand. The hand was warm and a particularly convincing imagined version of William's, but she couldn't let her delusions stop her from what she needed to do. She had to kill Thomas Lang. Her finger squeezed against the trigger as her hand was pushed downward, the bullet spearing into the floor at her feet.

The sound of the discharge was enough to rattle the windows and pull gasps of terror from those around her. It also pulled Emma from the trance she seemed to have fallen into, and slowly she turned to face the owner of the voice. She was a little surprised now to find that she'd not only conjured William's voice but the man himself.

Chapter 26

Emma opened her eyes. She had no recollection of how or why she was now prone on the settee. Long shadows cast across the floor suggested it was late afternoon, with magpies singing their last melodies for the day and a willy wagtail offering its own sweet song.

A gentle breeze teased the curtains at the French doors that opened onto the verandah, where the deep Scottish rumble of Doctor Fenning's voice drew her attention.

"From what I hear, the poor wee lass has had a hell of a time. It's not surprising at all that she went down as she did. But she'll be well enough after some rest. No more surprises, mind. Not until she's back on her feet. As for you, I think the leg is healing well. This Mama Maali or whatever the lad Simon kens her to be, has saved your life. I would have liked you to have stayed off it for a day or two more, but I think you'll heal right enough."

Emma had to assume she was the "poor wee lass" the doctor referred to, but who owned the leg that was healing well? And who was Mama Maali, and whoever she was, how did the silent Simon convey that piece of information to Doctor Fenning?

Emma pushed the blanket aside, fully intending to find out the answers to these questions, but the sight of the dress she wore let loose a flood of memories—Lang, the priest, the vows. There were some blank spots in her recall, she had to admit, but there was no hiding from the dreadful realization that she was Mrs. Thomas Lang, that thought as painful as if she had been beaten, and she groaned.

The sound of chair legs scraping across the floor came from outside, the curtains at the French doors were pushed aside, and Emma looked up.

"You're awake."

Now other memories began to fill the gaps—Simon, the deed, Maggie, the gun, and this man who stood in front of her. William. Emma closed her eyes for a moment, then opened them. "I'm not imagining you?"

William shook his head. He sat down beside her.

She stared at him silently for a long moment, then flung her arms around his neck.

"I thought you were dead," she whispered into his shoulder, the words too ugly to be said aloud.

She felt him nod. "I know. I'm so sorry I scared you, Emma. But in truth, if it weren't for Simon, I may well have been."

Emma pulled back to look at him. She frowned, "Simon?"

As if he had been waiting in the wings for his cue, the boy pushed through the curtains. William gestured for him to come closer. "It's a long story, and one he best tells. He knows it better than me."

Emma imagined the boy could communicate through gestures and mime, but she didn't know if she was up for a lengthy game of charades. Emma opened her mouth to say so, but Simon spoke first.

"I took him to Mama Maali," Simon said, his voice clear and strong.

If anyone was to be accused of being mute, it would have to be Emma. She recalled Doctor Fenning saying she was to have no more surprises. Obviously, no one had listened. But as shocked as she was to hear the boy speak, she kept to herself any questions about this sudden gift and waited for him to say more. And he did, the words flowing easily from his mouth, Emma now noting the soft French accent. The nationality of the boy had never been a question in her mind. Emma had assumed his mother was English.

"I was in the stables at the top of the lane. I have been hiding there since the fire. Lang knew I saw him set it, and I knew he would never let me tell anyone, if he got hold of me." His brown eyes darkened with hatred. "I heard a horse come along the track from your uncle's property, and I looked out to see who it was. I saw William, and he was talking to Lang. I couldn't hear what was said, but William looked angry. I saw William turn to ride away, and I saw Lang shoot him."

Emma turned to look at William for a moment but said nothing.

"Mr. Lang rode away, but Mr. Rideout just lay there on the ground where he'd fallen from his horse. He has always been kind to me, and I was so scared he was dead. There was a lot of blood. But when I got closer, he made a noise. I tried to lift him, but I couldn't. So I dragged him into a bush to hide him, in case Lang came back, and then I went for help. Mama Maali sent two men back with me and we took him to their camp."

Emma opened her mouth. She wanted to know who these people were and how the boy knew them, but that could wait, and she nodded to Simon to continue.

"I wanted to tell you he was there," Simon said, "but

when I told Will, he said it was too dangerous and he would be able to ride to see you in a few days. But he got worse, a fever, and Mama Maali gave him medicine. It made him sleep most of the time. So I waited. Then I saw you on the track that day, and I thought I would take you to Will anyway. But Mr. Lang came, and I heard what he said about marrying him. I begged Mama Maali to wake Will. I told him and gave him the pouch you dropped into the bushes." Simon took a breath. "He told me to go to Fremantle to speak with his mother and give her the note he'd written. I did, and she asked me to go with two men and point out Mr. Lang when he came along the road. Instead, it was Ned who came along."

"I didn't know what the men said to Ned, but he went with them to see Miss Swanson…Maggie. Then this morning Maggie told me to ride ahead and give you that piece of paper. She would be directly behind me after she'd spoken to Mama Maali."

"The title?"

The boy nodded.

"Who is Mama Maali?"

"There's a small group of natives," William said. "They have a camp in a clearing not far from here, but it's well hidden. Mama Maali is a healer. They watch over Simon, feed him and care for him when Lang becomes too dangerous to be around."

Simon nodded in concurrence to William's words.

Emma was quiet for a moment. There were so many things she wanted to ask, but one question stood out from all the others. She turned to William. "Where were you going? When Lang shot you?"

William sighed, his expression one Emma was familiar with, one that meant this was something he

337

didn't want to answer.

"William?"

William sighed again and stood up, letting her hand slip from his. "Go and see if Martha needs any help with supper," he said to Simon, who was beginning to look bored now his tale had been told.

Simon nodded and trotted from the room.

William didn't return to sit next to Emma, instead claiming a spot in front of the mantel.

Emma was a little surprised that he'd not just left the room along with Simon, leaving questions unanswered, something of a habit with him, but even though he stayed, he didn't look like someone eager to speak. Whatever thoughts he was having were troubling ones.

"William?" Emma said after a long moment of silence.

He didn't look at her, his focus on an empty vase on the mantel, moving it slightly to the left as if its position was of some great importance.

Finally, the man spoke. "I was riding to speak with my mother. I believe you know by now that my mother is Maggie Swanson?"

Emma nodded, not missing the simultaneous look of both anger and embarrassment that flashed across his face.

"For ten years I shunned and refused to acknowledge her. I didn't want anyone to know I was related to this woman, and I hated her for making me the son of a whore. But when I returned that night with news of your father, and saw the barn, I knew I had to do something to save this property. Anything. Even something I found as distasteful as asking my mother for help." He glanced at Emma, his gaze retreating just as quickly to studying his hands. "I lay awake most of the night thinking about it, and it was then I realized that as much as I was prepared to do whatever it took to save the people I care about from the streets, Marg…my mother had done the same thing. After my father died and there was no money, no food, I understood that for her to put food on the table, keep a roof over our heads, protect what she loved, she'd done whatever it took. However distasteful it was. And for that I respect her." He looked up at Emma and smiled, but it was a smile of sadness. "She did the best she could for me, and I hated her for it."

Emma said nothing. She wasn't expected to speak.

William shrugged. "Anyway, I didn't get far before I met up with Lang. He made it clear he was going to buy your uncle's property, to which I replied something along the lines of, 'I'll be dead before I let that happen.' " He half smiled, shrugging. "I guess Lang decided to make sure of that." He looked down at his leg, his fingers hovering over a point at the top of his thigh. His trouser leg was tight there, pulled over thick bandages.

"Does it hurt?"

William shook his head. "Not so much now, but I have learnt that it may be best to think before I speak, in the future."

Emma smiled faintly. She knew his attempt at humor was a mask. For what, she wasn't sure, and his silence offered no clues.

"I'm more than grateful for what you did, William. You gave us all back our home, a chance for my uncle to get better, and a safe place for their baby to grow up." What she said was the truth, but there was no hint of the pride or satisfaction she expected to see on the man's face. He just looked beyond her, lost in thoughts that again seemed distasteful. Emma reasoned he must be in pain, and there was no question he looked exhausted. The doctor had said he shouldn't be out of bed, let alone riding to Eden Hill from wherever this Mama Maali's camp was. "And I never thought you had abandoned us."

William looked at her. He was angry. Emma could see it. "Abandoned you? Why would you assume I had?" The anger in his words matched that in his eyes.

"I, I didn't." Emma stuttered. "I knew you wouldn't abandon my uncle." Her words did nothing to calm the man.

"Your uncle?" William glared at her. "And how about you? Did you think I would abandon you?"

Emma shook her head, wishing she could take back the words. "William, let's talk about this later. Neither of us are—"

"Did you?"

Emma sighed. "No, but I had no…no idea what… what you…" She took a breath. This conversation wasn't getting any better. She started over. "William, please. Listen. That morning on the verandah I told you how I felt about you and asked you the same question. But you said nothing. The night you broke the news of my father, you said I had people who needed me, people who loved me. I asked if you needed me, but you said nothing. But I always knew you would come back if you could, certainly for my uncle, and I accepted that. You made no promise to me." Again, her reassurance didn't have the desired effect. William's hands balled into fists at his side, his mouth set in a tight line, but he said nothing, just looked away from her, the ticking of the mantel clock marking the growing seconds of silence.

Finally, he spoke, his voice calmer now. "You know, Emma, I didn't expect you to be who you were," he said, talking to a point on the wall just over her shoulder. "When your uncle asked me to go and bring his niece and nephew to him, I expected to find two children, but instead, I found you." A smile flashed momentarily onto his face, elicited by a memory. Then it was gone. "I wasn't looking for someone to love. As far as I was concerned, that was going to happen at a time of my choosing, when things were right to do so, but I truly thought it would be my choice. Then you came along." He shook his head. "I did everything I could to keep you out of my head, but it was impossible. But until I knew if I could support you, was sure we had secured Eden, I vowed to keep that to myself. Only then would I say anything about it." He glanced at her for a moment, a vulnerability in his eyes that Emma hadn't seen before. "But the night I brought news of your father, and I held you, I knew I couldn't lose you. So I did the only thing I could think of." He took a deep breath in, letting it out slowly. "Not that any of it matters now." The man fell silent, showing no signs of continuing.

"William?" Emma asked after a moment. "What do you mean by saying none of it matters now?" She pushed herself from her perch on the settee, the hideous wedding gown billowing around her as she stood. "William?"

William sighed again. "Emma, after everything that has happened, I, I don't…" He turned toward the door. "As I said, it doesn't matter. If you'll excuse me, I'll go and check on your uncle."

Glancing around and finding nothing other than a cushion to hand, Emma launched it across the room, hitting William in the back. "No, I don't excuse you," she said, her voice rising. "You don't leave a person with half a sentence and expect them to accept that. I'm tired of playing 'Let's guess what Mr. Rideout is thinking.' Finish your sentence! You don't what, William?"

William didn't turn to face her, but he didn't make any move to walk away either. "Emma, you said we didn't have to do this now."

"Well, I have changed my mind," Emma said, even though she too knew this wasn't the time for such a discussion. Exhaustion was clouding clear thinking, but she couldn't stop herself. "After everything that's happened, I deserve to know why none of it matters. Today, I thought you were dead. Today I almost married a man who had assaulted me more than once and he made no secret of the fact that there was worse to come."

Now William spun around, anger clear on his face as he strode toward her, but Emma stood her ground, held his gaze, her anger matching his. He stopped in front of her, breathing hard.

"Goddammit, Emma! Do you not think I want nothing more than to wring his throat for putting his hands on you?" He raised his hand, his fingers barely brushing the purple mark on her face. "That I want to flay the skin from his back for, for this?"

Emma raised her chin. "You don't what?" she repeated.

For a moment they could only stare at each other in silence, fury robbing them both of further exchange. Then William sighed loudly, his anger dissipating with the breath. His shoulders slumped, and he looked down at his hands.

"Emma, I should have been here to protect you, and I wasn't. If it weren't for Simon, for my mother, Lang would have taken the only thing that really matters. We might have Eden, we might have a future, but after everything that has happened, Emma, did I lose you?"

Chapter 27

The woman gave a final scream, then fell silent.

Emma rubbed the newborn vigorously with a towel, unable to stop the tears that streamed down her face as the infant's lusty cry gave notice that she had arrived. Emma held her up for her mother to see. "It's a girl, Martha. She's beautiful."

Martha pushed herself up, leaning back against a pillow. Her hair hung limply over one eye, her brow glistening with sweat. "Oh, Emma! Is she strong, is she healthy?"

Emma swaddled the baby and placed her in her mother's arms. "Yes, she's…she's perfect."

Martha parted her gown and her new daughter latched on, suckling contentedly at her mother's breast. A knock at the door drew Emma's attention, and she quickly wiped her hands on her apron as she crossed to open it.

"I have someone eager to come in," William whispered.

Emma turned to look at Martha. After twelve hours in labor, Martha must have been exhausted, but her joy hid any hint of tiredness. She smiled up at Emma and nodded.

William pushed the door open farther and wheeled the chair into the room.

"You have a daughter, Uncle," Emma said.

Robert's smile matched that of his wife. "She's beautiful, Robert. She has your eyes," Martha said, holding her hand out to her husband.

Emma wheeled her uncle over to the side of the bed so he could see his newborn child. He'd made good progress over the past four months, Doctor Fenning citing rest and peace as the main reason for his promising recovery.

"Does she have a name?" Emma asked, looking from mother to father.

"Faith Elizabeth," Robert said, Martha nodding her agreement.

Emma smiled. "That's perfect," she said, looking down at the infant asleep now in her mother's arms, her belly full. "I will bring you some tea, Martha."

Emma removed her apron and gathered the towels, bundling them all together. "I'll be back shortly," she said and followed William from the room.

She dropped the laundry into the washroom trough, then went into the kitchen, putting the kettle on to boil.

"You did a wonderful job delivering that baby, Mrs. Rideout," William said, his arms encircling Emma's waist. He pulled her close. It had been little more than a month since their wedding, a quiet affair attended by her uncle, Martha, Daniel, Simon, and Maggie Swanson.

Maggie had been the one to purchase Lang's property, her wedding present to her son. The whereabouts of the previous owner were unknown. The police had come for him, but Lang had slipped away, leaving all his possessions behind, including his son. His house had been demolished, to be replaced by a new one being built high on the hill. It would be ready for them to move into within weeks, with room enough for Simon to join their family.

Emma looked up at her husband. She smiled, although a part of her couldn't deny the profound sadness at the memories of her mother and infant brother that sprang to life with the birth of Martha's daughter.

Some weeks back, William had taken Emma to Rockingham to visit the graves of her mother and baby brother, and of her father also. The land now was part of a new cemetery, and Emma comforted herself with the knowledge that they would rest peacefully together there, undisturbed.

"It must be all my experience delivering piglets," Emma said. "A fine job I did, too, if I do say so myself."

Will smiled. "Well, I'm grateful, to say the least, that a child being born didn't involve swimming. We both know how well you managed that."

Emma tilted her chin, pouting, and William obliged her with a kiss. She nipped his bottom lip. "You deserved that," she said with a lazy smile.

Despite the pained expression on his face, William laughed. "Maybe a few lessons may be in order."

"Swimming?" Emma said, one eyebrow raised in mock questioning. She held his gaze.

"In whatever the lady thinks necessary," William said, smiling slowly.

"Well, there are some endeavors that maybe require some guidance."

William bent to kiss her neck. Emma shivered as he nibbled the top of her ear.

"Such as…" he whispered.

"As we both agree, I certainly could use the swimming lessons."

"Uh-huh."

Emma squealed as her husband bit gently into the soft flesh of her neck, goosebumps rising on her arms. "Shooting instruction also could be useful."

"Noted."

"Umm, I believe I could do with some further tuition in horse riding."

William moved his attention to her shoulder. "You certainly could. Anything else?"

"Well, I was…"

"I think horse riding lessons first, Emma. They would be the most important. Or maybe swimming."

Emma stiffened. Her little brother was standing behind her. William straightened and Emma turned in his arms to face her brother. "Daniel." She felt her face warm. "Uh, Daniel, have you, um…seen the new baby?"

Daniel nodded. "Her head looks odd. Will she stay that way?"

Emma laughed. "No, she won't."

"Do you know how to swim, Will?" That seemed far more interesting to the boy than a baby.

"I do," William said, "and when the summer comes, I will be happy to show you how."

Daniel grinned at this piece of information. "When will you have a baby, Emma?"

Emma shrugged. "I'm not sure, Daniel. It's hard to know these things, but when I do, then you will be an uncle."

"Like Uncle Robert?"

Emma smiled. "Just like Uncle Robert. Oh, I forgot, the tea."

Emma slipped from William's arms and picked up the tray. She tiptoed into her uncle's room, but husband and wife were both fast asleep, their hands clasped.

The infant fussed in her cradle, a place she didn't seems happy to be, and Emma set down the tray and scooped her up, dropping into the rocking chair by the window. She rocked gently back and forth, a lullaby hummed quietly behind closed lips as the gray light of dawn gave way to the new day.

Later, that night, when the house was quiet, Emma slipped from her bed, careful not to wake Will. Saying goodbye to a friend was always hard to do, and she wanted to do this in private. Her diary sat on the dresser where she'd left it, a new page waiting for the news of the birth of baby Faith, but Emma hadn't written on this page. And she wasn't going to.

Diary in hand, she went into the sitting room. A fire burned here, not a ferocious one but one hot enough to consume the pages of a book. Her diary had been her companion and confidante through the darkest of times, but they were times she didn't want to revisit, nor did she want to share times of joy with days best forgotten. A new journal waited for that. News of her marriage, of the new child born to their family, of her hopes for one of her own would be written there. As much as her diary had been her friend, it was time to say goodbye, and with that whispered, Emma dropped the book into the fire. The flames licked at the pages, tasting them, then devouring them one by one until what had once been her memories and thoughts were nothing more than white ash and smoke.

Chapter 28

2022

"Look what I've got," Becca announced.

Sophie Harris swiveled around on her stool, her excitement at hearing the words equaling that in her assistant's voice. Becca carried a large cardboard box, her smile just seen over the top of it. She dropped the box onto the worktable, a flurry of dust particles erupting into the air. A man—tall, about thirty-five, Sophie would have guessed—followed her.

"And this is *Professor* William Sadler," Becca said, the emphasis placed on the man's title. "He's the owner of this wonderful donation."

Sophie held out her hand. "Thank you very much, Professor Sadler," she said, his hand warm in hers as he took it momentarily. "We are so grateful for donations such as yours. It helps give a voice to the past, every little piece telling another part of the story." This was the usual speech given when a donation to the history center was made, but she meant what she said. Donations didn't come often, time taking many of the treasures people left behind, so Sophie was always grateful when she was entrusted with those time had spared.

The man smiled easily. "Only my students call me Professor Sadler. Most other times I respond to Will."

Sophie returned the smile. She'd never met Will

Sadler before today, but he seemed familiar. Maybe they had gone to the same university. "Okay, Will. If you don't mind me asking, what do you teach?"

"Well, I lecture in French history and language, but my passion is tenth-century European history. Sounds a bit dull, I know, but I don't seem to mind it." He smiled a little self-consciously, then nodded toward the box. "As for the donation, you're most welcome. The box has been sitting for years in the shed in an old trunk. The trunk itself is over a hundred years old, so I'm guessing what's in the box is too. My father had a quick look and said there looked to be an old coat and some other bits, but he didn't want to disturb it. I don't imagine it's anything of financial value, but historically it might be of interest to you."

"Oh, it definitely will be," Sophie assured him. "Do you know anything about the people who may have owned whatever we find in there? We like to add some background information to donations where possible."

Will shrugged, shaking his head. "Not really. Apparently, one of my great-greats owned the land originally, so I imagine it's probably things that belonged to some ancestor or other." He laughed. "I know the succession of most European royal families but haven't a clue about my own family tree. I know that an Emma McLeod married a William Rideout, way, way back, but that's all I've got. I was thinking of looking into it at some point."

"Well, that's something to go on, at least, and yes, you should definitely look into your family tree. I'm a bit biased, but it's interesting and can become quite addictive. Just let me know when you want to start, and I'll show you how."

Becca cleared her throat, and Sophie was suddenly aware her colleague was still in the room. Sophie's attention had been focused solely on this man who seemed so familiar.

"Is your wife interested in genealogy as well?" Becca asked.

"My wife?"

"Oh," Becca said, "I assumed that's who I spoke to on the phone about the donation the other day?"

Sophie shot her friend a glance. Will Sadler wasn't only a history professor. He was also attractive. No matter how innocent Becca pretended her questions to be, Sophie could see right through her. Becca was on a fishing expedition.

"No, that would have been my mother," Will said, "and I'm not sure if she is."

Becca pouted as she considered this bit of information, Sophie fully aware her friend was contemplating her next question and pretty sure what it was going to be. She wasn't wrong. "Oh, so there's no other Mrs. Sadler?"

Will laughed. "I'm sure there is, but not one attached to me, if that's what you're asking."

"Prospective ones?" Becca ventured.

Will shook his head.

"And you speak French?"

"Becca, please," Sophie interrupted, before she turned to Will. "I'm so sorry. You will have to excuse my friend. She suffers from terminal matchmaking syndrome." Sophie didn't add that she was pleased the answers Will gave were all negative. That was for her alone to know.

Will chuckled. "That's okay. So does my mother.

We should compare notes." His smile was warm, as was his laugh, and again Sophie felt like she'd known this man for a long time. "Sorry, but I have to ask," he said. "Have we met before? You seem familiar."

Sophie shook her head. "No, I don't think so, although I did think the same thing. I can't place where that would be, though."

Will shrugged. "No, well, it's a mystery maybe we can solve sometime."

Sophie nodded, wanting to say she thought that a brilliant idea, and how about right now, but she could feel Becca's eyes on her and knew the smug look that would be painted on her friend's face. She wouldn't give her any more fodder to dine on. Unfortunately, Will did.

"You should come out to Eden Hill sometime. The original cottage is still there. It's been renovated a few times over the decades, and I did it myself about five years ago. I stay there most weekends, to help my father with the vineyard and that sort of thing. You might find it interesting. You could take some photos for your records. We also make a very nice wine, if you're a wine drinker."

"Oh, she is," Becca chimed in.

Sophie rolled her eyes. "Becca, you make me sound like an alcoholic." To Will she said, "Yes, I don't mind a glass or two occasionally."

"Well, come out sometime. We make a peach wine you might like."

"Oh, of course, Eden Hill," Becca said. "You make Sweet Will, don't you? I love that."

Sophie thought she could see a blush grow on the man's face. "Yeah, Sweet Will, that's us."

Sophie smiled. "Is it named after you?"

"Yeah, I guess. My parents' idea when I was born. Apparently, I was the child they never thought they would have." He shrugged, his embarrassment at telling the tale coloring his cheeks. "Apparently, I was sweet. Hence Sweet Will. It's a story my mother would tell with every bottle of wine if I'd let her."

"Well, it's a lovely story," Sophie said, "and one I'd definitely want to hear when I come and buy my bottle." She smiled at the man, the gesture returned with such a familiar intimacy she felt her cheeks warm. She looked away, completely flustered, aware that Becca was watching her with a grin that would have put the Cheshire Cat to shame. "Um, I'll, um, will give you a call when we've emptied the box?" Sophie said.

Will nodded. "Yeah, that would be good. I'll see you then."

He looked at her for a moment, a moment that rendered Sophie silent and she could only nod in agreement.

She watched the man leave, taking her time to turn and face her friend. She knew what was coming, and Becca didn't disappoint.

"He likes you, Soph," she teased, "and you like him too."

Sophie tried to hide her smile. "You're impossible, Bec, you know that?" but she couldn't deny to herself that Becca was right. She did like Will Sadler despite having known him for less than fifteen minutes, and she would certainly like to see the cottage and sample his wine, but that also was a thought she kept to herself. "Shall we do some work?"

Sophie opened a shallow drawer in the worktable and took out a pair of white cotton gloves and a paper mask, the gloves to protect the pieces they were going to handle, the masks to protect themselves from the layers of dust that oftentimes came with the items. She slid them across the table to Becca, then took another pair of gloves and a mask for herself, slipping them on. Laying a white sheet over half the table, she then took a pad and pen from the drawer. She opened the pad to a clean page, writing the date across the top and next to that the name: Sadler donation—Eden Hill Farm. McLeod/Rideout.

"Ready?"

Becca pulled the box toward them and took a scalpel, slicing through the brown packing tape that held the box closed. She opened the flaps, then glanced at Sophie, her own anticipation written all over her face. With care she reached into the box and, with two hands, lifted out what Sophie guessed was an oilskin coat, still wrapped around the items they were so desperate to see. Becca laid the coat on the white cloth and inspected it.

"There doesn't seem to be any water damage to it," she said through her mask. "Nor any perishing of the fabric."

Sophie nodded and wrote on the notepad. 1: Oilskin Coat. Brown. She would finish the entry after they had time to inspect it further. Right now, they had to see how willing the coat was to give up its contents. Becca slowly teased each fold back until the coat lay open, revealing all it had hidden for over a hundred years.

Sophie reached for a yellowed piece of paper. It had a rip in one corner and lines crossing it where it once had been folded in half. The ink that once would have been bold against the white background had faded, but the words at the top of the document were easy enough to read. "Certificate of Title" was written in an ornate script and below that was stated that the land was the property of Misters Robert J. McLeod & Edward A. McLeod.

"Well, we know who owned the land, at least," Sophie said. She took a clear plastic sleeve and opened it, ready to receive the document. Becca slipped it inside, and Sophie bent to add the document to the list on the notepad.

"Hey, check this out."

"What is it?"

"What is it? It's you."

Sophie laughed. "What are you talking about?"

"Look." Becca turned over the photograph she was holding to check the back, where faint writing informed only "McLeod-Rideout Wedding, 1865." She laid it down so Sophie could see what was, clearly, a wedding photo. The couple stared back at her. The man, tall and handsome, stood beside a young woman who without doubt was a spitting image of Sophie, right down to the small mole at the base of her neck. "See? It's you. The likeness is uncanny, bordering on super weird, don't you think? She could be your twin. And don't you think the man looks a lot like Professor Sadler?"

Sophie took the black-and-white photograph from her friend. The young woman's hair was bound up in a bun on the top of her head, but a strand had missed being captured and fell in a ringlet over her shoulder. Sophie's hair, too, fell in curls, and she spent ages trying to straighten them out. She wondered if this woman disliked her curls as much as Sophie did her own. The photo gave no clue to the color of the woman's hair, but Sophie imagined it could easily have been the same dark auburn as her own. "Yeah, I guess he does, a bit. He must be a descendant and not know it. He said he hadn't traced his family tree. As for the girl, I've traced my tree a long way back, and there are no McLeods or Rideouts that I know of. They look happy, though, whoever they are."

She handed the photograph back to Becca and opened a clear sleeve. Becca slipped the photograph into it, and it was added to the list as Wedding Photograph. Sadler: McLeod/Rideout Wedding, 1865. "What's next?"

"We may have struck gold, Sophie. I think it's a diary."

Sophie looked up, a flutter of anticipation in her stomach. Nothing gave a better snapshot of the time than a diary.

"You want the honors?" Becca stepped away from the table, Sophie taking her co-worker's place. She reached out for the book, which sat in the center of the oilskin coat, eager to hold it in her hands. The word 'Diary' was embossed in its red marbled cover, and she traced over it with her fingertip, then gently turned to the first page.

"My dearest friend," Sophie read aloud.

"I have so many wonderful things to tell you.

Baby Faith was born yesterday. She's healthy, and Martha and Uncle are overjoyed, as are all of us. Uncle Robert gets stronger each day, and now that Eden Hill is secured, he's full of hope and life. I too cannot be happier. I married William a month ago, and we hope also to welcome our own child into the world next year. Daniel is well, as is Simon. I miss Mama and Father, but I know they're together and watching over us. I feel that life will be better for us now, and having the love of William is more than I could have dreamt of.

E."

A word about the author...

From her first visit to a library at age five, Sarah's love of storytelling blossomed.

Winning her first prize for short story writing at ten, Sarah knew that writing stories for others to read was what she wanted to do with her life, which she fitted in between raising five children, obtaining a legal degree, and working.

Sarah has lived in Western Australia since she was a child, and when not writing, Sarah loves travelling with her husband, spending time with her family, and drinking coffee as she watches the world go by.

Sarah's other loves are genealogy, long walks in nature, Formula 1, and the family cat.

Thank you for purchasing
this publication of The Wild Rose Press, Inc.

For questions or more information
contact us at
info@thewildrosepress.com.

The Wild Rose Press, Inc.

www.ingramcontent.com/pod-product-compliance
Lightning Source LLC
Chambersburg PA
CBHW072311020726
47501CB00002B/475